HE WILL LIVE UP IN THE SKY

Christopher Loring Knowles

© 2019 Christopher Loring Knowles. All Rights Reserved
Photography by Elizabeth Victoria Knowles
This story is entirely fictional. Any resemblance to persons living or dead is purely coincidental.
ISBN: 9781705629734

PROLOGUE

Quincy, Massachusetts, April 1994

The gunman slipped like a shark through rolling waves of sweaty young bodies. No one seemed to notice the gruesome surgical staples in his shaved scalp, or the filthy bandages wrapped around his fingers and hands. No one noticed anything at all.

Instead, all eyes were locked on the band's frontman, "who burned with the charisma of a wasted angel," as one local critic had put it.

Still, the crowd parted as the gunman drifted towards the stage, unconsciously sensing the arrival of death in their midst. He locked his sights on the singer, whose serpentine blond dreads were swinging in lockstep with the relentless crack of the snare drum.

The gunman was painfully, alarmingly thin. He'd stopped eating in the hospital, and he had to be drugged into a stupor before the nurses could even get the feeding tube down his throat. But as emaciated as he was, he was filled with the terrible strength of someone who'd just found his one true purpose in life.

He drew his weapon from the pocket of his hoodie and aimed it at the stage. Someone screamed, "Gun!"

Someone else screamed, "He's got a gun!"

The singer emerged from his reverie just in time to look straight into the eyes of his assassin.

But he wasn't afraid at all. He couldn't possibly think of a better way to go than here, on this stage, with this band, playing this song.

A sudden flash burst at center stage; an eruption of white light so intense it left the entire room seeing nothing but spots in its wake.

The gun fired, but the bullet just bounced stupidly off a steel fixture hanging above the stage. The music ground to a halt while the crowd staggered and stumbled, grasping at empty air for bearings.

The bassist collapsed like a marionette. The guitar player hopped backwards when the drummer stumbled forward, sending his drums and cymbal stands crashing to the floor.

The gunman suddenly sensed strong hands on his wrist, then on his throat. He sensed sharp punches to his mouth, then to his ribs.

He sensed large bodies pressing him to the floor and pushing the air out of his lungs. His tongue sensed the coppery tang of blood.

But he never actually felt a thing.

A shrieking squall of feedback tore from the speakers before someone finally managed to cut the power. A murmur began to rise from the crowd as the house lights flickered on.

The gunman had been pulled outside and into an alleyway, his bony frame now being hammered by several meaty fists as a crowd of screaming young women cheered the beating on.

Back inside, the musicians regained their vision and looked around the half-empty room.

Someone finally said, "Where's Gary?"

CHAPTER ONE

Darja struggled with a road map with one hand, and the steering wheel with the other, as she made her way down Boondock Boulevard in beautiful downtown East Bumfuck, New Hampshire. She couldn't make heads or tails of the tangled mess of paper and was already ten minutes late for her interview. This whole job thing was not off to a great start.

She decided to toss the map into the back and try her luck again with the directions the placement agency had sent. Spotting a landmark from the list, Darja gripped the wheel with both hands and focused all her mental energy on not missing the upcoming turn. She also hoped she wouldn't get pulled over, seeing how she'd taken a few swigs of Southern Comfort at a rest stop in Massachusetts. She always got a little jittery before interviews, which is why she kept her trusty old flask under the driver's seat.

The turnoff was unmarked and brought her onto a very long gravel road winding through a dense wall of hemlocks. Darja wondered if she had somehow taken a detour into a bad horror movie and was heading for some tarpaper shack where toothless hillbillies hung human hides out to dry on wire coat-hangers. She was glad she brought her little Beretta with her. A girl can't be too careful these days.

Then she spotted a building through the treeline that made her heart sink. It was a crappy-looking old ranch, with moldy siding and a mossy roof that looked for all the world like Chez Serial-Killer. This had to be some kind of setup. Was her agent part of some Charlie Manson murder-cult or something? She did have a phone interview with the people she was supposed to be meeting with today, and it seemed legit enough.

Well, not 'people,' exactly. She actually spoke to a guy who sounded like he gargled with drain cleaner. He never did give Darja his name.

Maybe she should turn around.

She would've done, but the road was super-narrow and lined with deep, muddy ditches. She then happened upon an automatic barrier, the kind she recognized from Naval bases.

She saw a keycard box on the driver's side with a call button and an intercom.

Darja looked around for instructions of some kind and couldn't find any, so she simply pressed the button.

Maybe this was some kind of intelligence test.

The speaker buzzed, then a lightly-accented male voice said, "Insert the card in the slot and wait for the gate to rise." Darja went fishing in her purse for the paper keycard the agency gave her. After a minute of her digging, the voice impatiently repeated the instructions.

Darja muttered, "All right, all right, already," before she finally found the card and did what she was told. The voice then said, "Park on the left side of the house. Enter in the code at the back-porch door."

A glint of reflected sunlight caught Darja's eye as the gate rose; there were a number of surveillance cameras posted on trees overlooking the roadblock. She couldn't decide if this should make her more nervous or less. Maybe Drano-Voice was a tech-savvy serial killer. Darja drove on very slowly, seeing how she didn't much fancy driving into one of those ditches.

She reached the gravel lot and parked next to a Chevy Suburban the size of a Winnebago. It was brand new and had a fancy whip antenna around the back, leading Darja to wonder if maybe Drano-Voice was a tech-savvy serial killer with a lot of disposable income.

Granted, that all seemed rather low on the probability scale, but she decided to keep her purse unlatched anyway, just in case she needed to shoot herself up some rich-hillbilly-serial-killer ass.

It was showtime. Darja took two blasts of Binaca then sniffed her breath in a cupped hand. She couldn't really tell if the blasts were hiding the whiskey or not, so she took a couple more.

She inspected her makeup job in the rearview one last time, carefully removing a wide smear of lipstick on her front tooth with her pinky.

Finally, she checked her pits. They passed the sniff test, so she got out and headed towards this seriously ugly-ass house.

Darja was what old ladies liked to call "handsome," and wore her natural platinum-blonde hair in a conservative bob. This helped accent her high cheek-bones and her pale, hooded eyes, both a legacy of her family's Laplander heritage.

But at 5'10" she was a bit too tall for most guys, and no one ever seemed to drool when she walked into a room.

"Good-looking," she heard a lot. "Cute?" All the time. "Knockout?" Not so much.

Maybe a makeover was in order.

Either way, Darja was dressed to impress, or so she thought. She wore a white linen jacket with shoulder pads, a white silk blouse and a tight charcoal-gray skirt that showcased her tall, athletic figure while still lending her that elusive "professional" aura.

She broke out her padded bra for the occasion, on account of there being actual mosquito bites bigger than her boobs. Still, she was very proud of her body, and saw it as an asset in her line of work, even if some folks thought she wasn't particularly ladylike.

An effect, incidentally, that was only heightened when she started swearing like a sailor, which she actually once was. A sailor.

The keypad on the back door looked factory-fresh. Darja now began to wonder if she hadn't wandered from a horror-movie set into a James Bond film. She punched in the code and heard the door click.

She entered into a grubby kitchen area and was startled by a rather imposing man stepping out of the shadows. The guy wore black private security garb and was packing a Desert Eagle .50 in a leather hip holster. *A Desert Eagle*, for fuck's sake? Darja thought. What the hell was this guy expecting out here? Dinosaurs?

"Put your purse down on the counter, please," the guy said in a light accent Darja couldn't place. He looked Turkish or Arabic, ripped, young-ish, handsome, with dark olive skin, stylish crewcut and very intense black eyes.

She did what she was told and swallowed hard.

The guy opened her bag like it might be wired to explode and peeked inside. He pulled out her Beretta and dangled it by its butt like a dead fish. His indignant glare clearly demanded an explanation.

"Hey, I don't know who you people are," Darja said. "It was just a precaution."

"You'll get this back when you leave," Turkish or Arab Guy grunted with an annoyed tone. He put the gun back in the purse and walked with it into an adjoining room.

"I have to pat you down," Turkish or Arab Guy said as he returned, almost apologetically. He did the pat-down quickly and efficiently, without playing any grab-ass.

Then he pointed at a door.

"Go downstairs and take a right. Follow the tunnel to the end. The conference room is there."

A tunnel? For real?

This *was* a James Bond scenario.

CHAPTER TWO

The tunnel was disappointing. It was more like a glorified cinder-block hallway, lined with a clear plastic tarp and lit up with emergency lights. She ended up in a conference room, which was surprisingly large, bare, and definitely smelled like a basement. There was a swanky glass-top table, with four leather office chairs set up around it.

An attractive but severe-looking woman with long, jet-black hair sat motionless at the table. She looked young and foreign. Darja thought she might be Turkish or Arab like the guy in the kitchen and wondered if they were related.

Darja saw a small stack of folding chairs against the far wall. There was a black wooden podium in front of a small projection screen. On the far side of the room was a slide projector on a wheeled stand. There was also a weird-looking TV thing on a huge stand tucked against the other wall.

A trim older man with a flat-top and a severe, deeply-lined face stood at the podium sorting through papers. Darja had this guy's number right away; former military intelligence and most likely a management post at some alphabet agency.

In short, he looked like any number of total fucking assholes Darja had encountered in her Naval career; humorless bureaucrats who got their rocks off pulling rank on peons like her. And sure enough...

"Lundquist. You're late. Take a seat," the man barked in a familiar voice, without looking up. We meet at last, Drano-Voice.

"I'm sorry, I had trouble finding the turnoff," Darja replied, even though she wasn't actually sorry.

"Well, you got here first, anyway. The others seem to be having trouble, too. Make yourself comfortable."

Darja supposed that was Drano-Voice being amenable.

"Thank you," she said. She'd be god-damned if she called him 'sir.'

Darja sat down and smiled at the Turkish or Arab woman sitting opposite her. "Hi, I'm Darja Lundquist."

Turkish or Arab woman said nothing and turned her attention to the table top, which she apparently found utterly fascinating.

Darja was glad she didn't offer her hand. She hoped whoever else was coming would be a little chattier. She took a sip from the large glass in front of her. It tasted cold, clean and fresh, like deep-woods spring water. They probably had a well here.

Two men arrived in short order, a few minutes apart. The first was a youngish Eurotrash type, dressed in a snazzy, dark purple sweater and tight black slacks, a dark-gray windbreaker of some kind draped over his arm. He had short cropped dirty-blond hair, a soft, pale face and very German eyeglasses.

Darja figured he was probably planning to go clubbing after the interview. Either that or annex the Sudetenland.

The second arrival was a guy who looked like a college quarterback-turned-underwear model. He was dressed in a cheap and ill-fitted suit, but Darja could tell he was buff. He kind of looked like the guy who played Superman on that *Lois and Clark* TV series, but a little bit older and even better-looking.

What the hell was he here for? A Calvin Klein shoot? A guy who looked like that had no business in a musty basement in the middle of Hee-Haw, New Hampshire.

A very big, very mean-looking mercenary-type entered in after them, moving like he was expecting a firefight to break out any second now.

Mean-Merc wore the same outfit as Turkish or Arab Guy upstairs: tight, heavyweight black t-shirt, black fatigue pants and black SWAT boots. Only Mean-Merc here carried a SIG Sauer P226. Darja figured that if any dinosaurs happened by, this guy would just strangle them.

Mean-Merc took a look around like he was searching for explosive devices, then went over to stand at the door. Probably figured he could more effectively intimidate everyone if he was blocking their only escape route.

"Good, you're all here," Drano-Voice said. "Let's get started. My name is Robert Travis. I worked for the Defense Intelligence Agency for thirty years and now I'm hoping to bring those skills to the private sector. I hope to bring all of you along with me as well."

Darja wondered how many times this dude had rehearsed that introduction. The way Drano-Travis stood at his podium reminded Darja of a priest at a lectern. Or rather, priests at lecterns on television, seeing how she'd never set foot in a church in her life.

He turned everyone's attention over to a pulldown screen and clicked a remote until a slide came up that read, "The Bifrost Initiative: New Frontiers in Human Intelligence."

'The Bifrost Initiative?' Seriously? What the hell was all this about, switch-hitting Eskimos or something?

Travis then stared at the four recruits, as if willing their total attention, and began his spiel. "The four of you have been hand-picked for a very exciting project on the cutting edge of the intelligence industry," Drano-Travis preached.

"As you know, these are very exciting times, with the rapid growth of information technology, and the resulting options made available to professionals, whose very lives can often rely on the quality and quantity of information they are able to gain access to…"

Take me now, Jesus, Darja thought. She'd suffered through hundreds of these kinds of pep talks in the Navy. Everything was, 'cutting-edge-this' and, 'innovative-that' and, 'the best thing since canned tuna, bla bla bla.' It always ended up being the same old crap, only with more hassles and paperwork attached. And this pitch was as stiff and insincere as the rest of them.

Darja also found it a bit rich that Travis McDrano-Voice here kept using the word "exciting," when the guy projected all the excitement of a funeral director.

"…this mission you are about to embark on will employ the latest tools of information warfare available, both electronic and psychotronic…"

Wait, what? What the actual fuck does 'psychotronic' mean, Darja wondered. But she did notice Eurotrash Guy bolted up in his chair when that little buzzword dropped.

This Travis guy also kept droning on about that stupid Internet thing, which Darja couldn't care less about. Limp-dick nerd-boy crap. The placement agent had her thinking this was a security gig.

Drano-Travis then paused for effect and clicked to a slide of men and women sitting in what looked like high-tech school desks. They were wearing the kind of eye-masks Darja's grandma used for her naps. EEG electrodes were attached to their foreheads.

"What I'm about to tell you is highly confidential, and of the utmost sensitivity. But it cuts to the heart of your mission, and the work you are being called upon to do with us here."

Darja couldn't possibly guess what he meant. Clearly the guy was going senile. Too much Drano, maybe.

"For nearly a quarter of a century, the military and intelligence community have been conducting research into what is called 'remote viewing,' which is nothing less than the most exciting, most revolutionary tool ever developed. With little more than ordinary pen and paper, remote viewers have been able to gather intelligence completely inaccessible to our most advanced satellites and listening stations. Believe me when I say that some of the most decisive intelligence break-throughs of the Cold War came out of the remote viewing project. It's safe to say that without it, we'd probably all be speaking Russian right now."

OK, Darja thought, what in the holy living fuck is this coot actually talking about? Pen and paper more revolutionary than satellites? What the hell is this crap?

Travis paused for effect and began sermonizing again.

"Remote viewing is not only on the cutting edge of human intelligence, it's on the cutting edge of human potential. In fact, it's on the cutting edge of human evolution itself. It's been proven that the human mind is unbound by the laws of physics, that time and space are malleable, that operable psychic power is not only in our grasp, but may in fact be our destiny. Our birthright."

Wait: psychic powers? Is this some kind of a joke? This guy seemed about as New Age as a drill sergeant. Darja felt the floor beneath her begin to spin.

She wished now she took a few more swigs of booze before she wandered into this madhouse. And she wished even more that someone would give this nut a fucking throat lozenge.

"With the end of the Cold War, remote viewing technology is now going mainstream. Intelligence gathering is an imperative not only for governments but also for large corporations and other major business interests. It's in the economic sphere where the decisive battles of the coming century are going to be fought. And the psychic war has already begun, make no mistake about it. Remote viewing may be something we all can learn, but only a chosen few can perform viewing with the accuracy and predictability needed in an adversarial environment. The problem is that many of the those with the highest potential for remote viewing and other psychic skills are all too often unaware of their abilities. And there is already fierce competition to find those who may hold the key to full-spectrum psychotronic domination in the years to come."

Darja fought back a dry heave. Well, this is where you are now, she thought. This is what you've been reduced to, bitch.

All your years of training, hard work and achievement flushed down the toilet by all the wrong decisions and you end up in a mildewy basement in New Hampshire listening to some spook-ass nut ranting about mental telepathy.

The problem was that she didn't really get the impression she could just sashay out of this dungeon and chalk it all up to experience. This old coot might be a lunatic, but he was obviously a deadly-serious lunatic.

"This unit here has been set up to help find these people. Plain and simple. This isn't science fiction we're talking about, it's just good, old-fashioned detective work. Years of work with psychics and viewers has allowed us to develop reliable profiles that can help to locate and identify those individuals with the greatest potential for the gathering of non-traditional intelligence. The problem is that so many of these people exist on the margins of society. Many tend to develop substance addictions and dependencies. Many fall in with dubious, sometimes criminal elements. All because our society doesn't allow for the existence of their abilities, never mind their cultivation and exploitation."

Another dramatic pause.

"This team will be comprised of two field agents and two analysts," he continued. "The field agents' job will be to gather intelligence on persons of interest and then hand it off to the analysts, who in turn will provide reports to me. Decisions will then be made by an advisory board on how best to handle the situations that arise. It's just as simple as that. Now, does anyone have any questions?"

Yeah, where's the exit, Darja thought.

But no one at the table could think of any questions. No one seemed able to form any actual words, so they all just sat in stunned silence.

The Quarterback looked totally lost, as if this pitch had just been made in a foreign language spoken backwards.

Eurotrash Guy was studying his handout with an intensity Darja thought had to be feigned.

Turkish or Arab Lady sat stiff as a statue, staring at passing dust motes like they were a new life-form.

"Good. I'm going to let the four of you get acquainted. I have to leave town on business; but I expect to meet with all of you when I get back. Oh, before I forget..."

Travis took four standard envelopes from the podium and handed one out to each of his suckers.

"Have a look at those," he said. "My phone number is on the handout. I look forward to speaking with all of you individually when I get back."

Turkish or Arab Lady got up without saying a word and followed Travis out. Darja guessed she probably didn't want to get acquainted. Mean-Merc gave the remaining group another strong dose of scary-face and stomped off shortly afterwards. There were probably some grizzly bears out back asking for a knuckle-sandwich.

CHAPTER THREE

The three remaining recruits sat and stared at each other in mutual astonishment. No one knew what one should possibly say in a situation like this.

Darja tried to break the ice by telling this dirty joke she heard in the ladies' pisser of this crappy dive she got shit-faced in the other night. No one laughed, but Eurotrash Guy loosened up enough to inform Darja exactly how fucking stupid he thought her fucking joke was. She thought it was funny, at least. Maybe you needed a clitoris to appreciate it.

Still, it snapped the guys out of their trance and the three of them were able to have a not-entirely-excruciating little chat. Even so, they all realized this gig was a bust and they'd all be back doing whatever it was they usually did when they got up tomorrow.

The conversation died down and an awkward silence descended upon the room. Not really knowing what else to do, Darja opened her envelope. Inside was a computer-printed bank check, made out to her, for an amount she'd never seen before in her life. It was many multiples of any paycheck she ever got from the Navy. In the note section it read, 'six-month advance.' After watching Darja's face go snow-white, the other two immediately opened theirs.

"Hooool-lee shit," Eurotrash Guy yowled, and clutched his head in his hands. The Quarterback's jaw dropped, and stayed dropped. After a minute or two, Darja wondered if it'd become frozen in place.

"I guess it's time to start hunting for brainiacs," Darja mumbled as she got up from the table, and left the others to cope with their shock in private. She didn't want the boys getting embarrassed once they began to weep, which Darja promptly did shortly after she left.

Darja pulled into a nearby McDonald's, parked in the back and cried hysterically for a good twenty minutes. She cried like she cried at a wedding, only the kind of wedding where the bridesmaids are given $200,000 cashier checks in their swag-bags.

Ironically, Darja had actually applied for a job at a McDonald's, not two weeks before. She'd been going through a rough patch.

After she cried herself out, Darja drove to a local branch of her bank. She had no earthly idea how long it would take the check to clear, and she prayed her checking account wouldn't go into overdraft before it did.

The drive-through teller just burst out laughing when she saw the check, so Darja had to go in and spend an hour filling out a ginormous stack of documents while some fat-ass lech of a manager stared at her falsies. Her wrist hurt like hell by the time she got back on the road.

As she headed home, Darja tried to recall the insane spiel that this Travis guy laid on her and the others. She also thought about the halting conversation she had with the rest of the group after he left. Well, the two guys anyway.

The Quarterback's name was Porter Dunn, and he said he'd worked private security. Which seemed kind of funny to Darja, because 'Porter Dunn' actually sounded like the name of a private security firm. The guy seemed a little evasive about what kind of private security exactly, but he seemed competent enough.

The Quarterback was almost too good-looking, Darja thought, but also kind of blah. The two usually went together in her experience. If he'd found Darja attractive at all, he hid it pretty well.

Eurotrash Guy introduced himself as Bruehle, and indeed came from Germany by way of Toronto. Darja had no idea whether Bruehle was his first or last name. But she did notice he seemed the most dazzled by Travis' bullshit.

Bruehle spoke nearly perfect, idiomatic American English with a weird kind of sing-songy accent that reminded Darja of a slightly-warped record album. He also seemed a bit fruity, but that might have been because all of the zeros on his check. They were actually making her feel a bit fruity herself. But Darja did catch Bruehle sneaking glances at the Quarterback the whole time, too. She thought he actually licked his lips during one glance, but maybe he was just thirsty. Oh well, at least Darja wouldn't be distracted by interoffice romance on this gig.

She made the long drive back to her broom closet of an apartment in Weymouth, for once not feeling like the abject failure she was afraid she'd become.

CHAPTER FOUR

Joaquin Soares was a Sergeant with the Massachusetts State Police, currently working Investigative Services out of the Norfolk Detective Unit. Born and raised in the Portuguese community in New Bedford, Soares' family were descendants of the Berber Moors who had settled on Cape Verde before coming to America.

Soares was often mistaken for an African-American, which was both an advantage and a disadvantage in a racially polarized city like Boston. His wife always said he dressed like Columbo, with his rumpled suit and tan raincoat, but the effect was offset by his gray crewcut and the gold-rimmed glasses, which gave him the look of an adjunct professor.

Soares heard the stories about a rock singer disappearing during a concert, and took a drive to Quincy to see if there was anything worth his time. He doubted it, but there was also a shooting involved, and a few odd witness statements coming in that piqued his interest. Worth a quick look, at least.

The detective walked into the dark, empty nightclub and saw a tall, silver-haired man dressed in a plaid sports jacket and brown double-knit slacks standing near the small, elevated stage. He was jotting down notes in a small pad, occasionally glancing around his surroundings and taking in small details like a seasoned investigator.

But Soares could tell this was just a hassle for the man, just another rowdy downtown night in an unending string of them.

Soares approached and introduced himself.

"Inspector Cronin? I'm Sgt. Soares, State Police."

"How you doing?" Cronin said blankly, scribbling away at his notepad. "I'm just giving this place the old once-over. Not much to see."

"So you had a shooter take a pot shot at the band last night?" Soares asked.

"If he was aiming for the band, he wasn't much of a marksman. He hit that lighting rig up there."

"Some kind of explosion, from what I hear," Soares said, focusing on the fixture.

"Well, there was a bright flash. We're still trying to trace the source of it," Cronin said. "Didn't seem to come from that light. It flared out the video at stage level."

"All kinds of equipment around here," Soares noted.

"What I'm thinking," Cronin replied. "We're not exactly logging a lot of OT on this one, if you get my drift."

Soares glanced over at the stacks of electronics around the stage. "The singer still missing?"

"Well, not officially," Cronin offered. "It hasn't been seventy-two hours yet. There was a lot of confusion here last night. The general consensus seems to be the kid split when he saw the shooter and holed up somewhere, probably with a girl."

"Reasonable assumption."

"What we're thinking," Cronin grunted. "Lot of girls followed this bunch around, apparently."

"I'll bet," Soares chuckled. "Were those back doors open during the show?"

"No, they close 'em during the concerts. If it was opened, an alarm would sound. We checked."

"Was anyone hurt?" Soares asked, taking a survey of the room.

"Yeah, the shooter. Some of the local meatheads took him out in the alley and pounded him into jelly. From the looks of it, he recently had brain surgery. We're not expecting him to make it."

"Brain surgery?" Soares asked, incredulously.

"Yeah, his skull was being held together with staples," Cronin scoffed. "Guy looked like Frankenstein."

This detail didn't sit well with Soares. "Where is he now?" he asked.

"Quincy City. If he pulls through, I'm told they have a nice suite all ready for him at Bridgewater."

"Something with rubber walls, I take it."

"You got it," Cronin replied, still jotting in his pad.

"What's this I'm hearing about the weapon?"

"That's a weird one," Cronin said, finally looking up from his pad.

"Kid had a Russian PSM. Not something you'd ever see on the street."

"Any theories?"

"Not a one. Nothing in his jacket speaks to anything out of the ordinary," Cronin said.

"What's in his jacket?" Soares asked.

"Pfft, piddly shit. Shoplifting. Loitering. Domestic calls, bar fights. Been in and out of the nuthouse, though. Only thing he had in his pockets was a couple bucks and an expired driver's license."

"What are your people thinking?" Soares asked, scanning the room.

"He may have a family member who's a collector," Cronin said. "Hear his father's got money. But like I said, we're not losing any sleep over it."

Soares was silent for a minute. Something started to feel a bit off about this shooting.

"We're hearing reports of some kind of helicopter working the area, hovering just above the tree line," he stated. "Was that one of yours?"

"Funny, I was just about to ask you the same thing," Cronin said. "We don't have a chopper, Sergeant. We loan out from Boston if we ever need one. Not in our budget."

"Understood," Soares said and turned to leave. "Give me a call if the singer shows up."

"Right," Cronin muttered, his attention back to his notes.

Soares emerged from the dark club into the cold light of an early April afternoon in New England and walked around the grimy back alley. He scoured every corner for any visible clues to this very strange crime, but there didn't seem to be any.

The smell of fried food reminded him he hadn't had lunch yet, and he wondered if he had time to fetch himself a basket of fish and chips.

Soares reached the sidewalk and searched again for any-thing that might explain what actually happened here last night. He watched a smattering of cars and people pass by, but they had nothing to say about it either. Then he looked up at the spot where the aircraft was reportedly spotted just before the kid disappeared.

He looked up at it a good long time.

CHAPTER FIVE

With their orientation complete, the next step for Darja and Porter was to register as licensed private investigators. Darja was dreading all this, picturing long nights filled with deadly-boring coursework, just like her training for the NIS.

Travis had ordered Mean-Merc —AKA Evan — to get these two useless feebs squared away with their gear, so he took the opportunity to make Darja and Porter feel like the short-bus commuters at freshman orientation.

Evan had the taut sinew of a man who did more than just pump iron at the gym, and the healthy, ruddy glow of someone who spent a lot of time outdoors. He had close-cropped strawberry-blond hair, a square jaw, dimpled chin and steel-blue eyes. It was almost like he came off the Evan assembly line. Darja knew a lot of Evans in the Navy. She had a lot of fun with Evans.

Darja was disappointed to see this particular Evan wearing a fat, gold wedding band. She was even more disappointed by his ostentatious Christian tattoos ('In His Service,' 'Fightin' for the King').

Neither were necessarily disqualifiers, though the fact that Evan seemed to regard Darja with total disdain probably was. Then again, some of her best-ever lays were hate-fucks.

Evan seemed to want to barrel through this all bullshit as fast as possible so he could get back to wrestling sharks or kicking steamrollers to death, or whatever else it was he did when he left this dump.

"OK, c'mon over and let's get you two set up here," Evan barked impatiently. "First order of business, your licenses. Don't worry about the legalities. Your paperwork has already been processed."

Porter's eyes widened.

"Mr. Travis has a lot of friends in high places," Evan said. "You're both good to go."

Evan then handed them two 9-by-12 manila envelopes.

"Don't lose these. Put them somewhere very safe. I guarantee you any copies the State has have already disappeared into a black hole. I hate to break the news, but nobody out there likes P.I.'s much. OK, ID's..."

Evan gave Porter and Darja two folding leather wallets. Inside were brass shields emblazoned with 'Private Investigator.'

According to state regulations, 'Private' needed to be written in the same font and size as "Investigator," but the design clearly favored the latter word. The center was decorated with a graphic depicting an eagle and the scales of justice. Their actual licenses were inserted in the upper half of the wallets. 'Special Investigations Group' had been embroidered in gold thread beneath the cards. It wouldn't fool a damn soul who knew better, but it would put a scare into most civilians.

"Wait a minute; this has my driver's license picture on it. How did you get my picture?" Porter asked.

Evan stared at Porter like he'd just asked how Santa Claus could be at Sears and JC Penney at the same time, then put two oblong cardboard boxes in front of Porter and Darja.

"OK, first order of business are flashlights. Now these aren't some little Eveready's we picked up at the WalMart, so make damn sure you don't lose them. You do, it's coming out of your pay. And these suckers ain't cheap."

Next, the pair got leather notepads with the bogus logo embossed on the front. "I obviously don't need to explain these. But you just make damn sure your writing is legible. Mr. Travis will want to look these over now and then, and he'll take a slice out of your ass if he can't read what you wrote."

Evan reached into a large box on the kitchen floor and brought out two more items.

"All right, cellular telephones. If you don't know how to use one of these things, make damn sure you read the manual. Always keep them fully juiced but don't ever keep them on the charger overnight. You'll burn out the battery. Again, read your manual."

Evan then reached in his Santa box again and placed two small cardboard boxes in front of Porter and Darja.

"OK, handcuffs. You both have law enforcement experience, so I don't obviously have to explain how these work. But you need to read the State P.I. guidelines on their use. You get on the wrong side of the law with this and you'll end up in a world of hurt."

Next, Evan brought out two formidable-looking black plastic cases. He undid the snaps and displayed their contents with a loving glow.

"OK, now the fun part. These here are brand-spanking-new Glock Nines. You're both licensed to conceal-carry here and in the state of Massachusetts, so always keep them on your persons whenever you leave this building. No exceptions. Grab some extra ammo from the locker in the basement. You don't ever want to find yourself wishing you had more ammo. And like I said with the cuffs, make damn sure you read the state P.I. guidelines on deadly force."

Evan then put a large, rectangular wooden box on the table. With an air of reverence, he carefully removed the plastic sleeve from a large and imposing shotgun, fashioned out of polished matte black steel.

"Yeah, this baby. This little baby is a Mossberg 590 Tactical. Just a beautiful, beautiful weapon. Incredible stopping power, simply outstanding. Either of you ever used one of these before?"

Porter and Darja both nodded, but Evan paid them no never-mind as he swooned like a lovesick school-girl over the death-stick for a spell. He snapped himself out of his trance and turned his attention back to these two pencil-necks here.

"Good. Now, I honestly don't anticipate you ever having to use your weapons out in the field. But it's Boy Scout rules out there; be prepared. Either of you are rusty with your shooting, you'd best put in some practice time now. We got all kinds of land and you can go shoot at whatever you like out there. If you want to do some formal target work, we have a group member-ship at the local range. It's your call."

"OK, couple more things," Evan said as he took out a gold Kodak box and placed it on the table. "This is fresh from the oven; it's a camera that takes digital photographs. Take good care of this now, it ain't cheap."

He produced two more small white boxes.

"These are micro-recorders. You can use these when you need to do interviews or whatever in the field. There are batteries and extra tapes in the hall closet. Always keep them on hand."

"OK, we good to go? Read your manuals. Any questions you have, the answers are in there. All right. Have a good night, you two."

Of course, Evan didn't give a good quarter-fuck if Darja or Porter had a good night or not. He put on an olive-drab bomber jacket, grabbed a leather gym bag from the counter and marched out the back door.

"Wow, nice guy," Porter said. "Does he think we're both total retards or what?"

"He's probably an ex-SEAL," Darja offered. "That's pretty much how those guys treat everybody. Don't take it personally. I've seen SEALs treat Admirals like that."

CHAPTER SIX

Khoury rolled the big Suburban up in front of a small bodega in a working-class neighborhood in the Bronx. Travis glanced down the alley beside the little shop, then told Khoury to park off the street. While Khoury stood watch, Travis got out and knocked three times on a dented metal door marked, 'exit only.' It had no knob.

"¿Quien es?" a voice said behind the door. Travis identified himself and was let in. He had a few words in Spanish with the man at the door and took the stairway up. He came to another plain metal door.

An imposing young Hispanic man in track pants and a tank top sat on a lawn chair outside it, reading an issue of *Muscle & Fitness*. He had a 32 oz bottle of Gatorade and a fully-automatic Uzi lying beside him on the floor.

"Orlando, ¿como estas?" Travis said. "How we all doing up here? Any problems?"

"Not a one, sir. It's all good."

"Great, great," Travis said. "Anything you need, you call me, hear? Tell your mother I said hello."

Travis knocked on the apartment door. After a minute, a stout older woman appeared and let him in, and the two exchanged pleasantries. Travis handed her a very stuffed envelope and said, "And this is for you and your family, Señora Munoz. A small token of my gratitude."

The woman smiled and took the envelope. She walked over and placed it into a metal canister on the mantelpiece. She told Travis to wait there a moment before she disappeared down the hallway.

Travis clasped his hands behind his back and nervously tapped his foot in time with an inaudible rhythm, scanning the familiar apartment with mild interest. It was like a time capsule from the pre-Castro Cuba years, exuding a flavor that was both Old World and Caribbean.

Travis squinted at the morning sunlight coming through the bay window, heard the echoes of salsa-inflected pop music coming from the street below, and for a moment, he was taken back to Havana in its glory days. Travis basked in the glow of his fond memories until Señora Munoz came back to fetch him.

"She's ready for you now, Don Travis," the woman said, and waved Travis into the hallway.

Travis entered an empty room lit by a 40-watt bulb on a rudimentary fixture hanging from the ceiling. The floors were bare wood and looked well-trod upon. A cat lay on a pillow in the corner, sleeping.

In the middle of the room was a heavy-set young woman, early 20s, dressed in all-white, conservative Catholic attire. Her skin was as pale as her hair was black, which always got Travis worried about her health.

The young woman asked to be called 'Sister Esperanza,' as if she were in fact a nun. She wore a bulky turtleneck sweater, a hand-knit shawl, and an almost comically large crucifix. She also wore a satin scarf on her head, the kind women used to wear in Spain.

Mounted behind Sister Esperanza was a framed print of the Virgin Mary, surrounded a host of billowy blond angels. On the table in front of her were a leather-bound Bible and a glass of water.

"Mr. Travis, please take a seat. I understand you have some questions for the angels," Sister Esperanza said.

"I do, Sister. I've just embarked on a very... challenging project and I need guidance," Travis said.

"I understand," Sister Esperanza said. She adjusted the Bible so it faced her, took a deep breath and kissed the book. She said, "The Word of Our Lord," and then threw the book open.

She then ran her finger down the left-hand page, stopped and began reading.

"The Twelfth Proverb, verse twenty-three. 'One who is clever conceals knowledge, but the mind of a fool broadcasts folly.'"

She thought about the verse for a moment then said, "You're a man who trades in secrets, Mr. Travis. You must learn now to trust your own instincts, your own intuition. This enterprise of yours is a new kind of work, and there aren't any rules to follow. You must learn to write your own."

She closed the Bible, then threw it open again. This time she ran her finger down the right-hand page.

"Saint Paul the Apostle's Second Letter to the Church in Corinth, chapter twelve, verse ten.

'Therefore, I am content with insults, weaknesses, hardships, persecutions, and calamities for the sake of Christ; for when-ever I am weak, then I am strong.'"

Another thoughtful pause.

"You must be very careful in this new enterprise, Mr. Travis. You must be fully aware of your limitations and you must be very careful about those you choose to do business with. Realize your limitations may also be your greatest strengths if you trust the Lord and seek his counsel."

Esperanza didn't actually have to read the passages, she'd practically memorized the entire Bible. If Travis could figure out how, he'd be an extremely rich man. He rested his chin on his fists while Esperanza returned to her work.

"The First Epistle of Saint Peter, chapter five, verse eight. 'Discipline yourselves, keep alert. Like a roaring lion, your adversary, the Devil, prowls around looking for someone to devour.'" Pause.

"There is terrible danger lurking, Mr. Travis. There are powerful forces working against you, much more powerful than yourself. And these forces are close at hand."

Travis felt his guts churn. He wasn't expecting such a dire reading and he wasn't liking where this was headed now.

Esperanza flipped open her Bible again.

"The Epistle of Saint James, Brother of Our Lord, chapter one, verse twelve. 'Blessed is the one who perseveres under trial because, having stood the test, that person will receive a crown of life that the Lord has promised to those who love him.'"

"Our Father wills that you shall face many terrible trials and sorrows for his glory, as will all of those around you," Esperanza warned. "This is the path Our Lord has now chosen for you, and there is nothing you can do to avoid it."

Esperanza seemed especially concerned with that particular verse, so she waited a moment for her message to sink in before she returned to her divination.

"We shall let the angels speak through God's Word one last time, Mr. Travis," Sister Esperanza said, and flipped her Bible open again.

"The Twenty-Seventh Proverb, verse five. 'Wounds from a friend can be trusted, but an enemy multiplies kisses.'"

A particularly long pause here. "An enemy shall become a powerful ally, though the Lord may shield your eyes to this truth. But your enemies are hidden from you as well. They will not reveal themselves until the angels demand it."

Sister Esperanza sat silently. Bibliomancy was her chosen form of divination, but it was just a means for her to communicate her visions to others. The real driving force was her astonishing psychic power. Travis had worked with her long enough to know that her readings never lied, never failed.

He'd spent years trying to get her to submit to testing, not only for her gifts but also for her superhuman memory, but she refused to leave this apartment.

"Sister, I'm going to need more detailed information. Names, places, things like that. Can you provide those for me?"

"I will tell you anything the higher angelic powers choose to tell me, Mr. Travis."

"Thank you, thank you, Sister Esperanza. Now, is there anything I can get you? Anything at all that you need?"

"Our Lord in Heaven provides all that I need."

The room was now silent except for young woman's slight wheezing.

Travis stared into his own reflection in the black lenses of her sunglasses. He never ceased to be amazed by the fact that Sister Esperanza was born without eyes.

CHAPTER SEVEN

Travis called the first meeting with his new recruits to order. Darja had no idea why, but the bossman seemed particularly glum today. Maybe his cable provider dropped the Autopsy Channel.

"OK, I trust you're all geared up. Everyone had time to read all your orientation materials?" Travis asked, as if anyone would dare say no. "Good. Now let's get to work."

Travis handed the four of them a stack of letter-sized laser printouts. He sat down and leafed through his own copies, licking his forefinger to better separate the pages.

The first page was a headshot of what looked like the kind of junkie-bums Darja used to see while on leave in San Francisco: long, blond dreadlocks, scruffy goatee, ugly-ass piercings, dark brown mutton-chops.

"OK, subject: Gary Everett Sutton, lead singer for a rock music group named 'Cutter's Mill,' who apparently are popular among the local community. They're part of a new movement called 'the Grunge,' which appears to be connected to heroin trafficking and mind-control programs in the Pacific Northwest. So, why are we interested in this man?" Travis asked rhetorically, and then answered himself: "Because he fits a certain profile, he matches certain criteria that make him a person of very high interest for our project," he said, scanning the faces in the room for reaction.

No one had a single clue as to what that criteria might actually be, so Travis picked up a remote and aimed it at the large television which came equipped with a built-in VHS deck.

"Mr. Sutton also disappeared during a performance at a nightclub in Quincy, Massachusetts," he explained. "He hasn't been seen or heard from since, but is not yet officially listed as a missing person. Coincidentally, there are also reports of an unidentified aircraft observed by several area witnesses near the time of his disappearance."

Travis paused again to evaluate the team's reaction to this revelation, then played the video of the disappearance in slow motion.

"The disappearance was preceded by a shooting by an assailant who is the son of a prominent local businessman, who also had been reported as missing for several weeks," Travis said. "The gunman appears to have had major brain surgery recently, but no record of such can be located at any hospital in the continental United States."

"Do you think it was a black-market job, Skipper?" Bruehle asked.

Two days on the job and Bruehle had already taken to calling the boss 'Skipper.' Travis didn't seem to mind, so the nickname stuck.

"If so, it was done by very expensive doctors," Travis said. "The man's been scanned seven ways to Sunday, and the sutures were all intact, even though he took a major beating. The parents haven't a clue why he would need brain surgery or where he might have had it done."

"It was most likely performed in a private clinic, sir," Turkish or Arab Girl — given name Zaina Khoury — said in a pleasant voice that carried distant traces of an accent. "Probably a private clinic. Maybe somewhere the rich might go to have medical treatment without the news media getting wind of it."

Darja was stunned. She was seriously starting to think this chick was mute.

"That's an excellent theory, Zaina. Make note of that," Travis said. "The question then becomes why. Why would someone want to operate on him, and why would they do it in private?" Darja noticed that Zaina got to be called by her first name and felt weirdly jealous.

"What do we know about his institutionalization, Skipper?"

"Paranoid schizophrenia, apparently," Travis replied.

"Maybe someone operated on him to make him more schizophrenic," Bruehle said.

"That is certainly a possibility, sir," Zaina said. "Given some of the information we're been seeing about this individual."

"OK, then. Lundquist, Dunn; I want you down there, digging up any info you can," Travis barked. "I've arranged a meeting for you with a police detective in Quincy. He'll bring the two of you up to speed. Bruehle, Zaina; I want the two of you online getting every scrap of information on this man that you can. Family, friends, business associates, everything. Get to work."

CHAPTER EIGHT

Darja and Porter got to chatting about themselves on the long drive to Quincy. She could have written Porter's biography as soon as she met him. The quarterback guess was off, though; he was actually a running back.

Porter grew up in the northern suburbs of Virginia, father was some bigwig for the Census Bureau, mother was principal of a snooty private high school. First-string Varsity as a high school freshman, four years as All-State, all ultimately leading to a football scholarship at a halfway-decent state university where he majored in criminal justice and bench-warming. And like nearly all the other hometown superstars, he got cut from the team his sophomore year.

From college he went straight to the police academy, then did some time as a patrolman in Arlington for a couple years before finding himself recruited by one of the countless 'private contractor' outfits that hover around the Beltway like flies on shit.

From there, Porter got a little fuzzy with the details, a little evasive. Said he'd been doing some kind of security work in the area before getting a call out of the blue from Travis. Had no idea who Travis was or why the guy hired him, but he was happy to take his money all the same.

Darja had pegged the guy as a meathead but he really wasn't nearly as dumb as his life story might make him sound. And he seemed very interested in her own bio, even if she suspected most of it kind of flew over his head.

She told him that her parents were Marxist misfits of Finnish stock from Upper Michigan. They migrated to San Francisco to join up with the Beat movement, but it fell apart just as soon as they arrived.

They made a go of it there for a while but didn't really dig the whole hippie thing and hated psychedelic music, being crusty old folkies.

So they left the city to get real jobs in Marin County, just before the stork dropped their only kid down the chimney. Darja herself was a classic wild-child who started drinking, getting high and fooling around with boys in middle school.

Her parents were permissive even by Bay Area standards, and she had more than her fair share of run-ins with John Law. She was told she wasn't fit for college by pretty much everybody, so she decided to really piss her parents off and enlisted in the US Navy instead.

That little act of rebellion forced her mother to act as go-between between Darja and her father for years, since he refused to even talk to an imperialist-exploiter tool like her. So Darja decided she'd really twist the knife by signing up for Shore Patrol, then Master-at-Arms, and finally for the NIS.

All of which is to say she became a running dog in good standing for the capitalistic military police. Suck on that, Comrade Lardass. Hard.

She did two four-year bits, then moved up to Massachusetts after she was discharged and got work as a police detective for a suburban force. She did that for a while before trying her hand as a security contractor, doing some consulting for a few of the big companies around Boston.

At least that's what she told Porter. What Darja didn't tell him was that she'd earned a rep for being 'difficult' in the rent-a-cop racket and was having a hard time paying the bills when her placement agent first told her about this gig. And if this Travis thing didn't work out, she'd probably end up doling out handies at some Mass Pike truck stop.

Well, not really, but finances were getting a bit tight.

And so this is how their great partnership would begin, with the two of them lying through their fucking teeth to one another. Lies of omission, at least. Which Darja knew all too well were the worst kind.

CHAPTER NINE

Darja and Porter were instructed to meet this Sgt. Soares guy in the parking garage behind the main shopping area, of 'Quincy Center,' which looked like yet another once-thriving downtown strip killed off by the big malls. There certainly weren't any stores there that Darja felt like shopping in, but the fact that the local Woolworth's was still in business caught her fancy. Maybe she and Porter could go grab some some clam strips and grilled-cheese sandwiches at the lunch counter once they were done with this fool's errand.

Soares was parked in an unmarked sedan, a Crown Victoria the size of a houseboat. Darja and Porter got in the back, and Soares handed them two coffees and napkins before introductions were even made. Darja liked the guy already.

The car's windows were rolled down and a gorgeous breeze was blowing, but the sedan still smelled like sweet cigar smoke. Soares rolled them back up, started the car and put the fan on cool. He turned to face them and held his hand out.

"Sergeant Soares," he said briskly and shook Darja's hand.

She introduced herself as 'Darja,' like 'Madonna' or 'Cher.' Well, more like she always thought her surname sounded like some kind of cyst that heavy smokers developed.

Porter shook and said, "Porter Dunn."

"So you two wanted to talk to the shooter, right?" Soares asked.

"Yeah, if we could," Porter replied.

"Well, you're going to have to find him first," Soares sighed.

"What do you mean?" Darja asked, unsettled by this new plot twist.

"Well, the kid was taken to Quincy City and put under supervision," Soares explained. "Not under guard, mind you, because he was essentially comatose. What 'supervision' translates to is a patrolman drops by and looks in on you a couple times a day."

"OK, so where is he now?" Darja asked.

"He was transferred for emergency surgery. Only problem is that no one can seem to figure out where he was transferred to," Soares said, with a hint of frustration.

"Oh, you gotta be kidding me," Darja replied, successfully resisting the urge to drop a "fucking" in there.

"A private ambulance company came for him, a release order was arranged with QPD, and no one has seen or heard of him since," Soares said. "And to be honest, no one much cares."

"So why are you on this, Sergeant? I mean why do you care?" Porter asked, sounding nearly as unsettled as his partner.

"Listen; the shooting, the disappearance? Not really worth worrying about," Soares answered, waving his hand in dismissal. "By themselves. But my gut is telling me that they're pieces of a larger puzzle. Especially if a guy like Bob Travis cares enough about it to send a couple of hotshots out here to sniff around."

Darja ran a quick mental calculation and figured the guy wasn't using 'hotshots' sarcastically.

"To be honest, we really have no idea why he sent us out here, sir," Porter said. "We're brand new at this. We're just glorified information collectors, basically."

"Well, like I said, Bob Travis isn't going to waste time and resources unless he thinks there's something going on here," Soares said.

Are we talking about the same Travis? Darja wondered. The same crazy old fossil croaking on about psychic mind-powers and evolution? As far as she could tell, this entire fiasco was nothing but a waste of time and resources.

"How do you know him, sir?" Darja asked, thinking Soares didn't really know Travis that well at all.

"I was in 'Nam, getting towards the end there," Soares said. "Semper Fi. Bob Travis was the DI liaison to my unit. Our job was pulling out friendlies that Uncle Sam didn't want captured. Terrible, miserable work. The only thing anyone cared about was getting their ass on the next flight out. We couldn't even get our CO on the phone half the time. Bob Travis was the only guy in the whole damn place focused on getting the job done. It all went to hell in the end, but it wasn't because of him."

"Did you work for him here, stateside?" Porter asked.

"No. But he called me, I don't know, must have been the early 80s or so," Soares said, with a hint of puzzlement. "Said he was working down in DC and that if I ever needed a favor to let him know. Of course, what he really meant is that he would let *me* know if *he* ever needed a favor." Soares chuckled, "He sent me a nice card every time I got a promotion, when I got married, when my kids were born, which I thought was kind of strange. Then out of the blue, he calls me on this."

Darja thought the guy might be getting a little misty for a minute. But he switched gears and said, "So... you want a look inside the club?"

The trio made chit-chat as they walked the short distance to the club, which was apparently called 'Charlie's Da.' At least according to the sign out front, a carved wooden number decked in green and gold, sporting pseudo-Celtic script and an Irish harp.

Charlie's Da looked more like a repurposed hardware store than any kind of concert venue, with a small stage and a smaller bar. Compared to the sunny streets, walking into the place was like walking into a cave.

The black walls seemed to absorb whatever light escaped from the recessed ceiling fixtures. But the eyes adjusted and Darja and Porter shone their flashlights in corners where the house lights didn't reach.

"How many shots were fired?" Darja asked.

"According to the incident report, just one," Soares replied.

Porter lifted away a black mesh curtain behind the drum riser. There was an inch-deep bullet hole in the concrete pillar behind the curtain. Porter sifted through the folds of the curtain and noticed a hole there too.

"Sergeant, better take a look at this," he called out to Soares. "Looks like somebody took another shot here. Someone with a better aim."

Soares and Darja walked over to meet Porter and examined the fresh evidence.

"I'll be damned," Soares said. "But when was this fired? There was only one shot heard on the tape."

"The shooter could have been at the back of the room," Darja offered. "Maybe hiding behind that wall at the bar there. With all the noise from the stage you probably wouldn't hear a shot."

Porter stood at the center of the stage, facing the microphone stand. He took a sideways step. pointed one arm toward the bar and the other at the pillar.

"I don't know when that shot was fired, but if that kid was standing at the microphone here, he'd have caught it right in the chest," he said.

Soares walked back to look at the pillar. He inserted his pen in the hole. "There's no bullet in here," he said, disappointed.

He looked down at the floor and kicked the curtain out of his way. Finding nothing, he stepped behind the stage and scanned the area. Nothing.

Soares called out to the biker-looking guy behind the bar who was washing beer glasses in a tiny metal sink.

"Hey, excuse me. Did anyone find a bullet or a small piece of metal around? Maybe one of the cleaning people?"

"You're looking at the cleaning people," the Biker-Looking Guy said gruffly. "No, I didn't find anything. There were a lot of cops around this morning, picking through everything. If there was a bullet there, one of them probably hauled it off."

"Give me a minute," Soares said to Porter. He took out his cellphone and dialed.

After a moment he said, "Yeah, Inspector Cronin please." He listened a moment and said, "This is Detective Sergeant Soares, State Police. Yeah, thanks."

Soares held his palm to the transmitter and said to his companions, "This guy seemed pretty thorough."

He then turned back to the phone and said, "Inspector, this is Soares again. Yeah, good. Listen, your guys didn't find any other bullets when you were sweeping Charlie's, did they? Reason I ask is that we've found evidence another shot may have been fired, maybe by another shooter."

Soares listened for a few moments.

"OK, Inspector. No, no, I understand. If anything turns up, I'll get back to you. Thanks."

Soares hung up and said, "Asshole."

"What did he say?" Darja asked.

"He said his guys did a clean sweep and nothing turned up. He also says the Quincy Police Department doesn't have the man-power to worry themselves about a shooting in which nobody got shot. Especially since the shooter is now a vegetable. So if the Staties want the case, we're more than welcome to it."

"What do you think? There a case here?" Porter replied.

"That second shot definitely makes it a lot more interesting," Soares answered and rubbed his chin thoughtfully. "But my Captain is probably going to tell me the same thing the Inspector said. Unless Gary Sutton shows up with a bullet in his head that matches one of the weapons used here, there's no case. Just another bunch of drunk kids raising a little hell."

CHAPTER TEN

The trio left the bar and walked into the alley between it and the building next door, whose street level storefront was a fried-food joint. Soares pointed up at the roof's edge and explained the sightings there, while Darja and Porter tried to visualize a helicopter hanging over it.

Suddenly, a male voice addressed them from the shadows in a low, loud whisper.

"You cops? You looking into that boy going missing the other night?" the voice asked.

"Yeah. Why?" Soares replied into the shadows.

"Well, come on over here then."

The trio complied and met a tall, middle-aged black man in a dirty white apron and a yellow t-shirt that read 'Fish 'N' Chix,' using the same graphics as the joint's sign.

"That place is mobbed up, understand? That's Whitey Bulger's crew," the man said as he wiped his hands on his apron. "I don't want them seeing me talking to you."

"Did you see something?" Soares asked.

"I was out front, closing my place up for the night. I saw a flash come from that front door out there. Next thing I know a bunch of kids start screaming," the man said.

"What did you think was going on?" Soares said.

"I don't know, man. They get crazy in that place. But then I look up and there's this damn thing hovering right over the roof, about two-hundred feet up."

"Did you get a good look at it?" Soares asked.

"Not so much, because then all them kids came running out of there and started beating each other up. I got the hell away from there."

"People said it was a helicopter," Soares offered.

"Tssst," the man scoffed. "Listen, I did twenty years in the Air Force. Fixed everything that flew. If that was a helicopter, it sure as hell's something they ain't telling us about."

"What do you think happened inside there?" Porter asked.

The man thought about it for a moment.

"Ask me, it was all a show. I think that boy there was kidnapped, plain and simple. Somebody owes the wrong somebody-else money and they're not letting him go until they get paid. Like I said, that's Whitey's posse in there. Bad news, man. All day."

"Do you think the aircraft you saw has something to do with that?" Porter asked.

"Listen man, no offense, but the Mob, the cops, the government, the military? Same damn thing. It's all one big, happy family," the man said.

"Will you be around if we have any more questions?" Soares asked.

"Man, I just told you all I know. I'm just trying to point you fellas in the right direction."

Darja suddenly wondered if he thought she was a guy. Maybe she ought to wear more pink.

"All right, thank you, sir. We appreciate the help," Soares said. The man turned and disappeared back into the darkness.

"Seen enough?" Soares asked, lighting a cigarillo. "You want a look at the apartment?"

"Yeah, that would be great," Porter said.

"It's in Neponset, not too far from here. Follow me."

• • •

Following Soares through morning traffic was easier said than done. The man drove very fast, Massachusetts drivers were often aggressive to the point of hostility, and the streets here seemed to make no sense at all. Luckily, Darja had sharp eyes.

They all finally got there in one piece and pulled in front of a dumpy, badly-maintained apartment building in a gritty neighborhood.

Soares met Porter and Darja at the front entrance and the detective rang for the super. After a minute, a slovenly, middle-aged man in a dirty V-neck t-shirt and grimy work-pants let them in the door. The guy's four-alarm BO was making Darja gag as he led them up the narrow, airless staircase.

The winding hallway felt like it should lead to a Minotaur. The super let them into Gary's apartment and peeked curiously inside.

Already feeling a wave of stale heat from Gary's room, Darja said to the super, "We'll let you know when we're done."

As in, cops only, Bub. As in, take a hike, Stinky.

Gary's apartment was a depressing, rundown studio. His bed was a full-size mattress without a box spring or frame. The bed was topped with a tangled comforter but no sheets. Gary kept very little furniture and used Army surplus duffle-bags to store his clothes.

But amid all the squalor was some very expensive-looking stereo equipment of German make. Gary also had a Fender Stratocaster guitar on a stand, and a small Mesa Boogie guitar amp.

Gary also had a lot of exotic recording equipment and a sand-colored Macintosh Plus computer sitting on an improvised table made of stacked milk-crates and a small slab of plywood. There were a number of cassettes in a stand, all marked with dates and band names. Wires and patch-cords were tangled like noodles all over the room.

What most struck Porter and Darja, especially in light of the conversation with the cook in the alley, was the decor. There were posters of *Close Encounters*, *E.T.*, *Starman*, and *The Thing* pinned onto the cracked walls. Gary had also tacked up a lot of glossy photos of UFOs.

Darja took a look at the crate where he kept his books; they were all UFO-related. There was a high-end television and VCR, along with video tapes stacked in piles against the wall. Gary's viewing habits matched the decor. Nearly every tape he owned had something to do with aliens.

"What do you think of all this here, Sergeant?" Porter said, gesturing to the walls.

"What, the UFO stuff?" Soares replied, scanning the room. "Interesting."

"You think someone might have known about all this stuff and rigged up that little light-show at the club?"

"I don't know. It's a theory," Soares said, in a studiously non-committal tone.

"It could all have been some publicity stunt," Porter said, cynically.

Soares nodded sagely. "Could be."

"We sure this guy isn't just skipping out on a drug debt?" Darja asked, eyeing the squalor.

"We're not sure of much of anything, actually," Soares said, scratching the back of his head.

Porter rummaged through a shoebox full of artifacts, old photos, backstage passes, and clippings. He found a certain photo of two young men, smiling, arms tight around each other's shoulders. He held the photo up to Soares.

"Look familiar? Kinda looks like the shooter, no? At least going from the pictures Travis showed us."

Soares lifted his glasses and squinted at the picture.

"Yeah, you could be right."

"So maybe the two were friends at one point," Porter said.

"That doesn't surprise me. Most shootings are done by people who know their victims," Soares offered.

A pink carbon copy on the TV caught Darja's eye. It was a receipt for what looked like an abortion from a quote-unquote 'women's clinic' in Providence. Gary's name was the only one on the sheet, Darja assumed because he paid for it. There was no indication who the patient actually was. She jotted down the names, dates and locations listed on the receipt and put it back where she found it.

"Porter, why don't you go get the camera?" she said. "We can show all this to Travis."

Porter left and bolted down the stairs. He came back extraordinarily quickly by Soares' reckoning and handed off the camera to Darja, who promptly began taking snapshots.

"I think we got what we need, Sergeant," she said finally.

• • •

Outside, they said their goodbyes and Soares gave his new associates a list of names and numbers of people to contact; bandmates, family members, friends. The Quincy cops compiled the list and handed it off to the State Police, but no one had bothered to talk to anyone on it.

Porter and Darja were asked to copy Soares on their reports to Travis. Darja got the distinct impression Soares was essentially using them as his go-fers. He might think there was something bigger brewing, but apparently not anything big enough to waste his own time on.

Porter noticed that Darja seemed distant and preoccupied on the drive into downtown Boston.

"What's on your mind?" Porter asked.

"Just thinking about the apartment," Darja said.

"How so?"

"His stuff, it was all so well organized. Well, some of it."

"Some of which?" Porter asked, brow furrowed.

"His tapes and books and papers are neat but everything else is a wreck? Doesn't track," Darja said.

"I don't follow," Porter said.

"It just looks like someone had tidied up before we got there. Put things in nice little stacks."

"You think the apartment was tossed and then cleaned up? Kind of a stretch, don't you think?"

"Maybe. There's something else though," Darja added.

"What's that?"

"A receipt for an abortion. Why would he leave something like that lying around like that?"

"Maybe because he didn't think someone'd be going through his stuff," Porter offered.

"Maybe," Darja said. "Maybe not."

CHAPTER ELEVEN

Kernstock Productions Ltd., the agency that managed Cutter's Mill, took up the entire penthouse of the swanky Boylston Grove building in downtown Boston. The firm's lobby was huge, bright and well-appointed. Its ceiling reached about thirty feet high and its walls were mostly glass, which bathed the entire space in glorious sunshine.

The lobby was swarming with well-dressed people with expensive haircuts barking into cellphones as they rushed to and fro. Nary a slacker to be found here. The chrome reception desk was shaped like a giant 'C' and manned by four hatchet-faced young women, all of whom were yapping into headsets. None of them looked like they took even the tiniest spoonful of shit in their four-dollar coffees.

Porter and Darja walked up to the closest receptionist, a young woman with brown hair pulled back tight, a makeup-less face, and a concert shirt for a band neither Darja nor Porter had heard of.

The woman barked, "We'll get back to you," into her headset, then glared impatiently at her visitors.

"Can I help you?" the receptionist said in that tone librarians use on homeless people who wander in to use the toilet.

"Yes, we're from the Special Investigations Unit. We're here to see Mr. Kern," Porter said.

"May I see some identification?" the receptionist said in that tone liquor-store cashiers use on high school kids trying to buy beer.

Darja and Porter flashed their P.I. shields with Travis' faux-Federal design elements. It seemed to work just fine.

"Have a seat. I'll let Mr. Kern know you're here," the woman said, quite reluctantly. She'll fix your wagons next time, coppers.

After ten minutes or so, another woman came out to the lobby; this one a young, fresh-faced striver whose prissy bearing clashed wildly with her blatant Courtney Love fixation. She wore grungy togs, a bleached-blonde shag, and a diamond nose ring.

And she clearly never stooped to giving the common-folk her actual name. "Officers?" Courtney-Clone said. "I'm Mr. Kern's personal assistant. Please come with me."

Courtney-Clone impatiently checked her Swatch as the pair crossed the cavernous lobby. Darja wondered if all the women here were holding a contest to see who could act like the biggest cunt. The pair finally arrived at the door to the inner sanctum. Courtney-Clone buzzed them in with her keycard.

"This is a very busy time for Mr. Kern," Courtney-Clone sniffed haughtily. "May I ask what this is in reference to?"

"No, you may not," Darja said bluntly.

Courtney-Clone looked like she'd just been slapped. "Right this way, please," she said, stiffly. Courtney-Clone clearly wasn't accustomed to the commoners being cunts back at her.

They walked down halls lined with gold records, promotional posters and 8x10 photos of dumpy, hirsute men in white sport coats and Hawaiian shirts posing with celebrities, models and big-name rock stars. Courtney-Clone held open the door to Mitchell Kern's office for Darja and Porter. She stood silently at the threshold, waiting patiently for her boss to look up from his desk.

Mitchell Kern was a huge bear of a man. He remained seated but still looked well over six feet. His curly brown hair and thick beard was studiously un-groomed. He was more than a bit on the chubby side but looked like he could probably handle himself pretty well in a bar fight. Darja figured he liked to use his size to intimidate the weak and puny in his daily business dealings.

"That will be all, Lillian. Thank you," Kern said, without looking up from the papers he was shuffling through on his desk.

'Lillian?' She's a fucking *Lillian?* Darja decided to stick with 'Courtney-Clone.'

Courtney-Clone smiled tightly and left to lick her wounds, after having lost this particular grudge match with Boston's great unwashed.

"Agents, Mitch Kern. What can I do for you today?" Kern said as he shoved his paperwork aside. He held out an open hand, gesturing the two to have a seat. They did.

"We're here about Gary Sutton of Cutter's Mill," Porter said.

"I'm sorry, what about Gary?" Kern replied.

Just 'Gary.' On a first name basis with all his clients, obviously.

"The fact that he's gone missing." Porter replied.

"I'm sorry, when did this happen?" Kern replied, frowning in genuine confusion.

"He's been missing for nearly three days now, Mr. Kern," Darja answered.

"I'm sorry, no one's told me about this," Kern said.

This guy sure was sorry, Darja thought.

"He is one of your acts, isn't he?" Darja asked.

"I currently manage eighteen different performing acts. And to be perfectly frank, Cutter's Mill isn't exactly high on my list of earners," Kern replied.

"Well, we were told that you took out a general indemnity policy on Cutter's Mill worth two million dollars, and a life insurance policy on each member of the band," Darja said.

Kern didn't even twitch at the ambush. "That's just standard practice, Agent. It's simply a question of covering an investment."

"Well, that's nearly three million dollars for a band you say aren't high on your earners list," Darja pressed.

"Agents, can I get you something to drink? Water? Soda? Anything?" Kern said, swiveling toward a small refrigerator beside his desk. Obvious move to break her rhythm. Slick.

"No, thank you," Darja answered. Porter shook his head.

Kern swiveled back, rested his arms on his desk and steepled his hands together as if in prayer.

"Listen, I'll be frank; Cutter's Mill are a very, very good band, but they have pretty limited commercial potential. But they could have longevity as a cult act."

"If Gary Sutton turns up alive," Porter replied.

"Well, let's all keep our fingers crossed. See, there's a place for everyone in this business, big acts, small acts, all kinds, OK? You have U2 and Pearl Jam on one end of the spectrum and Cutter's Mill on the other. They probably won't go multi-platinum, but they've got a lot of talent, and I believe they'll still be selling records ten years from now. So I'm putting some money up front in hopes that it'll pay off somewhere down the road."

The superstar manager paused for effect, and then continued.

"I have to take out insurance because, as we've sadly seen recently, sometimes rock stars don't make it. And when they don't, the people who've spent a lot of money on them deserve some kind of protection."

Porter decided to sit back and study Kern's body language while Darja took the wheel.

"Well, hypothetically speaking, would a manager want to cash in on an investment that isn't paying off by doing away with the performer and collecting on the insurance?" Darja asked.

Kern shifted in his chair, obviously unhappy with the question.

"Well, hypothetically, such a person would be an idiot. Insurance companies tend to snap shut like clams if there's even a hint of foul play. They can hold up a case in court for years if they don't want to pay out. A lousy three-mill isn't worth the trouble you'd be put through in that situation," he replied.

'A lousy three-million?' Fuck this guy, Darja thought.

"Mr. Kern, we understand you're under investigation by the Royal Canadian Mounted Police for a club you operated in Toronto. They were concerned that it was used as a hub for drug smuggling by the Triads," Darja said bluntly.

Kern aimed his reply at Porter, as if he were the more reasonable one of the pair.

"That case went nowhere. Let me tell you what that was all about. The club scene is a zero-sum game. You have a limited amount of patrons and a limited amount of acts that draw. One of the ways you get a leg up in this business is by dropping the dime on your competition. In this case, the Mounties were all too happy to start talking Triads over a few crummy nickel-bag deals in the men's room. They always like to try to connect dots that aren't really there."

"But you got out of Canada nonetheless," Darja said, pressing the case.

This time Kern turned to Darja.

"Actually, I got out of the entire club business, because everyone in it had their damn hand out for a payoff or a kick-back. And that includes Mounties and Feds," he said acidly.

Ooh, testy testy, Darja thought. Taking a dig at the Bureau because he thinks we're Feebs. "Mr. Kern, we understand you're dealing with the IRS in relation to your connection with a Russian national by the name of Uri Chartov," she pressed.

"I'm not at liberty to discuss that as it's currently an active court case," Kern replied briskly.

"Well, we happen to know some things about Chartov and the people he works with. Is it possible that he might be involved in Gary Sutton's disappearance as a way of intimidating or silencing you?"

"Like I said, I had no idea Gary Sutton was even missing. I'm afraid you'll have to speak with my lawyer about all that. But I can tell you one thing..."

"What's that?" Darja asked.

"Cutter's Mill, and the entire scene around them, is like a goddamned Mexican soap-opera," Kern said to Porter again. "I mean, it's an absolute goddamn train-wreck. Those people are all seriously fucked in the head, even by industry standards. You're all assuming Gary has gone missing when he could just be hiding out from all the crazy bullshit that goes down with that band. You know why they call themselves 'Cutter's Mill?'"

"Not particularly, no," Darja said.

"Because their motto is, 'Music by cutters, for cutters.' Meaning *self*-cutters. So maybe I'd look into that before casting any more aspersions here."

It was time to end the interview. Kern was starting to get pissed off and Darja figured if they kept pressing him, he might want to find out if they actually had any jurisdiction in this case. Darja and Porter rose.

"Thank you, Mr. Kern. We appreciate your time," Darja said in her best *'OK asshole, you had your chance'* voice.

"Anything I can do to help," Kern said, suddenly sounding a lot more accommodating.

"I hope you find Gary safe and sound. Here, take my card, agents. Call me anytime."

Again with the 'agents.' Kern must be seeing a lot of agents lately, given all the trouble he's in. Darja just hoped they wouldn't run into any real agents on the way out.

The two took the elevator to the parking garage.

"What's the deal, Darj? You make him for this?" Porter asked as they got to the car.

"Nah, I just wanted to rattle his cage," Darja sneered. "It just really pissed me off that I'd ask the fucking guy a question and he'd address the answer to you."

"Well, I say we keep rifling through this guy's laundry, just in case," Porter said, starting the car.

"Fine by me. In the meantime, I think we have to talk to this Chartov guy," Darja said as she grabbed her shoulder belt.

"Well, we may get a chance to. Bruehle tells me he's coming to Boston soon to give a deposition in the Kern case."

"Jesus, that fucking Bruehle," Darja sighed heavily. "I sure hope to hell he never goes snooping around my personal records."

"Tell me about it," Porter sighed.

CHAPTER TWELVE

Travis bought a unit at an industrial park in Billerica to act as the Bifrost showroom. He was going to be meeting with corporate clients and needed a suitable venue for hosting.

He'd considered renting an office in the city somewhere — anywhere from Boston to DC would probably do — but had decided against it. It would have been impossible to keep secure. He was the only one with the keys to this space and no one got in or out without his say-so, not even the cleaning people.

Billerica was a sentimental choice for Travis, given his keen sense of history. It was halfway between Hanscom Air Force Base, where scientists brain-drained from Germany after the war worked on top secret technology with their American counterparts, and the old Scientific Engineering Institute farm in Andover, where the Company's Office of Research and Development dreamed up all kinds of creative applications for that same technology.

Those were very heady days for men like Travis; the entire world was at their feet.

The only problem with his new showroom was that he'd already held meetings in it and some of the other advisors knew how to get here. That's why Travis had state-of-the-art surveillance equipment installed, hardware that even most working agents were unaware of.

Unfortunately, he forgot to activate all that expensive gear when he arrived this morning. He was kicking himself for the oversight when an unwelcome face showed up at his office door.

"Bobby T! Fancy a day out on the links?" that face said, in an airy approximation of preppy bonhomie. "I've got morning reservations at Lexington," he said, holding up an orange golf ball like a summons.

The man, Don Morton, looked like a prosperous, late middle-aged accountant who played a lot of golf.

He certainly dressed the part, wearing reddish-brown loafers, tan double-knit slacks, a powder-blue Polo jersey and a Ralph Lauren navy cotton windbreaker. He stood around 5'11", and was trim, tanned, and energetic.

Morton's slightly weathered face was etched with deep smile lines and his graying blond hair was cut like a banker's. He gave the overall impression of a man who was having a great day and generally enjoying the hell out of his life.

"How the hell did you get this address?" Travis barked.

"A little bird told me. It also told me you might need some fresh air."

"Don't they have telephones in the Twilight Zone, Morton?" Travis replied impatiently. Morton actually lived in Connecticut.

"Like you'd take my calls," Morton said and sat himself down in the elegant leather chair facing the desk.

"You're lucky I'm talking to you now," Travis snapped. "And no, I'm busy. I'm always busy, in case you're wondering."

"Well, I was hoping to pick your brains about that," Morton said, leaning over to peek at the files on Travis' blotter. "I hear you drew the Bifrost assignment."

"I created Bifrost, Morton," Travis barked. "And no, we don't need any loose cannons aboard this ship."

"Come on, Bobby," Morton pleaded. "I'm dying for some action. I've got nothing to do since those tightwads in Congress shut down my unit."

"Why don't you retire and become a professional sex tourist, Morton? You can start in Bangkok."

"Don't be vulgar, Bob. It doesn't suit you," Morton said, carefully studying the ball as he rubbed it between his palms.

"If you're looking for work, the DoD is looking to open up a new UFO desk," Travis replied, offering Morton an envelope.

"Yeah, I've been thinking about it, but that's a pencil-pusher gig," Morton sighed, pocketing the document. "I was hoping to get out in the field a bit more."

Travis returned to his paperwork. "You're too old for that kind of work, Morton. Plus, most field supervisors think you're criminally insane."

"Better than not being thought of at all, I suppose."

Travis stared at Morton over his reading glasses.

"Have you ever been diagnosed for multiple personality disorder, Morton? I can never figure out which version of you I'm talking to."

"I went to a shrink once," Morton said. "He ended up retiring on me."

"Why? You tell him how many people you've killed?"

"No, I told him how many you did," Morton deadpanned. "He lost all hope for humanity."

"Well, it's been a real gas trading one-liners with you, Morton, but I have work to do," Travis said.

"Anything I can help with?" Morton asked hopefully.

"No, Morton. If I need your help, I'll call. Give my best to whatever you're fucking this week."

"I prefer to give them *my* best, Bobby-boy," Morton chuckled as he walked out without closing the office door behind him.

Travis rose irritably and marched over to shut it. Then he went over to the security console and made damn sure all the cameras, sensors and automatic locks were turned back on and in good working order.

CHAPTER THIRTEEN

Miraculously, Porter and Darja were somehow able to pick their way through downtown Boston's noodle-soup maze and retrace their steps back to Quincy Shore Drive, which the locals still called 'Wollaston Boulevard.'

Soares told them that Matt Conroy, bass guitar player for Cutter's Mill, was known to fish at the beach and had racked up a number of open-container citations there. The pair figured Conroy had nothing but free time now that his lead singer was missing, so they took a stab at tracking him down and hearing what he had to say.

Conroy stood barefoot at the edge of the low Wollaston surf, beside a small turquoise cooler and an old-fashioned corrugated steel Thermos. Darja couldn't possibly imagine what he'd be fishing for here. Certainly nothing you'd ever want to eat.

Darja figured the guy wasn't gunning for a GQ layout any time soon. He wore lime-green, acid-wash cutoffs, a maroon and gray baseball jersey bearing the AC/DC logo, and a hideous, gold-plaid flannel shirt. He also wore cheap RayBan knockoffs to cut the bright glare gleaming on the waves.

Darja was surprised to see Conroy without a radio or Walkman. Instead, he seemed tuned into the rhythm of the low surf, swaying his stringy brown locks ever so slightly to the beat of the waves. He turned when he saw Porter and Darja approach from his left.

"Hey, they told us we could probably find you here," Darja said, struggling to walk on the loose sand and still look vaguely authoritative.

"They told you right," Conroy said, and smiled at the surf.

"Hobby of yours?" Darja said, finding surer footing on the wet sand at water's edge.

"Yeah, I'm a fishing musician, baby," Conroy chuckled, and grinned at Darja.

"I assume you know why we're here," Porter said. "I'm sure you've probably talked to the cops already."

"That is correct, sir." Conroy's accent was thick, his syllables were faintly slurred, and his breath was ripe with hard liquor fumes.

"So, what do you think happened?" Darja asked.

"Well, I keep expecting to see Gary come floating in with the tide, such as it is," Conroy said. "Let's just put it that way."

"You think Gary was suicidal?" Darja said.

"Yeah, I think that fucking kid was a lot of things. Suicidal among them, yeah."

"But you just got signed," Darja countered. "Things were looking up."

Conroy shook his head slowly, as if he were dealing with children. "C'mon, you know how hard it is to make any money in this business?"

"Tell me," Darja replied.

"Listen, we got signed but none of us were getting rich. All of that money went back into the band. Hell, I could be making more flippin' burgers at Mickey D's," Conroy said grimly, his gaze again trained on the sickly gray waves.

"Well, isn't that how it works when you're starting out?" Darja asked.

Conroy's expression darkened as he pondered the grim reality of an also-ran alternative-rock band in the 1990s.

"I mean, the label all but told us we were a third-tier act. We won't get on MTV, least not on primetime. We'll always be a friggin' 'cult act.' We'll spend our lives opening for other bands that ain't half as good as us. Then we'll probably end up stuck on some crappy indie label who won't pay for beans. But most of us are pushing thirty, man. We don't know what else the fuck to do."

It was obvious this was a speech he'd had to make all too often.

Conroy sighed with exasperation. "I mean, we'll probably make an okay living out of it or whatever, but it's a rough life. And if Gary does turn up dead, we'll just have to find another singer. That's just the way the cookie crumbles, babe."

"Sounds kind of grim," Darja said.

"Sugar, life is grim," Conroy said, his grin returning. "It's why God invented fishing."

"So you think Gary is dead," Porter asked, more like a statement than a question.

"Yeah, I think that was all a big show he cooked up with his buddy there from the nuthouse. Go out in a blaze of glory and live forever as a local legend. The East Coast Kurt," Conroy scoffed.

"Wait, wait, back up a sec. What buddy from the nuthouse is this?" Porter asked.

"The gun guy. That was his old bunkmate there. You didn't know that?" Conroy replied.

Porter and Darja were momentarily taken aback. "No, we didn't know that," Porter replied solemnly.

"What nuthouse is that, Mr. Conroy?" Darja asked.

"I dunno, place out in the boonies," Conroy said. "Forget the name. The shooter guy used to come to rehearsals when Gary first joined. Just sat on the floor like a fucking retard and stared at Gary. Never said a word to any of the rest of us. Creeped everybody out."

"What did Gary have to say about him?" Darja said, her mind now whirring with possibility.

"Not much. Just said it was his boy from the hospital. That's what he called the nuthouse; 'the hospital,'" Conroy explained.

"How often did this guy show up?" Darja asked.

"Pretty much every day for the first month or so. He dropped out of sight after that. Gary said they threw his ass back in the banana-bin after he flipped his shit out on a guy at some biker bar in Weymouth Landing. Never saw him again."

"Did Gary mention him at all after that?" Porter asked.

"Nah, nothing," Conroy said. "I got the impression Gary tolerated the guy but was happy to finally get him off his dick."

"Is there anything else you might remember?" Darja said.

"Well, Gary did say his boy's family were loaded. I think Gary was mooching off the guy," Conroy said. "Then again, Gary was mooching off everybody."

"Mooched how?" Darja asked. This case was really getting interesting all of a sudden.

"I think Gary was squeezing a lot of money outta the guy," Conroy said. "Dunno what for. Gary wasn't using. That's one of the reasons he got hired. Junkies are band-killers, every single time. No exceptions."

"That it?" Porter asked.

"Well, pretty much. The only other thing that sticks out in my mind is that Gary said the guy was volunteering for some kind of drug testing trials."

"Really? With who?" Darja asked, somewhat stunned.

"I dunno. For the Army, I think. Some big-ass base out near Worcester there," Conroy said.

Darja and Porter stared hard at each other.

"Okay, thank you, Mr. Conroy," Darja said. "We'll be in touch if we have anything else we need to talk about."

"My friends call me Connie. You can call me Mr. Conroy," he said, grinning mischievously at Darja. "Hey honey, anytime you need a personal fishing lesson, you know where to find me."

Darja winked and flashed him a knowing grin in return.

"Thanks again, Mr. Conroy," Porter said, and guided Darja as she stumbled her way through the sand.

"Anytime," Conroy said to the sea.

• • •

"Well, that was informative, don't you think?" Porter said as he and Darja stumbled across the sand.

"I'll say. We gotta get Bruehle on all this shit," Darja replied. "It's starting to look like Gary kicked the shooter to the curb and maybe the guy didn't appreciate it."

"What I'm thinking," Porter chimed, before switching gears. "Come on, Darj. I'll buy you some lunch and we can take in the sights."

A sandwich truck parked in the lot and looked halfway sanitary. It seemed to be popular with the workers rebuilding the seawall near the yacht club, so they decided to try their luck.

Darja ordered a seafood roll, and Porter a footlong hot dog with onions and peppers. They split a dollar-sized bag of chips.

The pair took their lunch and sat on a bench facing the beach, and soaked up the sun and sea. The breeze coming off the water was a bit brisk, but otherwise it was a glorious day. It was easy to forget the grim work yet to be done.

They ate their food and sipped at their off-brand diet colas for a while before Darja broke the silence.

"Well, this has got me reconsidering the suicide angle," Darja said. "We know Gary's got a history of mental illness, and the two go hand-in-hand. But if this guy really had a hard-on for Gary, maybe it was all coincidental. Or maybe Gary owes a lot of money to someone who sent Kevin over to give him a scare."

"What about the videotape?" Porter replied. "That flash couldn't have been more than a second or two. Kind of hard to disappear in that short a time, especially in a crowded bar like that."

"I don't know, light can do a lot of weird shit to video cameras," Darja stated. "And that dump ain't exactly breaking the bank on their gear."

"Well, we have to talk to someone at the hospital Gary and this gunman were treated at, and see what's up with that," Porter said. "Who knows, maybe there's another former patient mixed up in all of this."

"Yeah, that's all we need, another mental case," Darja said, her voice heavy with resignation. "That Kern guy was right about this whole scene being like something out of a soap opera."

"Well, say there are more old bunkmates in the mix. Gary could be hiding out with them."

"Gary's a rock star, Porter. He could be hiding out with anybody. He's probably shacked up with some hot little piece of ass out in Woburn."

"Either way, we gotta do this thing by the numbers," Porter said, squinting at the sparkling waves. "I don't know about you, but Travis strikes me as a real by-the-numbers kind of guy."

CHAPTER FOURTEEN

That evening, Porter and Darja sat with Bruehle at the kitchen table, scarfing down Taco Bell. The two made small talk while Bruehle stared blankly into his laptop. Finally, he closed the computer and stared at his partners like they'd suddenly materialized out of thin air.

"So I hear you two were out at Wollaston Beach today," Bruehle finally said.

"Yeah, talking to Gary's bass player," Porter answered.

"That's quite a historic stretch of real estate there," Bruehle said, his tone clearly implying that he had a story he was itching to tell.

"Really? Didn't seem like much to me," Porter replied.

"Well, there's an island just off the beach there that played host to some very interesting people," Bruehle said.

"People like who?" Darja asked.

"Like Wernher Von Braun and his entire staff," Bruehle said. "Like several dozen top Nazi scientists smuggled into the US to ply their trade for your defense industry. You know, that kind of interesting, Sailor Moon."

Bruehle was big on giving everyone nicknames, preferably from TV shows. Darja had no idea who Sailor Moon was, though.

"Seriously?" Porter said. He was having difficulty picturing a secret Nazi lair in the gritty, working-class neighborhood running along the shoreline.

"Oh, yes. They were set up on Long Island there, while waiting for their marching orders. A place called Fort Strong. It was part of a project called 'Operation Paperclip' and it was highly secretive."

"Operation Paperclip?" Darja said. Terrific, more spook bullshit, she thought. Just what we need.

"Yeah, the name came from notes that were posted over the subjects' files with a paperclip," Bruehle explained. "The original file would say 'Reinhold So-and-So, committed Nazi,' but a note would then say, 'Reinhold So-and-So, NOT a committed Nazi.' Apparently, the whole operation drove Harry Truman cuckoo."

"Well, that's just a coincidence, right?" Porter asked. "You don't think this has any bearing on this case, do you?"

"It all depends," Bruehle answered. "Most of your Paperclip boys went into the space program. There's all kind of theories that UFOs are just secret aircraft they brought over with them. And the kinds of human experiments that the Nazis were messing around with started showing up in the States, especially the mind-control experiments. And many of the institutions involved in those experiments are located in the Boston area."

"Like who?" Porter asked, clearly taken aback by all this.

"You know, little mom-and-pop shops like MIT, Harvard, Boston University, Mass General, the Scottish Rite, and Worcester State Hospital. Then all kinds of Federal departments that have offices in Boston. And these are just the ones we know about. There could be dozens, maybe hundreds, more that we don't know about. Quite a coincidence, don't you think, Sails? That all these Nazis show up in Boston Harbor and a few years later everyone's suddenly doing Nazi experiments here?"

"Well, that's absolutely riveting, Bruehle, but how does this connect to what we're doing?" Darja asked.

"Again, it depends," Bruehle replied. "Some folks seem to believe that remote-viewing is actually a by-product of those mind-control programs. That it was accidentally discovered when they were running LSD tests on certain subjects. Many of whom claimed to be alien-abductees. Then there's the curious fact no one seems to have heard of remote-viewing before these mind-control experiments were held."

"I really don't get it. Why are all these people so worked up about this remote-viewing thing? It still doesn't make any sense to me," Porter said, clearly not drinking the Kool-Aid.

"If you find a remote-viewer who knows what they are doing, you have access to information you can't otherwise get through spying or signal intelligence," Bruehle answered. "A remote-viewer can steal all your secrets while he's holed up in a fish shack on some Norwegian fjord. They don't need to break into your office or hack into your network. They are invisible, untraceable and nearly unstoppable. The really good ones cannot only overcome space and distance, they can overcome time. They can view the past or the future.

Even if you have a viewer who's only twenty percent accurate, that's one hell of a lot more information than you'd have access to otherwise."

"Yeah, but any of this actually really work? I still don't see how any of this is practical," Darja said, not exactly sold on the concept either.

"Well, the US Government spent quite a lot of money on remote-viewing programs," Bruehle said, brushing Darja's skepticism away. "For twenty-five years, almost. And now there are a lot of companies out there that are willing to spend their own hard-earned dollars on it, and guys like Travis more than happy to take it. So I'd imagine that someone thinks it actually works, wouldn't you?"

"Yeah, well, I'll believe it when I see it. Believe-it-when-I-fucking-see-it, buddy-boy," Darja said tartly, then took a defiant sip from her 32 oz. vat of Diet Pepsi.

CHAPTER FIFTEEN

Morton had been working this gimmick for six weeks and now he was seriously starting to wonder if someone wasn't just pulling his leg. He had gotten a tip from a reliable snitch that some very nasty players were in the market for some brain-jobs; psychics, remote-viewers, the works. Word was they weren't just going to settle for hot stock tips, they were up to something witchy.

The chatter was spotty, but it looked like some very ugly business was bubbling up, some heavy-duty heathen-juju that may also tie into a rumored kill-cult out in the sticks. The only hard data he'd been given was a partial plate. But it ultimately led Morton to a pile of construction scrap overlooking a dirt road running beneath an elevated railway the commuter train rode on.

Morton came loaded for bear; he'd brought a Sony DAT recorder, along with a custom-made parabolic microphone and military-grade 20x60 binoculars with a built-in digital camera. And of course, his trusty old Browning, bless its soul.

Just about three hundred feet away from Morton's position stood a tall, late middle-aged white man dressed entirely in black; black suit, black shirt, black tie, black shoes. Morton couldn't say much for the color scheme, but the suit seemed cut well enough.

The man was standing beside a black Chrysler, casually smoking a cigarette with one hand, and flying a cheap plastic kite with the other. Morton thought his eyes were playing tricks on him but no; that man, looking all the world like a mobster's mortician, was indeed flying a kite.

Morton mentally ran through the range of possibilities: The guy was a nut. The guy was bored. The guy stole the kite from some poor kid to keep his larceny skills fresh. The Mortician turned to face the sound of an approaching car, then released his kite into the wind. Morton followed the kite with his spyglasses as it disappeared into the low, thick clouds.

When he looked back, the Mortician was leaning over an old Lincoln Town Car. Morton was thinking it was probably a '64.

Good year for Lincolns.

Morton couldn't make out the driver from this angle or see his plates. But he certainly could hear the two of them, due to the nice, quiet spot they chose to meet. Morton made a mental note to thank these fellows for being so considerate before he executed all of them.

"What do you have to tell me?" the driver said, his voice distorted by the distance but audible enough.

"We have a team in place," the Mortician said, in a low rumbly baritone. "Three viewers, and an influencer that shows a lot of potential. We're still working with the others, but it may take more time."

"How good are they?"

"Promising," the Mortician said. "Certainly, the best we could get under the circumstances. We're still training them. They have potential, but they're not the easiest people to work with. But we've gotten a lot of hits during their practice sessions, hits we've been able to verify. The question now is refining their skills."

"Are you having behavior problems, then?"

"Not so much, just some whining and bellyaching. We did have some major problems with one of the viewers, though. He was being extremely uncooperative, so we released him from his contract." Morton chuckled at the euphemism. He'd have to use that one sometime.

"You know how to reach me. Keep me posted," the voice said, punctuated by the metallic twanging of those old Lincoln electric windows.

The Lincoln backed away and out of sight. A gray cloud of gravel dust made the front license plate unreadable. The Mortician got into the Chrysler and took off to the south, but Morton already had his plate. Only problem being it was registered to an import firm that didn't seem to actually exist.

Don Morton put down his headphones and thought for a good long while about the conversation he just overheard. Something was clearly rotten in Denmark. Getting out here seemed like an awful lot of bother for such a short encounter. He hadn't heard anything actionable here, outside of the gag with the viewer released from his contract. But Morton was pretty sure that people involved in legitimate enterprises didn't conduct their business under railway trestles out here in the middle of West Nowheresville. Pretty damn sure, indeed.

CHAPTER SIXTEEN

Porter and Darja chose Cutter's Mill guitarist Adam Weaver for their next interview. Adam had founded the band and was considered a major talent, so far as rock guitarists go. He'd won 'Best Guitarist' in a poll in a Boston-based music magazine, beating out better-known national stars.

His bluesy style was being compared to Jimi Hendrix and Stevie Ray Vaughan, and *Rolling Stone* recently called him one of the 'Five Post-Grunge Guitar Gods to Watch.'

Adam's day-job was teaching guitar, and judging by his condo, a two-bedroom job in a waterfront complex in a gentrifying corner of Dorchester, it looked like he was doing all right for himself. He was thin but in a wiry way, like a high school track star dressing grunge for Halloween. He wore his dirty-blond hair in a ponytail and was dressed in old jeans and an Alice in Chains t-shirt.

Adam's girlfriend, a pretty brunette in grunge-peasant dress named Susan Driscoll, showed the investigators around the apartment. But Darja soon got the very strong impression that Adam was an arrogant prick, and that Susan was already planning her getaway.

Porter and Darja sat with Adam and Susan in the living room area and made small talk about the neighborhood and Boston real estate prices until Porter got to the point of the visit.

"So, Adam, your story is that you saw the flash, and then after the gunshot, Gary was gone?" Porter asked.

"Yeah," the guitarist replied.

"How long did it take for your eyes to adjust?"

"Oh shit... maybe five minutes or so?" Adam said.

"So, Gary could've gone into the crowd and left the building while you were in this daze, right?" Darja said.

"No man, it was like he was there and then he was gone. I didn't see him jump into the pit or anything like that. I wasn't that blind."

"Well, the video seems to substantiate that, otherwise we wouldn't be here. And there's no trapdoor in the stage," Porter offered.

"No man, it's just a bar,"

Porter felt a 'you idiot' hanging there, but Adam changed course. "But it's like home base for us, it's where we play for our real core fans."

"Susan, you're standing behind the amplifiers, from what we've seen on the video," Darja stated.

"Adam's amps," Susan specified.

"Right. What did you say happened?" Darja asked.

"Same as everyone else. Gary was there and then he was gone," Susan stated. "But I wasn't blinded by the flash because I closed my eyes when I heard the pop."

"You told the cops you covered your eyes," Darja said.

"You know what I mean," Susan responded.

"Why did you do that?"

"I thought it was a beer bottle, like some asshole throwing a bottle at the stage. And I didn't feel like getting broken glass in my eyes."

"There was a pop before the flash?" Darja asked.

"That's what I heard," Susan said.

"Because none of the other witnesses reported that," Darja said, pressing the point.

"Yeah, well, they were all getting blasted by the music, weren't they?" Susan said petulantly.

"Fair enough. You weren't?"

"No, behind the amps is the quietest place in the room."

"Quiet?" Darja said, cocking an eyebrow.

"Relatively. You know what I mean. I get bad headaches, so I stand there," Susan explained.

"So you had a good view of the crowd?"

"The bar. I can't really call it a crowd, there were only about fifty or sixty people there," Susan said. She clearly wasn't enjoying this.

"That's a crowd. And you didn't see Gary anywhere?" Darja said.

"Nowhere, because only the front doors were open and it would take him a while to get back in there if you were going to leave," Susan said. "There were bouncers at the back doors, and they would've definitely seen him if he tried to go out through there."

"So you weren't blinded, and you didn't see Gary?" Darja asked. "He didn't duck behind the stage or sneak behind the bar?"

"You'd have to ask the bartender that," Susan said. "All I can tell you is that he was not at the back of the stage and I didn't see him in the crowd. It's a small club."

Darja turned her attention back to Adam.

"Okay. What about your relationship with Gary, Adam? How did the two of you get along?" she asked.

"OK, I guess."

"You guess," Darja replied skeptically.

"We didn't really hang out or anything. Gary usually kept to himself," Adam said.

"He didn't hang out with the rest of the band, but the rest of the band did hang out?"

"We were a band already before Gary joined," Adam said, as if that should be common knowledge. "We had another singer before, but he left to go to cooking school to study to be a chef or something."

"When was this?" Darja asked.

"About two months before Gary joined."

"What did you think about Gary's whole UFO thing?" Darja pressed.

"We never talked about it," Adam said, clearly wanting to slam the lid shut on that particular topic.

"Never?"

"Listen, he came to practices, he came to gigs, he came to business meetings. But all we ever talked about was music."

Adam seemed like he was over this entire conversation now.

"So you have no knowledge of any of that UFO stuff?" Darja said, poking at the scab.

"Hey, everyone has their own trip, OK? He didn't bring it up, so I didn't ask," Adam replied irritably.

"It seems like a sore spot. Was it a bit of a sensitive subject in the band?" Darja pressed.

"Listen, he's a good singer and a good songwriter. After a while you realize that the good ones are usually crazy. Just comes with the turf," Adam said. He'd crossed his arms now and was glaring sullenly at Darja.

Darja ignored Adam's glare and turned back to his girlfriend.

"What about you, Susan? Did he discuss it with you?"

"What do you mean?" Susan replied, a trace of panic in her surprise.

"Did Gary ever talk about UFOs with you?"

"I mean, when are you talking about?" Susan suddenly reddened, clenched her arms together and began gnawing at her thumbnail.

"Well, the two of you were sleeping together, right? Did Gary ever talk about aliens or flying saucers with you then?"

"Oh my God," Susan cried, and buried her face in her palms.

"What the fuck?" Adam shouted. "You were fucking him?"

"No! I mean, it was just..."

"You fucking whore!" Adam shouted again and tore Susan's hands away from her face. "You *are* fucking him! How long has this been going on?"

"Hey, calm down!" Porter said and leapt to his feet.

"Shut the fuck up, faggot!" Adam spat, stabbing an angry index finger at Porter. "You're not a real cop."

"Tell him, Susan. Tell him about the abortion!" Darja shouted.

She'd had either gotten caught up in the excitement or felt it was time to lance the boil.

"A fucking abortion? You goddamn fucking whore!" Adam slapped Susan hard across the face, leaving a dark red handprint on her cheek.

Darja stepped forward, but Adam punched her in the side of the head. His large pewter rings tore into the skin beneath Darja's left temple.

Jesus, Darja thought as she reeled, that little hippie shithead can really throw a punch.

Porter suddenly leapt forward and grabbed Adam by his shirt, hurled the man down face-first, then pinned him to the floor with a persuasive right knee before anyone else knew what was happening.

Darja figured Porter had probably drilled that particular takedown a hundred times or more, but she had to admit it was still pretty damn impressive.

"Okay, that's assault and battery," Porter said, not even winded. "I'm placing you under arrest. Call the cops, Darja."

Adam quickly recovered from the shock of the hard tackle and started to buck, so Porter yanked his punching arm up and out in the wrong direction with one hand and pressed his face against the carpet with the other.

Darja cuffed Adam, then called 911.

Two young, somewhat-overzealous cops, one white and one Asian, showed up about fifteen minutes later. But they seemed more interested in hassling the investigators about their credentials than the blood red slap-mark on Susan's face or the open wound on the side of Darja's head.

Cops and their dick-size bullshit.

CHAPTER SEVENTEEN

Satisfied with Porter and Darja's bonafides, the cops finally took a closer inspection of Susan's bruise, Darja's wound and the dry blood on Adam's rings. They switched out the cuffs and hauled Adam off to the station. Darja was going to have to file an assault complaint, a formality she couldn't wriggle out of. This arrest, on top of Gary's disappearance, was going to keep Cutter's Mill in the local headlines for a while yet.

After dealing with some more cop-bullshit, Porter and Darja took the elevator down to the icebox-cold concrete parking garage and walked to the car.

"Jesus, what is wrong with that guy? Fucker really tagged me," Darja huffed as she dabbed at the bloody wound with a KFC wetnap. It stung like fuck.

"What's wrong with that guy? What's wrong with you?" Porter shot back.

"What do you mean?" Darja asked, taken aback by Porter's sudden flash of anger.

"Was that really necessary? I mean, what the hell was all that? A hunch? Woman's intuition?"

Darja sighed heavily and threw her arms down at her sides, as if to acknowledge she indeed had let the situation get out of control. She rubbed her brow, then turned to face Porter.

"No. I mean, partly," she said. "Gary had that abortion receipt from the woman's clinic. They went down to Providence for it, so I figured they obviously didn't want anyone to know about it. And yeah, I could tell by the way Susan was with Adam that she was probably stepping out on the guy. And Gary seemed like the obvious candidate..."

Darja stopped talking but only because she saw that Porter was utterly aghast at what he was hearing.

"Porter, please say something," Darja pleaded. This was not how she wanted to kick off their partnership.

Porter shook his head. He crossed and uncrossed his arms, lowered his chin to his chest. He rubbed his face with his palms. He obviously had no idea what to do with his hands.

"Porter?" Darja said, imploringly. She was starting to feel sick.

Porter took in a deep breath and said, "What... what exactly did all of this accomplish in finding Gary, Darja?"

"Well, maybe one of them killed him," Darja protested. "I mean, it speaks to motive, right?"

"No," Porter replied, shaking his head. "No, it doesn't."

"I mean, love or money, right?"

"Darja, unless he's a really good actor, Adam clearly had no idea Susan and Gary were seeing each other. So no, I don't see any motive here at all."

"OK, fine," Darja said curtly.

"Darja..." Porter said as he unlocked the Taurus.

"Fine, you're right, OK?" Darja said, getting into the car. "You win. Let's just go back to New Hampshire and have a fucking staring-contest with Zaina."

The two rode in silence in the dark, drizzly night.

Darja couldn't stand the quiet so she turned the radio to a college station that played hardcore metal and cranked the volume. Porter was annoyed but figured it was best not to poke at the hornet's nest again. Darja reclined back in her seat and flopped her foot up on the dash.

Finally, Porter lowered the pounding volume on the radio.

"Darja, you're a really good investigator."

"Oh, don't you fucking patronize me, dickhead," Darja spat. "I'm not in the mood."

"No, I mean it. That was an amazing piece of deduction there. And there may turn out to be something to it. But next time, I'd appreciate it if you let me know before you go dropping any bombs like that."

"Look, I'm sorry," Darja said. "It was a fucking mistake, OK? It won't happen again. Jesus."

"I'm just saying we have to keep the lines of communication open. I mean, that kid almost took your eye out with those rings of his."

Darja fell silent. He was right, but did he have to be such a fucking Boy Scout about everything?

It was going to be a long ride home.

CHAPTER EIGHTEEN

Darja and Porter took a drive out the next morning to the mental institution Gary and his would-be shooter had once spent time at. It was a pleasant drive and the leafy, idyllic hospital campus seemed more like a retreat center than an asylum. The lobby was clean, modern and staffed with friendly faces.

Things got a bit less cozy, however, when Darja and Porter had to surrender their weapons at the guard station and then fill out all kinds of intrusive paperwork. Darja had brushed her hair over her bruise, but everyone seemed to stare at it anyway.

But they were ultimately rewarded with guest passes and a perky, petite nurse who seemed to believe she'd been hired on as a tour guide. They couldn't pass a fire extinguisher without hearing its life story.

Darja wondered if this ditzy little chatterbox thought she and Porter were in the market for a new nuthouse. If so, this one would certainly be a good choice. It was bright, airy and refreshingly tranquil for a mental institution. No one seemed to be shrieking in Latin or flinging poop at passersby. The staff here probably called their patients 'residents.' Or better yet, 'partners.'

After an excruciatingly informative tour, Chatterbox finally showed them to the director's office. Porter and Darja sat in two leather reception chairs while the history lesson continued unabated. The chitter-chatter was so incessant that Darja thanked all the stars in the sky when a stocky, older man appeared at the door and asked them to come in.

Chatterbox smiled sheepishly and did a strange kind of curtsy, as if waiting for an invite herself. But the man simply said, "Thank you, Mary," and closed the door.

If Sylvanus Ivor Sanderson weren't a real doctor, he could play one on TV. He looked like he was in his early-60s and enjoyed a good meal or two. His thinning hair was a brilliant silver and he sported a white doctor's coat, horn-rimmed bifocals and a kindly, open smile. Everything about him screamed, "It's OK, I'm a doctor. You can trust me."

"Dr. Sanderson, we understand that Gary Sutton was a patient here," Porter said with his cop-voice.

Darja was content to tag out while she pondered why the hell people used to give their kids names like "Sylvanus Ivor." Sadism, probably.

"That's right," the Doctor replied. "On and off, since he was in high school. His most recent admission was a couple years ago. Maybe 1991, I'd have to check."

"And a man named Kevin Stuart was a patient here as well?" Porter asked. "We understand that he was friendly with Mr. Sutton."

"I'm not exactly sure if they were friends, but Kevin Stuart was also a patient here, yes," the Doctor said in his helpful voice.

Darja cut in, asking, "Is there anything you can tell us about Gary Sutton's condition or his treatment?"

"Not off-hand. That information is restricted under doctor-patient privilege," the Doctor said, with the obligatory tone of regret.

"We understand that, sir, but we're investigating serious crimes involving these individuals," Darja said, pressing her case.

"No, I get all that, I do," the Doctor countered. "It's just that if you want access to their files, there's a certain protocol to be followed. You'll need a court order."

"Sir, we're working against the clock here," Darja said urgently. "Gary Sutton's life may be in danger, and we..."

"Wait a minute; Lundquist? Dunn?" the Doctor said, a light of recognition flickering in his eyes. "That's right. You're working for Bob Travis. I'm sorry, I blanked out there. Senior moment."

"Bob Travis?" Porter sputtered dumbly, earning a dirty glare from Darja.

"I'm on the Bifrost advisory board," the Doctor said, earning blank stares from his guests. "I'm your boss, basically. One of them, at least."

"Sir, let's say this is true," Porter said. "Then why didn't you provide Mr. Travis or whomever with information about these patients." It was all Darja could do to avoid slapping her partner upside the head for pulling this lame-ass bluff.

"You see, that's Bob Travis for you," the Doctor sighed. "He could have found out everything he needed about these men with a simple phone call. But he's too bull-headed. So he has you two waste time running around doing it the hard way."

"Well, what else are you permitted to tell us that might help our investigation, sir?" Porter asked.

The guy really wasn't bowling Darja over with his interrogation skills here.

"Please, call me Sam," the Doctor said warmly.

"OK then, what can you give us on Gary Sutton, Sam?" Darja said, adding a touch of hard bitch to her voice.

"On the record, of course, I can't tell you much of anything. But off the record…?" Sam said, suggestively. "I'll tell you what, since we're all in the family here, why don't you come over to my place for dinner tonight? I'll tell you everything you need to know. And I'll tell you everything you need to know about Bob Travis, too. Believe me, that's a conversation we need to have."

Arrangements were made, then Porter and Darja walked out of the hospital and into a bath of golden light. It was afternoon now, and the sun glowed magnificently behind the fir trees lining the grounds. If anyone were depressed here it certainly wouldn't be on account of the scenery.

"Well, that was interesting," Porter said, shielding his eyes from the glare. "I certainly didn't expect to run into our secret boss here."

"Oh, it was captivating," Darja sighed. "But from now on, how about you let me do the driving on interrogations next time, OK? No offense, guy, but you really suck at it."

CHAPTER NINETEEN

Darja and Porter took the Taurus out to Sam's house, which was perched on Cohasset's posh Jerusalem Drive. Porter had Darja navigate, being unfamiliar with the myriad Byzantine complexities of suburban Massachusetts driving. It all just looked to Porter like a bunch of drunks threw a bowl of spaghetti on the floor and traced it off as their street plans.

Darja did most of the talking, complaining about their new jobs and the weird people they were working with. Porter found this big, brassy motormouth to be very entertaining, though he could do without all the foul language.

Darja and Porter dressed casually but presentably; Porter wore a brown corduroy sports jacket over a charcoal mock turtleneck and black chinos. Darja got the feeling Porter fell into The Gap and picked out this getup as soon as he dropped her off at the Lair, which was Bruehle's new nickname for the shit-box that Travis ran his freak-show out of.

For her part, Darja wore fashionably form-fitting black pants and matching jacket, and a frilly salmon blouse with three-quarter sleeves. She wore heels, so she stood nearly as tall as Porter, who was 6'1". Darja hated to admit it, but they looked kinda good as a couple.

After making several wrong turns, they finally arrived at the house. It was a beautiful Modernist number overlooking the ocean. It looked to Porter like a millionaire's spread. He wondered how a psychiatrist could afford these kinds of digs. Sure, the guy ran a unit in a fairly-large state hospital, but how much could that really pay? He couldn't imagine it paid this kind of money.

They followed a winding slate walkway to the front door and rang the buzzer, which set off a pleasant series of reverberating bell tones that reminded Darja of New Age music.

They soon heard men's shoes scuffing on tile and Sam opened the door, his face warmed by a soft alcoholic glow. He was wearing what looked to Porter like the kind of housecoat men wore at old-fashioned private clubs, complete with embroidered monogram patch. Almost like some kind of Hugh Hefner-wannabe.

Sam's house was decorated in a sparse but homey style, and there was a fire going in the massive stone hearth in the living room. The front hall was lined with photos of Sam's world travels; pictures of him in front of the pyramids, Greek temple ruins, Teotihuacan, Japanese shrines.

It must be nice to have money, Darja thought, and then was happy to remember that she recently came into a little of that herself. There were also pictures of Sam and some 70s Hollywood celebrities Darja vaguely recognized. She made a mental note to ask about them.

An attractive, black-haired and olive-skinned woman in her late 30s was setting the table. She wore a floral print dress with red flats. Darja tagged her as the trophy wife, seeing as how Sam seemed to be in his early 60s.

"Apollonia," Sam said. "These are my friends Darja and Porter. We're working together on a project." Apollonia smiled and everyone said their how-do-you-do's. Porter wondered if Sam didn't actually tell the missus who was coming over for dinner beforehand.

"Come, sit. Make yourselves comfortable," Sam said, pointing to the black leather furniture in the living space. "What's your poison?"

Darja asked for whiskey on the rocks, Porter a beer. Sam poured Darja a Johnny Walker Black and Apollonia brought Porter a sweaty Heineken wrapped in a linen napkin. Fancy.

"So, I want to thank you both for coming over tonight. I think I can help you two quite a bit with this investigation."

Sam took two fat manila envelopes off the coffee table and handed them to his guests. Darja and Porter opened them, finding stapled photocopies of charts and reports on Gary Sutton and Kevin Stuart. They both scanned through them.

"Doc, a lot of the stuff in these files is blacked out," Porter observed, frowning as he thumbed through the pages.

"Sorry about that, can't be helped," Sam said. "It's hospital policy to redact certain details on administrative copies. It has to do with privacy laws, doctor-patient relationships, and so on."

"So, it can say that Kevin Stuart was paranoid, but not what he was paranoid about? That's kind of odd," Darja countered.

"I wouldn't worry too much about it, Darja," Sam said. "You have plenty to work with there."

"Is there any way we can access the non-blacked-out copies?" Darja asked.

"I'll tell you what; I can try to track down their therapists and see if they can help you out. How does that sound?" Sam said.

"That sounds great," Darja said, her mood warming thanks to this very fine whiskey.

"Good, good. I have a vested interest in this case getting solved too. So, anything I can do to pitch in."

Sam then slapped his knees and rose from his chair. "So, what do you say; you two hungry? Why don't we go and see what Apollonia's fixed up for us tonight, OK?"

The foursome dined on Veal Marsala, rosemary potatoes and mixed greens in a balsamic vinaigrette. A fine Pinot Noir relaxed Darja and Porter even more, but both demurred when Sam started fishing around for their biographies. Neither wanted to be pulled into a game of *This is Your Life,* especially not with an experienced headshrinker. Tired of the probing, Porter decided to steer the conversation back to their case.

"Doc, we saw a lot of UFO kind of stuff in Gary's apartment," he said. "He seemed pretty fixated on the topic."

"I'm not surprised. It's quite a popular topic with the mentally ill," Sam said, somewhat wearily. "We get a lot of it, especially these days."

"Was he into it back when he was a patient there?" Porter asked.

Doc rested his chin on his forefinger and thought about it.

"Possibly, quite possibly. When did *E.T.* come out?"

"1982, I think," Porter answered.

"Well, that would have been before his first commitment, so it's entirely possible, yes."

"Speaking of movies, I noticed quite a few pictures of you in the hallway with some old movie stars, sir," Darja chimed, in a sing-songy, insinuating tone.

"Yes, that's right. I wrote a few novels that were based in part on my experiences in Vietnam," Sam said cheerily.

"Under an assumed name, of course. But one of them was made into a motion picture, so I got to meet some interesting people when I was hired on as a consultant for the film."

"What was the film?" Darja asked.

"It was called *Die in the Dark*. Have you seen it, Darja?" Sam replied.

Darja nodded, a bit too enthusiastically; she was already into her fourth glass of wine.

"I have. I watched it on an aircraft carrier in the middle of the Pacific Ocean with about forty other sailors."

"Outstanding!" Sam exclaimed. "That sounds like a movie scene in itself."

"Do you still write, Doc?" Porter asked.

"Oh no, not for years. And I used a ghostwriter in the first place anyway," Sam chuckled. "They were my stories, but the writer could actually make decent books of them."

Sam suddenly grew serious. "Now, I didn't bring you two all the way out here to talk movies. I have information the two of you need to know before you get any deeper into this project."

Sam then wiped his mustache with a napkin and firmly placed both hands on the table before him, as if girding himself for the moment.

"Right. Now, what I'm going to tell you is very important, so I need you both to listen very carefully," he said gravely. "Bob Travis is a... very *complicated* man."

"How so?" Porter asked.

"Well, what I mean he's complicated in that his motives are not... simple. This project you're all working on is not just another assignment for him. It's a... let's call it a quest. It's intensely personal to him. I think in a very strange way he's trying to redeem himself. Do you know what they used to call him?"

"No, sir," Porter said.

Sam winced. "'Hacksaw Travis.' Never to his face, of course."

Porter didn't like where this was going. "Really? I'm almost afraid to ask why."

"Oh, and with good reason," Sam said. "Let's just say it has to do with his interrogation techniques of enemy spies during the Vietnam War. The Vietcong were brutal, Porter. Barbaric. People back home never understood just how brutal they were. But men like Bob greatly admired the VC, and were determined not to be outdone by them when it came to sheer ruthlessness. He just couldn't stop himself. One of the reasons that Bob was eventually put behind a desk was because he had become a one-man blowback generator."

"Do you think he saw that as punishment?" Darja asked.

"Bob? Oh no, he's a true believer. And he could do as much damage behind a desk as he could in the field. Plus, was so far gone by the Iran-Contra deal, he didn't know the difference anyway."

"What do you mean?" Porter asked.

"One thing you will find with men who've lived the life Bob has is that they don't see the world like a civilian does. They see things, they experience things, that change their view of reality."

"What changed him?" Darja said.

"Bob had a near-death experience. An NDE. I'd love to tell you it was during a firefight or some police action, but it was a simple heart attack. Bob was so stressed out by the Contra thing; he had a coronary at his desk. He never spoke about it, but his behavior totally changed."

"How did you hear about it if he never spoke about it?" Darja asked, her cop-mind working even when she was half in the bag.

"Well, there was one person he did talk to about it; his ex-wife," Sam offered. "She told me about it, and she told me when Bob had begun to consult with psychics, channelers, people like that. Something obviously touched him on a very deep level, even if he still seemed like the same old hard-nut. But there were a lot of strange ideas circulating at the time, like the First Earth Army and Project Stargate, and all of that. Bob went through all of it in the same ruthlessly-efficient way he went through an interrogation. He was full-steam with the Bifrost Initiative as soon as he'd been deactivated. I don't think he even took a day off in-between."

"But why does he travel around with a couple of hard-ass types like Khoury and Evan? It seems like he takes it all a little too seriously. Does he really think that hunting for psychics is that dangerous?" Darja asked.

"Bob doesn't have bodyguards because your work is all that dangerous," Sam explained. "He has bodyguards because of all the enemies he made back in his DI days. Those men were working for him a long time before he started Bifrost. They're with him because they are intensely loyal to him, and for very good reason."

"How so?" Darja asked.

"Evan was part of a special SEAL team the CIA took out on-loan for drug interdictions. The interagency politics in Washington were getting very nasty with the Iran-Contra business, so the CIA decided the team was expendable. Bob disagreed, and put his own ass on the line to airlift them out of a very deep jungle in Guatemala after Evan and his men had come under heavy fire from drug bandits. The airlift alerted the local government that the Company was working the area, and Bob spent months dealing with the fallout. Bob has made enemies for doing the right thing just as often as the wrong."

"What about the other guy? Khoury," Porter asked.

"Khoury -- Peter -- is Lebanese. Bob worked with his father during the civil war there. Peter was just a young kid then, fighting in some god-awful street militia in Beirut. Bob got the entire family out of Beirut after the father was assassinated, and Peter is the type of man who never forgets a favor like that. Ever. Neither does his sister," Sam explained.

"OK, so why us, then?" Darja said pointedly. "We don't have a history with this guy. We haven't been through hell with him. I mean, even some random cop we just met has crazy Travis war-stories. What's the deal with us?"

Sam took a sip of wine, placed the glass down, then closed his eyes for a moment. He locked his gaze on Darja.

"Bob Travis is a very meticulous man, absolutely tireless. But what he prizes most, above everything else, is dedication. Which is a very hard thing to come by in our business, believe me. Bob knows your histories, probably even better than your own mommas, so he knows you both have very strong motivations towards loyalty."

"In other words, we're just a couple of fucking losers, a couple of broken toys who have nowhere else to go, right?" Darja snapped. "Right? I mean, that's why, isn't it?"

A sudden chill descended upon the party. Sam kept his eyes locked on Darja's. He waited a moment before speaking again.

"Darja, I don't know a single, solitary human being in this line of work that isn't deeply, profoundly broken. This business breaks everyone, believe it. The difference becomes whether being broken causes you to surrender your humanity. You two don't realize it, but you're just at the very start of your careers. Whatever happened before is irrelevant. It's like a juvenile record that's been sealed by the courts. I need you both to understand that."

Darja just crossed her arms and stared at her plate.

"So what are you worried about now, Sam?" Porter said, desperately hoping to change the subject.

"Let's just say I'm concerned, not worried, per se," Sam replied. "I'm concerned that Bob's quest is the only thing that matters to him now, and that everything else is just means and ends."

Sam paused and added, "I think he needs other people involved in this project who might approach the work with a little more balance. Bob won't let me get involved directly, but I am offering my services to you indirectly. And maybe in time I can take a more direct role."

Things finally settled down and the evening's equilibrium was regained. After dessert and cocktails, Darja and Porter said their good-byes on the front steps. It was a lot colder now, and the brisk wind whipping off the ocean wasn't helping at all.

"I meant what I said," Sam said in parting. "You two can call me anytime, day or night. And believe me, the time will come when you're going to need someone else besides Bob Travis in your corner."

CHAPTER TWENTY

Cutter's Mill's drummer's real name was Warren Cortese, but everyone called him 'Quattro,' a nickname he'd carried since junior high school. He seemed to exist apart from the nucleus of the band, living outside the Greater Boston area in Worcester, a mid-sized city some 50 miles west.

Worcester seemed a little run-down to Darja, a little tired. Past its city prime. Quattro lived in a two-bedroom apartment over the storefront of an electrical supply company. He let Porter and Darja in after they flashed their shields in the old-fashioned door viewer.

The walls and shelves of the apartment were all bare. Darja noticed stacks of packing boxes in the bedroom. It looked like Quattro was moving out, or had just moved in.

Quattro was short and gaunt, some five inches shorter than Darja. He wore some of his jet-black hair up in a semi-bun that reminded Darja of *Charlie's Angels* for some reason. His scrawny arms were covered in a dense mesh of illegible tattoos, and he wore a black concert t-shirt with a weird band name Darja never heard of. She thought they looked like Conan and his barbarians trying to look like KISS.

"Hey, did we catch you at a bad time?" Darja asked with her best *'we really don't give a single, flying fuck if we caught you at a bad time or not'* cop-voice.

"No, come on in. You know, just cleaning house," Quattro replied in an oddly-dippy voice.

"I'll say. It looks like you cleaned everything out," Darja observed. "What happened to all your books?"

"Oh, those were mostly textbooks. I resold them all at the school bookstore."

"Make a lot of money that way?" Darja inquired, as if he were some creeper she just busted for selling kiddie porn.

"I'm saving up for a new kit, so everything is kind of going towards that," Quattro shrugged.

"Makes sense. Hey, I hear you have a degree in archaeology. That's kind of unusual for a rock musician, isn't it?" Darja asked, as if Quattro were a fifty-year-old plumber who played with Barbie dolls.

"Yeah, there's really not much money in it, so I figure pursue the music thing while I'm still young, you know?" Quattro said, seeming to be growing progressively more intimidated every time Darja spoke.

"There's a lot of drama with Cutter's Mill, huh?" Darja said, getting to the point while Porter went to nose around.

"Ha ha, too much!" Quattro said and laughed nervously. "I try to keep out of it. It's really the other three. It's kind of like a soap opera, y'know?"

"Yeah, we've heard that line," Darja replied, as if Quattro stole it from his manager intentionally.

"Yeah, I just keep to myself and my girlfriend," Quattro said. "We really try not to involve ourselves in all the head games."

"Looks like you missed a spot," Darja observed, pointing to a glob of black wax on the coffee table.

"Oh, yeah. Yeah, my girlfriend is into, y'know, crafts and shit," Quattro explained. "The wax and glue and shit are always hard to get up."

"So, what do you think about the situation with Gary?" Darja asked, as if expecting a murder confession in response.

"Man, I don't know what to think," Quattro said, looking away. "It's crazy."

"You think maybe he was abducted by aliens?" Darja asked, implying being he couldn't possibly believe such ridiculous things.

"Hey, who knows?" Quattro shrugged. "Weirder things have happened."

"Weirder than being abducted by aliens?" Darja asked.

"You got me there, dude," Quattro conceded, and laughed nervously.

"Did he try to talk about aliens with you? Gary, I mean."

"Some, yeah," Quattro said, arms now clutched tight against his chest. "I could pretty much tell from the lyrics that he was talking about it."

"Really? How so?" Darja asked skeptically.

"Well, some of the terminology. It's kinda specific, y'know?" Quattro said.

"Can you give us an example?" Darja asked.

"Not off the top of my head, but it was pretty clear, I think. Do you have our demo?"

"Actually, we don't," Darja said.

"You should get a copy," Quattro said, offering it up like a peace pipe.

"Do you have any extras?" Darja said, noticeably peering at the boxes in the bedroom.

"As a matter fact, I do. There's no lyric sheet, but you'll hear the words clear enough."

"So where do you think Gary is now?" Porter asked as he returned from his snooping.

"I don't know, man," Quattro shrugged. "Up there?"

"Can we talk to your girlfriend?" Porter asked.

"She's actually out of town right now at a craft festival in Vermont," Quattro said. "But if you have a card or something...?"

"Here, give us a call when she comes back," Porter said, offering Quattro his card.

"Anything in particular you want to ask her?" Quattro asked.

"No, we're just talking to everyone," Darja answered. "By the way, what was your specialty in archaeology?"

"Oh, Ancient Egypt, mostly, and the Near East."

"Pretty crowded field," she replied, guessing.

"Oh, you know it. But it's where most of the paying work is," Quattro said brightly. "Egypt is such a huge cash cow, you have no idea."

Porter and Darja left the building and returned to the car.

"Why did you ask about his archaeology thing, Darj?" Porter asked.

"No reason, just a hunch," Darja said, pulling down the seat belt as they turned onto the Interstate.

"Hunch about what?" Porter asked, eyeing her peripherally as they ascended the on-ramp.

"Just a hunch," she said and took in the landscape.

CHAPTER TWENTY ONE

Roslindale reminded Porter of a drunk working a 12-step program, and working it hard. You could tell this Boston borough had hit bottom and was simply taking it one day at a time now.

And so it was that the downtown area had funky coffee shops and boutiques sitting cheek-by-jowl with long-abandoned store-fronts. Old rummies and street people sharing the sidewalks with yuppies and housewives. But it was still a long way from recovery, and the odds were still stacked against it. Porter could relate.

Gary's girlfriend lived in an apartment building that looked like it once had been quite the swanky address but now it sat on a particularly rough stretch of the main drag. But it was a beautiful spring day; trees and flowers were budding, birds were singing, and things were looking up for Roslindale, New England, America, and the whole wide world.

At least that's how Porter happened to feel at the moment. Of course, that feeling was always subject to change.

Porter and Darja entered the scuzzy lobby of the apartment building and immediately noticed the handwritten sign taped to the elevator. In a shaky ball-point line it read, *"Out of service. Please use stairs."* Someone had scrawled, *"Fix it already, you lazy fuck,"* beneath it.

"More stairs," Darja said, making a face.

"Aren't there any working elevators in this city?" Porter replied.

"Come on, Cowboy. The exercise'll do you good."

Darja and Porter heard the screams as soon they hit the fifth floor. Screaming, then glass breaking, and what sounded like the thumps of large pieces of furniture being overturned.

They ran to the apartment door. The screams were female, high-pitched and blood-curdling.

Porter and Darja drew their weapons and hugged the wall on opposite sides of the door. Wary of potential gunfire, Porter rapped on the door with a forceful backhand and leapt back into ready position.

"Police, open up," Darja hollered, with impressive volume.

"Fuck off, you cunt!" a deep male voice yelled in response. The doors here seemed especially flimsy. Whoever was behind it might as well have yelled in her ear.

"You got to the count of four," Porter shouted, hoping that guy in there would take another male voice more seriously.

The hallway suddenly went silent. Porter and Darja held their chins up and listened intently. Porter thought he heard whispers from inside.

He and Darja were straining to listen when the door suddenly flew open with a gust, and the grunge version of Andre the Giant stormed out and tackled Porter. The two men struggled on the ground as the giant tried to wrest Porter's weapon away.

Andre gave Porter several meaty punches to the side of the head before dedicating both his hands to ripping Porter's gun out of his locked fist.

"Hey, get off him!" Darja cried. "Get off him, you fat fuck!"

The ungodly shrieking kicked up again inside the apartment. Darja was beginning to panic. This gorilla outweighed Porter by at least eighty pounds, which could make all the difference in a ground fight.

"Give me a reason, you hippie asshole!" Darja screamed, then quickly leaped around the two men, clutching her Glock with both hands in front of her.

The mass of muscle and sweat quickly migrated across the floor and was now shoved up against an old iron radiator. With his gun-hand pinned down by the attacker, Porter grabbed the giant's face with his other hand and plunged his thumb hard into his eye before the monster realized what was happening. The larger man shrieked in agony and shock.

As the iron grip on his wrist momentarily loosened, Porter was able to whip his other hand free and smash his opponent in the mouth with his gun-butt. Porter nearly wretched as he felt the hard steel shatter most of the giant's front teeth. A sheet of blood and saliva whipped from the man's lips as his head flew back. The giant rolled onto his back, but somehow still managed to keep Porter pinned to the ground.

Darja positioned herself, took aim and then hammered her boot-heel down on the goon's crotch. He arched back violently and shrieked.

As the giant was about to lunge forward once more, Porter slammed him in the chin with a sharp palm strike that gnashed the man's mangled teeth together. Darja gave the beast another heel-kick, this one straight to the center of his throat.

Porter used the force of the kick to push the monster off him and leaped to his feet like a cat. Darja hopped around him, planted herself and again brought the heel of her boot square down on the man's groin.

The beast let out a weirdly high-pitched scream and curled into a fetal position. Darja wanted nothing more than to kick this fat fuck's face in, but Porter grabbed her by the shoulders and pushed her away.

Darja raised both hands in surrender and Porter quickly turned on his heels to make sure this gorilla no longer posed a threat. Porter then buckled over, placed his hands on his knees and took several sharp, deep breaths. He'd been in his fair share of fights, but this was like going one-on-one with the Incredible Hulk.

He didn't even notice Darja had run into the apartment and cuffed the woman, who began her shrieking again just as four armed cops came bursting from the stairwell.

"Hands up! Police!" one of them hollered, just before Porter collapsed face first to the floor. Darja emerged from the apartment with a handcuffed young woman and flashed her shield.

Porter may have heard bits and pieces of their exchange, but soon everything went black.

CHAPTER TWENTY TWO

Porter woke to the unpleasant sensation of a flashlight glaring in his eyes. He bolted up.

"Easy there, Rocky 4, easy," a female voice told him.

Porter then realized he was inside an ambulance and was lying on a cot. It smelled cold, like a mix of sheet metal, rubbing alcohol and cleaning solution.

"How's he look?" Darja said to a young black EMT that Porter was finally able to bring into focus.

"You said he took a few good ones to the head?" the EMT asked, brow furrowed in concern.

"Yeah, from that motherfucking Frankenstein fuck out there," Darja replied.

"His dilation is normal, eye movement is getting there, his reflexes seem OK," the EMT said. "Ish. But I definitely think he should get some X-rays and maybe a CAT scan straight away, just to be on the safe side."

Turning his attention back to Porter, the EMT asked, "How do you feel, sir?"

"A bit sick to my stomach," Porter answered.

"Any dizziness? Light flashes, dark flashes?"

Porter swung his legs to the side of the cot and stretched, as if he'd just had a nice nap. "Not so far."

"Hang tight, let's give it at least twenty minutes. After that, let's talk about getting you to the emergency room," the EMT said. "You had yourself quite a tussle there."

The EMT hopped out the back and joined a clutch of cops and paramedics staring down at the hairy hulk writhing on the sidewalk. He had an oxygen mask strapped to his face, and his feet and wrists were cuffed together. His tan flannel shirt was cut away from his chest so the EMTs could attach EKG diodes. But first the paramedics had to shave a rug of hair from his chest.

"Never a dull moment," Darja said, and smiled sweetly.

"So how much trouble are we in here, Darj?" Porter asked and took a swig from a cold bottle of Poland Spring the EMT supplied.

"Well, you just thank your lucky stars, Slugger. It turns out that rhino you just boogied with is a wanted fugitive. Like, he's a majorly wanted fugitive."

"Wanted for what?" Porter asked.

"Oh, you know, a few little trifles like attempted murder, aggravated assault, kidnapping, rape, statutory rape, possession with intent. A few other goodies here and there. The cops found a quarter-pound brick of black tar in his knapsack up in the apartment. Not to mention a snubnose they said had traces of spatter on it."

"Jesus, you're kidding me," Porter said.

"I kid you not, Rambo. I talked to a Captain who came down for the occasion. His feeling was that that fuck would have given his blues same what he gave your pretty little ass, so better you than them. Man wasn't real eager to be taken alive."

"Holy crap," Porter replied.

"Oh yeah. I got the feeling this Captain was pretty dazzled by your cage-fighting skills. Seems you did him a major solid," Darja said brightly.

"You helped," Porter said, and took another gulp. He was as thirsty as he could ever remember being.

"Ah what, a couple lousy dick-kicks? That's just a normal workday for me," Darja said, flashing her feline grin.

"What about the screamer out there?" Porter asked. "You know, the girlfriend."

"Blues say the bitch is toast. She's going down for the tar since it was found in her crib, and apparently she's got a few outstanding warrants for soliciting."

"I have an idea. Hold on a second," Porter said, patting his chest. "Damn, you got your phone? I left mine in the car."

Darja pulled out hers and handed it to Porter.

"Who you calling?" she asked. Porter silenced her with an index finger in response.

A blue appeared at the door and said, "Ma'am? Cap'n needs another word with you."

Darja returned to the ambulance after talking with the cops. Porter's color had come back, and he was working on a second bottle of water.

"What was all that about?" Porter asked.

"Well, yeah. How do I put this?" Darja said, scratching her forehead. "Seems the Captain would like to know if we wouldn't mind stepping back and letting the boys-in-blue take credit for the bust."

"You're kidding me," Porter said, wiping water from his lips with the back of his hand. "Why?"

"He said it just makes it easier for everyone, less paperwork and all that bullshit. Says a lawyer might make trouble if it came out this maniac got nut-stomped by a couple lousy P.I.'s. Says they really want this asshole behind bars, and he's got a couple plainclothes he can use as ringers if something about us comes up at trial."

"Did you run that by Travis?" Porter asked.

Darja looked at Porter like he'd just announced he was a magical flying unicorn from the enchanted lollipop forest.

"Travis? You better lie back down, tough guy. I think you got your eggs scrambled there."

Porter chuckled and offered Darja her phone back.

"Who'd you call?" Darja asked, pocketing the phone.

"The Doc."

"What Doc?" Darja asked.

"Sam, Sanderson."

"Yeah? Why, need some therapy?"

"Ha ha. No, I asked the Doc to talk to the cops," Porter replied. "Asked if he can arrange to have her remanded to his custody. So hopefully, the cops can just take her straight to the hospital for us."

"The fuck we care about that skank now?" Darja sneered.

"Well, she's a witness, and we didn't get to interview her and find out what she knows about Gary," Porter said.

"Shit, good work, Porter. Fast thinking."

Darja gave him a once-over; dude kept blooming like a rose. Fucker damn-well knew how to streetfight and seems he wasn't totally useless as an investigator after all.

Outside the ambulance, Gary's girlfriend was shrieking at the cops, her ungodly caterwauling piercing the daily bustle of the neighborhood.

She lunged at what looked like a TV reporter at one point, trying to head-butt the poor woman. Passersby began to gather and ogle at the fracas. A policewoman was called in to try to reason with the girl-friend, who Darja now officially dubbed 'the Screamer,' but that only seemed to make a bad situation worse.

Finally, a frazzled-looking young blue walked over to talk to Darja and Porter.

"You two privates the ones who want that psycho bitch hauled off to the funny farm?" the cop asked in a thick Boston burr.

"Yeah, is that a problem?" Darja asked.

"Yeah, it is," the cop said, clearly exasperated. "We can't take any more of her bullshit. I'm about to take out my fucking gun and shoot myself in the side of the head from the sound of all that screaming. We'd sure appreciate it if you two could ship her ass over there yourselves."

"Oh, no problem," Darja said, completely taken aback by the request. She turned to Porter, who seemed mildly shocked by it as well.

"She's remanded into your custody, then," the cop said. "You're responsible for her care and conduct. Any issues in transit are all on you."

"Understood," Darja said.

"Cap'n asked if you wouldn't mind leaving him your cards."

Darja and Porter both took out small leather wallets used exclusively for the occasion and handed out their business cards. The copper cocked an eyebrow at the rather dubious-looking cards for a moment, then placed them in his breast pocket.

"OK, she's all yours. Have Admissions phone my watch commander once she's been processed."

Two other patrolmen then handed over the visibly-disheveled young woman over to Darja and Porter.

The Screamer shot Darja a filthy look and shouted, "Where the fuck you think you're taking me, you big fucking dyke?"

Darja grabbed the Screamer by the cuffs and yanked her towards their car.

"For an attitude adjustment. Come on, bitch."

Darja took the wheel since Porter still didn't look right to drive. She forced the Screamer into the backseat of the Taurus, but the girl began writhing and kicking the chair-back. Then she started rocking the car with her entire body.

"Hey! Hey, Linda Blair! Calm the fuck down back there!" Darja shouted at the thrashing woman.

"Fuck you, you lezzie fucking cunt!" the Screamer replied, and continued kicking at the car door.

Darja took out her weapon and pointed it right up against the younger woman's head.

"I said, *calm the fuck down, bitch!* Do it now or I blow what's left of your fucking brains all over the upholstery! You tell me if those cops out there will give two flying fucks if I do."

The Screamer suddenly stopped her thrashing and silently stared down the muzzle of the weapon, as if hypnotized by a snake-charmer. Darja realized the woman probably never had a gun pointed at her before and had no idea how to react to one now.

She didn't scream a single time on the drive to the hospital.

CHAPTER TWENTY THREE

When they finally got to the hospital, Porter and Darja took the Screamer — Katie, it so happened — to admissions and had her processed.

Katie was changed out of her street clothes, bathed by nurses in surgical gear and put into a hospital gown. She was handcuffed to a metal chair that was bolted to the floor while the paperwork was done. A gaggle of imposing orderlies came and took the Screamer away in a special stretcher with canvas restraints.

Meanwhile, Sam sent down two pleasant young candy-stripers with a wheelchair to take Porter down to radiology. The girls seemed a bit hotted-up over him. Darja was thinking maybe they thought he really was the guy who plays Superman.

Radiology took several x-rays in what felt like record time, mercifully. Porter was then given some green surgical scrubs to wear. A nurse who looked dressed for hazmat duty hauled his bloodied street clothes away in a clear plastic bag to be incinerated. Probably come across some nasty shit here at the nuthouse, Darja thought. Can't be too careful.

Porter and Darja sat in the recovery room and sipped orange sodas out of large plastic cups filled with chipped ice, enjoying the downtime.

A neurologist dropped in to tell Porter that it didn't look like there was any damage to his brain, neck or skull, but also gave him a pamphlet with warning signs to look out for. Porter was given a stern admonition to call his doctor if he experienced even one of the listed symptoms, and warned that one should never fool around with head injuries.

The candy-stripers then returned with the wheelchair in tow and told Porter and Darja that Dr. Sanderson would like them to join him for dinner in the cafe. Darja noticed the girls brought a couple more friends with them this time.

The cafe was doing its best to look like a casual restaurant, like a Bennigan's without the dollar-shot happy hours. Darja guessed people coming here would be depressed enough already, so a more festive atmosphere might do some good.

The two agents apprised the doctor of the day's events and the three of them discussed bits and pieces of the case.

Sam had ordered them some cheeseburgers and fries that tasted one whole hell of a lot better than the garbage they usually served in these places. Darja figured you had to know the secret handshake.

After supper, two different orderlies arrived to take Porter and Darja down to interview the Screamer. After a trek through an endless maze of doors, floors, and corridors, they came to a cold, cinderblock dungeon the good doctor made available for them.

The Screamer — Katie — sat strapped to a wheelchair beneath a harsh fluorescent light, looking as lost and miserable as anyone Darja or Porter had ever laid eyes on.

"Can you please get me out of this?" Katie begged, tears streaming down her reddened face. "I promise I won't make any trouble."

"Your promises don't count for much, Katie," Darja said.

"Please, I can't take this. Please let me out of this. I'm seriously about to puke. I swear I won't do anything."

Darja nodded at the orderlies, who undid the restraints. The three of them sat down at a table while the orderlies went over to stand by the door.

Porter and Darja stared hard at Katie. Neither of them could figure out the legitimate use for this space. Or much wanted to. It seemed to be engineered for maximum discomfort; metal folding chairs, steel table, hideous linoleum tile, harsh fluorescent lights.

The temperature was maintained at a chilly 63°F. This was definitely not a room a junkie wanted to get dope-sick in.

Darja took the lead on the interview, which she taped on her micro-recorder.

Still feeling weak from his ordeal, Porter sat silently and gave the Screamer a dose of cop-eye. Though it was not like she needed anything else to be intimidated by.

"Don't I get a phone call?" Katie asked.

"No," Darja said bluntly.

"Don't you have to read me my rights?"

"No," Darja repeated.

"Don't I get a lawyer?"

"Fuck no."

"What the hell kind of cops are you?"

"The kind that can make your life hell if you don't start cooperating," Darja spat.

"Cooperate with *what?*" Katie pleaded hopelessly.

"Let's start with that bullshit at your apartment," Darja said. "Who the fuck was that goon?"

"He's my dealer. His name is Jag. I owe him money. Actually, I owe him a lot of money. He's fucking crazy, which is why he jumped you."

"'Jag?' He actually calls himself 'Jag?'" Darja shook her head in disbelief. "Is his last name 'Off?'"

That last quip earned Darja one of Porter's dad-looks.

"It's short for Jaguar," Katie said. "That's his actual birth name. I don't remember his last name."

Darja couldn't think of a snappy comeback for that particular piece of information. So she went with, "Is Jag Gary's dealer too?"

"No, Gary is clean. He kicked two years ago."

"What's your habit running you a day, Katie?"

"It depends. Two, maybe two-fifty," Katie said, meaning hundreds.

"Was Gary footing your bill?" Darja asked.

"Most of it, yeah. I paid some and Jag took the rest out in ass. But I guess he got sick of mine."

"You a working girl?"

"On and off, for a service. I'm getting too old for a lot of those guys, though."

"And how old is that, Katie?"

"I turned 23 in December," she replied glumly.

"Does Jag have anything to do with Gary's vanishing act?"

"I have no idea," Katie said, widened-eyes scanning for an escape route.

"Why were you screaming?"

"I dunno. It seemed like the thing to do."

"Why?" Darja asked.

"Dunno. To scare him away, like someone might go and call the cops if I made enough noise."

"Let's talk a bit about Gary," Darja said as she opened up a file folder. "What did he ever tell you about aliens or UFOs?"

"You're kidding, right?" Katie said.

"That's right, Katie. We brought you all the way down here to tell you jokes."

"I don't know, man," Katie said, raising her quaking hands again in distress. "Nobody but me pays any attention to that shit. They just figure it's his own trip, the way some guys are into model trains or baseball cards or whatever. Gary was into being abducted by aliens, I guess."

"Well, he obviously told you something. What did he say?" Darja pressed.

"He didn't remember the abductions themselves, just bits and pieces," Katie said, straining to remember. "He said they would take him places. He said they would, like, take him to the art museum when it was closed and tell him all this weird shit, like places he'd been to in past lives."

Katie posed in thought for a moment, then said, "Oh, I do remember this; he said they'd take him into stores at night and let him take all this shit."

"What kind of shit?" Darja asked, her interest piqued.

"Everything. Sports stuff, record albums, stereo equipment. He used to have a storage unit filled with all this, like, merchandise. He'd pawn some of it off whenever we needed extra money."

"And you never questioned that?"

"No. I mean, I just assumed he stole it all. I never believed he got it from aliens or some shit like that. But he supports me, and I support him, y'know? That's how it works."

Katie was wishing she'd brought her cigarettes, so she could channel her anxiety somehow.

"Did he remember the first time it happened? With these so-called alien experiences, I mean," Darja asked.

"He said he was, like, eight or something. He was coming home from grade school one day and these aliens were just waiting there for him in the field behind his house," Katie recalled.

"He said they looked like elves and they spoke to him in his mind, like ESP. The shrinks tried to tell him it was sleep paralysis, but he told them they never came to him in his sleep," Katie explained. "He started remembering more at the hospital, but they didn't take any of it seriously there, either. He'd get all moody and pissed off, and just stopped talking about it. He'd just sit alone at parties and mope out. But if you read his lyrics, they're all about his stories in one way or another. Music is a way for him to express his experiences."

"But you didn't believe any of it either," Darja pressed.

"No, I just think he's crazy," Katie said, staring hard at the floor. "Like the rest of us."

"Alright, we're going to need you to fill out some paper-work," Darja said coldly. "And a doctor is going to come to speak to you some more about Gary."

"Listen, can we do all this later?" Katie pleaded. "I mean, I'm seriously getting sick as hell here. It's been, like, almost two days now. In fact, I really don't think I can talk much more until I fix, OK?"

Darja checked her watch.

"I mean, you busted my only dealer," Katie said in utter desperation. "So I'm, like, in some serious deep shit right now. Pretty soon I'm not going to be able to tell you anything."

As if on cue, a heavy-set, ruddy-faced woman entered the room carrying a big white wicker basket.

"This nurse here is going to help you out, Katie," Darja said. "The doctor prescribed a little something to make you feel all brand-new. We'll be back. In the meantime, try and remember more of Gary's stories."

"You got a lot of work to do, Katie," Porter added, finally breaking his silence. "Try to get some rest."

CHAPTER TWENTY FOUR

Travis called a meeting in the basement conference room so he could be briefed on what Darja and Porter had found out from the Screamer. He threw a fit when he found out that they'd been working with Sanderson without consulting him. But the agents protested that they were unable to reach Travis when the shit was hitting the fan in Roslindale, and that they had to find a way to keep Gary's girlfriend out of jail so she could be interrogated about his abduction claims.

This mellowed Travis out a bit, but he warned them that they were not to talk to anyone outside the house again unless he knew about it first. Porter and Darja got the feeling that would be a hard order to fill, seeing as this was the first they'd seen or heard from their boss since he first put them on the Sutton thing.

"So, what do we know about Sutton and his experiences?" Travis asked the team.

Darja realized Travis wanted to know about Gary's UFO experiences, quote-unquote.

"Well, according to the girlfriend, his first so-called experience came around eight years old, daytime, coming home from school," she said.

"How reliable is she?" Travis inquired.

"She's not one of these UFO nuts, but she's also got a heavy habit," Darja said. "So take your pick. She thinks Gary's crazy. Apparently their whole crowd does, too."

"What did she have to say about his stories?" Travis asked, his frown growing ever-deeper.

"According to her, he claims to be a repeater," Bruehle said, tagging in with some stupid UFO lingo. "The girlfriend apparently says he told her about abductions throughout his school years, but they were weird."

"How so?" Travis asked, obviously feeling more comfortable dealing with someone who knew the topic.

"Gary reportedly claimed the aliens took him places like to museums or shopping malls after hours," Bruehle said. "Says he'd wake up with a bunch of weird merchandise with the price tag still on, things like that."

"Sounds like MILABs," Travis said.

"Could be, Skipper," Bruehle said.

"Do we have any evidence of MILABs?" Travis asked.

Neither Darja nor Porter had any clue what a MILABs was.

"Nothing on file," Bruehle answered, rifling through printouts. "I called your contact at the FBI office in Boston. They seemed vaguely aware of Gary, but only because of his manager."

"What's the deal with the manager?" Travis said, turning back to Darja.

"Some rumors of connections with organized crime, but he seemed genuinely surprised Gary was missing. Said the whole band were all a bunch of mental cases," Darja offered, grateful this conversation had returned to actual reality.

"What about the shooter? What's his story?" Travis asked.

"Paranoid-schizophrenic, apparently," Porter said. "First met Gary in the hospital, got his head filled with Gary's UFO stories. Went totally off the rails a few years ago when he started college."

"The funny thing is that he seemed to be the only one who believed Gary's bullshit," Darja offered.

"So why try to kill him?" Travis asked.

"Maybe he didn't," Darja replied. "It's possible he just wanted Gary's attention again, like the good old days."

"That's a plausible theory," Travis said. "A spin on the staged suicide attempt."

"This is interesting," Bruehle said. "First time the shooter was thrown back in the cuckoo nest was after he threatened an abductee support group with a baseball bat."

"Wait, wait, back up," Travis said, gesturing Bruehle to slow down. "What happened?"

"There was one of these abductee support groups that met in some Episcopal Church down in Hingham, all wannabes from the look of it," Bruehle said. "They'd kicked the guy out for his erratic behavior. So he came in one night swinging a bat around, so the cops came in and hauled him back to the nuthouse."

"They should've given him a medal," Travis scoffed.

"The shooter apparently told his doctors that he thought Gary was a fraud," Bruehle replied, summarizing the reports. "Gary was long gone by this time. Which takes us up to his recent hospitalization."

"What did the doctors say about Gary?" Travis said, turning now to Zaina, who already had the stack of hospital files book-marked to the hilt with Post-it notes. She was wearing black-rimmed librarian glasses that made her look even more deadly serious.

"The reports say Gary is a fantasy-prone narcissist who is otherwise emotionally stable," Zaina replied. "The prevailing opinion seems to have been that the alien-contact accounts were compensatory fantasies for a lack of peer support."

Travis frowned sourly at the psychobabble. "How many times has Gary been in?"

"He was first put in when he was twelve after a suicide attempt that the doctors felt was not serious," Zaina replied. "Superficial wrist slashing, barely broke the skin."

"The old cry for help?" Travis sniffed.

"Apparently," Zaina concurred.

"Sounds like precedent to me," Porter said.

"Possibly. Gary had a discipline problem, according to his file," Zaina said as she continued to leaf through the reports. "He was also repeatedly disciplined for engaging in improper sexual relationships during his stays."

"Improper how?" Travis asked.

"Well, leaving aside the fact that all sexual relationships are considered improper for patients, we have reports of a running liaison with a nurse's aide," Zaina answered. "Apparently, she was let go after the relationship was dis-covered. A number of reports concerning Gary and other patients. There was also some talk about him seducing his social worker as well."

"A total degenerate, like the rest of his generation," Travis grumbled. "What about his songs? Any mention of aliens in them?"

"The band has a publishing deal, but Gary just sent in gibberish for the lyrics," Bruehle replied. "Don't know if we'll get a chance to look over the real ones."

"What about the band?" Travis asked.

"Nothing. No files on them, no history to speak of," Darja said, desperately trying to get a handle back on this insane conversation. "The girlfriend is your typical junkie-whore. Occasionally tricks through an escort service. Nothing else particularly hinky on her."

"Actually, there is something," Bruehle said, shuffling his stack of printouts like a Vegas croupier. "I found one weird thing on the girlfriend; an old police report about a series of calls to her home when she was in middle school."

"What kind of calls?" Travis snapped.

"It's unspecified, but judging from the incident reports it sounds an awful lot like poltergeist activity."

"What went down?" Travis asked impatiently.

"There was a lot of mysterious damage done to the house," Bruehle said. "Family Services got involved, thought it was domestic violence. The social worker who was looking into the situation was put in hospital for nervous exhaustion about two weeks into the investigation."

"How did it all shake out?" Travis asked.

"Cops said the family left the attic windows open during windy nights which caused all the mysterious events," Bruehle explained. "But the social worker was discharged was put on administrative leave. She returned to work for a month, then took an early retirement."

"What was going on with the family?" Travis said.

"Parents divorced when the girlfriend was six. Mom remarried not long before the poltergeist events began."

"What do we know about the stepfather?" Travis asked.

"Apparently, the marriage split up before Gary's girlfriend left high school," Bruehle said. "Stepfather was later arrested during a prostitution sting at a hotel in Braintree involving underage girls from Honduras."

"So he was probably working on the girlfriend, too," Travis offered.

"Looks that way," Bruehle agreed.

"Zaina, call Sanderson and tell him I want that girl given a top-to-toe work-up," Travis said. "Tell him to run the gamut. I don't think she and Gary were together by accident."

"You think she has abilities?" Bruehle asked.

"I'd bet on it. It sounds like she manifested during the abuse situation with the stepfather," Travis said, nearly smiling. "Poltergeists eat that shit up. Maybe if we apply the right kind of pressure, she might manifest her abilities again."

"I'll make the call now, sir," Zaina said.

"Great. Lundquist, Dunn, you keep the pressure on the family and friends. There's blood in the water here, I can smell it. Let's crack this fucker wide open," Travis croaked triumphantly.

Travis then called the meeting to a close. He, Bruehle and Zaina got up from the table and left the conference room.

Porter and Darja sat and stared numbly at each other, stunned at what they'd both just seen and heard.

"Porter, what the fuck have we gotten ourselves into?" Darja finally whispered.

Her partner cradled his head in his hands and said, "I don't know, Darj. I really don't know."

CHAPTER TWENTY FIVE

Zach and Tracey entered the grand, old Catholic Church, located in a traditionally-Italian suburb just north of Boston. It was like stepping into a time capsule. The sanctuary positively radiated Old World energy, an ornate display of pink Italian marble and extravagant stained-glass windows and wall murals in the style of the Old Masters, The overall effect was warm, rich and radiant, which synched perfectly with the fat tabs of X the pair had downed earlier at a party.

The two were dressed in the downscale fashion of the fading grunge era, all denim, flannel and unkempt hair. They may have looked like homeless street urchins, but their outfits were bought at an upscale chain store on Newbury Street.

"Oh man, this place is a wicked trip," Zach said, his eyes agog.
"I mean, look at those windows!"

"It's so beautiful," Tracey gaped. "The colors are so vivid and amazing."

Tracey wore an oversized knit cap with an embroidered cartoon monkey patch on the brim. She looked like a school-girl dressing up like a lumberjack.

"Look at those paintings on the wall," Zach noted. "It's like the Vatican or something."

Tracey looked around the huge empty room and whispered, "Dude, this place is deserted."

"You know what?" Zach said, giggling. "We should totally do it here. That would be so friggin' hot."

Tracey agreed, so the two laid themselves out on the padded pews and began tearing at each other's belts and zippers. Just as they were ready to initiate contact, their liaison was suddenly interrupted by the slow creak of a door at the other end of the cavernous room.

"Shit! Shit!" Zach whispered as he and Tracey darted up and desperately fumbled to fasten up their pants.

A long-haired, goateed man in an olive-green Army jacket and worn denim jean-shorts emerged out of the sacristy. The first thought that entered Tracey's mind was, Holy shit, it's Jesus.

"Hey, look," Zach said, whispering in Tracey's ear. "That's that guy from Cutter's Mill. The one who's supposed to be missing."

"Are you sure?" Tracey whispered back.

"Sure, I'm sure," Zach said, confidently. "I've seen them a mess of times. Fuckin' pissah band. Wicked. Met 'em at the Paradise once."

The man then walked silently between the rows of pews, slowly and deliberately, like he was part of some invisible ritual procession. He locked eyes with the young couple as he approached.

"S'up?" Zach said, nervously.

The other man said nothing, but followed the pair with his eyes as he walked towards the front door and exited into the night. Zach and Tracey looked at each other in silent amazement.

"Shit. Dude's bugging out," Zach finally said.

"Should we call the cops?" Tracey asked. "Tell them we saw him? I mean, a lot of people are worried about the guy."

After a brief discussion, Zach and Tracey agreed that they would call the police and report their Gary sighting. First thing tomorrow, right after they'd resumed with their ongoing coupling at Tracey's parents' house.

CHAPTER TWENTY SIX

Gary's childhood home was a modest, slate-shingle Colonial with a white picket fence, flowers in a well-kept garden, and a one-car garage in Wilmington, an affluent suburb northwest of Boston. Porter and Darja were relieved to finally go somewhere that felt halfway-normal.

Gary's mother greeted them at the door, and invited them in without hesitation. The investigators were surprised to see that the woman was fit, busty and attractive. She also looked very young for her apparent age, and sported light makeup and a short auburn bob. She could easily pass for Gary's older sister.

Darja and Porter were shown into a sitting room, in what looked like a recent addition to the house. It was clean, airy, and bright, thanks to a large bay window in the back. Gary wasn't some rock 'n' roll vagabond, Darja thought. He clearly came from a good home, and judging from his mother here, from very good genes. Nothing about this house radiated any dark family secrets.

"Gary's father went missing, too," his mother said, sadly. "It must run in the family."

Well, scratch that brilliant deduction, Darja thought.

"I'm sorry, we didn't know about that, Mrs. Sutton," Porter said, in his best gentle-cop mode. Mommie Dearest just flashed him more sadface. Darja wondered if this bitch were a Pat Benatar fan, seeing how she stole the singer's old hairdo.

Darja also wondered if Big Mama Mammaries here had just been sweatin' to the oldies, or maybe she was wearing that size-too-small sweatshirt so she could show off those big, bouncy boobs to her guests.

Darja also wondered if she was just being a jealous bitch because her own boobs never blossomed. They never even sprouted. She wore an A-cup, but the sad truth was she didn't need to wear one at all. She didn't even qualify as an A-minus. Her mother always blamed herself for not breastfeeding her daughter, but Darja was pretty sure breastmilk didn't actually work that way.

Darja then wondered if she should get herself some implants now that she had some money in the bank. It was a thought.

"Mrs. Sutton, I'm very sorry we have to trouble you, but we're trying to construct a profile so we can investigate any potential avenues that might lead us to Gary," Porter said.

"No, I understand," Gary's mother said, then clasped her hands between her knees and shrugged her shoulders, which gave the jugs a little jiggle. She obviously wasn't wearing a bra.

Porter squirmed involuntarily in his chair.

"What I mean to say is, by that, uh... I mean, that is if we can retrace Gary's steps, then we can try, and, uh..." Porter said before falling off whatever train of thought he'd been riding.

Judging by his glassy stare, Darja figured that the guy wasn't thinking about finding a missing singer so much as he was thinking about titty-fucking the missing singer's mom.

And the attraction was definitely mutual; Big Mama cocked her head and rested her chin on her palm as Porter babbled, a cheeseball move Darja had seen a million cheap floozies pull on a million more drunken sailors in a million dives.

The bitch was clearly trying to make Porter feel like he was the most fascinating man in the world, and it seemed to be working like gangbusters.

Darja had to laugh; men could be so friggin' clueless. The widow-woman knew some cops would be stopping by, so she squeezed herself into clothes that didn't seem too slutty, but made damn sure everyone knew she was stacked. And nobody would stop to think about how outrageously inappropriate it all was. Not for a second.

And that perfume! Did Porter actually think women wore perfume like that around the house? Not to mention the artful makeup; just enough not to look trashy, but using the old tricks like slathering on the lip-gloss (*gloss!*) and pumping up the cheekbones with rouge. Oh yes, I was just doing the laundry, Officer. Oh yes, I'm washing my panties today. I swear it's true. Here, would you like to sniff them? What a joke.

Darja grew depressed when she realized that Mommie Dearest here looked like a slightly-older version of the girls she used to run with in high school.

This broad was pushing fifty? Jesus, Darja hoped and prayed she looked that good at fifty. The women in her family didn't age well. Their Scandinavian skin got ruddy and blotchy, and they tended to pack on fat in weird places. But Mama Mia actually looked younger than Darja did.

Porter was goddamn lucky she came along with him, Darja thought. Because if the dumb fuck had come here alone, Melons McGillicuddy here would have had his balls in her mouth by now and Travis would have kittens once he found out about it. Which, of course, he inevitably would.

Darja reckoned it was time to put her horn-dog of a partner back on ice. "Do you have any of Gary's old journals or diaries?" she interjected, "Anything he might have kept when he was institutionalized? We're trying to construct a profile."

A cloud of concern crossed over Gary's mother's face. What was this big-tittied cow's name again? Darja realized she'd forgot.

"I'm sorry, Mrs. Sutton, I didn't catch your first name."

"Grace," she said, sadly.

"Grace," Darja said. "Anything you might have could help us get Gary home. I'm sure you understand."

"There are some things in his old room," Grace said. She looked out the window as if searching for moral support, but there wasn't any out there. She suddenly looked a bit older, Darja thought.

Grace got up from her chair like she was carrying a load of bricks and walked towards the hallway. She took out a small keychain from her pants pocket and unlocked a bedroom door. That was a bit odd, Darja thought, but let it slide.

"The boxes are all over there," Grace said. "They're all marked."

And so they were. Staples-brand file boxes, all marked with *'Gary's journals'* and *'Gary's HS stuff'* and so on. This bitch was organized, Darja thought. And a neat freak; those boxes looked crisp and white as the day she bought them.

"Would it be OK if we borrowed these?" Porter good-copped. "We promise to return them as soon as possible. We just need a bit of time to look through them and determine what might be helpful to our case."

Grace said, "Please do," and Porter and Darja loaded up the trunk. Darja grabbed a couple journals from the top, one with '1990' embossed on the cover in gold, and tossed them on the front seat.

They went back and said their goodbyes to Grace, then drove off for the Lair.

Darja studied the journals as Porter tried to work his way through the suburban spaghetti. Darja wondered if any of his old writings held some kind of clue about the direction Gary would end up taking in life. For his part, Porter alternated between picturing how Grace's ample hips might look with those sweatpants around her ankles, and feeling guilty for doing so.

Darja looked at Porter quizzically. "Why would he leave all this stuff behind?" she asked.

"I dunno. Maybe he was trying to leave his past behind. Trying to reinvent himself," Porter suggested.

"Good handwriting for a guy," Darja said as she studied the book. "Huh; says here he contacted some famous alien-abduction researcher, some guy he saw on Oprah."

"Really?"

"Yeah, hold on," Darja said, flipping forward in the journal. "It says here he met with him in Boston, at some UFO conference or something. Says the guy was interested in hypnotizing him."

"Yeah? How did that go?"

Darja ran her finger up and down the pages, then turned to the next.

"Huh, says here he chickened out at the last minute," Darja replied. "'Is this real?' he writes. Maybe Gary figured this guy would have sized him up and figured out he was full of shit."

Porter didn't reply. This alien stuff was a total non-starter to him, just something some poor slobs used to get through the day. He didn't think it had anything to do with Gary's disappearance, and he was sure that people were seeing UFOs purely out of the power of suggestion. It was a fad, that's all.

A couple years ago it was satanic cults. This year it was aliens. Next year it would be something else. Maybe werewolves.

CHAPTER TWENTY SEVEN

Porter and Darja went out for a late breakfast after meeting with Gary's mother. They drove back to the Lair, and were going over their notes at the kitchen table. Neither had any experience with this kind of case, nor did they have any concept of the grunge subculture these people were a part of.

On top of that was all this UFO stuff, which just seemed like total science fiction to the both of them.

Either way, it all made for a very steep learning curve. So neither were much in the mood for Bruehle to come along and dump more information on their heads, but that wasn't what he seemed to have on his mind this morning.

"So I got in touch with a UFOlogist in Portsmouth, but she didn't have much to say about Gary," Bruehle announced. "But she did say that he sought out another one of these UFO buffs, an artist up around Franconia Notch. The artist guy made a home video of interviews with people who said they were alien abductees. Apparently, he and Gary met a number of times, and this guy taped their conversations. I rang him up and told him I was starting a new MUFON chapter in Rhode Island. I said I got his name from this other woman and that we were interested in his work. I know enough about the subject to convince him I was for real."

"Was that really necessary?" Porter asked.

"I thought so. These people can get really paranoid," Bruehle replied.

"Well, why don't we make a trip of it then?" Porter said. "I could stand to get out of this place for a little while."

Porter saw that Zaina was in the living room working on her laptop. He called out, "Hey Zaina, want to tag along?"

"Sure, let me get my bag," Zaina said, much to everyone's shock and amazement.

Darja figured Zaina was probably sick to death of being cooped up in this shithole and wouldn't mind taking in some godless Yankee mountain air.

The four drove through the stunning mountain scenery in relative silence, broken up only by Darja's impatient fiddling with the car radio.

Most of the stations you could get up here were big commercial outfits out of Montreal. Porter found it a bit surreal to hear the familiar 'Morning Zoo' format in French. After scanning the dial a least a dozen times, Darja finally found a decent classic rock station and kept it there, much to everyone's relief.

Mac Cullen's studio was nestled in the foothills of the White Mountains. It was actually an old hunter's shack converted into a comfy artist nook, and seemed to be the only structure of any kind for miles. There was an iron wood-burning stove in the corner and ceiling fans placed along the exposed rafters. The same cedar shakes that lined the outside walls lined the interior as well.

The pleasant, homey tang of wood fires warming bitter New Hampshire nights was baked into the walls. A sizable work-table stood at the center of the room, much the same as you'd see in any suburban basement.

To its side was a large wooden box lined with heavy-gauge plastic, where Cullen stored the native clay he used to sculpt his artworks.

Hanging from steel wires were masks modeled after aliens that Cullen's interviewees had described from their abduction accounts. There were a fairly wide range of variations, but most would look reasonably familiar to anyone who'd watched TV or been to the movies in the last twenty years or so.

Cullen sat working on a face sculpture as he spoke to the four visitors, looking very much like a hip, middle-aged art professor. His hands were caked in grayish white clay. He kept a plastic cup filled with odd wooden tools to his right side, and a large bowl of cloudy water to his left.

"Are these aliens that people have actually encountered, Mr. Cullen?" Zaina asked.

"Yes, but not always physically. Some encounters can happen during trance states or lucid dreaming," Cullen said.

Darja whispered to Bruehle. "Gee, ya think maybe *all* these encounters happened during dreams?"

Bruehle rolled his eyes, then went back to studying one of the alien masks. He had to admit it was rather eye-catching.

"Lucid dreaming," Zaina replied in a professionally neutral tone.

"Yes, I personally believe that these beings are shape-shifters and have assumed a number of different guises over time. What I try to do with my art is accurately portray all of the different alien races, as a form of therapy for experiencers," Cullen continued. "Being able to concretize the Visitors is an important part of the recovery process. This way we can understand who they are and what they want from us."

Bruehle's heart sank. His brief hopes that this visit might uncover some real information about actual aliens seemed to have evaporated.

Porter had heard enough; it was time to get to the point. "Mr. Cullen, we understand that you did a lot of work with Gary Sutton."

"Ah, the man of the hour," Cullen replied. "Yes, I did. Wild stuff."

"How so?" Porter asked.

"Gary could summon orange orbs during his regressions, totally unconsciously. Manifestations would appear right in this room. They'd even give off a smell, like ozone."

The group all perked up to this particular revelation.

"I don't suppose you have any evidence of this? Photographs, or whatever?" Zaina asked, taken aback but still deeply skeptical.

"Actually, I do. Quite a bit of it, in fact. After the first session, I made sure I got as much evidence as I could. But let's cut to the chase," Cullen said and looked up from his sculpture.

"I finished this head two weeks ago. I just needed something to work on so you wouldn't see my hands shaking," he said, his voice lightly quavering. "It's very warm in here, so I'm guessing that the two of you are keeping your jackets on because you're carrying firearms. Correct?"

Porter held his hands up, as if to say, 'You caught us.'

"You guys aren't MUFON," Cullen said bluntly. "I know every member east of the Rockies personally. So my question then is how fucked am I now? I know all about what happens when people like me get too close to people like you."

"Oh, the drama, the drama," Darja sighed under her breath. Porter shot her a look and stepped in to defuse the situation. He took out his ID and placed it on the table in front of Cullen.

"Relax, Mr. Cullen," Porter said. "We're private investigators. We're just looking into Gary's disappearance as it relates to a different case we're currently working on. You're not in any kind of trouble."

Darja cursed Porter under her breath, then plowed straight into Cullen's personal space in an attempt to make the guy nervous again. Which wasn't all that difficult, seeing as how Cullen didn't seem to be buying Porter's line about them being private eyes at all.

"But we would really appreciate it if we could have a look at any material you could show us pertaining to your work with Gary Sutton," Darja said sternly, clearly implying it wasn't an option.

Cullen walked over to a shelving unit and grabbed an oversized milk crate filled with cassettes, VHS tapes and manila envelopes.

"Please, take it. Take all of it. Please. You'll save me the trouble of digging a hole to bury it all myself."

"Why's that?" Bruehle asked, suddenly intrigued.

"Gary is what you'd call a strange attractor," Cullen said. "People who came into contact with him usually found their luck changing for the worse."

"How?" Bruehle asked, suddenly riveted.

"Gary's girlfriend was a health nut when I first met her. Practically lived in the gym. Wouldn't even take an aspirin. Two months in with Gary, she's smoking pot. Six months in, she's sniffing heroin and working as a prostitute to support her habit," Cullen explained. "It was like she suddenly fell down some kind of giant cosmic staircase or something. You probably heard that the guy who tried to shoot Gary was institutionalized, right? Kevin? Well, before he hooked back up with Gary he was studying for his MBA. Smart as a whip, super-motivated. He didn't blow his fuse until he met up with Gary again. Kevin was usually the one who drove Gary up to see me. Had a real nice car, too."

"Did Gary ever talk about his music career?" Zaina asked.

"In the short time I knew Gary, he'd been in five different groups," Cullen replied. "No one could handle him for too long. I was actually amazed this latest band could tolerate all his bullshit."

"What do you mean?" Zaina asked, rather urgently. "Do you think he was lying about his experiences?"

"No, Gary is a genuine experiencer. I have no doubt about that. But he's also a classic sociopath. And I'm not so sure about these beings he's been in contact with, either. So, please; take that box. I'm hoping getting it out of here lifts the curse I've had on my life since I first met that fucking guy."

"What do you mean?" Zaina asked, clearly very eager for something genuinely supernatural to take back to Travis.

"Gary's problem is that he lies incessantly. He lies even when he doesn't have to. And the lies he tells are almost specifically engineered to injure the people who love him the most. It all creates this invisible web of bad karma," Cullen said.

"What about Kevin Stuart? Did he say if he had any UFO experiences?" Bruehle asked.

"No, Kevin is a classic victim of childhood sexual trauma, which I would say then manifested itself as abduction fantasy," Cullen stated. "But I think he was just trying to bond with Gary. Kevin was clearly very deeply in love with him."

"What do you think about Gary's disappearance?" Zaina said. "Do you think it was an abduction, or did you think he staged it?"

"Knowing Gary, I'd say it was a fifty-fifty proposition."

CHAPTER TWENTY EIGHT

With the tension broken and the day's business now attended to, Cullen offered up some very fine gourmet coffee for his visitors, which he served in a random assortment of mugs. Afterwards, the visitors said their thank-you's, loaded up the trunk and took off for home.

They four sat in silence as they drove back through the majestic mountain country. All of them were processing the new information in their own way, so the quiet was prerequisite.

"Well, that was unexpected," Porter said, breaking the long silence.

"Do you believe him?" Darja asked no one in particular.

"I think he's too scared to lie," Zaina answered. "And not of us, he's obviously afraid of Gary."

"But come on, that bullshit about us being some kind of black-ops hit-squad out to prevent the truth from coming out about flying saucers?" Darja sneered. "That was embarrassing."

"Actually, when you think about it, he wasn't too far off the mark," Bruehle said.

"Wha...? What the fuck are you talking about, Bruehlie?" Darja asked, glaring at his reflection through the makeup mirror.

"Well, think about it. Even if you may not see yourself as such, you are in fact an armed agent for a black-budget operation sponsored by the US Military," Bruehle explained. "You lied about who you really were, so you entered his home -- carrying concealed firearms, mind you -- under false pretenses and without a warrant. And if something had gone wrong somehow, there's even an outside chance you would have pulled your guns out and shot him. You two've already been involved in violence with this case, right? So, when you think about this purely objectively, he's actually well within his rights to be paranoid."

"Oh, come on," Darja scoffed. "You're blowing this all way out of proportion here, Bruehlie."

"Am I? Bifrost is not really an independent entity, Darja, it's a cutout. Travis and this Doctor Sanderson you met are still on file as government employees. Neither of them have been officially retired. I know this for a fact because I cracked the health insurance database at the OMB."

"So? That still doesn't mean we're spooks," Darja protested.

Zaina weighed in: "I think Bruehle makes a good point. Hollywood has deliberately warped people's perceptions. If I gave someone your job description, they'd picture some action-film star, like Mel Gibson or Bruce Willis. But you are in fact field agents for an intelligence-gathering project underwritten by the Department of Defense."

"But why would that guy think we're some kind of death squad? It's nuts," Darja said, clearly not wanting to cede an inch to her arch-nemesis Zaina.

"Darja, you and Porter carry concealed weapons. We actually did lie to him about who we all were. And technically speaking, you lied again when you told him you were private investigators. We're not private. We are all military-intelligence contractors, the same as anyone working for Dyncorp or Wackenhut. The private investigator identity is only your cover. If any of us set foot in any other country in the world, we'd all be arrested as spies," Zaina said.

Darja fell silent.

"So what did you think about the UFO stuff, Bruehle?" Porter said, hoping to change the subject.

"I thought it actually ended up being a lot more interesting than I expected. I want to see if there really is all this evidence he was talking about. I mean, I've seen a lot of what counts for evidence with these people," Bruehle said.

"But does it get us any closer to finding this Gary guy?" Porter asked.

"I don't know. If these experiences were genuine, then there is certainly an outside chance he really was abducted by aliens."

"Awesome," Darja sighed. "Just fucking *awe*-some."

• • •

As they approached the Lair, the four saw Khoury's and Evan's SUVs sitting on the front lawn. No one was particularly reassured by the fact that they chose not to park in the lot or that their engines were running and their headlights still on.

And if Khoury were here, that meant Travis was here too, and he wasn't expected to be back until later in the week. It didn't seem like a particularly good omen.

"What the hell is Travis doing here?" Darja asked.

"I don't know but it can't be good," Porter said.

"Oh shit, check your phones," Darja said. "I have eight missed calls from him."

"We must have been out of cell range up there," Bruehle said, tapping away at his cellphone.

The team were barely through the front door before Travis jumped down their throats.

"Where the fuck have you four been? Why haven't you been returning my calls?" he barked.

"We were up north. I guess we were out of our service range, sir," Porter explained.

"Up north doing what?" Travis snapped.

"Interviewing one of Gary's former associates, sir," Porter replied.

"You picked a hell of a time for it," Travis growled.

"Why? What's going on, Skipper?" Porter said.

"Two kids saw Gary Sutton in a church in Saugus last night."

"Last night," Porter replied.

"This guy is the new Elvis," Darja said. No one laughed.

"How did they ID him?" Porter asked.

"One of the kids is a big Cutter's Mill fan," Travis said. "He's seen them perform a number of times. Met Sutton in person."

"What was Sutton doing?" Porter asked.

"Kid said he walked right past them without saying a word and left the church."

"What the hell is he doing in a church in Saugus?" Darja exclaimed. "Got religion all of a sudden?"

"There's something else; a surveillance camera at a McDonald's in Randolph took these," Travis said, and handed out black and white 8-by-10's.

"Randolph? What's he doing out there?" Darja asked again.

"Well, why don't you and Dunn get the fuck down there and find out? That's what I'm paying you for, isn't it?" Travis said.

"Will do, Skipper. We'll get on it first thing in the AM," Darja said.

"No, you'll get on it now," Travis said sharply. "We're not the only players on the board here."

"I'll pop onto the 'Net and see if there've been any other Gary sightings today, Skipper," Bruehle volunteered.

"You do that, Bruehle. And the rest of you damn well better let me know before you start writing up your own assignments. You're on call 24/7, understood? All four of you."

"It won't happen again, Skipper," Porter said.

"It damn well better not. I'll be back late tonight, and I want to see some new information, you hear?" Travis said. "Now get the hell to work."

Travis stormed out through the front door, with Khoury and Evan in tow. The drivers both tore out of the yard, ripping up divots of lawn. They seemed pretty pissed off at everybody, too.

Darja stood, arms folded, and frowned at nothing in particular.

"What are you thinking, Darja?" Porter asked.

"I'm thinking about the Skipper."

"About getting chewed out?" Porter said.

"Yeah," Darja answered, frowning more deeply.

"Don't worry about it. He's just pulling his tough-guy routine."

"No, it's something else."

"What else?" Porter asked.

"It was like he was afraid," Darja said.

"Afraid? Afraid of what?"

"Afraid when he couldn't reach us."

Porter was silent. "Why?" he then asked.

"I don't know. But it makes me wonder," Darja replied.

"Wonder what?" Porter asked.

"Wonder if maybe we should be afraid too."

CHAPTER TWENTY NINE

Travis kept his office at the Lair in what was once the master bedroom. It was absolutely bare except for a cheap glue-board desk, his leather office chair, and a hot seat he used to grill poor unfortunates. It was Bruehle's turn for the third degree tonight, so he sat and neatened his little stack of white laser prints waiting for turn at the stockade.

Much to Bruehle's shock and surprise, Travis was in a much better mood than before. Of course, with Travis a 'better mood' was on a different sliding-scale than it was for normal people. Bruehle had no idea why his boss seemed a bit less irritable tonight, and had no plans to ask him about it.

"What do you got for me, son?" Travis said and leaned back in his high-back chair.

"Um, yeah. Well, I've been seeing a bit of uptick in some of the psychic newsgroups and BBS boards. A bit out of the ordinary," Bruehle replied.

"What are they saying?" Travis asked.

"Hard to parse exactly, Skipper. These people aren't always what you'd call lucid, but there seems to be some chatter that psychics are disappearing. Like maybe they're being killed or kidnapped."

Travis' expression lost a bit of its luster. "Any pattern to all of this?"

"Not sure yet," Bruehle said. "These people all use fake names and tend to be paranoid about giving up any personal details. But I am getting a strong sense that this is mostly all going down on the eastern seaboard. Maybe Quebec, the Maritimes, places like that, too."

"What's the verdict on the haul from that UFOlogist?" Travis asked.

"Mixed. A lot of your typical saucer-cult talk. Trading conspiracy theories back and forth. The usual pseudo-religious abduction blather, super-naturalist worldview. I still have a lot of interview material to look through, though."

"What did he have to say about the situation with the shooter? Anything?"

"He seemed to think that Stuart was just dissociating his childhood trauma because he was obsessed with Gary," Bruehle replied.

"Never listen to a UFOlogist when it comes to psychology,. They're all lousy at it," Travis grumbled. "Now what's all this about Sutton calling up orbs?"

"That's a different story. The camera was on a tripod so it doesn't follow the flashes when they come around. A debunker might be inclined to dismiss them all as lens flares or whatever," Bruehle said. "But there is a lot of stuff on here I want to take a much closer look at."

"What's your gut tell you?" Travis asked, leaning forward.

"I'd probably say it was psychic overspray, manifestations of their latent potentialities," Bruehle said.

Travis winced at the jargon.

"Come again?"

"That they were manifesting these phenomena through some kind of telekinesis. Or more precisely, Gary was."

"Now we're getting somewhere," Travis said, assuming his approximation of a smile. "What's your take on this Cullen guy, then?"

"Sincere, intelligent, knowledgeable. A bit gullible, I'd say. Maybe more than a bit paranoid," Bruehle said.

"Good," Travis said. "He should be. So should you."

CHAPTER THIRTY

Morton was grateful for the rain. It had been coming down hard enough to mask his tail, and helpfully slowed to a soft drizzle while he set up in a clearing. His equipment was all top drawer, but the wind blowing through the marsh reeds here would make an utter hash of the recording, especially at the discreet distance he was trying to keep. He thought about bringing some video equipment along tonight but didn't want to bog himself down.

Morton was eyeing that same Chrysler sedan, which was soon joined again by that same Lincoln. A man got out of the front passenger side of the Continental, dressed in what looked like an old-fashioned chauffeur's uniform. The driver stayed put. It seemed like there were two figures in the back, but Morton couldn't swear to that.

But he was definitely intent on pinching that limo for his personal collection once he'd put some nice bullets in these men's heads.

Two other men came out of the Chrysler. One was a portly, bearded gent wearing a tacky silver blazer. Morton thought the chap looked like a doorman from some strip-joint in the Combat Zone. And the other was the Mortician from the trestle, looking his funereal self.

The Doorman went around the back and lifted the trunk. Morton wasn't overly shocked when he saw what the man had taken out of it. In fact, it was exactly what he was expecting.

The Doorman was carrying a squirming young redhead under his tree-trunk of an arm. She looked like she was in her early twenties and was dressed only in panties and bra. Her wrists and ankles were bound with duct tape. The Mortician fetched a green blanket and tried to wrap it around their struggling victim.

Morton, wishing like the devil he'd brought his hunting rifle, held the binoculars with his left hand and pressed the headphone to his ear with his right. Unfortunately, the audio wasn't all that great, what with all the drizzle and wind and such.

"Who are you people? Why are you doing this? Please, please let me go! My father has a lot of money, he'll pay you! I swear, I won't tell anyone!" the girl screamed.

The Doorman casually glanced at the terrified girl with detached amusement, like a bored suburbanite watching a neighbor's dog doing tricks. The two enjoyed a minute or so of the girl's desperate pleading, before the Mortician ripped off a length of duct tape from an enormous roll and slapped it across her mouth.

The Doorman slung the girl's bound body over his shoulders. Morton watched as a dark mass formed around the man's shoulder and realized the girl had just urinated on him.

"That's the spirit," Morton said, and smiled.

Morton fought back a powerful urge to gut-shoot all of these thugs, then piss all over them himself. That'd all be good, clean fun, but he was hunting bigger game here and didn't want to send any of these rats scurrying back into their holes. He did feel a momentary twinge of regret about that poor girl's fate, but it quickly passed.

The Doorman brought her over the limousine. A tinted window slid down with a grating, metallic whine. Morton's view was blocked so he couldn't make out who was in the back there, but he thought he heard someone say, "Put that in the trunk." He'd have to check the tape when he got home.

The other chauffeur popped the trunk and the Doorman forced the struggling woman inside it. He slammed the trunk shut and walked back to his car.

The Mortician looked at the Doorman's urine-soaked blazer, said something like, "Get that off," and pointed to the sedan. The Doorman went around to the trunk, took off his sport coat and donned a black windbreaker with a white logo Morton couldn't quite make out. But it looked familiar all the same.

The Mortician then strolled over to the limousine window and waited to be addressed. Protocol.

Morton strained to hear the conversation but only caught brief snippets of words. He hadn't planned on it getting so windy and didn't bring a mic-screen to compensate for it. The window went up and the limo began to back away.

The two men returned to their vehicle and appeared to have a conversation while the engine idled. Morton couldn't make it out.

This odd couple seemed awfully brazen to Morton, even cocky. They didn't bother to secure their location and didn't seem to care they were sitting ducks out here.

Morton wondered about their level of experience with this sort of work. The Doorman looked like he probably did a lot of strong-arm stuff, but the Mortician was a question mark. He seemed to be a bit too oblivious to his surroundings to be a real pro. Or maybe he was such a pro that he just didn't care anymore.

And of course, there was that whole kite thing, which Morton was hoping to ask the Mortician about before he shot him in the oysters.

Morton watched through his binoculars as the huge limo made a series of turns in order to get back to the access road. A fog was rising through the drizzle which made trying to read a license plate next to impossible.

He just hoped the Lincoln, which he already considered his property, didn't sustain any damage out here. Morton was sure as sunshine it'd be an absolute pip to get parts for.

CHAPTER THIRTY ONE

Porter wasn't exactly sure how it happened, but somehow he found himself taking a major detour towards Grace Sutton's house on the drive home. He wasn't even exactly sure where he was going until he was actually turning onto her street.

And he wasn't even exactly sure why he was going to her house until he found himself on her stoop, ringing her doorbell.

Grace Sutton answered the door and said, "Agent Dunn. Is there a problem? Have you found Gary?" She was wearing slippers and a white terry-cloth robe. She smelled absolutely wonderful, as if she'd just had a bedtime bubble-bath.

Porter stood mute, unsure why this was happening, or even if it actually were.

"No, I'm so sorry, Ms. Sutton, we don't know anything more," Porter finally said. "And I'm very sorry for the late hour. I just had a few more things I needed to ask you about."

"Of course, of course. Please, come in."

Grace and Porter sat at the dining room table. The lights were low and the antique furniture and decor made this all feel close, intimate and familial. Grace sipped at a cup of herbal tea while Porter struggled to collect his thoughts.

"Um, we really didn't discuss your husband's disappearance the other day," Porter said. "Do you think it had anything to do with what Gary claimed? About the UFO thing, I mean."

"No, Glenn — my husband's name was Glenn — worked for the government. I never knew what he did. He couldn't ever tell me," Grace replied. "You look surprised."

"I... we weren't given any information about this at all," Porter said, unable to meet her gaze.

"That's by design, I'm afraid," Grace said. "Glenn wasn't allowed to talk about his work. He was paid in cash. He was picked up early in the morning. We never knew where they would take him or when he would be back."

"And you still have no idea what he did. For work, I mean."

"I knew it had something to do with computers."

"He was working for Data Global?" Porter asked.

"Yes. We met there, in their London office."

"And he disappeared when Gary was thirteen."

"Yes. I think he was doing work on one of the nuclear plants," Grace replied. "I overheard him talking on the phone one day."

Grace stopped and stared into her teacup as if it were a crystal ball.

"Glenn was much older than me," she said. "I was just a few years out of college. He was always so secretive. He'd been married before. The company helped us take care of the arrangements."

Porter was shocked by the gaps in the dossier.

"We had none of this on file. And you never remarried?"

"No, I work too much."

"And you do what, exactly?" Porter asked gently.

"I work for a small software company in Dedham. I run the sales department. It's not really very glamorous, but it pays pretty well."

"Where is this now?"

"Dedham? It's down on route 128."

Was this a secret too? Suddenly Gary's disappearance made just a little more sense.

"I have some papers and things of Glenn's upstairs," Grace offered. "I don't know if it will help."

"I'm sure it will."

Grace bolted up. "I'll go take a look. Can I get you anything to drink? Coffee? Tonic?" she asked.

"No, I'm okay. Thanks," Porter said and folded his hands.

Grace disappeared up the spiral staircase to the attic. Porter soon heard what sounded like heavy boxes being moved around. That went on for quite a few minutes until he heard Grace call down to him.

"Agent Dunn? I'm sorry, would you mind giving me a hand up here?"

Porter began to sweat as he climbed the spiral staircase. The fog of estrogen this woman seemed to emit was intoxicating, but now it was making him feel extremely anxious. What the hell was he thinking coming here alone at this time of night?

Upstairs, Grace held out her hands like a real estate lady presenting a nice loft to a client.

"Like it? This was Glenn's study. He had the upstairs to himself. Isn't it beautiful?"

It actually was a very nice space, with polished wood floors, a wood-burning stove, exposed rafters, and high octagonal windows placed at both ends of the room. It seemed very New England, at least to this born-and-bred Virginia boy.

"There are actually some old floppy disks up there that have Glenn's information on them," Grace explained, and pointed to a high cabinet. "Can you reach them?"

Porter stretched up and grabbed a plastic case of old five-inch floppies and handed it to Grace.

Grace kept sneaking glances at Porter as she thumbed through the disks. He smiled stupidly, but was feeling a vise tighten around his chest as he sat at an antique desk in front of a hot and noisy vintage IBM PC.

Finally, Grace found what she'd been looking for and handed it to Porter. The disk had 'Glenn: Resume' handwritten on it in silver marker. Porter placed it in the drive and waited for it to load. It didn't.

"I can't get this floppy to load," Porter said.

"I'm sorry. That drive is a bit tricky. Let me do it."

Grace tightened her bathrobe, then reached over the desk and wiggled the protruded edge of the disk.

It still didn't seem to load, so she tried it again. No luck. Grace then leaned over a bit farther to wiggle the cable at the back of the drive. As she did, her firm breasts pressed against Porter's shoulder. He felt a wet, fragrant heat rising from her robe, and it struck him like a jolt of pure electricity.

Grace flinched away as Porter reflexively bolted upright in the chair.

"Um, that should do it," she said, embarrassed.

The disk loaded, but it was the absolute last thing Porter could think about at the moment. He swallowed. His mouth had gone desert-dry.

The drafty room suddenly became intolerably warm, the air felt unbearably close. He felt utterly humiliated by the pulsating hardness between his legs. Sweat began beading on his upper lip.

Grace stepped back and crossed her arms tight against her chest. She seemed to be scrolling through a range of emotions, from sheepish to guarded to confused. But a terrible kind of gravity had taken hold of the both of them, and all they could do now was play out the string.

Frowning intently at nothing in particular, Grace strained to choose exactly the right words.

"I'm not... *busy* tonight," she said, frowning at the floor and squeezing her lower lip between her thumb and forefinger. "Are you?"

Grace and Porter stared at each other in silence. This Rubicon had now been crossed and they both knew full well what stood on the other side. It's just that neither knew exactly what to say about it.

Grace turned to the stairwell. "Come downstairs," she whispered, and reached out a soft, warm hand to him.

Porter took it, stood up and followed her down the winding staircase like he was under some kind of hypnotic spell. He realized then that he'd never felt so devoid of self-will in his entire life, from the very minute he first laid eyes on this woman.

CHAPTER THIRTY TWO

Porter awoke to the cold, harsh reality of what he had done. He had slept — had *sex with,* rather — the mother of a man whose disappearance he was investigating, a man who may very well be dead.

He'd be thrown out on his ear for this were he still a cop. He had no idea what his new boss would think about it.

Porter went into the half-bath, washed up and got dressed. He returned to Grace's bed, and gently shook her shoulder. She turned over and Porter finally saw how magnificent her naked body truly was. He felt like he'd stuck a finger in a light socket.

He'd been with a lot of beautiful women, but her soft, supple figure and rosy-pink glow seemed practically engineered for maximum sexual arousal. Porter thought about kissing her, but the moment wasn't right. Should he tell her he loves her? This was all uncharted territory, and it took a minute for actual words to form in his mouth.

"Hey, sorry. Um, listen, I have to go. You've got my number. Give me a call if you need to talk."

"Are you coming back?" Grace asked.

"Uh, yeah. Sure. Whenever I can."

"Whenever you can," she repeated, her expression clouding.

"No, it's... I just don't know what my schedule's going to be today."

Grace took a pillow and clutched it to her bare chest. "I understand."

"I'll call you later. If I'm free, I'll definitely be over."

"Good. I'll fix us some dinner."

"Sounds good. It's been a while since I had a home-cooked meal," Porter said, hoping his smile was reassuring.

• • •

Porter hit the highway, wondering when the afterglow was finally going to subside. It was extremely pleasant but could be distracting at work. He then realized he should clean himself up before he showed up at the Lair, so he stopped off at his hotel room in Methuen to shower, shave and get changed.

He drove over to 'Manchester Esther's Coffee & Cakes' for morning breakfast, which had become his daily ritual now. Any ambivalence about his night with Grace had evaporated and a kind of euphoria was setting in. He didn't seem to notice he was going a little overboard with this morning's order, and wouldn't have cared anyway.

"OK, four extra-large regulars. Make that six. OK, give me a mixed dozen muffins. I'll have two corn, two banana, two blueberry, and two carrot. Let me have some of those donuts and Danish, too."

"Big day, huh? Fueling up?" a man behind Porter said.

"Excuse me?" Porter said, turning to face him.

"I hope that's not all for you," the man replied.

He looked like an optometrist on his way to the country club.

"Do we know each other?" Porter asked, hackles good and raised.

"Your money's no good here, handsome. Here; please take this. Keep the change," the man said as he handed the cashier a hundred-dollar bill, which she stared at like it had dropped in from another planet.

"Who are you?" Porter asked impatiently.

"A friend. I'm sorry to sneak up on you like this, Mr. Dunn, but I thought it best we meet face-to-face."

"You've got about sixty seconds before..."

"Why don't we sit down and talk a bit? I have something you need to hear."

"What exactly do I need to hear?" Porter said, unyielding.

"Well, let's just call it opposition research," the man said and flashed an ingratiating smile.

"I don't have time for this," Porter said and turned for the door.

"You're running a race, Mr. Dunn, but your opponent has got a big head-start. It... *complicates* your situation."

"Who are you, besides my friend?" Porter demanded.

"I know Bob and the Doctor. Quite well, in fact. I've worked with both of them over the years. Tell the Doctor you spoke to Morty. He'll vouch for me."

"What about Travis?"

"That's a bit more complicated. Please, let's go sit down so we can converse like gentlemen."

Porter and Morty sat down at a small table near the front window. Porter put his bags on the ground and gave this Morty a once-over.

"Tell me more about the race," Porter said skeptically, and folded his arms across his chest.

"You're racing to a certain goal, but you haven't found the right teammates yet."

"And our competition has," Porter responded.

"Yes, very much so. Unfortunately," Morty said, making what looked like a regretful expression.

"Do you want to give the team a scouting report?"

"I don't have much more to tell you at the moment. What I can tell you is that the game is about to reach a very... let's just say a very challenging phase. And you need the right players for your team if you're going to play this game."

"How do we find them?" Porter asked.

"You might have to bend the rules a bit. But first, you have to learn how that's done."

"I hope you realize I don't have a single clue what you're talking about," Porter said.

"I think you do. You just don't have all the pieces of the puzzle yet."

"So, this team you're talking about, what kind of players do you think we need to be looking for?"

"Well, that's where I come in, my friend," Morty said. "I'm a kind of a... talent scout, you might say. It's just that there are just certain... *difficulties* we need to iron out first."

"What do you mean, 'difficulties?'" Porter asked.

"That's something we'll have to discuss later, son. Oh dear, look at the time. I must be on my way," Morty said, and got up from his chair to leave.

"Is that it?"

"Here, this is a new kind of sweetener," Morty said. "Much better for you than that saccharine crap. Stuff'll kill you. Well, best of luck to you."

Porter watched as this 'Morty' walked out, crossed the street to the parking lot, got in a silver Mercedes CLK and drove off. Porter grabbed his bags, went back to his car and called Sam as soon as he closed the car door.

"Hey Doc, it's Porter. I just had a very strange conversation with a guy who said you could vouch for him." Porter said, and yanked on his shoulder belt.

"Is that so? What's his name?" Sam asked.

"He said it was Morty," Porter replied. "He gave me a sugar packet with a Connecticut phone number on it."

"My oh my, Porter. You're certainly drifting into very deep waters with this job."

"Why? Who is he?" Porter asked.

"Morty is Don Morton, who's a bit of a living legend in some intelligence circles," Sam explained. "Back in the Sixties, he was a young field agent working under your boss in Southeast Asia."

"He did seem to imply that Travis wouldn't be too happy to hear from him," Porter said.

"Bob hates everybody," Sam explained. "But he especially hates Don Morton."

"Why?"

"Well, it all boils down to the fact that Don Morton is one of the very few people in this world that Bob is actually afraid of. Then again, a lot of people are afraid of Don Morton."

"You're kidding me. Why?" Porter asked, stunned but intrigued now.

"How shall I put this? Don Morton has a penchant for... *overkill* when you cross him," Sam said. "I mean that literally. There's quite a lot of rage buried in that man's soul."

"Seriously? He seemed pretty easy-going to me."

"So does a lion, most of the time. Don Morton can be a real charmer, under normal circumstances. Just don't ever piss him off."

"Care to share some of these legends?" Porter asked. This was really getting interesting.

"Maybe some other time. Let's just say that Don Morton is a man you definitely don't want as an enemy. Don't be fooled by the whole preppie act. He has no compunctions whatsoever about killing anyone who ruins his day. Even now, well into his maturity."

"Understood."

"What did he have to say?" Sam asked.

"Well, we were in public, so he was being kind of vague," Porter said. "But he said we're in a race and that the other side had a head start. That mean anything to you?"

"It might. What else did he say?"

"He said we don't have the right players on our team, but the other side does."

"Did he offer any evidence of this?" Sam said.

"No. Like I said, we were in a public place. It was a bit awkward, actually. He also said the game was about to enter a very difficult phase, that we were going to have to bend the rules if we want to win it."

"I see. Well, this is not good news," Sam said, grimly.

"I've got a vague idea what he meant, but I get the impression that you know exactly what he was talking about."

"I do indeed. Listen, I need to speak to Bob. The three of us may need to get together on this problem. The three being Bob, Don Morton, and myself."

"OK, Sam" Porter said, uncertainly.

"Be extra careful out there, Porter. Don't take anything for granted. If what Morton says is true, we have a serious problem on our hands. Don't report this to Travis, let me handle it."

• • •

Porter's mind reeled as he hit the road. He wasn't sure what exactly was going on, but suddenly all those zeroes on his paycheck made a bit more sense. He decided to put it out of his mind.

The sun was shining, he'd just had some of the best sex of his life, and the coffee and muffins were smelling awfully good as he wound down the treacherous gravel road to the Lair.

"Breakfast is served," Porter said as he entered the kitchen and put the bags down on the counter. "Where's Darja?"

"Dunno. Running late," Bruehle said as he rifled through the morning's selections.

Porter reached into his inside pocket and pulled out the information Grace had printed out for him.

"Got a little present for you, Bruehlie. Fresh data on Gary's father. Looks like he might have been working for some of the nuclear plants around here. Off the books."

"Where did you get all this?" Bruehle asked.

"From Gary's mother," Porter said.

Zaina got up from the table and stormed out of the room.

"What's with her?" Porter asked.

"You fucked her, didn't you? That poor bastard's mother," Bruehle said, without taking his eyes off the printouts.

"What? Why do you say that?" Porter said, as he felt the floor plunge beneath his feet.

"Darja had a few too many last night and started in on how you and Mother Goose were eye-banging each other the entire time you were supposed to be interviewing her. She said she was worried the two of you were going to start rutting like terriers right there on the coffee table."

"OK, so why does she care?" Porter said, pointing in the direction Zaina walked out.

"She's very traditional. She has no time for you degenerate Yankees and your loose morals."

"So the three of you were discussing all this behind my back."

"Only because you weren't here," Bruehle said, then bit into a cheese Danish the size of a dinner plate.

"Oh God, what about Travis?" Porter said, as his afterglow switched off like a lightbulb.

"Don't sweat it, Studly Do-Right. We're all grown-ups here. If he asks, just tell him you took one for the team so you could pilfer all this deep background on Gary's dear old dad. All in a day's work."

CHAPTER THIRTY THREE

Darja had finally showed up at the Lair, a bit hungover. The warm sun had disappeared by mid-morning and a cold, dark rain-shower had descended suddenly, like a shroud. Once she loaded up on coffee and donuts, she and Porter drove to a wealthy neighborhood in the town of Littleton, Massachusetts to talk with Kevin Stuart's mother.

They pulled into the driveway, got out of the car, and then looked up. The Stuart family house stood only slightly smaller than the Taj Mahal. The roof didn't actually break the dark clouds overhead, but it certainly gave that impression. Whatever you could say about Kevin, you couldn't say he was depraved because he was deprived.

"Jesus, another castle," Darja said.

"This job is giving me serious house envy," Porter said.

"No shit. Especially since we have to go back to that depressing little dump every night."

Porter and Darja stood at the front door and rang the bell. A very worried-looking, late-middle-aged woman answered and invited the two in after they identified themselves. She ushered them through a long hall and into a sitting room. It was bathed in natural light coming in from the sliding glass doors leading onto the deck. Unfortunately, this particular natural light was quite a bit muted because it was a cold, rainy, miserable day.

The sitting room was essentially a Kevin shrine. There were photos of him placed all over the room, especially graduation pictures. Kevin looked like the gentlest, sweetest guy you ever met. There was a deep sadness in his eyes that seemed especially tragic when you considered the direction his life would ultimately take. All the more so seeing how the prevailing opinion at the Lair was that someone was somehow directing her son's actions.

Darja took the lead with Mrs. Stuart, adopting a gentle persona Porter found unfamiliar but appealing.

"Mrs. Stuart, looking back on Kevin's time in the hospital, do you remember any unusual events, any strange letters or phone calls?" Darja asked.

Unfortunately, Mrs. Stuart wasn't feeling very talkative. So much so that Porter soon suspected that someone had gotten to her.

"To be honest, it's not a time I care to remember," the older woman said. "It was a stressful time for our family, as I'm sure you understand."

"We understand, it's just that Kevin is a suspect in a potential murder investigation, which is why we need as much information as possible," Darja said softly. "It could mean the difference between Kevin's guilt or innocence. And we would hate to see him suffer for a crime he didn't commit."

Mrs. Stuart looked more crestfallen than ever. She took a sip of her coffee and said, "I see. Well, my husband is really the person you should talk to about that."

No sooner had she finished speaking than Kevin's mother suddenly noticed that the two strangers' attention had been turned to the sliding glass doors, specifically to the naked, anorexic man standing on the deck, peering into the house. Mrs. Stuart screamed.

Porter spotted the rusty staples in the naked man's scalp and realized that this was Kevin Stuart, literally in the flesh.

Porter very carefully placed his mug down on the coffee table and moved to the doors. He fumbled with the lock for a moment, then got out onto the deck, which was slick with rain. It was also cold enough out here that the drizzle was starting to ice, which made Kevin's nakedness all the more shocking.

Where the hell were his clothes? Where the hell had he come from? How the hell did he make it to his mother's house without the neighbors noticing a naked, bald, stick-figure scarecrow of a man running down the street?

The skin around the staples was red and inflamed. Kevin's genitals were shrunken to near invisibility from the cold and wet, and someone had shaved his pubic hair. In fact, Kevin didn't seem to have any hair on his body at all, not even any eyebrows.

Despite his nakedness and his emaciation, Porter felt a grave sense of threat radiating from this man. Kevin was frozen in an unnatural pose, his arms akimbo and his bony knees pressed together. But he was clearly freezing. His skin was white and mottled, the blood having drained from his flesh to protect his organs from the cold. Even the bruises on his face from his recent beating looked pale. If Kevin didn't get inside very soon, he was going to die of exposure.

Porter crouched down as if to minimize any threat he might present. He held his hands palms out, an unconscious display showing he wasn't holding a weapon. Kevin backed away; his back arched awkwardly.

"Kevin. Hey, hey, buddy, take it easy," Porter softly spoke. "It's OK, buddy. I'm here to help. Come inside, all right? Let's get you out of the rain, OK? Your mother would really like to see you, buddy. OK?"

Porter craned his neck backward and called to his partner, "Darja, get him a blanket!" but Kevin bolted the second Porter took his eyes off him. He was unnaturally fast; Porter had read in the file that Kevin was a runner before his breakdown. Even in this degraded state -- even naked in the cold rain -- he could move. But Porter was fast, too. They ran like wild deer over the rolling hillocks behind the giant homes.

They finally came to a tall, rain-slicked wooden fence that offered no purchase, running to the tree line in each direction. Kevin stopped and spun as Porter approached.

Porter crouched, held out his hands and said, "Kevin, wait. I'm not going to hurt you, I promise. But we really, really need to get you inside, OK?"

But Kevin had tensed his withered frame, as if to summon every last remaining reserve of strength. He took a flying kick at Porter with the expertise of a black-belt, a kick that might've done real damage had it not been so obviously telegraphed.

Porter easily ducked the kick and grabbed Kevin's bony ankle as he spun. Kevin tried to jerk free from Porter's grip but only managed to land on his head. Something made a sick, snapping sound as Kevin hit the grass. He was out cold, and Porter was terrified he might have paralyzed him. Porter removed his jacket and tried to cover up Kevin's bony, quivering frame. He was suddenly overcome by such a wave of pity for this tormented man that he felt hot tears stinging in his eyes.

Porter was already on the phone with 911 by the time Darja caught up with them. "For God's sake, Darja, go back and get some blankets now or he'll freeze to death before the paramedics even get here!"

Darja sprinted off.

Porter scanned the neighborhood, desperate to discover where Kevin had come from. Peering in the space between two houses, he thought he saw a dark shape atop the curve of a hill in the long distance. He reached into his jacket pocket and removed his fold-out binoculars.

Adjusting the focus wheel, Porter saw what looked like a black Lexus or Mercedes sedan.

He was shocked to see a man with high powered binoculars staring right back at him. The man was holding what looked like a two-way radio or cellphone in his other hand.

Porter tried to sharpen the focus, but the man and the car were obscured by the distance, the bad light and the soft rain. The man had put the radio in his pocket and the binoculars back in the car and pointed defiantly, letting Porter know he saw him, too.

From what he could make out, the man was black or dark-skinned Hispanic, wore a black ball-cap and a black leather trench coat over black-and-grey Army-issue fatigues. Yeah, not trying to stand out or anything, Porter thought sardonically. The man then got in his car and drove away, without any apparent sense of urgency or alarm.

By this time, Darja had sprinted back with a blanket and a heavy, quilted comforter. She carefully laid them atop Kevin, hoping not to make his situation any worse. She then crouched to rub Kevin's paper-white feet in order to restore his circulation.

Two cops came jogging over from the easterly direction. Porter sniffled and wiped away his tears while he held out his ID wallet,

"The paramedic unit should be here within 10 minutes. Is there anything we can do, sir?" one cop asked. Porter realized he hadn't looked very hard at his ID, and assumed Porter was a Fed.

"Suspect sustained a head injury from a fall. I think it's best we leave him be and let the paramedics handle it." Porter replied.

"We can tape off the area and keep foot traffic out of your way."

"That would be great. I appreciate it," Porter said.

"Let us know if you need anything else," the cop said helpfully.

"You bet. Thank you, guys," Porter said, then turned his attention back to Kevin Stuart.

CHAPTER THIRTY FOUR

Twilight had fallen hard, as did a nasty freezing rain. Porter was trading small talk with random cops and firefighters while Darja was engaged in a serious conversation with a female paramedic. Neighbors had gathered on the far side of the street despite the very cold sleet and rain. Kevin's mother stood with an umbrella and a rain slicker, a look of utter devastation on her face as she listened to a fireman pass on the bad news from the ambulance crew.

From the looks of it, Kevin had very possibly sustained a broken vertebra in his neck. He would need emergency surgery since the skull sutures from his recent brain surgery had still not properly healed. The paramedics were alarmed by his physical condition and said he was showing signs of advanced anemia; his tongue and gums were a very light pink. Mrs. Stuart now realized that she may well be burying her only child before the week was out.

A middle-aged cop with a thick mustache and salt and pepper hair introduced himself simply as the Chief of Police. He took Darja and Porter to a nearby gazebo so they could talk freely, away from the mob of cops and fire personnel.

"I understand you two were looking for this guy in connection to a shooting in Quincy," the Chief said.

"Yes, I'm Special Agent Lundquist and this is Special Agent Dunn," Darja said, nearly biting her tongue.

"OK, well, I have a problem. This kid's family's in bed with the state government and his mother's having a fit over there about her son. She's talking about suing you, me, the town, the county, the state, everyone. I also need to know how a stark-naked anorexic can run around my town without anyone ever seeing where the hell he came from. On a freezing cold-ass day, I might add."

"I may be able to help you with that, Chief," Porter said. "I spotted a black sedan parked up on that hill over there. There was a subject watching the neighborhood with high-powered binoculars. Looked to me like some kind of military contractor."

"Jesus, this really is some James Bond shit. huh? Is there anything more you can give me on this Quincy thing, so I can get this crazy woman off my back?"

Porter and Darja looked at each other.

"Her son may be involved with a terrorist organization that the government is presently monitoring," Darja said in a severe tone.

"Whoa. No shit, eh? Well, that at least makes some kind of sense. Some kind of militia thing, I gather?"

Porter shrugged off the speculation. "It's really not something we want out there right now," he said, knowing full well that everyone in town would be expecting an imminent invasion from a terrorist army by breakfast tomorrow.

"Let us handle the mother," Darja said. "We can deal with her through channels."

Actually, she was fully intending to never set foot in this godforsaken burg ever again. "But just remember, we don't want anyone knowing this suspect may be involved in terrorist activities," she added gravely.

The Chief rubbed his chin thoughtfully. "No, I hear what you're saying. I appreciate you sharing all this with me, agents. It's not the kind of thing we usually hear about around here. "

"We'll keep you posted if we learn anything more that might impact your jurisdiction," Darja said. "But as of this moment we really don't have much more to share. We're only at the very beginning of this case."

"Well, I'll have my men keep their eyes peeled for anything out of the ordinary."

"We appreciate it. Thanks again, Chief. We'll be in touch," Darja said.

Porter shook his head in disbelief as they walked back to the Taurus.

"Remind me never to get on your bad side," he chuckled.

"What do you mean?" Darja said.

"'Terrorist organization?' That poor woman's going to get run out of town on a rail."

"Serves her fucking right," Darja snapped. "She's holding out on us. And anyone who raised a five-star fuckup like Kevin can't be all that right in the head herself."

"She's scared, Darja. I think she's holding out because she's afraid of somebody. I don't think Kevin grew up that way. I think something happened to him."

"What are you getting at?" Darja said, frowning.

"I think he's in real trouble, worse than we thought. I think we're up against something big, bigger than we know."

"What, the flying saucer people?" Darja snapped, and rolled her eyes.

Porter ignored the dig. "That guy over on that hill was clearly some kind of operative. And he obviously just dropped Kevin off. That changes the entire complexion of this case, if you ask me."

"OK," Darja snapped. "Let's say that's true. So what does some 'operative' care about some crappy grunge band on the South Shore for?"

Porter bypassed the question. "I think we're being tracked, don't ask me how. But I think they knew we'd be out here today, and so they dropped Kevin off, knowing exactly how this would all turn out."

"But *why*, Porter?" Darja asked urgently.

"I don't think they want us out there looking for him, because that in turn might then lead us back to them," Porter said. "There's something going on we're not supposed to know about here. And God knows we certainly won't get any more cooperation from Kevin's mother now."

"OK, so they take Gary out of the picture, throw up a bunch of smoke around him, and now they take Kevin off the boards. Why? What for? What's the point of any of this?" Darja pressed, impatiently.

"I don't know. I just know it's part of a much bigger puzzle, Darj."

Darja thought it all over for a minute.

"OK, let's just say you're right," she admitted. "But right now we have a job to do, and that's finding that dumbass fucking longhair for Travis. That's what we're getting paid for. I don't know about you, but I've never seen the kind of money that crazy old fart is paying. A few more years of this and I'm buying me a nice cabana down in Costa Rica."

CHAPTER THIRTY FIVE

"Knock, knock, Sammy," Don Morton said as he peeked into Sam's office door.

"Ah, the man himself. Come in, Don. Been a while, no?" Sam said cheerfully.

"Sure has," Morton said as he flopped himself down on the sofa. "Just like old times, eh Sam?"

"You mean you sticking your nose in Bob's business and me trying to keep the two of you from killing each other? Those old times?" Sam asked.

"The very same," Morton said with a mischievous grin.

"So I hear you accosted one of Bob's men this morning. What have you got?"

"I've got proof that the bad guys have a team in place. A good one."

"Let's see it," Sam said, beckoning with his hand.

"I may've been born at night, but I wasn't born last night, Sam. It's going to cost."

"I'm not the man with the checkbook," Sam said wearily. "Besides, Bob already assumes other groups are putting together teams anyway."

"Travis doesn't know what I know, old chum. It's much worse than he thinks. This isn't just a bunch of ordinary viewers he's dealing with. It's heavy-duty heathen juju, the blackest of the black magic. Bad medicine, Kemosabe."

"So what do you want, Don?" Sam asked, quickly losing patience.

"I want to direct the team in the field, Sam. Bob's not a people person. That's not his thing. Never has been."

"I don't have the authority, Don. I'm not directly involved in this myself. I'm merely advising on an informal basis, and barely at that."

"Well, you have Bob's ear," Morton pressed.

"Not really."

"As much as anyone does, Sam. Listen, if what I'm hearing is true, Bob is going up against the dirtiest players in the game; sickos, fanatics, kill freaks. Those poor, dumb kids of his have absolutely no idea what they're up against."

"I'll see what I can do," Sam said, resignedly.

"Listen Sam, you just get on the phone today and tell Bob that his little glee club is about to walk straight into a wood-chipper. No two ways about it."

"What do you have to offer? Besides yourself?"

"I've got a line on some top-rank remote viewers. I just don't have the resources to do anything about it. And some of them have special needs."

"Jesus Christ, Don. You messing around with junkies again?"

"The good ones always need to numb out, old boy. It comes with the territory. Otherwise they overload."

"You never learn. You and Bob Travis are peas in a pod," Sam sighed.

"Hardly. You think I'd ever pick a name like 'The Bifrost Initiative'? Good God, Sammy. Who the hell does Bob think he is, Hammond Innes?" Morton exclaimed.

"Robert Ludlum, actually. You know how much Bob loves his Ludlum."

The two men wrangled on for a while. Morton left Sam's office with both men angry and frustrated. Sam damn well knew that Morton only wanted to get back out in the field so he could kill other human beings with impunity. And get paid for it.

But Sam had to admit that Morton was right about Travis. Bob was now an errant knight on his own personal Grail quest, not a General fit to lead troops into battle. He was going to get those fine young people killed and Sam could not have that.

Don Morton, one the other hand, was a diagnosable sociopath and seemed to be somewhat more than mildly dissociative at times, but so were any number of great leaders throughout history.

Sam fidgeted and fussed in his chair. He picked up the phone a few times, thought better of it and hung up again. Finally, he figured out how best to approach the problem and dialed.

"Bob, it's Sam."

"I'm busy. What do you want?" Travis asked, predictably irritably.

"I just received some disturbing intelligence directly relating to Bifrost."

"You shouldn't even be talking about Bifrost, Sam."

"Do you want to hear what I have to tell you or not?" Sam asked impatiently.

"What is it?"

"I've been informed that someone else might already have a team in place, Bob. A heavy duty one."

"Where did you get this?" Travis growled.

"I can't divulge that yet. I'm still trying to get confirmation."

"When will you have confirmation?"

"Can't say. The intelligence is patchy," Sam admitted.

"Call me when you sew it up, Sam. I'm hearing all kinds of rumors these days and can't go around chasing after every single damn one of them."

CHAPTER THIRTY SIX

Bruehle kept his workspace in the basement, on the other end of the tunnel from the conference room. With its exposed ceiling, fluorescent lights and electronic equipment everywhere, the space looked like some mad scientist's laboratory, only vaguely more suburban.

Porter had come downstairs because Bruehle was going to dig up some dirt on this Morton guy. Everything the Doc had told him had only fueled his curiosity. Bruehle was sitting at one of his computers, which he'd disassembled for repairs. Wires and circuit boards were scattered all over the place. Porter wondered how Bruehle could keep it all straight.

"What's the matter, Supes?" Bruehle asked. "You look like you still got coitus on the brain. Must've had quite a roll with the Sutton widow there."

"You got a girlfriend, Bruehle?" Porter asked, glancing around the chaotic workroom.

"Had a boyfriend, actually. He vanished the last time I got arrested," Bruehle said, concentrating on soldering diodes to a flat green piece of plastic. Porter couldn't make out what it was. Some kind of motherboard or something, he supposed.

"How does Travis feel about that?"

"Well, that is the question, isn't it?" Bruehle said, without looking up. "How Travis feels about that."

"OK, if this is the part where you tell me Travis is secretly gay, you can save your breath," Porter scoffed.

"Well, it's interesting," Bruehle said. "He's been married four times but has no kids. His last marriage ended in 1975, so he's been single nearly twenty years now. That doesn't exactly throw me off his scent."

"You want to know what I heard?"

"Ooh, do tell." Bruehle perked up and locked eyes with Porter.

"I heard he's got a former prostitute that he keeps in an apartment in DC. Apparently, he keeps her on the DoD payroll as a counterintelligence consultant."

"Ha! No kidding. And she's a woman?"

"She's a woman," Porter said.

"A *biological* woman?"

"Ha ha. I'll have to look into that."

"One thing about the spying game, Supes; gay men are very good at it," Bruehle said.

"So I've heard. Why is that?"

"Practice, from a very early age. Living undercover. We're natural born double agents. As to your original question, Travis doesn't give a shit one way or the other about me being gay, he just cares about the job and who can best get it done."

"I know what you mean. So, what did you find out about this Don Morton?" Porter asked.

"Well, funny you should ask. I couldn't get much. We'll have to take the good doctor's word that he's on the payroll somewhere."

"What did you find?"

"Mostly just media clippings," Bruehle said. "Something intentionally vague about Vietnam service in his hometown paper. Apparently, he was also some kind of executive at the big public television station in New York for several years. Which is interesting, because he doesn't seem to exist much before then. Or much after, actually."

"Sounds pretty typical for a spook."

"Possibly, but he also seems to have had some kind of involvement with the Skeptical Investigations Committee, which some people in the newsgroups believe is a DoD front."

"I'm not familiar with it," Porter replied.

"It's a group made up of a bunch of prominent academics and scientists. They got a lot of exposure in the Seventies and Eighties debunking things like pyramid power and alternative medicine. All of that hippie-dippy, New Age bullshit."

"So why would the Pentagon get involved in something like that?"

"Well, the consensus seems to be to muddy the waters in case any fringe stuff the military were working on leaked out into the mainstream media," Bruehle said.

"OK, whatever."

"But this is weird; Morton was married twice, and both wives met violent ends," Bruehle said, and set down his soldering gun while a tiny dab of silvery metal hardened. He then began to rifle through a stack of file folders.

"You're kidding. How?" Porter said, shocked.

"First wife was killed by Contra rebels in Nicaragua." Bruehle said, as he scanned a sheet of print-out and put it back in a folder.

"Holy shit. What happened?"

Bruehle found the file he was looking for.

"Yeah, well, let's see. Wife was attached as a lay leader to a Catholic mission accused of aiding communist rebels in El Salvador. It got raided, everyone inside was raped, tortured and beheaded, not necessarily in that order. It caused a huge international scandal at the time. Pope John Paul himself apparently tore Ronnie Reagan a new one over it," he explained.

"Reports have it that one of the big Contra generals personally shoved each one of the accused raiders off a ten-story apartment building in a rebel-held neighborhood, then ordered their bodies to be left in the street for nearly a week. To make an example of them, you see. There were about a dozen, all told. The oldest of them was only seventeen, apparently."

"Oh my God. That's insane," Porter said. "You think this guy Morton was involved in that?"

"Well, seems the good *Comandante* had been seen in the company of a blond gringo around that same time, so you tell me," Bruehle said. "OK, Morton later remarried, but the second wife and a daughter were later killed in a motor crash on the Saw Mill Parkway in New York State, just a few years ago. The news stories are interesting; some unnamed sources dropping subtle hints it may not have been an accident, exactly."

Bruehle thumbed through the folder, then continued.

"That crash was mentioned — apropos of absolutely nothing, mind you — in a story on a Macedonian arms smuggler who died when a fire broke out inside his Federal prison cell in Ohio. This was about two years back. The news syndicate claimed it was a typo. And that little barbecue party in Ohio was held just a couple weeks after stories ran that that very same smuggler's family were found in a shallow grave in a garbage dump outside Skopje. Papers said they'd all been buried alive. The guy's wife, two kids, his mother, a sister. A few cousins. It's safe to assume they were probably planted there by your new boyfriend, or at least on his orders."

"Jesus. I can see why Travis is afraid of this guy," Porter replied.

"This is interesting," Bruehle said, rubbing his chin as he read a file. "Apparently, a whole bunch of Bush Administration people attended the wife and daughter's funeral."

"Pretty impressive," Porter said.

"But here's why I asked about Travis; there are a few photos of this Morton guy with Mika David. Fairly recent ones, actually."

"Who's Mika David?" Porter asked.

"Big disco diva from the Seventies, huge on the gay scene in Berlin," Bruehle explained. "Romantically linked to a lot of the big pop stars of the time: Bowie, Marc Bolan, David Cassidy, various celebrities, politicians, football stars. Appears on various record covers for various rock groups, some German films."

"OK, so good for Mika David. Why do I care?" Porter asked.

"Well, you probably don't. But it's widely rumored that Mika David was born David Miguel Alcala in the Philippines to a Dutch mother and Filipino father who worked high up in the Marcos regime."

"Yeah? Well, when I was a kid it was widely rumored that Rod Stewart had a gallon of semen pumped out of his stomach," Porter said, dismissively.

"Who says it was a rumor?" Bruehle deadpanned.

"It's weird; I'm having a really hard time squaring all that with the man I met. I mean, the guy reminded me of my youth pastor," Porter said, getting back to his main topic of concern.

"Well, like I said, the spy business. You get all kinds of actors," Bruehle explained. "But if this guy lost two wives and a daughter, I don't think it was a question of really bad luck, oh-so-terribly-sorry. If someone went after his family like that, it was probably payback. And probably paying back something quite very nasty indeed."

"What makes you say that?" Porter asked.

"The bad guys know messing with spooks' families is generally a death sentence, as you can probably see," Bruehle answered. "It usually brings the whole bloody government down on your head. If they do it anyway, it's usually for a vendetta worth dying for. It's just that maybe these particular bad guys didn't realize a whole lot of other people would die as well."

"You'd make one hell of a detective, Bruehle."

"Oh, I'm quite happy where I am, Supes. I don't much fancy getting shot at."

CHAPTER THIRTY SEVEN

The girl reminded Darja of something she once saw on some nature documentary, like a lemur or a marmoset. Mostly because her eyes looked twice as large as they should have in proportion to her face.

Her skin was pale, and her hair was thin and mousey-brown. Tiny beads of sweat seemed to be fixed to her forehead. She was small and frail, and didn't look a day over thirteen.

Darja's immediate impulse was to physically shelter this girl from the men in the living room, but she let it pass. For the time being, at least.

"Have a seat, Celeste," Travis croaked in what he probably thought was a comforting, paternal tone, but Celeste seemed alarmed by everyone and everything. She hesitantly chose the nearest armchair and sank into it. She held her bony arm out, palm up. Travis knelt down and produced what looked like a shaving kit from his briefcase.

The group watched with alarm as Travis unsheathed a fresh plastic syringe, then stabbed it into a vial emblazoned with Japanese writing. He then gingerly wrapped Celeste's arm with a rubber tourniquet and waited for a vein to present itself.

When a tiny bump materialized, Travis injected Celeste, and she seemed to brighten a smidge and relax.

"Celeste has an endocrine imbalance. She needs these injections four times a day," Travis said, scanning his team's blank faces for reaction.

Not a single soul believed for a second that Celeste actually had an endocrine imbalance, but no one was keen to argue the fact with a man who wasn't exactly famous for enjoying a good argument.

Travis reached again into his bag and pulled out a strange sample of electronic equipment, something none of the group had ever seen before. Like the medicine, all the writing on the instrument panel was in Japanese. Travis plugged an imposing DC adapter into its side, and then plugged the adapter into the outlet in the lamp on the small table beside Celeste's armchair. He produced a length of thick telephone cable, plugged it into the side of the machine then reached down and plugged the other jack into the phone outlet at the floorboard.

Then he pressed the sides of the black box and two speaker-like devices rose from their wells of a closed-circuit telephone unit, something else none of them had ever seen before.

Travis pressed the 'call' button and waited. "Bob?" a voice sounded, in startlingly clear audio fidelity.

"Yes, we're ready to start," Travis replied.

The voice said, "Test: Celeste DeBella, remote viewer. Supervisor, Robert D. Travis, Administrator, Bifrost Initiative. Facilitator: Jon Aaron Silverman, Consulting Agent, Defense Intelligence Agency. OK, Celeste, we're going to start with something simple, OK? I have six cards laid out in front of me. Just read the cards, from my point of view, from left to right. OK?"

Celeste closed her eyes and lowered her chin to her chest. Her voice sounded like some kind of squeaky toy.

"From your left, Two of Swords, Ace of Wands, Three of Wands, Nine of Coins, Four of Cups and... I can't. I can't see the sixth card."

"Keep trying, Celeste," Travis said, encouragingly.

"It's not clear," Celeste squeaked.

"Keep looking."

"Umm...ahh, it's the Fool," Celeste finally said.

"Very good." The muffled sound of applause burst from the speaker. There was obviously an audience on the other end as well.

"What was the problem?" Travis asked.

"I had my hand over it, Bob," Silverman said over the phone.

Travis laughed at this with a deep, guttural guffaw, which the group found far more disturbing than the unnatural phenomenon they had just witnessed.

"OK, let's try a series of coordinates," Travis croaked. "Just like we did before. I'll call out coordinates and you just tell us what you see there, OK...?

When it was all over, Celeste left with Khoury and Evan. The poor girl seemed to utterly vanish between the two black-clad man-mountains as they took her out to the parking lot.

The four sat in the dimly-lit kitchen, sharing pizza and garlic knots. Travis came in to join them. He grabbed a slice and a plate and sat down with his group. He was uncharacteristically ebullient, nearly giddy, which his team found even more intimidating than his usual demeanor.

"Isn't she amazing? I've never seen a viewer before with that kind of accuracy," he said, and took a healthy bite of his pie.

Bruehle said, "It was incredible. I mean, you read so much about remote viewing but it seems hardly anyone takes it seriously."

Travis suddenly darkened.

"We spend a lot of money to make damn sure people don't take it seriously. It's bad enough civilians even know it exists."

"So, what's the plan?" Bruehle asked.

"She'll be kept in a safehouse for the time being," Travis replied, recovering his enthusiasm. "If everything goes right, you'll be able to communicate with her using the new speakerphone unit I brought in today. So Bruehle here can patch her into your cellular phones when you're in the field, whenever necessary."

"Will Celeste be needing a tutor in the safehouse, sir?" Darja said acidly.

"Meaning?" Travis replied, setting the remainder of his slice down as if readying for a bar fight.

"Well, she at least needs a high school diploma to work here, for this here Bifrost Initiative, doesn't she? Sir?"

"She's got one, Lundquist," Travis said, his eyes glowing with a simmering rage.

"Oh, goodie-gumdrops for her, sir. That must have been very difficult, sir, what with her 'endocrine condition' and all," Darja said, flashing sarcastic finger quotes.

Darja then compounded the felony by sneering, "Will you need me to babysit for her? Sir?"

Porter felt a sudden stab of panic. Darja had always come across as a little erratic, but now she was really running off the rails. Travis trained his black, soulless eyes on Darja, who stared back in defiance. No one else in the room dared breathe.

Finally, Travis said, "Miss Lundquist; a word, please."

He rose and walked out of the room and down the hall into his office. Darja hesitated, stared imploringly at the others a moment, then followed him and shut the door behind her.

The group sat at the table and stared down the hall in fear, not to mention utter astonishment. Unfortunately, Travis' office had been soundproofed so their conversation could not be heard.

After five interminable minutes, Darja stormed out of Travis' office with thick, hot tears oozing mascara down her reddened face.

She grabbed her car keys from the counter and nearly flew out the back door. The group were all shocked, accustomed as they all were to Darja's rough, tough-chick exterior.

After she'd left, Travis walked from the bedroom and into the living room. He collected his things and put them back in his case, his own face as blank as a page. He also left without saying goodbye, leaving the rest of the group dumbstruck.

"What the hell did he just say to her?" Bruehle said, speaking for everyone.

No one felt hungry anymore.

CHAPTER THIRTY EIGHT

Porter performed his daily ritual of bringing coffee and muffins to the group the next morning. Darja arrived a little bit later than usual and did her best to pretend she hadn't been completely humiliated by her boss the night before. The rest of them went to great lengths to accommodate her. It was a small group in a small house. They all felt her pain, even if they still hadn't a clue what had been said in that office last night. After breakfast, Porter and Darja conferred with Bruehle and worked out the day's itinerary. Barring any unforeseen events, they would meet back at the house at 1900 for a status meeting.

Porter and Darja took the Taurus out and headed back to Massachusetts. Porter was content to take in the scenery, the scrub pines and salt marshes, all the strange and elusive beauty of southern New Hampshire. The sunshine helped, and Porter took time to wonder at the oddly-obtuse lighting of the hilly country. It never looked quite right. Something about this state was just a little bit off. Porter couldn't account for it.

Porter wondered if it had something to do with all these flying saucers people were seeing up here. He also wondered if the magnetism from all the granite somehow affected the brain. This state was said to be some kind of UFO hotspot; Porter decided that these people were all hallucinating, their minds somehow affected by the strange geology of this ancient land.

Darja broke his reverie. "What do they have on you, Porter?" she asked in a muted, chastened tone.

"What do you mean?" he replied, unsure what she was getting at.

"I mean they clearly have the four of us by the short and curlies. So, what is it with you?"

"What is it with *you*? What the hell did Travis do to you last night?" Porter asked.

Darja almost spoke but then cupped her mouth, as if willing her own silence. She was clearly trying to stop what she'd started, but there was a momentum now that could not be derailed. She had to get it out.

"I had a friend. She was a good sailor. But she was also a woman and there were some men who didn't like that. And one of them decided he was going to do something about it. The guy raped her, off-base, in Okinawa. But she couldn't ID him. He wore a mask and gloves and used a condom. But she knew who it was. So she came to me for help. The guy she said raped her was a grade-A scumbag, always just one fuck-up away from a court martial. Total washout. And a disgusting sexist pig. All the other men thought he was trash, too. So we arranged a blanket party for him. Unfortunately, someone whacked him a little too hard in the head and he ended up a vegetable."

"Well, it sounds like he deserved it," Porter opined.

"Actually, yeah; he might have. But not for the rape. The guy wasn't even on the island the weekend it happened. He was in Hawaii at a friend's wedding. She didn't even bother to check because she hated this guy so much already. But it turns out it was somebody else. Actually, it turns out it was probably the guy who put the other guy in the produce department. Because that guy ended up going down for the rape and murder of a local schoolgirl about a month later. Like, maybe my friend was just a test run."

Darja stopped to gnaw at her thumb, then continued. "Either way, the shit hit the fan and everyone but me got tossed out on their fucking asses, including my friend. Someone obviously put the whammy on her because she can't get any kind of decent job anywhere now. She was bagging groceries for minimum wage last time we spoke."

"So why didn't you take the fall?" Porter asked.

"Because my CO and I were... we were *fucking*, Porter. Not to put too fine a point on it. I loved that man. No, actually, I fucking *worshipped* that man. He was literally like a god to me. Hell, he was like a god to everybody who served under him. But he was married and had five kids. And he also had his eye on the Admiralty. So he knew if I went down, he'd go down with me. Oh man, we thought we were such ninjas, sneaking around like we did, fucking in all kinds of crazy places. But men like Travis know everything that goes on in the military, I mean *every-single-fucking-thing*. Hell, in every single branch of the Federal government. They can't tell you if a terrorist is about to blow us all to Kingdom Come, but they damn sure know who's fucking who, right down to the toilet-scrubbers in the VA hospitals. And more often than not, they have... evidence."

"You're saying they have pictures of you and your CO?"

Darja stared hard out the window, saying nothing. Porter saw her fighting back fresh tears. "Officers are under constant surveillance. The higher you go, the worse it gets. It's a total fucking police state."

Porter wanted to change the subject, immediately. "You think they have something on Bruehle and Zaina?"

"Bruehle?" Darja scoffed. "He's up on so many major felony beefs, it's all Travis can do to keep his faggot ass out of prison."

"Zaina? Seriously?"

"You heard the Doc; her and that crazy brother of hers would follow Travis off a cliff if he asked them to."

"I guess."

"So, what *do* they have on you, Porter?"

"Nothing that I can think of. I mean... no, nothing. Really."

Darja was silent for a moment, processing. Suddenly, a light switched on. "No, no, no. They definitely do have something on you. Oh, yeah, they do..." Darja nodded her head triumphantly, as if she'd just solved a particularly vexing calculus equation.

"What do you mean?" Porter asked.

"Your new fuck-buddy? Mommie Dearest? *Hello?*"

"What do you mean? I mean, we just met because of the case..."

"The case!" Darja scoffed. "Listen to you! You still think all this bullshit is actually a *case*?"

"What do you mean?"

"Every rock we pick up there's a goddamned spook hiding underneath it, Porter. This isn't a case. This is just some nut-bar spook-bullshit. This is where your tax dollars are going. To a bunch of crazy old farts chasing after mental cripples who think they have magical mind-powers."

"I don't know. I mean, I think it's more than that, don't you?"

"Forget it," Darja said, turning her attention back to the scenery.

"Just take me to our next assignment. Our next futile fucking assignment."

CHAPTER THIRTY NINE

Darja and Porter lined up for another caffeine fix at a donut shop in Medford. Porter checked his watch; the day was speeding by too quickly.

Behind them, a tall, stout, goateed. crewcut young white man — wearing a black nylon wind-breaker festooned with *'Mall Security'* patches — was staring intently at the back of Porter's head.

He finally leaned over and tapped Porter on the arm.

"Yo! Hey, Porter! S'up, dude?" the gigantic man-child said cheerily. "Jeez, we all thought you fell into a hole somewhere, bro."

"Hey, what's going on, Richie?" Porter mumbled, hoping to God no one overheard them.

"Yeah, man. Hey. So, yeah; you just vanished, bro. What'cha doing now, cuz? Back in sales, or what?" Richie said, oblivious to Porter's humiliation.

Darja was staring at them both now, her mouth agape and her feline eyes wide with utter astonishment.

"No, I'm doing this thing...," Porter muttered.

"Yeah, what thing? There any openings or what?"

"Uh, I don't know, Richie. I'll have to let you know," Porter said, debating whether to skulk away now before the situation got any worse.

"So yeah, what's the dilly, cuz? This your new girlfriend or what? You're hot," Richie said to Darja, grinning jocularly.

"So are you, cuz. *Wanna fffffuck?*" Darja said, purring like a sassy porn star. An old lady shot them a dirty look, so Darja pulled the zipper on Richie's jacket up and down, just to piss the bitch off some more.

"Right on! Hey, I like this one! She's a keeper, dude," Richie said, his face flushed with embarrassment and delight.

"Is this line ever going to move?" Porter said to the ceiling.

Richie put his hands on his hips and suddenly grew serious and reproachful, which Darja found absolutely hilarious. He looked like a giant angry baby with a beard.

"So yeah, bro, we were all wondering where you went. I mean, you just stop showing up for work, y'know?"

Richie crossed his meaty arms in anticipation of Porter's reply.

"Yeah, like I said, I got another gig. Needed to pull in a bit more cash," Porter said, avoiding eye contact.

Mercifully, Darja was suddenly at the register, giving their order.

"I hear that, my dude," Richie offered meaninglessly, then spotted Porter's holster under his jacket and blurted, "Shit, bro, you packing?"

Darja abruptly turned and shushed Richie.

"Dude, you seriously packing now?" Richie stage-whispered, as if everyone else in line weren't already hanging on every single word of their conversation. "Holy shit! What they got you doing there, cuz?"

"It's, uh, corporate security," Porter mumbled, already planning his escape route.

"Oh man, movin' on up," Richie sighed wistfully. "That's where the real money is, bro."

"Yeah, I guess it is," Porter agreed, desperately wishing for a hole to crawl into.

"C'mon, Mr. Corporate Security Man," Darja said as she rescued Porter with one arm and carried their coffees with the other. "We got us some corporations to secure."

"We miss you, bro!" Richie bellowed, and added, "Hey dude; that little honey over in the food court? Man, she *really* misses you!"

"Thank you," Porter said, and immediately felt like an idiot for doing so.

"Call me, cuz!" Richie hollered, miming a phone with his stubby thumb and pinky as Porter and Darja walked out.

Porter and Darja got back into the car and were both silent for a moment. Porter then emphatically stabbed his right index finger at her and said, "Don't... don't say anything."

"I'm not saying anything," Darja said, feigning innocence. Then she blurted, *"Rent-a-cop, cough-cough,"* and flashed Porter another Cheshire Cat grin.

"It was a... stop-gap, OK? I really needed a job," Porter said, red with humiliation.

"Well, that wasn't in your file. Actually, there wasn't much of anything in your file. Bro."

"No, of course not," Porter said as he started the car. "And I was the supervisor there, OK? I ran the security force."

"Ooh, the 'security force!' Hmm, wasn't that a Chuck Norris movie?" Darja said, eyes skyward, forefinger at her lips in mock contemplation.

"Hey, it was actually very good experience for me. I got a lot of good management experience there."

"Oh, sure. I bet you got all kind of experiences there. So how little was this little honey from the food court? Still-in-high-school little? Middle-school little?"

"Don't be disgusting, Darja."

"Hey, just asking... cuz," she giggled.

"She was twenty, not that it's any of your business," Porter said as Darja tittered. "She was just a bit on the petite side, is all."

"Can I ask you one thing though?" Darja said, her face now a question mark.

"What?" Porter said and sighed heavily.

"What the fuck *happened* to you?" Darja asked. "You're still the missing piece in this puzzle."

"Nothing."

"Bullshit. C'mon; out with it, dickhead."

"I don't want to talk about it."

"*Bullshit,* Porter," Darja said, emphatically. "You know everyone else's life story. Including mine. You can't just duck out of the sharing circle like that, asshole."

"Drop it, Darja."

"C'mon, Supes. What was a hot-shit hired gun like you doing working at a mall? You've obviously had some serious training."

Porter said nothing and pulled into the noontime traffic.

CHAPTER FORTY

Darja and Porter drove into Boston, parked in an overpriced underground garage and walked over to the hotel where Uri Chartov was staying. Travis heard through his contacts in law enforcement that the man was in town, even though he wasn't due to give his deposition until next week. No one seemed exactly sure why Chartov flew all the way out from California so early. Probably just to make Mitchell Kern nervous.

Chartov's suite was surprisingly accessible, with no protective layers of stone-faced secretaries running interference on his behalf. He probably just wasn't used to being approached, either that or he wanted to seem cooperative in light of the rumors painting him as a shady underworld figure.

Darja and Porter handed their P.I. shields to a stone-faced ex-boxer type who glanced at them, grunted softly and handed them back.

A couple of other ex-boxer types with flattened Slavic noses reclined on armchairs in the spacious hotel suite, looking utterly bored. This suite offered a magnificent view of the city, Darja thought. Those guys must really be jaded.

Chartov looked like a recent immigrant from the far side of the Iron Curtain unused to modern American attire. He wore dark gray slacks and a vest, with a blue shirt and tie, Soviet-issue bifocals atop his balding head.

He was sitting at one of those nondescript all-purpose tables that hotels provided to traveling businessmen, copying figures from stacks of receipts into a ledger book with a #2 Ticonderoga pencil.

Wow, old school, Darja thought. Not a laptop in sight.

"Agents. What can I do for you today?" Chartov asked, without looking up from his ledger.

"You could tell us what you know about Gary Sutton," Darja replied, taking the lead.

"Nothing. I never heard the name before. Anything else?"

"Yes," Darja added. "What about Mitchell Kern?"

"That name I know," Chartov said, scribbling numbers almost faster than the eye could see.

"Sutton is one of Kernstock's clients."

"That's unfortunate," Chartov said, his pencil grinding. "Send him my condolences."

"We will once we find him," Darja said. "He's missing."

Chartov put down his pencil and regarded his guests.

"Ahh. And you think that that has something to do with me," he said, without inflection.

"You and Mitchell Kern are in a bit of a jam, no?" Darja said, with a tight, sardonic smile.

"No, *Mitchell Kern* is in a bit of a jam," Chartov replied brusquely. "Mitchell Kern is in a jam, so he draws me into his mess. But I am already in the process of digging my way out of Mitchell Kern's mess, since I did nothing to put myself there in the first place. Go ask your superiors in Washington. They will confirm everything I am telling you."

Darja pressed on. "Mr. Chartov, we know about your business…"

Chartov ran his left hand down a column of numbers and waved his pencil in the air with his right.

"Oh, you have a crystal ball that tells you all you need to know, eh? Who is this Gary person and why should I know anything about him?"

"He's the singer in a band called Cutter's Mill and he's gone missing in Quincy," Porter said, joining the conversation.

"And we are in Boston and I do business in California and I never heard of this Cutter's Mill," Chartov snapped. "I remember the name of every band that plays every single one of my halls, and Cutter's Mill is not one of them."

"And you would have no reason to want revenge on Mitchell Kern?" Darja said.

"Oh, on the contrary. I have many, many reasons to want revenge on Mitchell Kern," Chartov said, heat rising in his voice. "And I'll get my revenge; in a court of law. Believe me, getting revenge on Mitchell Kern is very high on my list of priorities."

"Do you have any other associates or business partners in the state of Massachusetts?" Porter asked.

"Massachusetts is a one-horse town when it comes to my line of work," Chartov said, turning a page in the ledger. "You have Boston and a bunch a little nothing towns where you can't make a nickel from a dollar. I'm trying to expand into New York, but the competition there is brutal. Texas, I'm looking at. Florida interests me. Massachusetts? Fah. Give it back to the English, see if I care."

"Then why are you here, sir?"

"Business," he said bluntly, and lowered his glasses to the bridge of his nose to inspect some numbers on a bad photocopy. The bifocals made him look like either like a professor or a KGB torturer, Darja couldn't decide which. She also noted how well Chartov spoke, despite his rather pronounced accent. There were a lot of foreigners on this case speaking better English than she did and it was starting to give her a complex.

"Let me ask *you* a question, sir," Darja interjected. "Your English is nearly perfect. Where did you pick that up, since you've only been in the country a few years and we have no record of what you did in Russia for a living?"

"What did I do for a living?" Chartov answered, almost dreamily. "A little of this, a little of that. You did what you had to, to scrape by."

Chartov put down his pencil again and regarded his visitors quizzically.

"Let me ask *you* a question, Agents. In Russia, we have bands filled with musicians who have mastered their instruments and can play every kind of music, from classical to jazz to old folk songs. So why do they call these little packs of screaming monkeys 'bands'? I still don't understand that."

"That's not really our job to decide, sir," Porter said. "I don't much care for the new music myself, either."

"No? What do you like then?" Chartov asked, with genuine interest.

"Beatles, Rolling Stones, The Who..." Porter answered.

"Fah! What's the difference?" Chartov said and waved his hand dismissively, a look of disgust on his face.

"So why then are you involved in the rock music business?" Darja asked.

"Because there's no market for real music in this country, it's all shrieking rock oafs or that terrible rap music, which I don't book. If you Americans had any taste, I'd be more than happy to book classical music or jazz, I can tell you that," Chartov snapped.

"Thank you, sir. We'll be in touch if we have any more questions," Darja said as she and Porter turned to leave.

Chartov got up from the desk, brandishing a handful of shiny fabric patches.

"Here, take some passes," he said cheerily. "You two definitely look like you need a vacation. Those are good at any of my halls, no matter who's playing. You just peel the back and stick that on your jacket there. All access. You come out to California, maybe you stop listening to no-good punks like Mitchell Kern."

"Thank you, sir, that's very kind of you," Porter said, pocketing the passes. "We don't really get out to California much, though."

"No? That's a shame," Chartov replied, looking disappointed. "OK, you two have a nice afternoon. It was very much a pleasure meeting you. You give me a call if you ever get tired of working for peanuts. I have a lot of former Federal people working for me."

Darja and Porter said their goodbyes and walked out into a misty drizzle on Boylston Street. A strange aura settled over the city, a vague sense of unreality. The skies had darkened considerably, and the cars had all put their headlights on and the sidewalks were filled with umbrellas, like a garden of anemones drifting to the gates of Boston Common.

"What was that little talk about, an attempt to sound like a naïve immigrant?" Darja asked Porter.

"I dunno. Maybe just making friendly conversation," Porter said, shrugging.

"I think maybe we need to look into this guy. He has a KGB smell to me," Darja said, thinking Chartov might have been a former interpreter for the Russian spy agency.

"I doubt he'd hand those passes out if he had something to hide."

"So, what's he doing here then?" Darja asked.

"Making money, from the looks of it," Porter replied.

CHAPTER FORTY ONE

It was after midnight and Porter and Darja were driving down a very deserted and desolate Route 28, on their way back to the Lair. As usual, Darja was fidgeting and scanning the radio dial through channel upon channel of dead air, talk shows and static. Somehow, she still failed to grasp the fact that radio was terrible up here.

Darja finally gave up and studied the road ahead of them.

She spotted an empty storefront a few hundred feet ahead, and said to Porter, "Pull in over there."

"Why?"

"Just do it, Porter."

Porter pulled into a crumbling, weed-infested lot and put the car in park, letting the engine idle. They both sat in silence for a minute.

"Come on, then. Out with it, mall-cop," Darja said.

Porter shook his head, knowing exactly what she was referring to.

"Porter, I'm going to count to ten..."

Silence.

"Porter, if you don't start talking now, I swear to Christ I'm going to pull out my Glock and shoot you in the fucking leg. I'm not even remotely kidding."

Porter stared away from her, biting his lip. Finally, he summoned his courage. "I did... something... terrible. Somebody got killed."

"Fuck. I mean, what did you...? Who...?" Darja stammered, totally taken aback by this.

"Someone who... *I loved*," Porter replied.

And as Darja watched, Porter collapsed over the steering wheel and began to sob. Terribly and heavily, and for a very long time.

A fucking eternity, by Darja's reckoning.

Darja awkwardly placed her hand on Porter's shoulder, very much regretting she went nosing around this particular Pandora's box, whatever the hell it was.

When he was all cried out, Porter told his partner the whole story.

He'd scored a plum gig with a major security contractor in DC, and one summer drew bodyguard duty for a prominent ambassador's family in Georgetown. The man in question was involved in highly sensitive work and had been the target of a very serious assassination attempt during the Cold War. He was still considered a major target, due to the nature of his job.

There'd been a brutal heatwave and sporadic blackouts all throughout the area, particularly following a series of hairy electrical storms. There was also a B&E crew working the neighborhood, so Porter and his new partner Dennis got set up in an apartment in the carriage house.

They soon became friendly with the Ambassador's teenage daughter Martina, who began to think of the handsome young bodyguards as the big brothers she never had. Porter and Dennis took the girl on outings when her parents were busy or away, to the beach, to the movies, to restaurants, concerts, everything.

It was a magical summer; three strangers who very quickly came to love each other like family.

Porter was tasked with surveying the house and grounds for vulnerabilities and had written up security and safety protocols for his supervisor to pass on to the Ambassador. Everyone in town was getting paranoid about the burglaries, especially since one of them had escalated to a gang rape. Local nerves were getting very frayed.

One night the Ambassador and his wife were invited out to a party in Virginia and weren't expected back until morning. They left their daughter home, secure in the knowledge that two heavily-armed pros were never more than a hundred feet away from her at any given time.

Porter and Dennis planned to set up in a sedan parked in front of the house, holding vigil in case the house-creepers showed up. Porter had second shift and spread out on the living room couch to catch a few Z's, so he'd be fresh and alert for the changeover.

During Dennis' shift, some obvious non-locals came stalking down the street. There were four of them; Dennis made them as residents of some DC housing project, and they seemed a little too interested in the cars parked along the street.

When the bunch of them got to his position, they peeked into a sedan and were shocked to see a smiling Dennis flashing his Uzi.

They immediately bolted off. But Dennis never made them for the B&E squad, just a bunch of kids exploring the other side of the tracks, hoping to see something heavy go down with these crazy gangsters everyone in town was talking about.

But there was a disaster lying in wait that all the guns in the world would never fix.

The shower stall in the bathroom upstairs had sprung a leak and made the very expensive marble floors very slippery and very dangerous. The Ambassador and his wife always put down a towel on the floor while showering, so they didn't notice the puddles.

Porter was concerned about the leak, the surprisingly-thin frosted glass in the stall door and the slick marble tile, and said as much to the boss during his safety evaluation. But his supervisor didn't think it was a problem worth bothering the harried Ambassador over, and didn't include it in his report.

Porter meant to fix the leak himself but forgot about it during all the excitement over the storms, the blackouts and the burglaries. It would have taken him five minutes to repair.

Martina had a riding lesson early the next morning and was taking a shower before bed. But for some reason, she forgot to put a towel down. A slick of water collected on the polished marble and she slipped and fell backwards against the thin glass door as she was coming out of the stall.

The panel shattered and a huge shard of glass tore through a major artery. She suffered a number of other serious wounds as she fell to the floor of the stall. She bled out in complete and utter terror, atop a pile of broken glass.

"She was lying there bleeding to death and I was asleep, not fifty feet away! She died on my watch! *My* watch! Died a stupid, horrible, absolutely meaningless death. And it was all my fault!"

Porter started hammering his palms against the steering wheel. Then he grabbed the wheel until his knuckles went white and shook the car violently. Then he stopped, popped the trunk and got out of the car.

Darja didn't know exactly what to expect as he marched towards the storefront, tire-iron in hand, but then Porter started in on a Dodge Caravan parked to the side of the building.

Darja was shocked by his animal ferocity, by the amount of damage this guy could cause with just one of those stupid little tire-irons you get with your spare. And she couldn't help but notice he never cursed the entire time he was beating that poor minivan to death.

Sure, the guy was a square and a wet blanket and a pussy-whipped little bitch, but he had a lot to get off his chest. She decided to let him.

Jesus. Of all the luck. Of all the dumb, blind, stupid-fucking luck, Darja thought. Of the million-and-twenty fucking things that could have gone wrong with that gig, and that's what happens. Those are the times when you know, you just fucking *know*, that your name is on some devil's list somewhere, down there in Hell.

Darja felt a hot flush of shame. She and her friends had done wrong. They -- she -- had gone out of their way to break the rules. They knew they deserved what they got.

Porter, on the other hand, was a victim of the cruelest of bitches, Fate. If what he said were true, that poor girl was dead-meat the minute she hit the floor. You slice up a major artery like that and it's sayonara, Sammy. At the very best, a paramedic team would have gotten there in ten minutes. That little girl probably would have bled out before the call was even made.

And this is the world they lived in, where a sweet little pearl of a girl bleeds to death on a bathroom floor for no good reason at all. It was such a cliche, but she suddenly knew then why so many cops ended up eating their service revolvers. See enough shit like that and it's really not that hard to get sick of this fucking world.

Porter, breathless and spent, returned to the car. He rested his sweaty forehead on the steering wheel. After a moment, he continued on with his story without looking at Darja or lifting his head.

"We were told we'd never work again," Porter said, referring to himself and Dennis.

"They made it clear in no uncertain terms that we were lucky to be getting out of town with our lives. We were just thrown out on the street. Everything was taken away from us; our jobs, our certification, our bank accounts, everything. I was afraid they might change their minds and come after me at my mother's house, so I came up here and lived in my car for six months. I showered at this gym I used to sneak into. I was so damn lucky to get that mall job, believe me. It was like a miracle. Dennis went off to work for some South African drug cartel. He's dead now. So's his wife. And their baby."

Porter stared at Darja with a weird, unhinged light in his eyes she didn't recognize -- or welcome -- at all.

He flashed her an odd, leering smile, then said, "Glad you asked?"

CHAPTER FORTY TWO

After a long day of chasing bad leads with Darja, and an equally pointless meeting with Zaina and Bruehle, Porter went over for supper and sex at Grace's house.

The sex was great, but not quite as amazing as it had been. The two were clearly preoccupied with other business. They lay in bed and Porter wondered if whatever fleeting magic they'd shared was drifting away. Grace now seemed to be focused on a point in space and time that Porter had no access to. This wasn't particularly unusual, he had sensed this the first time they met.

But the glare from that hidden star seemed to burn especially bright in her eyes tonight, even as she hummed softly and traced her fingertips around his naked torso. Porter thought the tune she was humming might be "Rhiannon."

For his own part, Porter was trying to exorcise the unspeakably obscene image of Martina's bloody, naked corpse atop a pile of shattered glass, the look of abject terror in her still-opened eyes, and the absurdly large stain the flow of water and blood had made on the Ambassador's rare and expensive hallway carpet.

But that wasn't because of anything Darja had said or done. This was an image that came to him, unbidden, several times a day.

And it was an image he knew would haunt him on his deathbed. And it would continue to haunt him in Hell, where Porter knew for sure he would be going for letting a beautiful young angel die such a horrible and utterly preventable death.

One of the girls from the mall he went with for a while — the one at the nail salon who drove that souped-up Mazda — was a Scientologist, and she tried to teach Porter all of these tricks to get the image off his mind. It actually worked; he did OK for a while.

But then Martina began to come back to haunt Porter in his dreams.

It was always the same plot line, even if the exact details changed. Martina was always alive and well, and took care to tell Porter not to worry, that it all had been a great big misunderstanding. She hadn't bled to death atop shards of shattered glass, silly.

In fact, she was hoping Porter and Dennis could take her to the park because she'd fixed them all a nice box lunch, and wasn't the weather just perfect for a picnic? Or for a concert under the stars? Maybe they should go see that new movie everyone was talking about. And then afterwards they could all go out for ice cream at that new place that just opened up downtown. I hear their new banana cookies 'n cream flavor was just to die for.

And the dream always ended the same way; Porter jolted awake, lying in a pool of sweat with Martina's dead eyes staring into his own from every corner of the room.

Porter finally fell asleep, but Martina didn't come to him tonight, Dennis did. He had crawled up from Hell to stand in this very bedroom and warn Porter that a giant serpent was coming for him and his friends. The serpent had a thousand heads and could see in the dark. There was nowhere to hide from it.

Dennis then told Porter that this new job of his wasn't really a job, it was just a trap the serpent had laid for him. And now it was coming to take Porter and the rest back down to Hell, where they all belonged.

Dennis said the serpent was going to cut all their heads off; Porter, Darja, Grace, Bruehle, all of them. He was going to cut their heads off because he'd grown new necks for their heads to sit on. And they'd spend all of Eternity with the serpent, helping him hunt for even more heads to chop.

And it was because Porter and his new friends were all just monsters, deep inside. Demons, really. And they'd had all been damned for their sins, which were unforgivable. This phony job of his was just the cheese in the serpent's mousetrap.

There was a figure standing in the shadows behind Dennis. Porter couldn't see it, but he just knew it was Gary Sutton, whispering Porter's name, over and over.

Porter sprang up from his pillow, his heart racing with terror. He looked out the window and saw the first glimmer of dawn breaking above the tree line.

He turned to his right and saw Grace standing before him in the gloomy half-light, dressed in her robe.

She held her forefinger to her lip for a long moment, exhaled, then said, "There's something I need you to see."

Grace walked out of the bedroom and into the kitchen. Porter slipped into his chinos and followed her. She sat silently at the breakfast table as Porter took a seat. After a moment, she pushed an old, battered envelope in front of him.

Porter eyed Grace quizzically. "What is this?"

"It's a letter from Kevin. He was still in the hospital after Gary got out," she replied, eyes bereft of expression.

"What does it say?"

"Kevin said that he had remembered things in the hospital that he'd repressed. Like that he and Gary had known each other as young boys and had been part of some kind of experiment on a military base."

"Well, Kevin is schizophrenic. That's exactly the kind of thing that a schizophrenic would say."

"I realize that. But even so, there's one detail that's bothering me. Glenn had sent Gary to a boarding school called 'Sunshine People' near Worcester, in the sixth grade. We had to go out of the country for a project the company was working on and taking Gary wasn't really an option."

"Were you OK with that?" Porter asked, scanning the neat handwriting on the page.

"I had no choice, really. And the school was very prestigious. It was an alternative school that was trying out some cutting-edge methods."

Porter felt another shoe about to drop, and drop it did.

"I later found out it was a front for a CIA mind-control operation, through old friends of Glenn's," Grace said, without affect. "I never found out if Gary was ever involved in the experimentation, most of it seemed to go on after he left. But I definitely believe Kevin was. And so did Gary."

"So, what happened"

"Well, we got back, and Gary came home again. But I do remember that that about was the time that he changed. He became very angry and withdrawn. The music was all he cared about; heavy metal, punk kind of stuff. Dark, angry stuff."

"Well, he was hitting puberty."

Grace ignored him. She was lost in her own reverie.

"Kevin's letter... he knew things about Gary's school, his teachers, the grounds, the classrooms. Thing she couldn't have known unless he'd been there."

"Or Gary told him," Porter suggested.

"Well, here's the thing that got me; Gary threw out all of Kevin's old letters but kept this one. Gary told his girlfriend that his experiences began in third grade, when he was coming home from school. I didn't know exactly when... I mean, I thought that was..."

Grace trailed off.

"So, your husband puts him in boarding school after these experiences begin, this school has some kind of connection to mind control experiments, and then after Gary comes home, your husband goes missing. What do you think it all means?" Porter asked.

"I don't know, but it means something." Grace insisted. "It has to."

CHAPTER FORTY THREE

It was a clear, crisp night and Darja and Bruehle stood on the back deck, sharing cigarettes and a two-liter bottle of Merlot that Bruehle had found in an abandoned cupboard in the basement.

There was actually a nice little selection of dust-coated bottles of wine stashed away down there, apparently forgotten. Bruehle didn't like to drive unless he had to, so he'd just help himself to the basement stash whenever he needed to calm his nerves. There weren't any wine stems around, so they drank out of old Mason jars.

"I didn't realize you were a smoker, Sails," Bruehle said.

"I'm not," Darja replied. "I used to be, but only when I drank. But this stupid gig is making me want to smoke, drink, snort coke, shoot up…"

Bruehle laughed. "It suits you. Gives you that *femme fatale* kind of vibe."

"Spend enough time in the service, you eventually get sick of it," Darja said. "I just have to hide it from Porter, my new dad. Actually, he's worse than my dad. When my real dad caught me smoking, he went out and bought me a carton of Virginia Slims. He said he was proud that I was 'yearning to express my budding feminist autonomy.' Which is to say he's totally full of fucking shit. Cheers."

They both laughed, clinked their jars in a toast, then sipped at their wine. It was surprisingly good, and Bruehle was very, very picky about his Merlot.

"So where is our little stud-muffin tonight?" he asked.

"Where do you think? He's getting his pipes cleaned over at Madame Sutton's pleasure palace."

"That wouldn't be a wee little hint of jealousy I detect there, is it, Sailor Moon?"

"Hell no," Darja scoffed. "Not at all. I just the think the bitch is fucking with his head. When she's not giving it."

They both giggled, then Darja turned serious.

"I don't know what it is, Bruehlie. I just get a seriously bad vibe from that woman. Something very, very off about her."

"You said she's pretty hot stuff, right? I mean, she's got all the right bits in all the right places and all that, right?"

"Yeah, but come on, Bruehlie. Look at that guy. I mean... OK, so the other day we run into this fat douchebag Porter used to work with, right? And it turns out that Porter's most recent fuck-buddy was some hot little twenty-year-old. Who I kind of got the distinct feeling might actually have been a hot little eighteen-year-old."

"Some fat douchebag Supes used to work with? Seriously?"

"Yeah, that's a whole other conversation. My point is that woman's got her hooks into him and they barely just met. It's not like he's ever been lacking for pussy, least far as I can tell."

"Yeah, I hear you. But I'll tell you, Zaina seems even to be more upset about that situation than you. I think she's got a wee little crush going on, herself."

"I kinda doubt that, Bruehle. I think you might be projecting a bit there, buddy," Darja scoffed.

"No, I don't think so. She's always asking after him, asking me if I think he's in any danger out there. That death-cage match he had seemed to rattle her up a bit. Then the kung-fu fighting with Herr Shrinky Dink. Of course, she never seems to give two shits about your fat ass."

They laughed again, then fell silent.

"What does Zaina think about all of this crap anyway? I mean, you can never shut the bitch up at meetings and then it's like she switches off like a robot the rest of the time."

"Some people are just wired that way, Sails. I think she's very compartmentalized, by necessity," Bruehle said. "But as to your question, she's only doing all this out of loyalty to Travis. She's very much a product of the Syrian Orthodox Church and they are very, very traditional. They all think the Vatican's a viper's nest of Satanists and kiddie-fuckers. I mean, it's not exactly like she opens up to me either, but I have had a few conversations with her. She's actually a very fascinating person. She has a very unique way of looking at things."

"Yeah, what did she say about this mess?" Darja asked.

"She thinks all this is the Devil's work, that it's all just another Anglo-Zionist plot to break down traditional religion and morality," Bruehle explained.

"What Devil's work, exactly?"

"All of it; remote-viewing, UFOs, alien abductions, you name it. She despises heavy rock and thinks Gary got exactly what he deserves. But it doesn't seem to color her work; she's actually a very, very good tactical analyst. The Lebanese are natural-born conspiracy-theorists, you know. I tend to think it comes naturally when all your neighbors actually are all plotting to kill you."

"You think she'd be too biased then to be much use for a guy like Travis then," Darja said and sipped at her Merlot.

"Zaina seems to be able to triangulate, to separate her personal feelings from the work she's asked to do. Her father was a mathematician who did a lot of important cryptography work for Travis, even though the man absolutely despised the US in general and the US government in particular. So I suppose it runs in the family."

"I guess it does," Darja said as she stared into the black.

"Being stuck out here in the sticks is driving me batty, Sails."

"Boston's really not that far a drive, Bruehlie," Darja said reassuringly.

"I don't have the time. Travis is driving me like a dog. He's got me doing all kinds of crazy shit that has nothing to do with Bifrost. Some of it's really fucking creepy, I'll tell you," Bruehle said, shivering a bit.

Darja nodded. She didn't need the details, knowing full well how really fucking creepy Travis was.

"Let me ask you a question, Bruehlie. If all this remote-viewing shit is real and Travis really does have some enemy out there that has their own psychics, what's stopping them from spying on us?"

"Ah, very good question, Sailor Moon. From what I've been told, Travis put in special equipment to jam remote-sensing."

"You're kidding me. How the hell do you do that?"

"He's got transmitters set up all over the grounds. They operate on the same electromagnetic frequency that remote-viewers and influencers' brains operate when in scan mode."

"Oh, come on," Darja scoffed. "That all sounds like a bunch of total bullshit."

"Not at all. If any of us had those kind of abilities, we would have terrible migraines all day. Travis has these things set up all over New England, actually. They create all these false feedback zones. Only the very best of viewers can tell the difference. The top one-half of one-percent."

"Yeah, well, whatever," Darja said resignedly, then stared out into the night. She listened to the sounds of distant traffic and wondered exactly where it was coming from.

"I really need to get laid, Sails," Bruehle said.

Darja snickered. "Wish I could help you out with that, Bruehlie. You want me to run out and pick up a strap-on somewhere?"

Bruehle laughed. Darja offered him one of her Marlboro Lights, which he'd never tried before. They smoked quietly and stared at the night sky.

"Porter really is working his ass off on this case," Bruehle finally said. "He seems very highly-motivated to find this guy alive."

"There's a reason for that, Bruehlie," Darja said and sipped at her wine. "He's got some heavy debts he's trying to pay."

"I assume you're not talking about his overdue Jordan Marsh bill," Bruehle said.

"No, but I think you should probably ask him about that yourself. Just be prepared to get shot down."

"So you can't be more specific?"

"Let's just say there's a damn good reason his resume's so thin. And an even better reason a manipulative prick like Travis has Porter under his thumb," Darja said, quite darkly.

They went silent again, and brooded on the implications of it all.

Suddenly, Bruehle pointed up to the stars.

"Hey Sailor Moon, take a look up there," he said.

"What is it?" Darja asked as she watched the excessively large, excessively bright orange star slowly glide across the heavens.

"You tell me, you're the detective."

"Shit, there's another one! Are they airplanes?"

"Well, I don't know how you filthy Yanks like to do it, but in Europe we generally try to put wings on our aeroplanes," Bruehle said.

"You don't actually think they're UFOs, Bruehlie," Darja said incredulously.

"Can you identify them? If not, they're UFOs. We're certainly in the right neighborhood for it."

"There's an airport in Manchester," Darja said. "They're probably just airplanes in a holding pattern."

"Sure thing, Sails," Bruehle said, smiling indulgently. "Whatever you say."

CHAPTER FORTY FOUR

Porter sat at the kitchen table in the Lair and scanned through his notes on the case, which he'd collected into a Word document. He strained to read between the physical lines of text, trying to detect some kind of pattern, something that might point to Gary Sutton's whereabouts in some secret code. Otherwise, he had no clue where, or even *who*, the guy was.

More and more, Porter feared Gary was most likely dead, that someone created a diversion, nabbed him, blew his brains out and disposed of the body in some way it would never be found. So he welcomed the sound of Bruehle bounding up the stairs, hoping he'd have some hot scoop to brighten the day.

Bruehle entered the kitchen, slightly breathless.

"I can't find any official records on that school online, Porter."

"You think Gary and Kevin made it all up?" Porter replied, and closed his laptop.

"Oh no, there are plenty of conspiracy theories about it in various newsgroups. There's just nothing verifiable in them," Bruehle said, then he handed Porter a stack of fresh printouts. "There's a lot of rumor and innuendo, some of which might even be true. But to be honest, my first inclination was to think that our Kevin came across some stories online and concocted a fantasy around them in order to bond more completely with his rock star lover, who had real life stories to tell."

"Did something change your mind?" Porter asked.

"Research, sir! It moves mountains!" Bruehle exclaimed. "First of all, that letter the good widow-woman passed to you was written in 1990. It's possible that Kevin was nosing around some BBS with his 1200 bps modem, searching for conspiracy theories to spice up his love letters, but not very likely."

"Unlikely but not impossible," Porter offered.

"The law of parsimony, Supes," Bruehle said. "Now, your letter says that kids were bussed from the school to the base for experiments. But this school was apparently pretty exclusive. It's said everyone who went had parents involved in some kind of military or intelligence work."

"So what about Kevin then?" Porter asked.

"Well, before he went and became a computer millionaire, Kevin's father was a Staff Sergeant in the Yoo-nited States Army. Care to take a guess what his title was?" Bruehle asked, with an insinuating tone.

"Besides Sergeant? I don't know, UFO pilot? What?"

"P-O-S, Psychological Operations Specialist. Yassuh, ten-hut," Bruehle said, mockingly.

"Guy's got an interesting career arc, that's for certain," Porter said. "Think we should bother the Skipper with any of this?"

"Not until we get more data," Bruehle replied. "I'd have a talk with the good doctor if I were you and see what he knows about all of it, Supes. Seems right up his alley."

• • •

"The Sunshine People School. Now there's a name I haven't heard in a long time," Sam said.

"You know it?" Porter asked. He sat on the front steps with his cellphone, casually eyeing the area surrounding the Lair, from force of habit. 'Situational awareness,' they called it at the academy.

But the only situation here seemed to be a wall of pine trees and the occasional squirrel or bird flitting past.

"Of course. Everyone in the business did. It was one of those unique institutions that arose out of the whole 'Today's Army' mentality in the early 1970s," Sam answered.

"What was it exactly?" Porter asked.

"It was an attempt to engineer young minds," Sam said, dolefully.

"Engineer young minds? To do what?" Porter asked, not liking the sound of this.

"ESP, telekinesis, precognition, you name it. There was a standard curriculum, if you can call it that, at least at first. But its real purpose was pushing the envelope."

"Pushing the envelope how?" Porter asked.

"Well, at first, through gentle persuasion, standard types of psychic testing," Sam sighed. "But when that didn't produce the desired results, some old CIA hands came onboard to consult, so to speak. Soon there was all kinds of nastiness going on. Electroshock, sleep deprivation, sensory deprivation, induced coma, induced fever, isolation, starvation, name it. Things got really ugly after a time; very heavy drugs, rampant sexual abuse, horrific beatings. Staff pimping young kids out to local perverts. Rumors of a murder, or maybe two, at one point."

"My God," Porter said.

"They'd originally claimed to be following the protocols set by a CIA psychiatrist named Ewen Cameron. Very prominent fellow, very highly credentialed, considered a leader in the field. He was president of a number of different psychiatric associations, including the APA," Sam explained.

"So what ended up happening there?" Porter asked.

"Well, some four-star General got wind of what was going on there and made a surprise inspection one day. He ended up putting the entire staff in leg irons. People say the place had become an absolute house of horrors, just Bedlam incarnate. Regular discipline had all but broken down altogether. The General flew in a special intel company from Germany to scrub the place out, from stem to stern. He had the entire staff — I mean, every single one of them — either cashiered, court-martialed or shipped off to the most gruesome hardship posts he could find. And then the Joint Chiefs themselves arranged a payoff for the parents of every student, to the tune of $75,000 a pop. That was real money back then, believe it."

"Did you know Gary or Kevin were involved?" Porter asked.

"No, that's the first I'm hearing about it," Sam replied. "The Army had all the records from the school destroyed. No one's sure who went there. No one's even sure who actually worked there. The fact that the Army destroyed all the documentation has only fed the rumor mill. From what I understand, most of the gossip and speculation is a lot less horrific than what actually went on in there."

"Do you think Travis knew about it?"

"I think that's a safe bet, Porter. Bob was more deeply involved in those circles than I was at the time. He's probably been keeping an eye on Gary for a very long time."

CHAPTER FORTY FIVE

A storm was picking up as Porter and Darja sped through the lightless night of backcountry New Hampshire. Darja got tired of Porter's silence and listening to the rain hit the roof, so she started in with the radio, desperate to find a decent station amid all the static. It was really starting to get on Porter's nerves.

"Jesus, Darja, you already know there's no reception in these hills. Put a CD on if you want to listen to some music," he said irritably.

"Yes, Dad," Darja snarled and dug a Tori Amos CD out of her bag.

There was a sudden and massive burst of light and the car came to a violent, wrenching stop. Porter and Darja were slammed back in their seats as both airbags blew up in their faces and the windshield exploded into a thousand tiny polygons.

As they recovered from the impact, the car began rolling into the opposite lane then onto the shoulder. Porter reached under the airbag and jerked the steering wheel sharply, sending the vehicle into an abbreviated tailspin. He kicked down the emergency brake then collapsed against the airbag like it was a pillow.

"Are you OK?" Porter asked, weakly.

"I think so," Darja said, somewhat dazed. "Thank fuck for airbags. What the hell did we hit?"

"I have no idea. I think it might have been a deer."

The two shoved the airbags away and got out of the car. If they hit a deer it must have gone airborne. All of the damage was centered around the windshield, and the portions of the hood and the roof closest to it. There was no damage to the fenders or the grill.

Darja circled the car and scanned the woods.

"I don't see any deer, Porter."

Porter retraced Darja's steps. He didn't see any either.

"Do you think someone was shooting at us?"

"It doesn't look it," Porter said, peering into the darkness. "And if they were, they could have tagged the two of us by now."

Darja checked her cellphone. "I'm not getting a signal."

"Great. Come on, let's lock the gear in the trunk and find a house."

"I hope to fuck someone's awake," Darja groaned.

They spotted a house just as the real downpour started. Neither were dressed for it. This wasn't just any kind of rain, it was a hard, heavy, freezing New Hampshire rain. The pair both jogged to the house and were relieved to see the lights on through the windows. Better yet, there was a porch to shelter them from the sky's assault.

Porter got out his ID and knocked on the door. The porch lights blinked on and an old woman opened the front door. She was short, stout and wore her hair in an anachronistic beehive hairdo. Her glasses were so thick it was like looking at eyes through a funhouse mirror. She was wearing a fancy green dress and heeled shoes, as if she were getting ready for a night on the town. In 1943.

"Hello," the old woman said. Succinct.

"Good evening ma'am, I'm Agent Dunn and this is Agent Lundquist," Porter said, flashing his P.I. shield. "We're with the Special Investigations Unit. We've had an accident and need to use your phone, if it's not too much trouble."

The woman gestured them inside without speaking. The house was warm and cozy and looked every bit like an old lady lived there.

"The phone is over there," the old woman told her guests.

"Thank you very much," Porter said. "I won't be a minute. Can you tell me exactly where we are?"

"You're right here," the woman answered.

"No, I mean what street this house is on and what number?"

"This is a rural route. It doesn't have a name. The houses here don't have numbers," the woman replied.

"Does the route have a number?"

"It does," the old woman said, searching her memory banks. "It starts with a one, I think." Well, that certainly narrows it down, Darja thought.

Porter was a lot more than a minute. He was on the phone with Bruehle, struggling to pinpoint their exact location. The old lady came up to Darja and glared at her, her head bobbing involuntarily. Darja suddenly felt like she was back in kindergarten, getting stared down by the teacher.

After what seemed like a lifetime, the woman finally spoke.

"Our people once lived in caves. Do you agree with that?" the old woman said, still glaring.

Huh? What the fuck was that all about?

"Um, sure," Darja answered, as neutrally as possible.

The woman glared at Darja, clearly unsatisfied with the answer. She waited for Darja to correct herself, then said, "George Washington once slept in this very house. Do you agree with that?"

Do I agree with *what?* Darja thought. The house seemed old, but not that old.

"Um, yes, I do," Darja said, nodding politely. "I do agree that George Washington slept here."

Wrong answer. Again. The woman's anger seemed to boil. She stared at Darja as she struggled to formulate the next riddle.

"This town gets the fewest sunny days of anywhere in America. Did you know that?"

Darja was pretty sure that it was somewhere out in Oregon that got the fewest sunny days, but didn't want this crazy old bitch to stab her with a knitting needle or something.

"Actually, I didn't know that," Darja said, attempting to sound contrite.

The woman changed gears. She suddenly seemed a lot more cogent and focused, regarding Darja with a clear light of recognition.

"You made them angry, Darja," she hissed.

Wait; did she give this batty old coot her name? In all the stress from the accident and its aftermath, Darja had to admit she was a little frazzled.

"I beg your pardon," she said politely. "Made who angry?"

"The Gentry. The Good Folk. They're all over these woods. They watch over the forests. You clearly angered them."

I angered them? Darja thought. Porter was the one driving. And who the fuck were 'the Gentry' anyway? Some Klan-ass neighborhood watch group or something?

"Well, I'm sorry about that. I didn't mean to."

"They're made of light," the woman said. "Not just light, but firelight. They were living here thousands of years before the Indians. Do you agree with that?"

It was then Darja realized that this woman suffered from senile dementia and was having an episode, probably from the stress of having two tall strangers dressed in black leather jackets show up at her door in the middle of the fucking night. Darja had been through a similar ordeal with her great-aunt when she first got out of the Navy, and things could get pretty screwy when the fuses in her head blew.

"They can see into your soul. You can't hide yourself from them," the old woman said, still glaring.

Jesus H. Christ, Porter, will you get off the goddamn phone already, Darja thought. Standing out in the freezing rain started sounding like a better deal than listening to this old crone babble. And like magic, Porter finally hung up.

"Evan's on the way," Porter said.

"How's he going to find us?" Darja asked.

"It looks like Travis had Lo-Jacks installed in all the cars so Bruehle was able to pinpoint our location. I told him that the house was about a thousand feet north of the car."

The woman shifted gears yet again, this time lurching into happy-hostess mode. "That's wonderful," she chirped. "Why don't you and your young lady have a seat by the fire until your friend comes. I was just about to put on some tea. Would you care for some?"

"Um, sure. Yes, please," Porter said.

"Miss?" The woman smiled at Darja as if their little confrontation never happened.

"No, thank you," Darja said. One of them needed to be alert enough to shoot the bitch, just in case she poisons the tea.

"Oh, that's fine. Let me get the two of you some towels so you can dry your hair. How do you like your tea?"

"Just plain is good. Thank you," Porter said.

The old woman left the room and Darja gave Porter her wide-eyed 'alarm' stare. She whispered, "Bitch is crazy," and spun her forefinger around her temple.

Porter had been so busy arranging their rescue on the phone that he hadn't paid any attention to Darja's conversation with the old woman, who had suddenly came back with towels.

"So now, you poor souls had an accident out there in the pouring rain," she said, stating the obvious. "Oh dear, that's just awful. Here, dry yourselves off. Porter, would you care for some Vienna Fingers with your tea?"

What the fuck was it with old ladies and cookies? Darja wondered. And then she tried to remember when Porter gave this old goose his first name.

Porter sipped his tea while everyone sat in complete silence. The woman simply smiled at her guests as her head shook with a mild tremor, which, along with the coke-bottle bifocals, gave her the appearance of a cartoon character.

Darja was relieved when she saw the headlights from Evan's truck appear in the windows.

"Looks like the cavalry is here... I'm sorry, I didn't catch your name, ma'am," Porter said.

"Edith, dear. Edith Brown," she replied with a grand-motherly smile.

"Thank you, Mrs. Brown. Is there anything we can do to show our appreciation?" Porter asked.

"Oh, you two just get home safely, dear," the woman said.

Porter ran out to the truck to talk with Evan about the crash.

The rain had eased up a bit but was still pissing down as Edith Brown called to Darja as she walked to the porch stairs. "Darja..."

Darja turned and asked, "I'm sorry, did I give you my name? I really don't recall..." But suddenly, all the ambient sound seemed to drop out, as if Darja had dove into a swimming pool. All she could hear now was the old woman's voice, which sounded remote and metallic, like it was coming through an intercom.

"Remember what I said, young lady. Whatever it is you're doing is making them very angry, and you'd do well to stop."

Edith Brown turned and closed the door. Darja felt frozen like a still-frame. She couldn't hear anything at all now and the truck was weirdly receding into the distance.

Evan and Porter were inside the vehicle, wondering what Darja was doing standing there alone in the rain. Darja shivered involuntarily as the sound suddenly came back on. The rain seemed especially loud; had it picked up again? And what the hell was that just then? Was that vertigo? Had some rainwater gotten in her ears during the downpour?

More importantly, who the fuck was angry at her and why?

Porter was suddenly at her side and hustled her to the truck. He opened the rear door, ushered her in and quickly got back into the front. Evan backed out of the driveway.

Porter stared at Darja and asked, "You OK?"

Darja couldn't seem to form the right words. "Yeah, I...um..."

Evan stopped the truck, turned in his seat and grabbed Darja by the jaw. He flipped on the overhead light and studied her eyes.

"Shock," he said bluntly. "Delayed reaction."

He flipped off the light and put it back in gear. Hey Evan, terrific fucking bedside manner there, Darja thought. Thanks.

The truck crawled up to the ruined Taurus. Evan advised Darja to sit and relax while he and Porter fetched the gear from the trunk. She was in no mood to argue. Evan then took his flashlight out of the glove box and stepped out to inspect the damage for himself.

"Looks like you hit a deer. It may have lost its bearings in the downpour," Evan said, studying the Taurus.

Porter thought Evan seemed oddly sympathetic tonight, or least uncommonly non-judgmental. But then Evan leaned in and examined the broken glass, noticing an odd discoloration, as if from intense heat.

Evan wiped some rain away with his jacket forearm and leaned in for a closer look. Porter wasn't liking the grim expression on the man's face.

"I'm gonna have this towed back to the house. We're going to have to have a talk with Mr. Travis." Evan said, frowning so deeply it was nearly a scowl.

Porter even thought the brawny merc actually looked a little bit frightened, if such a thing were even possible.

CHAPTER FORTY SIX

The morning sun was boiling the previous night's rain to a fine mist as Porter, Travis and Bruehle stood in the parking area and watched as Evan closely examined the Taurus and its shattered windshield. Travis looked grimmer and more funereal than usual, clearly unsettled by this latest turn of events.

"It looks like it was some kind of microwave burst," Evan said as he worked his finger around what was left of the windshield.

"Maybe a directed energy weapon. The edges around the hole there are melted, smooth."

"Would that have stopped the car like that?" Porter asked.

"Sure, the force of a DEW could do a lot more than that, definitely," Evan said as he stared at the glass.

"Then why didn't it fry us?" Porter asked.

"Whatever it was it was probably based on some kind of electrical charge," Evan explained. "Glass is a nonconductive material. So the force of the beam was powerful enough to shatter the windshield and stop you dead in your tracks, but most of the energy probably just bounced right back into space. If it hit the hood, the engine would have exploded and the two of you would've been Kentucky-fried," Evan said dispassionately. "You said there was a flash, like lightning, right?"

"Yeah, it was pretty intense," Porter agreed.

"Couldn't it have just been lightning, Evan?" Travis asked, frowning ever deeper.

"It's possible, but lightning always seeks out the shortest route to the ground," Evan said. "Driving out in those hills with all those trees and houses and light-poles? There are literally thousands of better targets up there. And look at your impact zone here; it's practically a geometric circle. Lightning is a lot messier when it hits a car, more random."

The men stared carefully at the shattered windshield. They all saw the same effects Evan was describing, but no one could figure what caused them or why anyone with such a powerful weapon would bother gunning for a couple private dicks.

Porter noticed that Bruehle seemed to be smoking his rancid French cigarettes with a peculiar intensity this morning. He turned and said, "Bruehle, you look like you have something on your mind."

"Some other time, Supes," Bruehle grumbled in response. He flicked his cigarette butt into the bushes and walked back into the house.

• • •

Darja came back after breakfast and reported to Travis, recounting the strange conversation last night with the old woman. But it got even stranger. Darja drove up to the house this morning and noticed it looked different in the daylight. The yard was overgrown, and the house seemed as if it had been deserted a long time ago.

Darja went to the front door and knocked. No one answered. There wasn't a car in the driveway last night so where could the old lady be? Darja had peered in through the windows and saw the same furnishings as the night before but she got the distinct feeling no one had lived there for years. She couldn't say why; it was just a vibe.

"It was just plain weird, Skipper," Darja said, surprised to notice that Travis seemed unusually interested in her story.

"Well, old women living alone aren't exactly famous for lawn maintenance," Travis said. "The grass could have been tamped down by the heavy rain. And Evan did say you were in shock."

"I guess," Darja replied. She never had much interest in all this paranormal bullshit, and even less now. "Yeah, I guess you're right. Still, weird."

"Put it all down in your report. We'll keep an eye on the situation, see if anything pops up," Travis said.

• • •

Porter walked down to Bruehle's workshop after lunch. He'd sensed some tension out in the yard and wanted to make sure that it wasn't somehow being aimed at him.

"What's up, Bruehle? You looked a bit perturbed out there this morning," Porter asked.

Bruehle stared at an arcane wall of data on his monitor, chin in hand, and ignored the question. Porter waited.

After a minute, Bruehle turned in his chair to face Porter.

"A DEW is a fucking huge machine that you mount on a giant lorry or a battleship. It's not something you can just point and fucking shoot at passing cars," he said, with heat in his voice.

"That's Evan's opinion. I'm not sure I..." Porter said.

"It's not Evan's fucking job to offer his opinions on these matters, it's mine," Bruehle replied, cutting Porter off. "Evan might know DEWs exist, but he doesn't know where the fucking technology is. Believe me, I've done the research and there wasn't some fucking super-spy in a trench coat and fedora hiding behind a tree with a directed energy weapon, waiting for the two of you to drive on by."

"Well, maybe there's some new kind of weapon out there we don't know about yet."

"Maybe. I have work to do," Bruehle said dismissively and swiveled back to face his computer.

• • •

Some hours later, Porter and Darja sat at the kitchen table reviewing their field notes when Bruehle came up and joined them, open laptop in hand. He seemed back to his old ebullient self, pointing at a digital scan of an old newspaper clipping.

"Look at this, it's amazing," Bruehle said. "Aleister Crowley actually had a letter printed in *The New York Times* complaining about the ball lightning in New Hampshire."

"Who the fuck is Aleister Crowley?" Darja asked. Bruehle scowled at her.

"What are you thinking, Bruehle? That we were hit by ball lightning?" Porter asked, having no idea who Aleister Crowley was either.

"Oh, fuck no. I just can't believe I found this story. What an amazing coincidence, don't you think?"

"Just out of curiosity, what *do* you think hit us last night, Bruehlie?" Darja asked.

Bruehle looked at Darja like she'd just asked him if water were wet.

"The *aliens* did, stupid," he said. "They put that whole entire show on, just for you."

Oh shit, Darja thought. Breuhlie's finally gone over to the dark side.

CHAPTER FORTY SEVEN

Kaitlynn Murphy was stirred from sleep by the bright light shining through her window. She sat up, rubbed her eyes, then went to see where the light was coming from.

She walked over the window and looked outside to the street below. There she saw a man with long blond hair and a beard standing under a street light. He was wearing a green coat, brown shorts and black boots.

Kaitlynn couldn't really tell from this distance, but she was pretty sure it was Jesus. He didn't move or speak, but somehow Kaitlynn knew he wanted to talk to her. Kaitlynn knew he had something important to tell her.

Mommy always told Kaitlynn never to talk to strangers, but she thought she would probably say it was OK to talk to Jesus.

Kaitlynn put on her fuzzy-bunny slippers and walked down the stairs. The house seemed lit up with a weird glow, like how it looks when there's a full moon after it snows.

She opened the front door, careful not to make any noise and stood on the porch. She called out and asked Jesus why he was just standing there in the street like that, but he didn't answer.

She wouldn't remember exactly why, but Kaitlynn walked down the porch stairs, then across the walkway out to the empty street. Jesus held out his hand for Kaitlynn, and she took it. Neither spoke a word they walked away into the dark.

Not out loud, at least.

CHAPTER FORTY EIGHT

Porter and Darja both got to the Lair at the same time, which was unusual seeing how Darja usually ran twenty minutes late any given morning. Darja gave Porter a hand with the breakfast bags and the two entered the kitchen. They were greeted by Bruehle, wagging his finger in playful accusation.

"Well, well, well; look who arrived together this morning," Bruehle said, his voice dripping with insinuation. "Anything you two would like to confess?"

"Yes. I let Bobby Stephens finger me in the library one time when I was in tenth grade," Darja said breezily.

Bruehle ignored her.

"Well, don't you two get too settled now, because it looks like this little caper of ours just broke wide open," he said, then tore into an apple fritter big enough to feed a platoon.

"Really? What happened?" Porter asked.

Bruehle held a finger up while he chewed. He took a gulp of lukewarm coffee then said, "Well, a four-year-old girl went missing out of her bed in a town about an hour south of Boston. Don't worry, now; she's back, all safe and sound," Bruehle said, stuffing his face with some more fritter.

"Yeah? And?" Porter said.

Bruehle held up another forefinger up and took another gulp of his coffee. Unsatisfied with the results, he repeated the process.

"And she told her parents that she and a friend were off to see the Wizard while she was missing," Bruehlie added, then attempted to work pieces of fritter free from his teeth with his finger.

"Are you seriously just fucking with us now, Bruehle?" Darja snapped, quickly losing patience with his nonsense.

"Well, you haven't asked me who her friend was yet, dummy," Bruehle answered then tore back into the last of the fritter.

"OK Bruehle, who was this little angel's friend?" Darja asked impatiently.

Bruehle paused meaningfully, then said, "Gary Sutton."

Porter and Darja scoped out the perimeter near the house where the little girl who said she saw Gary Sutton lives. They looked inside storm drains, behind fences, in bushes, and under trees, and saw not one scrap of evidence that anything even remotely out of the ordinary happened here.

They hadn't yet talked to the family because Travis said Sam wanted to make contact with them first. The pair then walked into a wooded area between two newly-erected McMansions.

They didn't get far. A dense wall of brush blocked their path after they'd walked about forty feet, so they returned to the street.

"Well, this complicates things," Porter said gravely.

"Do you think Gary was really here?"

Darja glanced around the street, as if expecting Gary to suddenly appear on it.

"I don't know how she could've known about him otherwise," Porter said. "They put a press blackout on the whole UFO angle."

"Maybe some friend or relative was at the show that night," Darja conjectured as she scanned for clues.

"Have Bruehle look into it," Porter said. "But I have a strong feeling it won't come up with anything."

"What about the details with the abduction?" Darja asked, feeling totally at sea.

"She could get all that from TV. That stuff is everywhere these days."

"So where's the actual deal-maker here, Porter?" Darja asked. "How do we nail this thing down?"

Porter's cellphone rang. It was Travis.

"You still in Bridgewater?" Travis asked, without saying hello.

"Yes, sir."

"The Caspers are out there. Call them. Stupid cops are looking in the wrong woods."

Click.

Travis occasionally worked with a group of so-called 'freelance paranormal investigators' out of Western Massachusetts. They were basically just a bunch of amateur ghost-hunters with an arsenal of funky, homemade electronics that allegedly measured fluctuations in magnetism, background radiation, temperature, and so on.

They even claimed they could capture ectoplasm. Bruehle had looked through their pamphlet and gave them the now-obligatory nickname; he called them 'The Casper Crew,' or simply 'The Caspers.' The name stuck. Even Travis took to using it.

Travis had the Caspers do a read at Charlie's Da to determine if there had been a genuine paranormal event there. The results were unsurprisingly inconclusive. They picked up elevated levels of radiation in there, particularly near the stage area, but explained that could be radon leeching up from the basement, or EMF radiation from all of the electronics lying around. They'd need to do more testing to know for sure. Travis passed. Gary was abducted by aliens or he wasn't. If he was, there was nothing they could do about it anyway.

It all seemed like pseudo-scientific gobbledy-gook to Darja, but the boss seemed to be happy enough with their work. Darja still didn't know from ghosts or aliens or witches, and didn't much care to, either. She sensed that Porter was getting a little weary of all this drive-in movie stuff as well. He was basically a cop at heart and was simply trying to solve a case. A case that kept blowing up in everyone's faces.

Porter called the Caspers' home office, which was actually one of the members' apartments, and spoke to their secretary, who was actually the member's wife. He got directions to where the team had set up, because they apparently didn't bring their cell phones.

They certainly brought everything else, though.

Porter and Darja followed directions to a cul-de-sac. They entered the wooded area by way of a break that someone seemed to have recently cut through a wall of pricker bushes. They stepped through carefully and followed a small trail into the cool, damp woods.

The forest floor was dappled with mottled patches of noontime sunlight, and the ground grew progressively muddier with every step.

"Aw shit, I just got these shoes," Darja said. "And they weren't cheap."

There were a series of small orange flags planted along impressions in the mud, which were apparently footprints. But the mud was so wet that the shapes were somewhat impressionistic, at least in Darja's view.

Just two of the Caspers were out today. One was a bearded, balding, bespectacled man who looked like a professor on early retirement.

He introduced himself as 'Rod Wilsher.'

The other was just a kid, who was trying and failing to tame his unruly ginger mop with a Boston Red Sox cap and seemed to be the techie of the two.

He didn't introduce himself, but the professor kept calling him 'Sean.'

"Hey, what do you guys got there?" Darja asked.

"A lot of weird shit, actually," Wilsher said. He removed his tan fishing cap and scratched his head. "We got footprints, a male's boots, look like size-10 Doc Marten's coming into the swamp and stopping right over yonder. And smaller feet, wearing slippers. Then we got nothing. Neither the girl, nor the male leaving the swamp."

Darja wondered why the cops didn't do any of this. Probably because the girl was telling a story no one could take seriously. Or maybe the cops didn't know where to look. Or maybe they didn't recognize those shapeless dents in the muck as footprints.

Darja squatted and looked carefully at the prints. It was faint but you could make out a boot tread. Impressive. She figured Travis knew from good investigators, and that these guys were probably a couple steps up over the local blues.

Porter took shots with the digital as Wilsher directed him to various points of interest. He hadn't a clue about whatever the Caspers were up to, he simply treated it like a crime-scene investigation. Wilsher did too, but for very different reasons.

"How far is the house from here?" Porter asked.

"That's the other weird thing," Wilsher said. "There's no good access road or footpath coming from the direction of the house. But that's the direction the footprints are coming from, south-southeast. But look; they start right at that marshy spot about ninety feet away there, which is another hundred feet or so from the clearing there where you came in."

"So how is that possible?" Porter inquired, studying the distances.

"Logically, it's impossible. They shouldn't have been here. But they were."

"The ground is harder there," Darja countered. "Could it be they didn't leave prints there?"

"Take a look," Wilsher said, pointing. "The two of you left very, very good prints. That soil there is actually what we call 'squatch-dirt,' since it's the best medium for lasting Bigfoot impressions."

The reference flew over Darja's head; she thought he was talking about people with large shoes.

"What about these 'elves' the girl talked about?" she asked. "Could they have been small animals? Squirrels? Raccoons?"

"Well, we're running tests," Wilsher said, scanning the tree line for some reason. "Usually these kinds of things come and go without leaving a trace because they don't really exist in this dimension."

Yup, here we go, Darja thought.

"But look over there," Wilsher added. "It looks like someone singed the ground with a flamethrower. See there? In a circular pattern?"

"Goddamn," Darja said, smiling. "You guys are good." She had walked past that thing and missed it entirely.

"Sean, let's get some samples for our friends here," Wilsher said. "In all likelihood, the soil has become hydro-phobic."

"It's got rabies?" Darja asked. You never could tell with these people.

"No, it means it won't absorb water anymore," Wilsher said, patiently. "Classic fairy ring. Or possibly a saucer nest. Either way, looks like we got some hard evidence of paranormal activity."

"Or a bunch of kids having a bonfire," Darja said.

She wondered how such perceptive site-investigators could believe in such insane crap. Then again, insane crap was keeping her fat ass out of the poorhouse, so she kept her stupid mouth shut about it.

"This is certainly the place for this kind of thing, I'll tell you that," Wilsher said, brightly. "You're standing on ground zero for unexplained phenomena in the Northeast United States."

"How so?" Porter asked.

"This is the Hockamock, dude," Sean said, finally speaking. "There's been, like, wicked crazy shit going on here since Indian times."

"It dates back to the late 1600s, during what was called King Philip's War," Wilsher said. "Philip was a local Indian chief who was trying to beat back English colonial expansion. The war got very nasty. Lots of horrible atrocities on both sides. The Indians eventually lost, and Philip was promised safe passage if he surrendered to the governor at the time. But some militant Pilgrims had other ideas, and Philip was killed. They stuck his head on a pike and hung it at Plymouth Plantation for twenty years. That was said to be the start of a curse that opened a dimensional gateway, in what a prominent paranormal researcher from Maine calls 'the Bridgewater Triangle.' Since then, every kind of weird creature or phenomena you can name has been spotted here. Bigfoot, UFOs, gremlins, the whole kit and caboodle, really."

"And there are, like, mad Satanists in the Triangle! For real," Sean offered breathlessly. "There was, like, a whole cult of Satanists that were offing hookers and, like, dumping their bodies here back in the day. Serial killers, mob hits; man, you name it. It was like a friggin' Freddie movie or some shit."

"Is that true? About the Satanists?" Darja asked the older man.

"Unfortunately, yes," Wilsher said. "Occultists seem to be drawn to the inherent power of the Hockamock. They believe it gives their rituals a little extra *oomph*, a little more bang for their buck."

That rang a distant bell of recognition in Darja's mind. Why exactly, she couldn't say.

CHAPTER FORTY NINE

Porter and Darja schlepped downstairs for their nightly debriefing with Zaina, who was taking Travis' seat at meetings more and more often.

The boss seemed to be coming around less and less often, and certainly spending a lot less time with the hired help when he actually did show up.

Darja didn't like where all this was going. She'd seen too many cases in the Navy where the CO would fuck off to god-knows-where and let a second-in-command take charge of a unit. And more often than not it was a bitchy woman, at least that's how it seemed in those last few years of her service.

Darja didn't like working under women, probably because women in positions of authority invariably didn't like her. Of course, a lot of men didn't either, but Darja had ways of getting around that if push came to shove. But that shit never seemed to fly when it was a woman calling the shots.

And tonight, Darja was in no mood to deal with all the hoodoo-mambo bullshit, especially since what was going on with this little girl seemed clear as glass to her.

"I think we have a serious problem on our hands here, Zaina," Darja said.

"What do you mean?" Zaina asked, neutrally. She was in robot mode tonight, perhaps to compensate for Darja's obvious irritation.

"Gary is clearly not an abductee, he's an abduc*tor*," Darja continued. "He's going around snatching little girls out of their bedrooms, and from the sounds of it, pumping them full of drugs. I think all of his abduction fantasies have reached a tipping point and now he's going around acting them out."

"Well, that's certainly a compelling theory, Darja" Zaina replied. "But there's only one problem; how is Gary seeming to vanish into thin air, and then appear and disappear on muddy ground where he should be leaving footprints?"

"Well, I would guess he probably has an accomplice," Darja said.

"Well, I'm willing to go there. But his accomplice would need some kind of aircraft," Zaina said.

Porter weighed in. "Not necessarily. He could use a plank or a board to walk on. That would keep him from leaving footprints in the mud."

"OK, but in that terrain we're going to see evidence of that. It seems as if the ground's been wet enough that the mud would set around the edges of a board," Zaina said.

"Maybe he used cardboard. That'd be easier to carry around," Porter surmised.

"Agreed, but then we have the problem of where they end up and how they get there," Zaina countered. "Let's say he can hide his footprints somehow. The girl didn't say anything about him carrying anything. They're going to run a toxicological on her, and I'm guessing it will come up clean. It's very hard to drug a small girl like that without serious aftereffects. Nausea, catatonia, cataplexy, the list goes on. Children her age simply don't handle heavy drugs well."

None of this was sitting well with Darja. In fact, it was just pissing her off all the more.

"I know where you're all coming from," Zaina said. "This is part of your police training, looking to solve a crime. You're looking for the quickest route from point A to point B in order to land a conviction. But that's not our job here."

"So what are you saying went down there?" Darja snapped.

"I don't really know. It's not my job to figure that out," Zaina said. "Bruehle and I will present a number of options, but the final decisions will ultimately be made by Mr. Travis and the board."

"So you actually think this fucking girl was taken up into a fucking spaceship? You think she went for some fucking flying saucer ride?" Darja bellowed.

Zaina held up a defensive hand, as if Darja were physically assaulting her.

"I'm sorry, could you please do me a favor and watch your language, Darja?"

"Sorry," Darja muttered, then crossed her arms and sulked in silence.

"Thank you," Zaina said with a tight, mirthless smile.

"Now as to your question; no, of course I don't. But Mr. Travis isn't paying me to decide these things. He's paying me — and you as well — to gather information, analyze it, and pass it up the chain of command."

"So what then? What do we do now?" Porter asked.

"Well, here's what we're going to do; we're need to get a full physical workup on this child," Zaina stated. "We're going to recommend that the girl be hypnotized by someone we trust. And then we're going to suggest to the local police that they put out a warrant on Gary Sutton for endangering a minor."

"Fair enough. Let's do it," Porter said, and the meeting was adjourned.

Darja got up, went out to the lot without speaking, and got into her car. She sat and stared at the middle of the driving wheel for a moment, then muttered, "Stuck-up bitch," and tore out of the lot.

CHAPTER FIFTY

The department informally known as 'Media Management' were set up in a nondescript office building in downtown Washington. This was a vestige of a time before electronic media really took off and it was easier to monitor the books, newspapers and magazines being published when you were physically closer to all the newsstands.

In fact, the entire operation was a vestige; most of this kind of work was being digitized now and processed by huge Cray supercomputers out in the deserts of Utah. But the Government's philosophy was always you should never spend just a dollar when you could throw fifty-thousand more down a sinkhole. Plus, the redundancies kept key agents flush enough to resist the ever-present lure of bribe money from hostile foreign powers.

Wojeczki, a thin and nervous man in his mid-30s aptly called 'Revenge of the Nerds, Part 4' by his fellow agents, didn't much like to bother his supervisor in person, so he usually just sent memos.

His boss, Director Fricke, was pushing seventy and not in the best of health, but everyone agreed that his laser-beam eyes could drill holes into your very soul if your courage was found lacking. And so it was that Wojeczki stood out in the hallway, summoned what little courage he had, and rapped on the translucent pebbled glass of the vintage door.

"Come," a voice called from inside the office.

Director Fricke's office was a bit small for a man of his position. On the other hand, it was furnished with beautiful, vintage office fixtures. One might have thought they walked into a time portal back to the 1940s, if not for some of the state-of-the-art electronics sitting around collecting dust. Fricke himself looked like a prison warden from some Forties film noir, in keeping with his decor.

"Sir, there's a situation up in Boston that's getting some media attention," Wojeczki said nervously.

"What is it?" Fricke asked, without looking up from his work.

"Little girl in a town called Bridgewater claims she was taken to a swamp by that missing rock singer and encountered what she called 'elves,' sir," Wojeczki said.

"Why are you wasting my time with this?" Fricke barked.

"Normally I wouldn't, sir," Wojeczki said. "But it coincided with a series of recent UFO sightings. And the local authorities leaked some details that look a bit anomalous. And some black budget groups seem to have taken an interest in the case. It's kind of got the local rumor mill all riled up."

"I'm still waiting to hear the reason I care."

"It's the Hockamock Swamp, sir," Wojeczki said nervously. "It's kind of a local paranormal hotspot. And like I said, the black-bag activity has not gone unnoticed."

"Are they ours?" Fricke asked, lasers now trained on the agent.

"I don't believe so, sir. But I've heard talk that Bob Travis is involved. And there's been some chatter than Don Morton is nosing around up there as well."

"Oh, for fuck's sake, the two of them," Fricke sighed and slapped his pen to the desk in exasperation. "Who's available?"

"Hocus Pocus is always available," Wojeczki offered.

"Hell no. I'm tired of cleaning up his messes with the little boys and the hotel rooms and all the rest of it. Who else you got?"

"I just spoke to Dick Kooper last week, he was complaining we haven't been using him lately."

"We haven't been using him because he's a goddamn fossil who looks like death warmed-over on television. And a walking sexual harassment suit to boot," Fricke snapped.

"He's very good at what he does, sir. He does all his own legwork."

"Don't we have anyone who was born *after* the First World War?"

"He's helped us a lot in the past, sir," Wojeczki protested.

"All right. Cut him a check. Tell him he's on his own if he insists on acting like a caveman towards the female help."

"Right away, sir," Wojeczki sniveled.

"And when you're done with that, get on the phone with some of your Pentagon contacts and find out what the hell those two goddamned maniacs are up to up there," Fricke barked, then refocused the lasers back on his paperwork.

CHAPTER FIFTY ONE

Porter and Darja were driving down to Bridgewater to meet up with Sam. The plan was to talk to this little girl and see if she could tell them anything that might lead to Gary.

Porter, who hated any music recorded after 1979 like cancer, was actually listening to a brand-new CD from some group out of Seattle. He said he liked this band because they sounded like a combination of Led Zeppelin and Black Sabbath. He also pointed out that the singer sounded quite a bit like Gary. It was a little raw for Darja's taste, but it sure beat hearing "Smells Like Teen Spirit" every five seconds on the radio. She hated that song from the get-go, but now it was your religious duty to listen to that whining crap all day.

Either way, she had to admit she was kind of getting into this new Beatles kind of song Porter was playing when her phone rang.

"Could you turn that down, please?" Darja asked Porter. "It's Bruehle."

Darja listened to what Bruehle had to say, told him she'd tell Porter, and hung up the phone.

"We've got a problem," Darja said. "Now our drummer friend is dropped off the radar. He's nowhere."

"What about the girlfriend?" Porter asked.

"That's the other thing. She doesn't seem to exist," Darja said. "Apparently, Quattro broke up with his last girlfriend months ago because he couldn't keep his dick out of the groupies' mouths."

"That little snot has groupies? I'm in the wrong line of work. What about family or friends?"

"His family is in Florida. Bruehle's working on the friends," Darja said.

"You think the archaeology thing might give us anything?"

"What do you mean?" Darja asked.

"Maybe he might avoid the music people and hang out with the archaeologists?"

"Maybe. But here's yet another thing; the Screamer says Quattro came out of the satanic black metal scene in Florida. Apparently, Cutter's Mill was a major departure for him."

"Well, that certainly changes things," Porter observed.

"It gets worse. Bruehle tracked down an interview with his previous band and apparently this Quattro guy was a true believer, at least when this interview was done."

"In the occult?" Porter asked.

"Yep. Not your usual metalhead kind of devil thing either, according to Bruehle," Darja answered. "Heavy stuff. Weird stuff. Sick stuff."

"Wow, this guy just shot to the top of the most-wanted list, eh?"

• • •

Sam met up with Porter and Darja in front of the kid's house to brief them on how it would all go down inside. The understanding was that if anything emerged that seemed pertinent to the case, Sam would arrange for a hypnotist to come in and try his hand at it.

A police cruiser sat diagonally across the street from the Murphy house. It looked wildly incongruous in this suburban paradise, like a mud wasp in a perfumed garden. The trees were beginning to bloom, the lawns starting to green, and generally the entire neighborhood looked as if any kind of paranormal madness was not just extremely unlikely, but in fact unimaginable here.

Sam had already spoken with the officer and explained his business. Now he briefed Porter and Darja in hushed tones, in the unlikely event the cop could hear them through his closed windows.

"OK, the understanding here is that I'm me, and you two are my associates," Sam told the two investigators. "If anyone gets touchy, I'll say you're investigating the possible kidnapping angle. So far there hasn't been much attention on this case past the local level. But I'm not going to identify you as FBI just in case the actual FBI ever bother to show up here. Plausible deniability, OK?"

Porter and Darja had no objections.

"OK, now let me take the lead here," Sam advised.

"You have your recorders, right? Just sit back and get all this on tape. I'm not expecting any breakthroughs here, but often-times those don't really come until you've gone over the material a few times."

Sam motioned towards the house, and the three walked up to the front porch together. Sam knocked on the screen door. A harried, soccer-mom archetype came to the door. Sam held up his hospital ID.

"Mrs. Murphy? I'm Dr. Sanderson, from the state hospital. We spoke earlier today?"

"Of course," Soccer-Mom said a bit nervously. "Please, come in."

Hellos were exchanged and the trio went inside. Another, nearly-identical Soccer-Mom was sitting at a dining room table.

"My husband's out of the country, so my sister came by to help," Soccer-Mom explained.

A television entered into earshot, as did the happy murmur of children. "Kaitlynn is in with her cousins," Soccer-Mom said.

Sam put on his most grandfatherly pose and said, "Mrs. Murphy, I want you to understand that there's nothing to be afraid of. The police are right outside, and we don't believe that man meant to do your daughter any harm. We think, given the media attention and so on, that it's also highly unlikely this person will ever come back here. My job here is to get as much information from your daughter as we can, so we can make sure that he doesn't. That whoever was with her can get the help he needs in a con-trolled mental health environment."

Translation: my job is to help nab this disgusting freak so we can toss his pervert-ass back in the nuthouse, Darja thought.

"Now, I don't want to take up too much of your day. Could you take me to see Kaitlynn so we can get out of your way? I promise to keep it short," Sam added.

Soccer-Mom led Sam and his companions into a bright and clean, yet utterly-sterile living room. Kaitlynn was on the floor next to the sofa, playing with brightly-colored plastic blocks. A Hi-C juice box sat at her side.

"Kaitlynn, this is Doctor Sanderson," Soccer-Mom said. "He just wants to ask you about what happened the other night, OK? Mommy will be right here. Just tell him what happened, OK?"

Sam took his coat, laid it on the back of an upholstered chair and sat down on the sofa next to the girl.

"Hi Kaitlynn, you can call me Sam. And these are my friends; this here's Porter, and this nice lady here is Darja," he said. "They're both here to help."

Soccer-Mom walked over to turn off the television. She stood over against the wall closest to her daughter and crossed her arms. Her tired face was an icon of worry, but Kaitlynn was clearly enjoying all of the attention.

Sam said. "Now, Kaitlynn, we just want to ask you a couple of questions. OK?"

"OK!" Kaitlynn said brightly. Whatever actually happened didn't appear to traumatize her all that much.

"Why did you leave the house?" Sam asked.

"Gary called me," Kaitlynn said. "But I went to talk to him because I thought it was Jesus."

"Gary looked like Jesus?"

"Yes, but he told me his name was Gary, not Jesus."

"Are you a fan of Cutter's Mill?"

"I don't know what that means," Kaitlynn said with a frown of confusion.

"Can you tell us more about what Gary looked like? Besides Jesus?"

"He had a green coat, and brown shorts, and boots like the Army," Kaitlynn replied breezily.

"Where did you go with Gary? Can you describe it for me?"

"He took me to the bright white room. The elves live in a hole inside the air."

"In the air? Up in the air?" Sam asked, pointing up at the ceiling.

"Like this," Kaitlynn said, making circles with her arms. "This is air."

"What did you do in the white place?"

"I talked to a elf. He was nice," Kaitlynn said and beamed.

"Like Santa's elves?"

"No, this one was real. It had really big eyes!" Kaitlynn said, throwing her hands in the air.

"What did the elf say?" Sam asked.

"It said I was very special and they would come to visit me so I could teach everybody about God and Jesus and the... ape... chocolate...?"

"Apocalypse?" Sam said.

"I don't know that word."

"OK. What else did the elf say?"

"He said I was a brave little girl, and he was proud of me."

"And what did you say?"

"That I was a big girl!" Kaitlynn said, throwing up her arms again.

"Do you remember anything else Gary said?"

"He told me he was a famous singer! Then he asked me if I liked to sing."

Sam paused a few moments, then said, "Kaitlynn, did anyone touch you, maybe someplace that made you feel uncomfortable?"

"No," Kaitlynn replied, sing-songing the word and picking up a rag-doll. She'd clearly grown bored of telling the story again.

"And after that?"

"I don't remember," Kaitlynn said, then brushed the doll's yarn-hair with a toy comb.

"You don't remember anything more?" Sam pressed.

"I remember waking up in the yard, on Daddy's hammock. And that Mommy was mad at me," Kaitlynn said, clearly finished with story time.

Sam tousled Kaitlynn's hair, rose from the sofa and said, "OK, then. We're going talk to your Mommy now. OK, Kaitlynn?"

Sam, Darja and Porter stood and spoke quietly with Soccer-Mom in the front foyer. The woman didn't seem particularly reassured by Sam's interview with her daughter.

"Is your family religious, Mrs. Murphy?" Sam asked.

"I mean, we attend church, but..."

"Does Kaitlynn go to Sunday School?"

"Yes, but what does that have to do with someone trying to kidnap my daughter?" Soccer-Mom pleaded.

"It's possible the individual in question was not this Gary person, but perhaps someone she might know from church. Or someone who may know her, or know of her," Sam answered.

"My God," Soccer-Mom said. Her eyes were beginning to glisten with tears.

"Now, I'm going to have someone look into that," Sam continued. "This person might have been impersonating Gary Sutton, or may have used a picture of him to confuse her. Children's memories are very malleable at that age. But there are clearly some religious overtones to this scenario here."

"Should we stop going to church? I mean...?"

"No, no, no. Just make sure that you keep a close eye on her when you're there."

After saying their goodbyes to the Murphy family, Sam conferred with Darja and Porter outside in the front yard.

"Well, that was creepy and disturbing," Darja said. "Do you really think someone from her church is behind this?"

"It's possible," Sam said. "I want to keep all our options open."

"Well, I'll tell you my 'option.' My 'option' is that Gary Sutton likes diddling little girls and needs to be put down like a dog," Darja spat.

"That's one option. But there's also the question of how he got here in the first place. He doesn't have a car; he hasn't been sighted in the area. It seems like an unlikely place for him to pop up," Sam said.

"So what do we do next, Sam?" Porter asked.

"The local police are going to keep an eye on the house for a couple days," Sam replied. "But I have to tell you, everyone seems to think this girl went sleepwalking on top of a weird dream, and I'm afraid I can't really make a compelling argument otherwise. Kids generally don't leave their bedrooms in the middle of the night to traipse off to Fairyland with rock 'n' roll singers. The media coverage and the obvious concern from other parents in town is keeping this thing on the front burner for now, but I suspect the police probably won't be devoting a lot more manpower to this case. We might have to pick up their slack."

CHAPTER FIFTY TWO

Porter and Darja sat in their brand-new Ford Explorer and watched the Murphy's house, in the offhand chance that Gary might materialize again for another sleigh-ride to the Twilight Zone. For some reason, the night seemed darker in this neighborhood than it did elsewhere. There was a kind of gloom that Darja just couldn't place.

Porter had a sports talk station playing at low volume, which Darja found not only annoying, but clichéd. She expected better of him.

"Sports talk, Porter? Seriously?" Darja whined.

"You're right, mindless habit," her partner said as he switched to a classical music station. Darja was surprised by the alternative.

"You like classical music, Porter? For real?"

Porter frowned. "Yeah. I mean, I don't know anything from anything else, but it helps me think."

Darja stared at him in disbelief. She just couldn't get a handle on this guy. After a few minutes of sickly-sweet violins, she switched it to a local alternative rock station. As fate would have it, a Cutter's Mill song was just ending, and the DJ updated listeners on the recent Gary sightings. Of course, he had to sneak in a few homilies to Saint Kurt, things being the way they were.

Porter didn't seem to notice, because at that very moment a black Cherokee rolled up into the driveway outside the Murphy's house.

Two tall, lean, bald, and extremely dangerous-looking men in black bomber jackets got out and walked quickly up to the front steps. Darja almost had time to wonder if they were aging skinheads on their way to a hardcore show before she and Porter whipped out their Glocks and sprinted over to intercept them.

Soccer-Mom came to the front door and was staggered to see four imposing figures standing before her. The two bald men turned to face Porter and Darja as they approached but weren't going to bother to do the pair the dignity of acknowledging them.

"Excuse me, gentlemen; what's your business here? May we see some identification?" Darja barked, hoping they wouldn't hear the undertone of panic in her voice.

"Mrs. Murphy, get back in the house and call the police!" Porter shouted, more emphatically than he had wanted.

The two men glanced blankly at Porter and Darja with cold, black eyes, clearly weighing the pros and cons of killing these two fools now or waiting to do them later. They didn't seem fazed by the drawn guns at all; they probably felt like they were close enough to disarm these two amateurs before any shots were ever fired. Their main concern was that the element of surprise had been lost, and that the lady inside had probably already dialed 911. They didn't seem to think it was feasible to whack the two snoops, then kick down the front door and ice everyone inside before the cops got there.

So the two men stepped around Darja and Porter and headed back to their car. Porter made a move after them, but Darja put her hand on his shoulder and shook her head emphatically. The Cherokee pulled into the dusk without putting its lights on. Porter quickly took out his flashlight and shined it on the back license plate as the car sped away.

"Get it?" Porter asked as Darja was jotting the plate down into her notepad.

"Most of it," she replied.

Soon after, Soccer-Mom appeared again in the front door, but kept the security chain locked. She seemed on the verge of full-blown panic.

"Mrs. Murphy, you remember us, don't you? We were here this morning with Dr. Sanderson," Darja said, and held out her ID.

Soccer-Mom nodded, then skipped straight to the more pressing question: "W-who were those men?"

"We're going to find out. In the meantime, we're going to see if we can't get you to a safehouse to spend the night," Porter offered.

"A safehouse? My God!" Soccer Mom said, and placed her palm over her mouth.

"No, no, don't worry. It's just like a hotel," Porter said, in what he hoped was a reassuring tone. "But we would like you to maybe find somewhere you can stay for a week or so until we can straighten this all out."

"My God, this is like a nightmare," Soccer Mom said and promptly burst into tears.

CHAPTER FIFTY THREE

Dick Kooper and his entourage marched into the lobby of the local CBS affiliate and waited to be received like royal dignitaries on an official state visit. Tall, red-faced, white-haired, and sporting a scowl that seemed frozen in place, Kooper looked eerily like a dyspeptic George Kennedy.

When nobody rushed over to bow and scrape at his feet, Kooper strolled up to the front desk to see if he couldn't have a word or two with this snooty receptionist here. The receptionist, a stern-looking, middle aged woman in a loud patterned blouse, stabbed out her forefinger and said, "Just one moment, sir."

'One moment' became more like ten minutes. The receptionist fielded about a dozen phone calls while Kooper stood there in his 1970s-vintage casual attire and made a big show of checking his Rolex every twenty seconds.

The receptionist finally leaned forward and said, "How may I help you today?"

"Dick Kooper? Here to see Harlan Bickert?" Kooper said, as if it were self-apparent. After all, this certainly wasn't his first time here.

"Just one moment, sir," the receptionist said and looked up Bickert's extension.

Again with the 'one moment.' This time it was only three minutes. Lucky for her, all right.

Kooper stood and scowled as a chipper young ginger in black jeans and a green turtleneck came out to greet him, holding out her small, thin hand. Kooper scowled at that, too.

"Hello Mr. Kooper, I'm Lucy Greenwald, Mr. Bickert's assistant," the woman said, now holding both hands behind her back. "It's such a pleasure to meet you. Just so you know, I'll be producing your segment tonight, in case there's anything you would like to ask me now."

Kooper seemed to boil inside his leisure suit as he listened to this petulant child, with her uppity razzmatazz.

"Sweetheart, you're obviously new at this, so let me bring you up to speed; I produce my own fucking segments, OK?" Kooper barked, jabbing an angry forefinger at her. "You just stand there and smell pretty."

Kooper then took a video tape cassette out of his satchel and pointed it towards the young producer the way an exorcist would point a crucifix.

"Pay attention now. Here's the montage that you'll be playing for my intro."

"And w-what's on it?" Lucy asked, swallowing hard.

Kooper admired the tape like it was a fine family heirloom, then said, "This? This here's a montage of gags from *My Favorite Martian, Mork and Mindy, ALF,* crap like that. There's some clips of dogs wearing tinfoil hats, kids dressed up as spacemen, nutty stuff. You've got some witness videos?"

"Yes," Lucy squeaked.

"Okay, have my boys here go over it with you. We only want weirdos, faggots, bag-ladies, hippies and drunks. If you can't scrape any of them up, just eighty-six the witness segment. Who am I debating?"

"We called Brian Mackey. He's in the area," she replied,

"Nix, doll. Too smart," Kooper said, then produced a preprinted pamphlet from his jacket pocket. "OK, here's a list of some real nutbags around town. Now, get your pretty little ass on the horn and drag one of these stiffs down here, pronto."

"But they won't have any time to prepare."

"*That's the idea*, sugar," Kooper said emphatically. "And I want them looking as freakish as possible. Have Fido here handle the makeup."

A rail-thin man with an unruly shock of black curly hair and dark circles under his eyes flashed Lucy an alarmingly-toothy, lecherous grin.

She immediately turned back to Kooper. "Anything else?"

"Yeah, send out for some tuna-fish sandwiches, will you please? I'm famished. The fucking food on the plane was like garbage. And then you go tell that fucking pussy boss of yours I want the full twenty minutes. He shorts my slot again and I'll ram my foot so far up his ass that I'll kick his fucking teeth out. OK, you run along now, girlie," Kooper said, shooing the young woman away with the back of his hands.

Lucy froze, dumbstruck.

"*Sandwiches*, toots," Kooper said, still shooing. "We're all starving here."

CHAPTER FIFTY FOUR

The Mortician stood inside a forest clearing beside his big black Chrysler, growing clearly impatient. He and his Doorman friend were staring at the entrance to the clearing, which led to a gravel-covered access road.

This place was a bitch to get to and that damn unpaved road was murder on the shocks. The sun had already set, so they kept the headlights on and the engine idling. The Mortician hoped they wouldn't run out of gas before their contact bothered to show.

"He's late," the Mortician said, looking at his watch. "He was supposed to be here thirty-five minutes ago."

"Did you hear what I said?" The Mortician turned to face the Doorman, but the man seemed to have disappeared.

A rustling sound caused the Mortician to look down. He saw that the Doorman had fallen to the ground and was twitching violently in the grass. The Mortician thought the Doorman might be having a seizure, but then an obscene ejaculation of blood and saliva burst from his mouth.

"What the hell...?" the Mortician said, just before he heard a voice greeting him from behind.

"Hello again," the voice said pleasantly.

The Mortician turned and saw a figure not twenty feet away, half-draped in shadow. The figure had some weird green halo and seemed to be carrying a silenced pistol at his side. He raised it, carefully aimed, then shot the Mortician in the solar plexus. The Mortician fell to the ground atop his partner, feeling like someone had stabbed him in the liver with a flaming railroad spike.

The figure came out of the shadows, capped by an eerie pair of night-vision goggles. He waited a few moments, removed the glasses then set them carefully atop a tree stump. It was Don Morton.

Morton walked casually towards the car, carefully stepping around his writhing victims. He stopped to regard the dying men with the same mild attention one might lend a newspaper ad for double-knit slacks. Morton then took out a penlight in order to evaluate his aim on the Doorman. He was very pleased with his marksmanship.

Distance with a silencer was always tricky, but he'd been practicing to compensate, and it all seemed to pay off with two very lovely kill-shots.

Again, another textbook case of practice makes perfect. Good, old-fashioned Yankee stick-to-itiveness.

Morton then heard a thumping coming from the back of the Chrysler and figured he'd best attend to it. But before he did, Morton crouched beside the Mortician and asked, "Before you go, old chum, I just have one question for you."

The Mortician's face was contorted in unspeakable agony. Blood was oozing from his nose and lips.

"Sorry, friend. Just one quick question," Morton said. "What was that bit with the kite all about?"

"F-f-f-fuck y-y-you," the Mortician gurgled.

"That's what I was afraid you might say. Oh well, can't blame a fellow for asking. As you were then, old boy," Morton said and smiled.

Morton turned to walk away but stopped dead in his tracks, hit by a sudden realization. He turned back to the Mortician, snapping his fingers.

"It was a signal! It was a signal to alert that limo to your location! Ho-ho, what a clever, clever dick you are, eh?" Morton said, beaming at the Mortician with what looked like genuine admiration.

The Mortician, his mouth and chin now soaked with blood, stared back in horror at Morton, who then bent down to pat the dying man on his shoulder and said, "Clever."

Morton paused a moment, as if he might have something else to add. But he didn't, so he got back up and left these two men to die, writhing in agony.

He walked over to the car, opened it, and popped the trunk latch. Then he went around the back and lifted the trunk open.

Inside it lay a young woman, who'd been stripped to her underwear and hogtied with duct tape by her captors. Her mouth had been taped shut, making it hard for her to breathe as her crying had caused her sinuses to swell. The trunk reeked of piss and terror.

The girl shrank away as a cold gust of air rushed in. Were they going to kill her now?

As her eyes adjusted to the light, there was a pleasant-faced, middle-aged man she'd never seen before. He was focused intently on a metal tube at the end of a handgun, for some reason Melissa couldn't begin to understand.

"Hello there, young lady," the man said to Melissa, smiling kindly. "I'll be with you in just a jiff," he added, refocusing his attention on whatever it was he was doing there.

After pocketing the tube and the gun, Morton carefully peeled the tape from the girl's mouth.

"Sorry about that, love. Melissa, isn't it? Well, this is your lucky day, darling. I've come to take you home. Would you like to ring your mother? I have a cellular telephone here you can use," Morton said and tapped at his jacket.

Melissa stared at Morton, utterly speechless, while the man just stood there and smiled beatifically at her, like a proud papa whose daughter just won a local spelling bee.

"Oh, damn it. Listen, I'm so sorry, Melissa. Where are my manners?" he said, his face furrowed with concern. "Please, let me take care of that for you, sweetness," as if Melissa had a choice.

Morton took a Swiss Army knife from his jacket and began carefully sawing away at the thick layers of tape.

"Beautiful night, isn't it?" Morton said, smiling cheerfully as he freed the woman from her restraints. "Nice to have some clear skies after all that rain, don't you think?"

CHAPTER FIFTY FIVE

It was a gorgeous spring morning. The sun was burning off the recent accumulation of rain, lending a dreamlike quality to the otherwise grim New Hampshire byways. Darja and Porter decided to head out and take advantage of the nice weather. They'd just placed their orders at the local IHOP, handed the menus to the waitress, then took careful sips of the very hot coffee.

Darja was just about to add a bit more sugar to her mug when her cellphone rang. It was Bruehle.

"The fuck you want, dick-lick?" Darja answered breezily.

"Listen, you filthy whore; I need you two back to the Lair, ASAP. In fact, right now would probably work best for me," Bruehle said.

"Jeez, can't it wait, Bruehle? We just ordered our food."

It wasn't bad enough Zaina had started throwing her weight around, now they had to answer to Bruehle, too?

"Ah-ha, stepping out on the Breakfast Club, are we?" Bruehle replied. "Well, try to eat fast, Lady Cop. Something big's come up."

"Something big's come up on what?" Darja asked skeptically.

"On the Bridgewater situation, stupid. And there's another little tidbit I'd like you and Studly Do-Right to have a little peek at," Bruehle offered.

"You can't tell me what it is now?" Darja asked, impatiently.

"I really think you need to see it for yourself."

Darja and Porter took their time with their breakfast. They also took advantage of the free refills of coffee and chatted about non-work-related topics. Then they took the scenic route back to the Lair.

Bruehle was waiting at the kitchen table and asked them where the hell they'd been, he called them over two and a half fucking hours ago.

Darja politely informed Bruehle that he should go and fuck himself. Sideways, if he preferred.

Porter chuckled and presented his young friend with a white styrofoam take-out box, bursting to the seams with blueberry pancakes and jumbo sides of sausage and bacon.

Without ceremony, Bruehle dumped the entire contents of the box onto a paper plate, threw it in the microwave, slathered the whole mess with the several packets of butter and syrup, then gorged himself while Darja and Porter watched and chuckled.

"You're gonna get fat, you know," Darja said.

"What difference would it make, you silly cow?" Bruehle replied. "It's not like anyone is ever going to see me naked again."

Darja and Porter took a seat and waited as Bruehle cleaned off the kitchen table with spray cleaner and paper towels. He then took a manila folder off the top of a cabinet and sat down to join them.

"OK, first order of business. I drove down to Ayer and visited the public library there, seeing if I couldn't dig up anything on that Sunshine People School," Bruehle said. "Anything that might have surfaced in the local media, any scandals, arrests, the whole business. But all I can find was an old puff piece on the place in a local paper."

"OK, so what good does that do us?" Darja asked.

"Patience, Grasshopper, patience," Bruehle pulled out his leather bag and fished out a manila folder.

"Have a look, old chums," he said and handed Darja and Porter two sheets of printout.

They stared at a ragged, high contrast, low-res Xerox of an old news clipping, but the name listed was legible enough: *"Noted Psychiatrist Dr. S.I. Sanderson and a Sunshine student discuss the school's revolutionary new curriculum."*

"Sam never said anything about working for Sunshine," Porter said.

"You think it maybe slipped his mind? Maybe he's getting a wee bit senile?" Bruehle asked. "Or maybe there are other things the good doctor isn't telling us."

"I'm going to find out," Porter said, resolutely.

"I wouldn't recommend that. Not at the moment," Bruehle said.

"Why not?" Darja asked.

"We need more information, Sails. This could just have been a photo-op."

"You're saying you're not struck by the coincidence here, Bruehle?" Porter asked.

"Oh, of course I am. Why do you think I brought it home for you, stupid? It's just that we already knew the good doctor is a spook and all of this business is spook business. So hold off the lynch mob until I get more data," Bruehle replied, sternly.

"You said you had something on the Bridgewater case," Porter said.

"Oh, I do indeed," Bruehle replied, then fished out another file of printouts from his folder. "What time did that kid's mother say she noticed her missing?"

Porter looked at Darja. "Around midnight," she said.

"Well, guess what; we had another Sutton sighting that night, around the same exact time," Bruehle said.

"Where? Around Bridgewater?" Porter asked.

"Try North Adams. At least a three hour drive west."

"What the fuck are you talking about?" Darja said, incredulously.

"A student there called the hotline, said he was drinking in a pub with Sutton. Knew of him from the music scene. Took a picture of him with some friends," Bruehle said.

"What time was this?" Darja asked.

"He said they were playing pool, from about 9:30 until closing time. He said he invited Sutton over to a friend's house, but our man took off on foot."

"And he's sure it's Sutton," Porter said.

"Positive ID. Said he called after he saw the news report on the Hockamock incident."

Darja turned to Porter: "Could be covering for a friend."

"Could be. You two might want to get those sweet asses up to North Adams and find out," Bruehle said and smiled knowingly.

The witness' name was Malachi O'Hara, and he attended the state college in town. The itinerary was set; they could be in North Adams by 3:30 PM, shake this bozo down, and be back at the Lair before ten.

It would involve a lot of driving, so Darja brought along an audiobook she'd just picked up at Borders.

Porter was relieved to see the one she chose was *The Alienist* by Caleb Carr, which was about a serial killer investigation in the 19th century, and not *Bridges of Madison County* or some other girly thing like that. Darja wisely bought the unabridged version and the two soaked it in, chewing over the various plot points between cassettes.

Darja and Porter rolled into town and called this alleged friend of Gary's. The kid agreed to meet with them at a local coffee shop at four, but was more than a half-hour late. The pair were ready to write it off when someone suddenly appeared at their table.

"Hey, you Porter? Moe," the kid said and offered his hand.

'Moe?' The fucking guy actually calls himself 'Moe?' Darja thought. Who the fuck intentionally calls themselves 'Moe?' Then again, Darja had to admit that Moe was better than 'Malachi.'

"Glad you could make it. Have a seat, Moe," Porter said, his hands cradled at his sternum.

"Thanks, man," Moe said. The kid slunk into his wooden chair, took his jacket off and rested it carefully on the seat-back.

Moe fished out a pack of Kents and lit one up with a Bic lighter while Darja and Porter waited for him to get settled. A waitress came by and asked Moe if he'd like anything, and he ordered a regular coffee.

Darja wondered if this joint would be closing up before they ever got around to talking with this tool.

Moe relaxed back into his chair, exhaled and gave a Darja and Porter a look that told them now — *now* — he was ready to bless them with his wisdom.

Porter waited a few beats before he kicked it off.

"So, you said you were with Gary Sutton here in North Adams the night he was seen in Bridgewater."

"Yeah. Until the bar closed," Moe said, sucking a drag from his Kent.

"What time was that?"

"Around 2 AM, I think," Moe said, casually exhaling blue smoke from his nostrils.

"Were you alone with him," Porter asked.

"No, I was with some buddies from school."

"And they saw him as well?"

"Sure." Inhaling, squinting.

"Would they be willing to testify to this?" Porter said.

"I don't see why not. Sure. Absolutely."

Exhaling. Tapping his ashes, lovingly.

"How would you describe his demeanor?" Porter asked.

"What do you mean?" Moe said, his puzzled expression draped in smoke.

"His mood," Porter explained.

"Oh, sure. Yeah, he was in a really good mood. He was psyched about the band, about getting signed. It was all good, brother."

Another elegant ash-tap, this time with a deft little twist of the wrist. The tender way Moe was making sweet, sweet love to his cigarette there really got Darja jonesing for one herself.

"Mind if I bum a smoke, Moe?" Darja said, earning a shocked look from Porter.

"Oh, yeah. Sure thing," Moe said. He fished out his pack and tapped out a fresh one.

"Need a light?" he asked.

Darja nodded, and Moe duly flicked his Bic.

"Did Gary say anything about his disappearance?" Porter asked. He side-eyed Darja, who was gazing lovingly at her cigarette as if it were nothing less than the Bluebird of Happiness.

"Yeah," Moe said, sucking another drag. "He did, actually."

"What did he say exactly?" Porter asked.

"He said it was all a publicity stunt," Moe said, exhaling. "His manager thought it up to get some media attention. Hey, worked, right?"

"Did he say what he was doing in North Adams?"

"He said he was scouting out places to play. They're really looking to work the college circuit." Deep inhale.

Porter looked over to see if Darja wanted to tag in, but she seemed too enraptured by her coffin-nail to give a damn what Moe here had to say.

"There was nothing odd or unusual about him?" Porter asked.

"In what way?" Moe asked, exhaling. He hovered his dying cigarette over the ashtray and studied it like a math equation.

"Any way," Porter said.

"No, not at all." Inhale. "He was totally normal."

"How well do you know him?"

"Well enough," Moe said defensively, then stubbed out the Kent, emphatically.

"Define 'well enough,'" Porter said.

"I don't know. I mean, how well do you know anybody?"

Porter shot Moe a skeptical look.

"I've seen the band a whole bunch of times, OK?" Moe finally explained. He suddenly looked naked and vulnerable without a cigarette.

"Can we see the picture you took?" Porter asked.

"Sure. Keep it. I got copies," Moe said. Tapping out a fresh Kent. Lighting it.

Darja and Porter stared at the photo and then at each other.

The snap was clearly not taken on a very good camera. The bar was dark, the light poor. But there was a guy who looked every bit like Gary Sutton posing with Moe here, along with a few other smiling young men. A Celtics game was ending on the TV behind them. The final score was legible so the date could be confirmed.

"You called the State Police because you saw the news story about that girl in Bridgewater," Darja said, entering the fray now that she was finally finished with her delicious, savory cancer-stick.

"Yeah, crazy," Moe said.

"Why?" Darja pressed

"Well, it obviously wasn't Gary. And I didn't want you guys thinking Gary was some sicko pervert or something. He's a good guy."

Moe felt so strongly about this last fact that he resolutely kept his cigarette hand at rest.

"The girl identified him," Darja replied sternly.

"Yeah, well, she obviously must've seen his picture on the news," Moe said, shaking his head and taking a dismissive drag.

"You're sure this is the same night?" Darja asked.

"Absolutely."

Darja and Porter seemed uncertain where to go next with this.

Moe exhaled meaningfully, then hit them with the *coup de gras*.

"Listen man, my nephew used to sleepwalk all the time. It was a real problem for my older sister," Moe said. "The kid'd end up in the most fucked-up places. He'd tell her the craziest stories because he was dreaming the whole time. He almost set the fucking house on fire one night. It's actually pretty common with kids at a certain age. No big mystery there at all."

Moe then sat back and took a slow, triumphant drag off the Kent, obviously rewarding himself for his rhetorical kill-shot.

"And you think this girl was sleepwalking when she saw Gary?" Porter asked.

"Don't you?" Moe replied.

CHAPTER FIFTY SIX

It was showtime. Dick Kooper watched in dismay as a reasonably objective report on the Hockamock situation ran in place of his montage. He shifted uncomfortably in his chair. The anchor didn't look like the usual seat-warmer he was used to. She paid close attention to the report and even took notes.

The only thing that comforted Kooper was the occupant of the chair next to her. It was some hippie shithead, swaying around like an imbecile. Kooper couldn't wait to chew this dirty derelict up and spit him out. Nice to think that stupid little assistant bitch could follow one order at least.

"Welcome to *Boston Spotlight*, I'm Barbara Coyne," the anchor chimed, as theme music swelled in Kooper's earbud.

"With us to discuss this very unusual story are two very special guests. First is Dick Kooper, who some of the older folks in the audience may remember as a UFO debunker from the 1970s. Also joining us tonight is Mr. Apollo Star-Fire, a local energy healer and UFO channeler. Gentlemen, thank you for being here tonight."

'UFO debunker from the 1970s?' Had this goddamn skirt just said what Kooper thought she just said?

"Mr. Star-Fire, what did you think of the witness testimony of the sightings in Bridgewater?"

"They're hee-ere. Oh yes, indeed," the Hippie said, as he undulated in his chair.

Kooper gazed over at him with a mixture of relief and contempt. The moron was stoned out of his gourd.

"Who exactly is here, in your opinion?"

"Oh, our space brothers, my lovely lady. They've come here to spread conscious enlightenment to the entire planet! It's time that people open their minds to their cosmic vibrations."

"Thank you, Mr. Star-Fire," Coyne said, without affect. "Mr. Kooper, what did your on-site investigations reveal about this case?"

"My on-site investigations," Kooper replied blankly. He just got here, for fuck's sake.

"Well, you're a self-proclaimed expert in this field," Coyne pressed.

"We would like to know what kind of evidence you've gathered, and what your own interviews with the witnesses have revealed."

'Self-proclaimed?' What the fuck...? There'd be hell to pay.

"My own...? Kooper muttered. "I had a video that was supposed to..." he squinted and shifted around in his chair, scanning behind the glare of the studio lights for that punk-ass producer.

"We're more interested in hearing about your investigative work, Mr. Kooper."

Kooper squinted; he could've sworn he saw a face from his past standing behind the cameras. But it couldn't be. It must've been a mirage. But he was rattled all the same.

"I, uh, just flew into town. I haven't been able to talk to any of these people," Kooper said, then flashed his withering stare, which had always worked so well with these people in the past.

"Just flew into town," Coyne repeated, looking decidedly un-withered.

"Yes, that's right..." Kooper bumbled.

Coyne shuffled some papers, dramatically.

"Mr. Kooper, you're used to flying around quite a bit, aren't you? Time was whenever a case like this hit the news you'd fly into town, practically right away. Must've really racked up the frequent-flier miles, no?"

Kooper continued to stare, hoping to intimidate this stuck-up floozy. No such luck.

"I was curious, your resume lists you as an independent documentary film producer, but we couldn't find anything that you actually produced. Would you say your UFO travels overshadowed your other work?"

"Are we going to talk about this case or not?"

"Well, I don't know how we can. You just flew into town and you haven't done any investigation, by your own admission. But maybe you could clear another mystery up for us. Maybe you could tell us how you could afford to travel around the country like you did, on an independent producer's salary for a studio that never actually produced anything."

"I flew economy class," Kooper sneered.

"Oh, I bet," Coyne said, chuckling professionally. "This is *Boston Spotlight*. We'll be right back after these words from our sponsors."

Kooper ripped the microphone away from his lapel and stood up to confront Coyne.

"Okay, what the fuck is this? Who do you work for?"

Don Morton emerged from a dark corner of the studio.

"Hello, Dick. Long time, no see."

"I thought I smelled cock on somebody's breath," Kooper sputtered bitterly. He turned to face Coyne again, and stabbed his thumb in Morton's direction.

"You have *any* idea who you're dealing with, you stupid cunt? Do you have *any* fucking idea who this goddamned lunatic is? I'm finished here."

"Oh, you're just plain finished, Dick," Morton said cheerily. "I warned these nice people that you don't behave yourself well in the company of women, so they taped your conversation with Miss Greenwald."

"You mean *you* taped me, you fucking freak. That's against the law, you know," Kooper shot back.

Was it actually against the law? Kooper wasn't sure.

"I guess you didn't read the new disclaimer before you signed it. We had it made especially for you, Dick."

"Gentlemen, can you please take this elsewhere? We're almost back from the break," Coyne asked forcefully.

"Fuck you, whore," Kooper answered. "You haven't heard the last of me. And you can bet your ass your boss is going to hear about this."

"Oh, her boss already knows all about it, Dick," Morton said, smiling. "So does yours."

Kooper stormed out of the studio. Morton followed, stepping gingerly as the red 'on-air' sign flashed. He softly closed the studio door behind him, so as to not make any noise.

"Welcome back to *Boston Spotlight*," Coyne announced cheerily, before assuming a pouty look of mock concern. "Sadly, Dick Kooper had to return to the field and won't be joining us for this segment." Changing gears again, she said, "But Mr. Star-Fire has offered to demonstrate some wonderful new meditation techniques."

She got up and joined the happy hippie, who was sitting in a lotus position on a small stage to the left of the anchor desk.

"So, I understand you have a way for us to communicate with the space aliens, Mr. Star-Fire," Coyne said, neutrally as possible.

"Yes. This is all about freeing the chakra kundalini energy so that we all may become as one with our space brothers..."

Kooper turned to confront Morton in the hallway. Sure, he'd heard all the scary stories, but this motherfucker was messing with his livelihood now. And Dick-fucking-Kooper wasn't going to let paying work dry up without a fight.

"How the fuck do you know who I work for, Morton?" Kooper seethed. His face turned a deep, unhealthy crimson and the veins in his neck began to bulge.

"Who you *work* for? Jesus Christ, Dick, I *created* you," Morton said, flashing a perfectly ingratiating smile. "I was the one who set up the SIC back in the early '70s, before you even joined."

"Bullshit."

"Go ask your friend, Hocus Pocus. He was there."

"Oh, fuck you, Morton. You've really lost your marbles. Have you got the AIDS or something?"

"Calm yourself down, Dick. You're looking a nasty shade of red. Go enjoy your retirement. You've earned it. Ed Brauner said to say hello, by the way."

A wave of ice water suddenly flushed through Kooper's veins.

"Fuck this. I'm out of here."

"Regards to the missus, old boy," Morton said with in his customary facsimile of good cheer.

Kooper almost blurted out something really stupid, but caught himself in the nick of time. He might have been sick to death of living, but he wasn't quite ready to die today.

As Kooper exited through a dark glass door he caught Morton's reflection as the man stared coldly at his back; the phony geniality was utterly erased from his face. Kooper would later swear he didn't see anything recognizably human in Morton's expression.

CHAPTER FIFTY SEVEN

The young, thin, long-haired man drove home in a daze, spots of light clouding his vision. It started in the morning, as a queasy feeling in the pit of his stomach. By lunch, he was seeing auras and his head was pounding like a hammer.

But this wasn't a migraine, it was an alarm bell. Something was terribly wrong.

After barely avoiding two collisions in traffic, he finally landed in the parking lot, the undercarriage of his 1980 Plymouth Duster scraping violently as he drove over a concrete divider. He ran up the stairway of the two-family house to his apartment, his vision still reeling from explosions of light.

Inside, his girlfriend sat motionless on the couch, staring at a blank TV screen.

"Get your suitcase out, Dale. Pack everything you need, we have to disappear," the young man said as he rushed in, breathless. "C'mon Dale, I'm not fucking around! Something's coming down. We gotta get the fuck out of here. Now!"

Dale's silent attention turned to the apartment door. The young man spun, as if struck from behind. A burly man who looked like an off-duty personal trainer was suddenly at the threshold. He was wearing black Nike's, black running pants, a white tank-top and a black nylon windbreaker. His auburn hair was cropped into a crewcut.

But the man wasn't waving his fists around. Instead, he was smiling and laughing, as if he were about to grab a stool and knock back a few cold ones with his best buddy Tommy here.

"Where exactly do you think you're going, Tommy?" the man said, chortling like he was just about to crack the funniest joke ever heard.

Two rather-intimidating men then appeared out of the bedroom, men whom Tommy thought might have been Samoan or Maori or something like that. But they weren't laughing. Or smiling, for that matter.

"I told you already, I'm not gonna work for you people, Darren," Tommy said, voice thick with panic and defiance.

Darren grinned warmly as he studied the cartoon character knick-knacks Dale had displayed atop a bookshelf. Whatever else one might say about the guy, Tommy had to admit Darren had a very ingratiating smile.

"Well, I'm afraid that's not your decision to make, Tommy," Darren said, with the utmost cheer and sincerity. "Tell you what; how about we all sit down and talk it over, hmm? Whad'ya say? Dale? How you doing there, babe?"

Dale just continued to stare at the blue TV screen.

Darren pointed to the kitchen then said to his companions, "I think Tommy here could use a drink of water."

The two looked at each other and drew mental straws until one of them finally disappeared into the nook. He came back shortly with the glass and handed it to Tommy, who nodded a thank-you and took a sip.

Darren sat down in a wicker chair facing the couch and motioned to Tommy to sit next to Dale. Tommy looked at his girlfriend, pleading for support, but she was lost in some kind of trance.

Darren waited for Tommy to get settled before his jovial tone grew just a tad more serious.

"Listen, Tommy...there's a kind of... well, let's say there's a war being fought out there. Only it's a secret war that no one else knows about," Darren said, as if talking to a child. "Now in a war, men get drafted. It's a bummer, but that's war. Can't be helped. So you see, Tommy, we're drafting yourself and your lovely lady-friend here to fight on our side. That's actually what's going on here, OK?"

"What do you want with Dale?" Tommy said meekly, unable to meet Darren's cheery gaze.

"Well, we believe she's just like you, Tommy. We believe that she has abilities, too."

"I don't believe you. I don't," Tommy said, petulantly shaking his head in defiance.

"Look at me, Tommy, at us," Darren said, gesturing to himself and the other two men. "Do we really look like the type of people who would go to all this trouble for no good reason?"

Darren leaned forward and rested his elbows on his thighs.

"Listen Tom, I realize you're afraid, but I'm here to tell you that you absolutely have no reason to be. No one wants to hurt you. No one wants to hurt Dale. I swear it to you, Tommy. On the life of my mother, I swear it. The two of you are very, very important to us. You're very special to us. I really need you to understand that. OK, Buddy?"

Darren got up from the chair and chuckled again.

"Now, we've already packed your bags, and we even have a nice stretch limo waiting for you out back," he said warmly. "Everything's been taken care of, Tommy. You really don't have to worry about a single thing. You two won't have to worry about paying your rent or your bills or about your lousy jobs anymore. So please, just come along with us and don't make a scene, OK? None of us want to do anything we all might regret."

Darren then gently placed his meaty hand on the younger man's bony shoulder.

"Tommy, I can absolutely guarantee you one thing, my friend. In the very near future, you and I will look back on this night and laugh."

CHAPTER FIFTY EIGHT

Porter and Darja drove back to the Lair in silence.

When they got back, they sat with Zaina and Bruehle at the kitchen table and stared at the photo Moe had given them. It lay there like a silent accusation, making a mockery of all their work. Their entire lives, even.

Gary was alive and well, his disappearance was just a publicity stunt. That little girl hadn't been whisked off to Neverland in a flying saucer, she'd simply been sleepwalking and dreamed of a face she half-saw in Daddy's newspaper.

After the group got a good eyeful of the shot, Bruehle and Zaina launched into a debate, with Bruehle clearly clinging to the UFO abduction explanation when it came to precious little Kaitlynn Murphy.

"Well, what about the bootprints?" Bruehle protested.

"Who knows how old they are?" Zaina said. "They could be some hunter's. The girl could have simply walked in the same path."

"Well, how did she get to the other side?" Bruehle asked.

"Sleepwalkers can do strange things," Zaina said.

"Oh, come on. That's not an argument, Zaina. Plus, how do we even know this Moe guy is telling the truth?" Bruehle protested.

"Why would he lie?" Zaina said sharply. "What's more credible, Bruehle? That a little girl was merely sleepwalking or that a group of men a hundred miles away somehow conspired to fake a photo and cook up an alibi for a crime that isn't even a crime?"

"There are some sick men out there," Darja interjected.

"Think about it," Zaina said. "By her own account, this girl left the house of her own volition. She never claimed Gary entered the house and took her away. And let's not forget the obvious fairy tale elements of her story. The public might think she's very cute, but once she gets to part about the elves, her credibility goes straight out the window. I think this Moe person was right, the girl probably saw Gary's face on TV, associated it with his disappearance, and that entered into her dreams. There's no reason to think his presence in the story is any more believable than the fairies."

It was really starting to get on Darja's nerves how Zaina seemed to just slip into the command role with Travis being who-the-fuck-knows-where, doing who-the-fuck-knows-what. What the hell experience did she have out in the real world?

"Can I say something here?" Porter asked.

"Go ahead, please," Zaina replied.

"OK, a week after Kurt Cobain died, I saw his exact look-alike in a CompUSA," Porter said. "I mean, *everyone* in the store was staring at him. But it was just some kid who worked there and had the hair, the clothes, the scruffy beard. Gary had a look; the dreads, the goatee, the sideburns, the notches in his eyebrows, the tattoos. It's not hard for any skinny kid in his 20s to adopt that look and be mistaken for someone people have only seen onstage. Especially when everyone's been drinking all night."

"Well, that is something to consider," Zaina said thoughtfully.

"You've got that look on your face," Porter said. "What are you thinking, Bruehle?"

"I don't think this story is cut and dried either way," Bruehle said. "I don't think it's anything you two need to spend any more time on, but this is definitely something Travis and the board are going to want to take a long, hard look at."

"OK, just humor us idiots and tell us what do you think is going on here," Darja spat.

"That swamp has a very long history of weird business, is all. Long before the white settlers showed up there were legends about elf-like creatures and strange lights and all the rest of it."

"Yes, but what does it add up to though, Bruehle?" Zaina asked.

"Some more weird stories for the local folklore, I suppose." Bruehle conceded. "But those two bone-crunchers showing up at that family's house? They didn't sound like your average UFO nuts."

"No," Darja said. "They were very bad news. *Serious* bad news."

"Well, that's what I'm saying," Bruehle said. "We know there's someone else on this case out there, and somebody is paying their tab. Those guys probably weren't there just to sniff the roses. I say we hold off making any kind of conclusions here until we have more facts."

CHAPTER FIFTY NINE

Darja arrived at the Lair the next morning and joined Bruehle in the living room. He was fast-forwarding through a recording of a local talk show covering the Bridgewater situation, and seemed especially interested in some pissed-off old fart who looked like he was about to stroke out on live TV.

Bruehle then paused the tape and turned to Darja.

"Oh, you are not going to like this," he said.

"What?" Darja replied.

"Kevin was originally sent to the intensive care unit at Mass General, OK? Well, it turns out he was misplaced a few days ago and then discovered back in his bed, fully conscious, day before yesterday."

"Just like how he went missing the other time," Darja said.

"Exactly. Only this time he ended up back in hospital, not parading his teeny-weeny around for the good burghers of Littleton. Then Kevin got his bony ass transferred from Mass General to a rehabilitation unit in North Andover."

"Let me guess; he's gone missing from there now, too."

"I've trained you well, Sails," Bruehle said. "Staff at the Andover facility said his behavior was quite unsettling. It seems he had long and detailed conversations with people who weren't there. The night nurse said, and this is a direct quote, Sails: 'Kevin was being disturbingly coherent.'"

"Well, I just talked to Porter. He's leaving the whorehouse now," Darja said. "We can cruise on down to North Andover once he gets his ass over here."

"Tell you what; I have a few things to take care of, but I'd like to tag along with you two," Bruehle replied. "I have to see this for myself."

• • •

The head of security at the rehab facility was a stocky, thirty-ish black man named Khaleef. He wasn't really sure who these three weirdos thought they were, or what they were actually doing here, but he was so freaked out by this messed-up little white boy that he appreciated having somebody to talk about it with.

The whole thing was just off-the-charts weird.

Porter, Darja and Bruehle sat with Khaleef at his station. From what he said this place had to have closed-circuit cameras going everywhere at all times for insurance purposes, but security couldn't show anyone the actual recordings.

"So, like I was saying, this guy walked down the hall, real stiff and awkward," Khaleef explained. "This here's a rehab facility, so we're used to a lot of strange shit, but the nurses were all saying he was moving like a puppet. Kinda looked as if he were straining against something. But then the lights all go out, and the patients on the wing all started screaming bloody murder for like a minute. Lights come back on, and this Kevin guy was gone. Staff couldn't find him anywhere. Everyone pretty much went into full-panic lockdown when the guy's mother came looking for him a few hours later."

"And the only way he could've left is if he was released?" Bruehle asked.

"Right," Khaleef agreed. "The kid was in a special restricted unit reserved for patients up on criminal charges. The administrator went to the tapes; kid's in his room, then there was about twenty minutes of this weird mix of shots from all around the facility. Kinda looked like someone switching TV channels. I mean, just picture *that* for a minute. There was a screen of noise, then nothing. Then the screen switches back to the kid's room, with an empty bed where he should've been."

"What about these conversations?" Bruehle asked.

"Yeah. Well, I wasn't here for that, but I talked with all the nurses about it," Khaleef explained. "They said they'd see him in his room just carrying on these long conversations with nobody. They didn't even think he'd be lucid, the guy was so incredibly messed-up. But check this out; most of the day he's pretty much catatonic, right? But one minute he's practically a vegetable, next minute he's practically giving speeches. It's freaky, man. I've never seen anything remotely like this guy. No one has."

"And you're sure we can't have a little peek at the tapes," Bruehle asked, a conspiratorial tone in his voice.

"Sorry, man. You need a court order for that. Them's the rules," Khaleef said, and leaned back decisively in his chair.

"I get it, no worries. Can't hurt to ask," Bruehle said and smiled innocently.

The three said their goodbyes to Khaleef, then stood out on the front walkway to hash it all out.

Darja was jonesing hard for a butt so she took the opportunity break out her Marlboro Lights. She offered one to Bruehle, then offered another to Porter, only to get some Dad-face in return.

"Sounds like someone was messing with their systems by some kind of remote control," Porter offered.

"Yeah, someone with some very sophisticated kind of remote control," Bruehle said. "Quite possibly using microwaves or some kind of low-frequency sonics. Speaking of which, I've been thinking quite a bit about those metal staples you saw in his head."

"What are you thinking about them?" Darja asked.

"I don't think they're just surgical staples. I also think they might be electrodes," Bruehle said and meaningfully dragged on his Marlboro.

"Electrodes? What the hell for?" Darja said.

"I think someone is physically manipulating Kevin, using these electrodes as neural stimulators. I think they are using them with some kind of advanced microwave technology to remote-control this guy, just like a kid's toy."

"Is that even possible?" Porter asked.

"Experiments have been done with animals for years," Bruehle explained. "A CIA doctor named Delgado did all kinds of tests at Yale with radio waves and electrodes planted in the brain. He could get lab monkeys to do whatever he wanted, and that was twenty, thirty years ago now. He even got a charging bull to stop dead in its tracks."

"Jesus. Motherfucking CIA again," Darja said.

"It's possible they were using a remote-influencer here, and a very good one," Bruehle continued. "With that, they were able to fuck with the video monitors long enough to get a team in there and get Kevin out of there before anyone noticed."

"Uh, yeah; that's a little too *Star Trek* for me, big guy," Darja opined.

"It's a brave new world out there, Sails," Bruehle said, then took another dramatic puff on his Marlboro.

CHAPTER SIXTY

Porter kept checking the rearview as he and Darja drove down a particularly grim and isolated stretch of highway under a colorless New England sky. Porter seemed quietly worried. Darja noted his concern, but didn't think it was a major issue until Porter began alternating his gaze between the rearview and the sideview.

"What's the matter?" Darja asked.

"It's that Cherokee again. I've seen it since we crossed over into Lawrence," Porter said, glancing in the rearview.

"Lot of Cherokees around here. Sure it's the same one?"

"It's the same one."

"What do you want to do?" Darja said, nerves now slightly-jangled.

"Let's see if we can't get ourselves some supper," Porter said, then pulled onto the exit lane for a roadside diner. He watched as the Cherokee drove past. He had a feeling they were just looking for a U-turn.

He found a spot in front and parked. He and Darja sat silently for a moment and scanned each other's faces for signs of undue alarm.

"Bruehle run those plates yet?" Porter asked.

"Not that I know of," Darja said, in a subdued tone.

"All right. Let's just try to get a table where we can keep an eye on our car."

Porter kept a wary eye on the foggy road as they entered the diner. Porter and Darja sat down at a booth and ordered.

After the waitress left, Porter noticed two men enter the diner. Sure enough, it was the same thugs from the Murphy house.

They were wearing the same bomber jackets, upper sleeves emblazoned with embroidered logo patches Porter didn't recognize. They wore black fatigue pants with standard police-issue boots, which Porter found a bit unsettling.

Some might mistake their outfits for skinhead or punk rock gear, but in the cold light of day they looked more like paramilitaries from some war-zone in the Balkans.

The pair casually surveyed the dining room and spotted their prey. They then strolled over to a table at the other end of the room, one which gave them perfect eye-lines to Darja and Porter's table. They sat and took two menus from the hostess.

These men had the effect of bull sharks in a kiddie pool. The other diners seemed to instinctively lean away from them, from the aura of utter menace the men radiated. They didn't belong in a cozy Bridgewater *cul de sac,* and they certainly didn't belong here.

Luckily, the walls were mirrored so Porter could keep watch on them without risking direct eye contact.

Porter used the mirrors to try to take a reading of the men as they pretended to study their menus. He still couldn't quite tell their nationality, but knew they weren't Americans. For some strange reason, he thought they might be Bulgarians or Romanians who came over here to work as mercenaries when the Wall fell. Maybe they did the kind of gigs you got working for drug gangs or for men skirting the line between high finance and organized crime. These guys would likely be very well-trained in martial arts, firearms, knives, the works.

Porter sized them up and concluded there was no way in hell he and Darja could handle them, short of walking over there and blowing their brains out now. They'd probably have their hands full taking on either one of them, the way they did with King Kong Cobain in Roslindale.

Porter and Darja's dinners came quickly, and they ate as calmly and naturally as they could. But Porter couldn't help sorting through worst case scenarios.

He knew the goons would act like they were only here to eat. They wouldn't let their prey catch them staring. They might steal a glance at Darja and lament having to send such a nice-looking woman off for a dirt nap. They might be debating whether or not they should rape her first, may figure it might be fun. Or maybe they'd just rape Porter instead. Or both of them. You could never tell these days.

The goons both ordered gyros and rice. They didn't take their eyes from their plates when Porter excused himself, apparently to go to the men's room. They'd be certain he wouldn't leave without the woman.

Plus, they had a clear view of Porter's car from their table.

Porter was pleased to see a longish hallway leading to the kitchen doors, which in turn were next to the restrooms.

He ducked through the kitchen and out through a wooden screen door that let out onto the back parking lot. No one paid him any attention.

He was very, very happy to see the Cherokee parked back in dark corner, a good distance away from the building.

Outside, Porter ducked beneath their SUV and undid the strap on his holster, just in case he was interrupted in his work. He took out his heavy-duty folding knife and stabbed it into the sidewall of the driver's side front tire. Doing so was a bit harder than it might look on TV. He jerked the knife back-and-forth until a rush of compressed air exploded past his face.

Satisfied, he bunny-hopped to the rear and repeated the process.

He got up, brushed himself off and stared closely at the diner. There were no windows facing this end of the parking lot, so he strode back into the kitchen and returned to the table. He'd made it back inside just before those low black clouds had finally burst.

Darja was counting her change and parceling out three singles as a tip. Her hands were shaking ever so slightly.

Porter fixed her with a solemn gaze and said, "Come on."

They left the restaurant and drove back onto the access road. The goons waited a beat, then made their way to the exit and out to the parking lot.

Dusk and drizzle were killing the light, so it took them a moment to notice that their vehicle was leaning at an odd angle. They both jogged over to the driver's side and realized their ride had two flats.

One cursed and punched the air in impotent rage, while the other held his fingertips to his temples, as if all this were some kind of misunderstanding he could mentally will away.

Suddenly, the passenger side of the Cherokee was drenched in a dirty splash, as the Explorer they'd been tailing sped through an adjacent puddle and came to a skidding halt.

Darja rolled down the window and called out to the goon in front.

"*Hey, fuckface!*" she yelled, her Glock pointed directly at his head.

The front goon took a step towards the car just as Darja ripped two bullets through the center of his forehead. The rounds blew most of the back of his head out. He fell to the gravel like a bald bag of bricks.

The back goon stumbled against the Cherokee, as if bowled over from the impact of his partner's death. He slid on the dewy slick of drizzle and blood, then scrambled to regain his balance.

Darja aimed again with both hands and shot the back goon three times near the side of the face, just as he managed to partly wrest his own pistol from his jacket. The bullets tore his right eye, cheek and ear away, producing a grisly spray of blood and bone.

Darja then pumped two more quick rounds into his body mass as he was doubling over. He collapsed into a sizable puddle, creating another muddy splash.

"Tear ass, Porter!" she shouted, bracing herself against the dash, gun still in hand.

Porter tore ass out of the parking lot, spraying gravel in every direction. He was immediately grateful that the back lot wasn't visible to anyone in the restaurant, nor was the exit road back onto the highway.

"Jesus, what the hell did you just do?" Porter shouted.

"I just killed those two fucks before they killed us," Darja shouted back, her voice shaking.

"What? Why? I already disabled their car; they weren't coming after us. Jesus!"

"You really think a fucking flat tire would have stopped those two animals, Porter?" Darja screamed. "I'm sorry, but I don't feel like taking a shotgun blast in the cooze from some fucking psycho hitman!"

"This is murder, Darja! Murder!" Porter screamed as he pounded the steering wheel. He was reaching a state of near-blind panic: they were in serious trouble. He never signed up for murder.

"For fuck's sake, Porter!" Darja yelled, dialing down her own panic a notch. "Why the fuck do you think Travis gave you a fucking *Glock*? As a fucking fashion statement?"

Porter sped down the highway until the rain forced him to slow to a near crawl.

"We are so screwed, so screwed..." he said, breathlessly.

"Calm the fuck down, Porter," Darja said, gesturing frantically with open hands. "Please... just calm down. If there's any trouble, Travis can handle it."

"Handle two murders? Are you serious?" Porter shouted. "This isn't the movies, Darja. Travis can't just wave some magic spook wand and make two murders disappear."

Darja bit hard on the knuckle of her thumb. The hair around her temples was soaked with sweat. Shooting those two didn't seem like such a great idea anymore.

"We have to tell him," Porter said, straining to calm himself. "No way he'll bail us out of it if we lie to him about this."

Darja thought long and hard about it.

"Yeah, you're right, you're right," she agreed. "Call him."

"Me? You're the one who shot them!" Porter replied.

"Right. So that means it's your turn to man the fuck up, you fucking pussy!"

"Jesus." Porter took the phone out of his jacket and pulled the antenna out with his mouth. He had Travis on speed-dial.

"Skipper. Yeah, it's Porter. W-w-we, uh, we have a little *situation* here. Me and Darja. We need to talk it over with you, OK? Where are you now, Skipper?"

Porter listened and then said. "OK, OK, good. We're on the way back now. We'll explain everything when we get there."

Porter hung up and said, "He's at the Lair. I sure as hell hope he's in a good mood tonight."

CHAPTER SIXTY ONE

Back at the Lair, Travis and Darja sat at the kitchen table and told Travis the whole story.

He listened impassively, stone-faced, like an irritable elementary school principal dealing with two Kindergarteners who just couldn't seem to stop themselves from eating all the Play-Doh.

"Are you two pissing your panties about doing your goddamned job? Is that what this is?" Travis finally asked, in a tone of utter exasperation.

"Skipper, we're not cops, we can go down for murder," Porter said, still visibly shaken.

Travis sunk in his chair and scowled ever-more-deeply at Porter.

"You are a trained and certified security professional carrying a licensed firearm," he said in a resigned tone. "You were confronted by two armed men who'd displayed malicious intent. They probably had all kinds of weapons in the car, not to mention rope and duct tape and chainsaws and God knows what else. I absolutely guarantee you that the cops are going to run their prints and find out they're both world-class scumbags. They'll probably just figure that those two finally got what they deserved."

"Yeah, but we also fled the scene, Skipper," Porter said.

Travis actually rolled his eyes at this.

"Jesus Christ... Bruehle, could you come in here, please?"

Bruehle trotted up to the table and stopped short in a campy manner that seemed completely out of character.

"Right here, Skipper," Bruehle said.

Darja half-expected him to break out into show tunes. She was really starting to worry about the kid.

"Tell them," Travis said, then he scowled some more at Porter.

"The Cherokee is registered to Loroles LLC, apparently to their motor pool," Bruehle said, clearly excited by a juicy new scoop.

"Wait, Loroles?" Porter asked. "Aren't they a computer company or something?"

Travis ignored the question.

"Here's how this is going to go down, Dunn; the cops aren't going to give two shits who actually blew those two assholes' heads off. Why? Because they're going to be a lot more interested in figuring out what the hell two lowlifes were doing driving around in a Loroles company car in the first place," Travis barked. "They're eventually going to figure the shootings are part of some larger conspiracy, and will be subpoenaing Loroles' goddamn scotch-tape invoices by the end of the week. This is the only reason D.A.'s get up in the morning, Dunn. Nothing they love more than big, juicy corporate-conspiracy trials."

"OK, I hear you, Skipper," Porter said, suitably contrite.

Darja just sat and nodded numbly. Her adrenaline rush was wearing off, leaving her with the cold realization that she shot and killed two men tonight. She'd never shot at anyone in her life. She wondered exactly why she was starting now.

"Now stop being such a goddamned fucking pussy about this, Dunn," Travis growled. "Unless someone was out there taking pictures, it never happened. In the meantime, go talk to Evan and tell him I said to trade out your weapons."

Travis got up and placed a fatherly hand on Darja's shoulder.

"Well done, Lundquist. Good instincts out there."

Darja's lips smiled but her eyes did not. She choked out something vaguely grateful to the back of Travis' head as he left the room.

The full measure of what was actually going on here hit Bruehle like a bucket of ice-water. Travis hadn't mentioned Darja killing anyone when he ordered him to get the story on that Cherokee. Suddenly, Bruehle was in a totally different business than the one he signed up for. This wasn't a game anymore.

See, all along he'd thought this was all some kind of lark, running about tracking down psychic superheroes to be press-ganged into some corporate spying program.

But now, his good pal Darja, the same Darja who loved to drink wine and trade filthy jokes with him into the wee hours of the night, had just blown the heads of two total strangers off and gotten a literal pat on the back for doing so from the very scary old man paying his salary.

Maybe it was time to start looking into other career alternatives.

Bruehle stopped to consider those alternatives. There were a grand total of two. It was this crazy damn job or thirty years in an American prison.

Bruehle really, really, really did not want to go to an American prison. He knew he would not go over very well in an American prison. He'd just as soon slit his wrists than spend thirty years in an American prison.

Plus, he got to play with such cool toys here, didn't he?

Well, that was that, then.

He'd better get back to the Dungeon; he wanted to dig deeper into this Loroles thing, and Travis wanted data on geomagnetic anomalies in pre-Colonial New England first thing in the morning.

CHAPTER SIXTY TWO

The four sat at the big conference table in the Batcave. As was now becoming customary, Zaina took Travis' seat at the table and set the agenda. The four had to be content with coffee because Travis had forbidden any food being brought into the Batcave, for some reason.

"So, what did you find on Loroles, Bruehle?" Zaina asked, looking as meticulously groomed and styled as ever.

Bruehle opened a thick manila folder of laser-printed documents and began his presentation. "Let's see, Loroles AKA Lorenz Electrics, Ltd AKA Lorenz Digital Industries, Incorporated, AKA LDI," he said. "They were established as the 'Von Eckstein Brothers Metal Salvage Works' during the Spanish-American War by Lorenz, Roland and Lasko Von Eckstein, who'd recently emigrated from Austria. They started off as scrap metal dealers, then landed a contract to resell surplus military equipment to foreign buyers. Started manufacturing copper wiring for telegraph concerns, went on to do the same for telephones. Brothers sold out early and Lorenz and his rather sizable family took the reins.

"They made a killing selling to both sides during the First World War, then moved into fashioning parts for business machines, telephone switching systems. A little of this, a little of that. Set up an LA branch and provided a lot of lights and wires and all that for the early film studios. Got rather huge during the Second World War, seemed to specialize in radar and sonar applications. Early adopters during the initial postwar computer revolution, but never got the glory companies like Bell Labs garnered."

"Anything hinky about them? Any scandals, bad press?" Porter asked.

"Nothing out of the ordinary. But they seem to have lost their edge in the Eighties, got complacent," Bruehle said.

"Didn't really anticipate the effect that PC's and networking would have on their business. General consensus is that they're running on fumes, but still have a lot of fumes left to run on. Recently changed their branding from LDI to 'Loroles' to cash in on the hot trend of giving your rapacious multinational corporation a meaningless name that vaguely sounds like a feminine-products line."

"So what the hell are they doing sending hitters after us?" Porter asked.

"Who says they are?" Zaina said. "Those men could have stolen the car, or it could have been loaned to them by a Loroles employee who had no idea what it was going to be used for."

"Come on," Porter said, slightly exasperated.

"I'm just trying to offer alternative scenarios here, Porter," Zaina replied, sounding a bit wounded by Porter's dismissive tone.

"OK, but what does your gut tell you, Zaina?" Porter asked.

"That someone at Loroles doesn't want anyone looking into Gary Sutton's disappearance, for whatever reason," Zaina said. "This company is still neck-deep in government and intelligence work. It's more than likely someone there is after the same thing we're after."

"Doesn't that seem sloppy to you?" Porter asked. "Why risk exposure like that just so a couple goons can have some wheels for the day?"

Zaina thought about it, and then said, "Well, everyone involved was probably confident that nothing would go wrong. That you and Darja were just a couple of small-time private investigators who could be easily disposed of."

Darja wondered if 'small-time private investigators' was a dig, then figured it probably was.

"Yeah, but a company car...?" Porter asked.

"My guess is that these men insisted on it," Zaina said, locking eyes with Porter. "And it seems to have been a pretty shrewd move on the killers' part. They wouldn't want to use their own car to commit a major crime and they certainly wouldn't want to be left exposed if something went wrong. So using a Loroles company car makes the company an accessory to murder by default."

"Can't they just claim the car was stolen?" Bruehle asked.

"They can, but the police have heard that excuse a million times before," Zaina observed. "And why steal a car from a secured corporate parking lot when you could steal one from somebody's driveway twice as easily? No, believe me; Loroles has a real mess on their hands. Someone there was certain these two would get the job done and that would be the end of it."

CHAPTER SIXTY THREE

Twilight was beginning to fall over the mottled, dappled gray skies, and the air was feeling unusually damp and heavy. Porter and Darja had just left the Lair and were on the way to their cars when Porter's cell buzzed.

He listened for a moment, then murmured, "Okay, I'll be there in an hour."

"Phew," Darja said. "Bitch's got you whipped."

Porter stared at his partner for a moment. He forgot exactly when Darja gave herself permission to insult him the way she always did, but he wished she would stop.

He turned towards his car, then said, "I gotta go."

Porter arrived at Grace's and noticed it was dark inside, but for a faint light coming from the back of the house. He went to the front door and noticed it was slightly ajar.

He stuck his head in and called out to her. No response.

He walked into the foyer and called again.

"I'm in the kitchen, Porter," he finally heard in reply.

Porter entered and walked to the kitchen. Grace was sitting at the table, frowning intently at a stack of Polaroids. For a moment he thought they might be pictures of Gary.

"What do you have there?" he asked softly.

Grace just shook her head and slid the snapshots over to Porter as he joined her at the table. He went numb when he saw what they actually were.

The Polaroids were of a series of young kids, all standing in front of an interior cinder-block wall. Boys and girls, some as young as five, were posed standing in front of men in military fatigues, almost as if they were being presented as items for sale. Each held up eight-by-ten cards with their first names scrawled in magic marker -- *Jimmy, Mary,* and so on — and a four-digit lot number written underneath.

Judging from the kids' clothing and hairstyles, the photos had been taken sometime in the late-1970s.

It made Porter think of some kind of modern-day slave auction, maybe being conducted through a mail-order catalog.

None of the kids were smiling. In fact, most of them looked pretty miserable. The implications were chilling.

"Where did you get these?" Porter asked.

"In the crawlspace," Grace replied, her voice sick with worry.

"They were in a day-planner of Glenn's. I don't know where he got them and I don't know who any of these people are, Porter."

Suddenly, Porter understood: Glenn Sutton had come across these Polaroids somehow. He knew that something sinister was going on and he wanted to stop it, but instead got himself disappeared. The problem was that the men somehow kept their faces out of frame. That was almost certainly on purpose.

One shot got Porter's attention. It was a little boy, around eight years old, looking absolutely terrified. The name on the card read, *Kevin -- Lot 1082.*

"Kevin," Porter said. "Kevin. Tell me something, Grace; does that look like Kevin Stuart as a kid to you?"

"I have no idea. I suppose it could be," Grace said. "Maybe if the picture were a bit clearer. Why? What are you thinking? Do you think that Gary might have been mixed up in all of this, too?"

"I'm going to need to take these, Grace," Porter said, without answering her question.

"Please; get them the hell out of my house. All of them," Grace said, shuddering. "Porter, I need... I need to get out of here. Can you please take me with you?"

"Yeah, just let me do something first." Porter called Bruehle and gave him the barest thumbnail of recent events.

"The gift that keeps on giving, eh? So what do you want to do, Studly?" Bruehle asked cheerfully.

"We need to get these looked at. We need to get these to Travis and his people."

Bruehle went silent for a moment, then said, "OK, come meet me at LumenX in Sharon. It's a photo-imaging lab, right off the highway. You can't miss it. I'm going to need to see that day planner, too."

"Give me a few minutes of your time and then you two lovebirds can go dance the night away."

• • •

Porter went inside to meet with Bruehle at LumenX while Grace stayed in the car. There were dozens of work-stations manned by very serious-looking people, working late into the night. Bruehle was staring into some arcane computer interface with a youngish Asian man who didn't introduce himself. He swiveled around to greet Porter as he stalked in.

"Where's the fire, Supes? You look a bit stressed."

"Yeah," Porter said, holding out the day-planner with the photos. "Have a look."

Bruehle's eyes widened as he studied the photos.

"Umm... right. OK. This is rather... shocking stuff, Supes. Funny, I just recently read a rant on a conspiracy newsgroup that was going on about children being ab-ducted by the military to be trained as super-soldiers."

"You think that's what this is?" Porter asked skeptically.

"Of course not," Bruehle replied. "But there's clearly something very, very dodgy going on here. I can't think of any legitimate reason for what we're looking at."

"What can you get from those?" Porter asked.

"I won't know until they're scanned and converted. This is a different process than your normal photo scanning. We scan at 2400 lines per inch and 48 bits of color. It's definitely overkill for a Polaroid, but you'd be surprised what you might find."

"Are you expecting anything in particular, Bruehle?"

"I can't say. Maybe nothing. Or maybe a birthmark or some other identifier the naked eye can't perceive. Maybe the kids' clothing might tell us something, I don't know. Maybe I can spot some kind of giveaway on those uniforms."

"In case anyone asks, we found these in Gary's place. I don't want his mother getting mixed up in all this, Bruehle," Porter said sternly.

"Not to worry, Supes. But I'm keeping a log of all these special favors you're getting. I may have to take the balance out in trade."

CHAPTER SIXTY FOUR

Porter had Bruehle modem the photos to Travis. On a hunch, he had them sent to Sam as well. It couldn't hurt to get two old intelligence hands set to work on the same problem. Travis actually made a rare appearance the next morning. He sat with Porter and Bruehle in the Batcave and scowled at the Polaroids for a very, very long time.

"This case suddenly got a lot more complicated," Travis said, leaning back in his chair.

"How so, Skipper?" Porter asked.

"I can't say for certain, but I strongly believe these photos were taken on an Army base that became a major problem back in the Seventies," Travis said grimly.

"A major problem how?" Porter asked.

"A cult -- a *doomsday* cult -- had infiltrated the ranks and was using the base as a staging ground for some very nasty business."

"Nasty?"

"Nasty," Travis grunted. "Sex trafficking, illegal arms-smuggling, dope peddling, contract killing, the whole nine yards. We found out that they were embedded all over the goddamn place, in every branch of the service. Took quite a lot of doing to put them out of business."

"Was this the Temple of Set?" Bruehle asked.

"No, that's an Army Intelligence operation. I'm talking about an actual cult. They were called the 'New Rites of Apophis.' These bastards didn't waste their time going on TV talk-shows, believe me. Real hardcore death-cultists. They liked to hunt down devil-worship types and carve them up like Christmas turkeys, believe it or not. Some kind of pissing-match thing, I guess. We found out they were making plans to infiltrate nuke sites and attempt unauthorized launches. They were dead-set on starting a hot war with the Soviets."

"How high up did it go?" Porter asked.

"Not very. Mostly non-coms, maybe a few lieutenants here and there. It was a big thing with enlisted men, sergeants, petty officers, men like that. We had them profiled, and the prevailing opinion was that the cult was basically made up of a bunch of grunts deeply pissed off about the

Vietnam thing. And they bore a lingering resentment of the officer corps. But they also were placed into a lot of biker gangs, particularly the ones popular with vets and ex-cons. A few prison gangs, too."

"Any connections to intelligence, CIA, that kind of thing?" Porter asked.

"Not so far as we could tell. And I'll tell you, thank God for that. These were some very sick bastards who did one hell of a lot of damage. It took a multi-agency task force about ten years to flush most of them out."

"This is wild, I never heard of these guys before," Porter said.

"No, this was all before your time. And we all worked damn hard to keep it out of the press. A lot of these men had to be killed. Most of them were absolutely incorrigible, real true-believers. I had to write up a lot of phony press releases about soldiers dying in training accidents or plane crashes to account for it all."

"Well, this opens up a whole can of worms when it comes to the Gary Sutton situation," Porter offered. "Do you think this cult had anything to do with that school he and Kevin Stuart were sent to?"

Travis stopped to consider this possibility.

"You know, it's never occurred to me before. But yeah, I'd say that's entirely possible. Especially given the timeframe and all the insanity going on out there."

Travis looked like he was captured by a stray thought, but let it go.

"Good work, men. Bruehle, see if there's any fresh internet chatter about Apophis. Send me whatever you find. I'll be at the off-site office the rest of the day."

Travis collected his things and left. Porter noticed that Bruehle seemed lost in thought.

"What's the deal? You got awfully quiet there, Bruehle. You know something about this Apophis thing?" Porter asked.

"Not much. Just what I've read online and in conspiracy newsletters for the most part. Word is they were extremely efficient at keeping themselves secret. But the general consensus was that they were the King Hell-motherfuckers of all Seventies cults."

"Where did this all come from?" Porter asked.

"From what I've gathered, the cult first formed on a US Army base in Germany, as an alliance between Neo-Nazis in the American military and plain old Nazi-Nazis left over from the war. But they weren't ideological or racial, they were religious. They'd take in Nazis, Communists, socialists, fascists, anarchists, gay, straight, whatever. Just so long as you were willing and able to kill for their cause."

"Kill who, exactly?"

"Everybody who wasn't them, pretty much," Bruehle replied. "They made the papers in the early Eighties, I remember. There was a big scare that some people on the S&M scene in West Berlin were involved in a heavy snuff thing. A bunch of runaways went missing at the time, kids who the cops knew were on the game, Things got really paranoid. It was all part of this huge dark cloud that seemed to prophesy the AIDS crisis in a strange way. A lot of very heavy shit was going down around '79, '80."

"A little before your time, isn't it, Bruehle?" Porter asked.

"Well, I was old enough to read. I'd take the train into Hamburg and pick up the gay papers and smuggle them into the house."

"A little data-pirate from the start, eh?"

Bruehle obliged with a mild snort. Then he turned serious.

"I just hope like Hell they aren't active again, I'll tell you that."

"Any particular reason? Aside from the obvious?"

"There's no doubt that most of them were Americans, but to me there's something very German about Apophis. The dark underbelly of Germany, of course, not the regular, normal, everyday kind of Germany. But it's still there, anyway," Bruehle said, almost wistfully.

Bruehle stared at nothing for a moment, trying to find the exact words. Porter let him have the floor.

"It's a virus planted very deep within the Teutonic psyche. But when I see those old newsreels from the Thirties, the night rallies and the rest of it, I don't see a desire for world conquest or any of that bullshit, no. If you're German, you understand where it's really coming from."

Bruehle leaned back and closed his eyes, as if trying to visualize the exact words.

"It all comes from... it comes from some suppressed, unconscious desire for mass suicide."

Porter spent a lot of time running angles on the photos, wondering why Glenn Sutton may have kept them. From what Travis said, the cult had been broken up back in the Eighties. That made them unlikely suspects for Gary's abduction.

But it was possible Glenn Sutton had been consulted on the Apophis investigation or had been asked to review the Polaroids. Possible, but unlikely.

There was also the more disturbing possibility Glenn Sutton was a member of the cult.

Porter was mulling that scenario over when his phone rang. It was Sam.

"I know these men."

"You know them? Porter asked, confused. "Know them how? You can't see their faces, Doc."

"Well, I know who they are, let's say," Sam answered. "They belonged to a cult within the Army that believed that they could bring about the Apocalypse."

"Yeah, we got that from Travis."

"Good, good. They also ran a murder-for-hire business while still on active duty," Sam said.

"Where are they now?"

"Nowhere. They were all purged a long time back. Rumor had it the rump of the bunch had moved down to South America and worked for Pinochet in Chile, Straussner in Paraguay, that crowd. Heavy death-squad work. They did the work the locals were too squeamish for, which is really saying something."

"Any connections to UFOs?" Porter asked.

"You got me there," Sam said. "Probably not. These types probably think UFOs are for sissies. These are people who ate Satanists for breakfast. I sincerely wish that were just a figure of speech."

"I believe this cult may have killed Gary's father, possibly because he had threatened to expose their operation with these kids, whatever the hell it actually was," Porter said.

"I'd say that's a highly likely scenario. They may have even taken him out in a plane or helicopter and dropped him in the ocean. That's a little trick they learned from Pinochet."

"What else can you tell me?" Porter asked.

"Well, I can tell you that most of the men in the photos are probably dead. And not dead of natural causes or old age."

"How so?"

"In the early Eighties, a secret society of sorts was formed inside the intelligence services," Sam said. "They had a very clear and singular goal of getting rid of Apophis for good. They even set up branches overseas. When you're trying to fight a group whose ultimate goal is to start a nuclear war which only they would survive, you find a lot of unlikely allies."

"Do you know how we could contact some of these secret society-types to see if they knew anything about these photos?" Porter asked.

"They're extremely secretive, Porter" Sam said. "I really can't promise anything."

Porter got the distinct impression he was talking to one of these secret society-types at this very moment. "Where are you now?"

"On the way out the door. I just wanted to get back to you as soon as I could on these pictures you sent. You want I should call Bob on this?"

"Sure. That's probably a good idea, yeah."

"Good, good. Just out of curiosity, where did you find these photos?"

"They were stashed in some CD cases in Gary's apartment. He hid them in the booklets," Porter lied.

"Amazing," Sam said. "Well, keep in touch."

CHAPTER SIXTY FIVE

It was a glorious spring afternoon, so Don Morton figured he might go and pitch a few at that new range in Lexington before he lost the light. He'd just pulled into the lot when his cellphone rang. Morton pulled the antenna out with his teeth and hoped whatever this fresh hell was, it would be brief.

"Sammy boy. What can I do you for?"

"I heard you made Dick Kooper soil his shorts over on live TV the other day," Sam said, chuckling.

"Yes, ol' Dickie did look like he got a little brown, the poor chap," Morton replied.

"Apparently so. What I'm hearing, Kooper told his handler he's retiring from doing any media. What was up with the hippie, though? Trying to shame the public off the scent?"

"Of course. Do we really want a bunch of damn rubber-neckers stomping around the Hockamock, hunting for little green men?" Morton said, gazing longingly up at the golfers on the driving platform, then over at the rapidly-descending sun.

"In this case, I thought the more attention that case gets the better," Sam said.

"That so? What's your thinking there, Sammy?"

"The more civilians you have around that family's house, the less likely the bad guys will make another move on the girl."

"And what else?" Morton asked. His spirits suddenly lifted as he watched powerful flood lights flicker on over the concourse.

"Well, we should wait and see what bubbles to the surface when we turn the heat up a bit, Don. If things start getting a little weird down there, we can keep an eye on who might come sniffing around."

"I don't know, Sam. Way I see it, having a bunch of amateurs down there will only muddle up our case."

"'Our case.' Jesus, Don. You better not let Bob catch you talking like that," Sam warned.

"Let's cut the crap, Sam. OK?" Morton said, a trace of heat in his voice.

"Bob's in way over his head and he knows it. He had absolutely no idea what he was getting himself in for with this project of his, and now he's going up against a death-cult that the entire United States Government had real trouble taking down."

"You do have a point there," Sam conceded.

"I mean, you really think Bob's little Mickey Mouse Club can handle Apophis? Frankly, I'm amazed any of them are still alive."

"You're preaching to the choir, Don. But the thing is, I'm a little uncertain how you found out about Apophis being back in the first place."

"Well, you know that Solomon girl, the one who was recently returned after going missing?" Morton said, with a hint of mischief.

"I saw her on the news. What about it?"

"Who do you think rescued her?"

"Oh, come on. Are you serious, Don?"

"As a heart attack, old boy. I started working this gimmick just before that girl got nabbed," Morton said, neglecting to tell his friend he'd also witnessed the abduction of another young woman. "It all stank like a witch-job to me. So much so that we asked the family not to talk to the press about it. They told the reporters she'd gone off her meds after a fight with her sister."

"Hence the story about the blackouts and the getting lost in the woods," Sam said.

"Exactly. Curious at all as to where I found her?"

"I am."

"Pepperell," Morton said, as if he couldn't believe it himself. "Right out there in the middle of the sticks. Obviously some rendezvous point where these sickos pass on these poor girls to whoever the hell is paying their tab."

"Jesus," Sam replied.

"That's not the half of it, old chum. These kidnappers had a long list of names printed on a spreadsheet. Three of the names were girls who have already gone missing. A fourth name was Melissa Solomon. We've contacted the families of the other girls on the list."

"Who's 'we,' exactly?" Sam asked.

"Oh, just yours truly and a few humble associates of mine," Morton said, lying through his teeth and enjoying it.

"So, I'm still missing the bit here where you found out about Apophis, Don."

"Well, after I handed the Solomon girl over to the State Police, I went back to look in on the hooligans. They didn't have any ID, but I took a peek at their persons and they both had the Apophis markings," Morton said, and checked the sun's progress again.

"You're kidding. In what way?"

"Well, they both had that full-coverage tattooing on the left arm, Sammy. I guess what's called a 'sleeve' nowadays. They had all those nasty damn scars with the hieroglyphs, and the serpent symbol at the base of the spine. Lots of piercings too, which I don't remember from the old days. Even on the boy bits, believe it or don't."

"Any kind of literature? Any kind of, I don't know, Apophis bibles?" Sam asked.

"Negative. But they did have themselves a nice little arsenal, some heavy drugs and a gym bag full of cash in the car."

"What kind of drugs?" Sam asked, with a hint of alarm.

"Good lord, Sam; Scopolamine, Rohypnol, some nutty kind of ether, looks Russian-made. Not exactly the kind of thing you want a couple of land-sharks to be rambling around with, my friend. Some bennies, but I got the feeling those were being saved for personal consumption."

"Were they carrying cellular phones?"

"They sure were, Sam. Custom gear, nothing I've ever seen before. Get this, Sammy; these little jobbers they had were programmed to go dead if you entered the wrong key code. Pretty far-out gizmos, actually."

"Where are the bodies, Don?"

"Last I checked they were cooling their heels out by the state morgue in Worcester," Morton said.

"Meet me there in two hours," Sam said and hung up.

Morton was more than happy to do so, since that meant he could sneak a few swings in for the next hour or so.

CHAPTER SIXTY SIX

The state morgue had no such official name. The sign outside said, 'Commonwealth of Massachusetts, Office of the Chief Medical Examiner,' and the facility was actually staffed and operated by the State Police. Most of the corpses it stored were connected to cases currently under active investigation, but an alarming number of them went unclaimed.

The building itself was a cinder block leviathan near the city limits. The building was surrounded by razor-wired topped hurricane fencing, and you needed to get past the guards at the gate to get into the lot.

Once you got inside the aura of death wrapped around you like a cloak. It was cold, it smelled of decay and Pine-Sol, and the staff seemed nearly as listless as the corpses.

"Can I help you gentlemen?" said a bored desk-attendant, more as a statement than a question. He was your generic Statie, in that he looked like a wannabe Marine and seemed to clock in at 35 years of age or so.

Sam produced his ID. "There are a couple JD's in your freezer we need to have a look at."

"Have a seat. I'll call the boss."

After a few minutes, a man in a crisply-starched uniform came striding in from an elevator. This one was in his mid-to-late 40s, shortish and stocky, with a ruddy, freckled face and a close, black crop tinged with shoots of white. Straight out of Central Casting.

"Gentlemen? Sergeant Rafferty. I understand you need to take a look at a couple of our guests."

"That's right, Sergeant," Morton said.

"Do you mind if I ask why? And why at this particular hour?"

Morton flashed his ID. "National Security."

Rafferty squinted at the ID a moment and looked over at Sam, who just smiled reassuringly.

"What are the names?" Rafferty asked.

"Probably John Doe #1 and John Doe #2," Morton replied.

"OK, we have several JD's in the facility at present. Do you have any idea what day they might have come here?"

"Last Thursday," Morton said.

"Are you sure?"

"Very much so, friend. I'm the reason they're here," Morton said cheerfully.

Rafferty looked again at Sam, who was still smiling with fatherly reassurance.

"Mind if I take another look at that ID there?" Rafferty said.

"Be my guest, constable. Please," Morton replied, cheerfully as ever.

"Thank you."

"Sammy, old boy, why don't you let the good man get a peek at yours as well."

Sam obliged.

Rafferty put both IDs on the table and studied them intently. For a moment or two longer than necessary, for obvious dramatic effect. Finally, he handed them back to the men. He went over to a computer terminal and began typing.

He nodded ever so slightly and said to the visitors, "Follow me."

Rafferty flicked on the overhead fluorescent lights in the cold, damp morgue, walked over to a numbered drawer and yanked it open. He walked a few spaces down and repeated the process.

There lay the Mortician and the Doorman, their skin as white as chalk. Except, of course, for their bullet wounds, which were a shocking bluish-magenta.

"There you go. I remember these two because of the tattoos and the, uh, piercings," Rafferty said.

"Yes, kind of hurts to look at," Sam said amiably.

"That's really not safe, you know," Rafferty said, wincing.

"You don't need to tell me. I'm a doctor."

"So, who are these guys?" Rafferty asked, eager to change the subject.

"Two of the most diabolical men you will probably ever lay eyes on, Sergeant," Morton replied.

Morton then produced a small but expensive-looking camera from his inside jacket pocket. "You mind?"

"Be my guest," Rafferty waved his left hand over the corpses, as if in benediction. "What exactly did these guys do, if you don't mind me asking."

"They're part of a human sacrifice ring," Morton answered. "They were caught red-handed with a female victim bound and gagged in the trunk of their car."

"Jesus," Rafferty said, visibly blanching. "I thought that was just the kind of thing you only see in the movies."

"Would that it were, my friend, would that it were," Morton said, clicking away.

"You came just in time," Rafferty said. "We were about to process them out of here."

"To where?" Morton inquired.

"To a cremation facility out in the boonies. They're homicide victims, so they'll be kept on ice for at least another 30 days. But this case's been given a low priority. I guess now I know why."

"No one's inquired about them besides us?" Sam asked.

"Not a soul," Rafferty said.

"Come take a peek at this, Sammy boy," Morton said, pointing to a tattoo on the Mortician's right shoulder, depicting the decapitated head of a cartoon devil. Sam leaned over and read the stylized writing arced around it.

"'*Satan Is Dead. Apep Ate Him.*' Words to live by, I suppose," Sam said and smiled at Morton.

Morton handed Rafferty his card.

"Sergeant, if anyone else happens to come looking for these men here, you give me a ring," Morton said.

He placed his hand on the officer's shoulder to emphasize his point. "Anytime, day or night."

Morton and Sam stepped out into the brisk night air and stood beneath the glow of a sodium light as a light mist began to fall.

"Well, there's no mistaking it. Those are Apophis men," Sam said grimly.

"So are you impressed yet?" Morton asked, as he casually scanned the area.

"I feel like a man whose cancer has come back after a long period of remission," Sam said, staring down at the cracked walkway.

"Well, tell that to Travis."

"It's all a symptom of a much greater disease, you know," Sam said, again grimly.

"What is?" Morton asked.

"Apophis," Sam replied, a flush of anger rising. "They're just an opportunistic infection. The host body is wracked with sickness. The patient is terminal."

Morton studied his old friend for a moment. The doctor's grandfatherly pose had dropped, replaced by something cold and hard.

"It's not my job to heal the world, Sam," Morton said, finally. "My job is making sure the right people are aware that Apophis are back in business, and making damn sure they put them back out."

"You just be very careful, Don. Bob starts to feel like you've been poaching on his land he just might put a bullet in you," Sam said.

"He's always welcome to try."

CHAPTER SIXTY SEVEN

It didn't take a psychic to guess who was coming down the metal staircase into what was euphemistically called 'the Dugout.' Steffie, an irritable bottle-blonde with sharp, angry facial features, heard the footfalls as she sat on a leather beanbag chair, flipping through a fashion magazine with supreme disinterest. A can of Diet Coke and a half-eaten take-out salad sat sadly on a metal TV tray to her left.

Her companion, a portly man-child with a mop of black curly hair, seemed utterly hypnotized by his handheld computer game, and barely ever said a word anyway.

The Dugout looked like a repurposed sub-basement at a utility station, its bare brick walls lined with archaic steel pipework. The Dugout was furnished with a large-screen TV and console stereo, as well as a half-sized refrigerator. There was a small bathroom off the side, with toilet and sink, but no mirror. Everything was black; the walls, the carpet, the beanbags, the fixtures, all of it.

Not the cheeriest of places, under any circumstances.

The approaching man looked like a reanimated corpse, at least so far as the young woman reckoned. He was gaunt and sickly, with wispy strands of greasy black hair combed tight against his skull.

His clothes could have been black or blue or brown or gray, for all Steffie knew. They seemed to absorb all light and deny any claim the color spectrum might make on them. He was of average height and seemed to speak with an accent, but his voice was so low and guttural that you couldn't really tell.

Steffie made him for some kind of ethnic from one of those countries no one's ever heard of, at least back when he was alive. But you couldn't really tell that, either.

The ghoul's sunken eyes hung over dark, ugly bags. He also looked like his liver was starting to crap out on him, giving his skin the dark-yellowish tinge of a prescription cough medicine Steffie hated when she was a kid. 'Marax,' it was called.

And since the ghoul never offered his name, she decided to call him that; Marax.

"We have some work for you," Marax said in a deep, phlegmy tone.

"Friggin' finally," Steffie sneered, in her own whiny, entitled way. "What work?"

"Here. Take a look," Marax said as he handed Steffie a letter-sized sheet of paper with a string of numbers written in black marker.

"What's this about?"

"It's about someone who needs to be taken care of," Marax said. "Someone who needs to stop talking."

"What are these numbers for?" Steffie asked.

"They're coordinates. They're to help you find your target."

"How?" Steffie whined. "I don't know what they mean."

"You don't have to. It will all work out. Don't worry."

"When do you want me to do whatever it is I'm supposed to do?"

"Tonight," Marax said and nearly smiled. "We're going to prepare the way for you."

"How?" Steffie had no idea what the fuck Marax meant by that. She didn't want to either.

"You don't have to worry about that. And this is for you," Marax said as he handed Steffie a prayer card. "Do you like it?"

"No. It's tacky as shit," Steffie spat. "I fucking hate Catholics and their tacky faggot bullshit."

"Good, good. You should feel a strong emotional response from it. Very good, Stephanie."

"What am I supposed to do with it?" Steffie asked, frowning.

"You're going to find somebody with it," Marax said.

"Who?"

"You'll tell us who."

"You really like to talk shit, don't you?" Steffie said and scowled.

"Someone will be along in an hour or so to help you prepare for your journey," Marax said.

"Oh fuck, not those drugs again," Steffie moaned. "They make me fuckin' puke."

"I'll make sure someone brings you a bucket," Marax said. "Good evening, now."

"Go fuck yourself, now," Steffie said mockingly, as Marax climbed back up the metal stairway.

"I hate that creepy prick," Steffie said to her companion. "He always smells like smoke."

"Cigarette smoke?" the Manchild asked.

"No, like a fire," Steffie said, curling her nose. "Like a fire in a fucking sewer."

"I don't smell anything," her companion said.

"You wouldn't," Steffie sneered.

Marax walked down a lightless corridor then entered an office filled with security monitors and filing cabinets. He encountered Darren, who was two-finger tapping away at a computer keyboard.

"What's the deal? They all set?" Darren asked expectantly.

"For now. But I think we might need to have an attitude-adjustment session with that woman," Marax noted.

"Yeah, I think you're right. I'll talk to the boss about it. What about the new ones? They online yet?"

"No, they're still being prepared," Marax said blandly. "It won't be long, though. They both have real talent."

"See? I told you about them, didn't I?" Darren said, flashing his 100-watt grin. "Man, this is all falling together beautifully. Absolutely perfect. Praise Apophis."

"Praise Apophis," Marax replied, with sudden, ghoulish cheer.

CHAPTER SIXTY EIGHT

Bruehle seemed excessively exuberant when he invited Darja and Porter to come on down to the Dungeon and have a peep at some of the interesting discoveries he'd made while snooping around online. In fact, Darja had noticed Bruehle's excessive exuberance quite a lot lately, and worried it might be a sign he was starting to crack under all the pressure he'd be under. She could relate.

"Well, it looks like Loroles won't be hawking their wares as computer security experts anytime soon," Bruehle said, leaping up from his chair as Darja and Porter entered the Dungeon.

"Why do you say that?" Porter asked.

"Because my eight year-old nephew could hack into their network. I mean, it's just comical. And I found some interesting little items while I was poking around in there."

"Such as?" Porter said.

"Position papers, Supes," Bruehle said as he handed out stapled stacks of laser prints. "Unsigned, undated, but all very, very interesting. Some-one is looking very far ahead."

"This one is called *New Roads to Apotheosis*, which is a very odd word for a technology concern to be using. It means 'to become godlike,'" Bruehle said. "Let that bit of trivia sink in for a moment. This paper essentially maps out a very detailed strategy -- rather, *strategies* - for the eventual mainstreaming of ultra-high-speed Internet. Now I don't know if this was meant as a proposal for Loroles specifically or just something some think-tank was pitching around to all the big firms, but either way it's somewhat alarming."

"How so?" Porter asked, feeling a bit lost with all this.

"They're talking about using the Internet for total, full-spectrum surveillance. That any device attached to the 'Net could pull data from the user and collect it in a centralized system. That every bit of online traffic, every connection, every email, every chatroom message, and every phone call can be gathered, sifted and analyzed by massive mainframes running very, very sophisticated algorithms. A Panopticon, basically."

"But that's crazy, isn't it?" Darja asked. "I mean, can that even be done, Bruehle?"

"Whoever wrote this paper seems to think so, they're also talking about essentially steering almost everything we do onto the Internet. Everything you read, everything you watch, even everything you buy. Maybe even everything you eat."

"Good luck to them," Darja said. "I only spend as much time on a computer as I absolutely have to. And even then it's a struggle."

"I tried America Online once. My laptop kept crashing. Drove me nuts," Porter said, glumly.

"Apparently what they are selling here is total centralization, massive consolidation," Bruehle said. "It's all about building monopolies and doing away with competition. They're also talking about sending all the manufacturing jobs offshore, even sending all the white collar jobs to countries like China and India and connecting them to companies in America and Europe using the Internet."

"It sounds like someone's selling a bunch of hype," Porter stated.

"Maybe, maybe not. There are more where this one came from," Bruehle added. "There's one called *Nine Reasons to Automate*, which is all about advanced robotics and computerizing labor. And then there's a really creepy one called *The Next Revolution in America*, which lays out a rather disturbing scenario about concocting widespread social and economic crises, as well as creating and financing fake radical movements to foment political extremism and racial violence."

"Why would they want to do that? It sounds insane," Porter said.

"Apparently so they can break down all the pre-existing cultures and replace them with a highly-controlled, highly-centralized monoculture," Bruehle replied. "I have to say, it all reminds me of *The Report from Iron Mountain*."

"What's that?" Darja asked.

"It was a white paper that was leaked in the late Sixties. It was written by some super-secret panel who determined that perpetual war was the only way to maintain world economic and social order. It also laid out a number of alternative scenarios as a replacement for war, including faked alien contact, believe it or not," Bruehle explained.

Both Darja and Porter seemed to tune out as soon as they heard the dreaded "A" word, so Bruehle reached for the big rhetorical guns.

"There was a lot of controversy over it, but your President Johnson and a famous economist called John Kenneth Galbraith both believed it was real. A lot of people did. If you read it, there's not a hint it's any kind of hoax. Of course, then some joker came forward in the Seventies and claimed it was all a satire that he had written. *Allegedly* written. The papers used his confession as an excuse to bury the story."

"Interesting," Darja said in the tone people usually reserved for things that are in fact not very interesting at all.

"It actually is," Bruehle said, defensively.

"What's this with the names here? These titles all start with N, R and A," Darja asked.

"New Rites of Apophis," Porter said.

"You get star for the day, Supes," Bruehle said, grinning.

CHAPTER SIXTY NINE

Darja and Porter were cruising down to the South Shore to track down some of the guys who played in bands with Gary before he joined Cutter's Mill. A few of them put in calls to the 1-800 tip line, and their names eventually made their way to Soares' desk.

The pair were speeding down I-93 and enjoying some of New Hampshire's very weird sunshine when Darja's phone rang.

"Tell me something good, Breuhlie," Darja chirped.

"OK, try this; your list of suspects is shrinking," Bruehle said. "Someone seems to have sliced and diced two of the members of Cutter's Mill at their rehearsal room. Ironically enough."

"Jesus, you're fucking kidding," Darja sputtered.

"Not one bit, Sails. Your old pal Sgt. Soares says you and your partner need to get those supple, round butt-cheeks of yours down at the crime scene in Quincy. Like ASAP."

"Got it," Darja said and hung up. She then looked meaningfully at Porter.

"What is it? What's going on?" Porter asked.

"Two of Cutter's Mill just got ganked in their practice room," Darja replied, and returned the phone to her jacket pocket.

"Oh, my God. Who?"

"Dunno. Bruehle didn't say," Darja said, frowning. "He says Soares wants to meet with us down there."

"Well, we were headed in that direction anyway, right?" Porter said, then hit the gas a little harder.

The Cutter's Mill rehearsal space was on the fourth floor of a recently-remodeled office building, catty-corner from the Masonic Lodge and across Hancock Street from the hideous Quincy Center subway station. There was a musical instrument shop on the bottom floor, and a number of names with 'studio' in them in the lobby's directory. Luckily, this particular building actually had a working elevator.

Darja and Porter ran straight into a wall of blue as soon as the elevator doors opened on the fourth floor. There was a riot of squawking radios and scuffling cop-feet on the new marble tiles.

A local patrolman spotted the pair and held out the old stop-hand at them.

"Whoa, hold up there. Who are you?" he snapped.

Darja held up her shield. "I'm Lundquist and this is Dunn. We're here to see Detective Sergeant Soares."

The cop stared sourly at the ersatz IDs, but Soares popped out of a doorway and called out, "Good, you're here. C'mon, over this way."

The patrolman shot a hot glare at the interloping black Statie, but Soares didn't even seem to register it. He was too used to all kinds of static from these clowns.

Two young female officers stood at the door like funeral ushers, next to some kind of metal cart filled with cardboard dispensing boxes. Soares flashed his shield and the trio were handed disposable plastic gloves, mesh hairnets and elastic-rimmed paper booties.

Inside, a crime-scene unit was doing a hair and fiber sweep. Other techs were dusting for prints and scraping samples from the innumerable splatters and writings on the walls.

Soares said, "Sorry for the party favors, but the crime-scene techs are still finishing up. Just watch your step, there's a lot of blood around."

"Who are they, Sergeant?" Porter asked, referring to the corpses.

"Adam Weaver and Matthew Conroy, according to their IDs," Soares answered grimly.

Porter shook his head in resignation. It looked more like a bizarre operating room than a murder scene.

The rehearsal room itself was featureless, a 15-by-20 white box distinguished only by its contents. There were amplifiers and microphones and a trimmed-down drum set. In fact, all of the practice equipment looked miniaturized. The band would probably go deaf if they tried to use their stage gear in here.

The room's other distinguishing feature was two dead bodies lying under heavy duck-canvas blankets. The blankets had 'Quincy PD' stenciled in large orange letters, and were lined with a plastic film to keep the blood from soaking through. Which was a good thing, because there was one hell of a lot of blood around.

Soares motioned to a tall, gangly man dressed in a long-sleeve, black shirt buttoned to the top, black denim jeans, black leather vest, and big, black boots with large, silver buckles. He had black hair, and a black goatee flecked with silver. He wore a bolo tie with a Masonic-looking clasp. However, the guy's attempt at the goth look was thwarted by the thick, unfashionable eyeglasses perched atop his nose. Not to mention the paper booties and hair-cap.

"Porter, Darja; This is Rohnaldo, he's a bit of an expert on the occult," Soares said. "I called him up from the Fall River Lodge to have a look at some of the ritualistic aspects of the scene here."

"Is there some kind of occult slant to these killings, Rohnaldo?" Porter asked as they shook gloved hands.

"It's Ron. And yeah, you could say there is. In the symbols and the setting."

"What are these symbols on the wall here, Ron?" Porter asked. "I'm assuming that's the victims' blood."

"It seems to be. And that's Enochian, a language allegedly given to the Medieval alchemists by the Archangels themselves. It's used quite a bit by magicians, white and black," Rohnaldo said. He wasn't referring to skin color.

"So we have some obvious ritual element here," Porter said.

Darja let Porter do the talking because this Ron dork was already getting on her nerves.

"We're also across the street from the Quincy Masonic Lodge," Soares noted.

"That lodge is a real trove of history, dating to the Revolutionary War," Rohnaldo said, nodding sagely. "It's also the place where Betty and Barney Hill first told the world of their alleged abduction by aliens back in the Sixties. Little did anyone realize what would come of that."

"And you're thinking this connects somehow to Gary Sutton's disappearance?" Porter asked.

"Well, the word on the street is that Gary Sutton claimed to be an alien abductee," Rohnaldo said.

"There's some evidence that he may have believed that, yeah," Porter replied in a guarded tone.

"It gets better," Rohnaldo said. "No less than Aleister Crowley himself was famous for his work with Enochian magic. And Crowley also spent a summer in New Hampshire in a town called Hebron, named after the village in the Bible ruled by the Anakim, who were said to be descended from fallen angels. That's the very same town the Hills claimed they were passing through when they awoke from their missing time episode. They were driving on what is now Interstate 93."

"Wow, Aleister Crowley again," Darja blurted, waving jazz hands. "Was there nothing he couldn't do?"

Porter shot Darja a dirty look. Rohnaldo ignored them both and continued on with his history lesson.

"We're also near the Southeast Expressway, which is an extension of I-93. Ninety-three is a very important number to Crowley's followers," Rohnaldo added. "And Crowley is now considered by UFOlogists as one of the first extraterrestrial contactees, having allegedly summoned an ET during a ritual not long after he vacationed in New Hampshire."

"So our killer really knows his occultism, then," Porter replied. He felt totally lost with this stuff, but let the details slide and focused on the basic psychology at work here.

"Killers. I'd say there were at least two, maybe more," Rohnaldo said. "There are Enochian sigils carved there into the bodies. That's hardcore ritual magic, blackest of the black. Whoever killed these people is trying to accomplish something. I'm thinking it's all going to add up to a very specific message, maybe one we can ultimately decode. Hopefully, it helps catch the bad guys"

"I don't get it. What connection does all this black magic and devil worship have to UFOs and all the rest of it?" Porter said. "It seems like a bit of a leap to me. This could all be totally unconnected. Maybe some Satanists had a beef with Cutter's Mill. Like bikers or some heavy metal band or something."

"Well, there was an Air Force report on UFOlogy back in the 1960s," Rohnaldo said. "The woman who compiled it said the UFO phenomenon had nothing to do with science or technology, and everything to do with the occult. Maybe at least one other person out there agrees with her."

CHAPTER SEVENTY

After the look-see at the crime scene, Darja, Porter and Soares walked outside to touch base on the investigation. It was a crisp, cool, sunny afternoon and Darja was wishing she were anywhere besides at some dump where two dumb longhairs got themselves carved up like Christmas hams by devil-worshipping fruitcakes.

"So, what do you two have for me today?" Soares said, with his usual preternatural calm. "I was hoping to hear from you sooner. Where are you at with all of this?"

"Well, we got lost down some pretty long side streets, Sergeant," Porter replied. "You got our report on the Kevin Stuart situation, right?"

"Yeah, Jesus. What a freakshow," Soares said and shook his head.

"Well, things have only gotten freakier," Porter said.

"OK, send me an up-to-date situation report," Soares said quietly but firmly. "I'm starting to get a lot of static from my Captain about all this hell breaking loose the past couple of weeks."

"Absolutely, sir," Porter said, as he and Darja turned to walk back to their car.

But Soares had one last order of business.

"Before I forget; you two wouldn't happen to know anything about a couple fuckups that got themselves iced behind a diner up in Burlington, would you?"

"Um, who exactly?" Porter said, squelching a sudden panic.

"Couple'a skinhead-looking guys, turned out to have a lot of occult tattoos and piercings all over. One of 'em even got his johnson surgically split in two. Real sweethearts, apparently rented themselves out as button-men to the local drug kingpins. There's even some talk of these two being involved in some kind of political death squad overseas a while back. Word is they moved over here when the Wall came down."

"First we're hearing about it," Darja said, as neutrally as she could manage.

Soares fixed his companions with an unreadable stare, for what felt like an eternity.

"OK, now that's very interesting to me," Soares finally said. "It's very interesting because a number of witnesses describe a couple eating at the diner same time these two got chilled. Real good-looking couple, apparently, in leather jackets. Kinda stood out a bit. A busboy said the husband looked like 'the guy who plays Superman.' The wife was a tall blonde, with what their waitress called 'Chinese eyes.' Not ringing any bells?"

Darja and Porter looked down at their feet in shame. Soares continued to stare silently at them, without heat or expression.

"Walk with me," he finally said.

The three walked to the end of the block, crossed the street then stopped to convene under the awning of an empty storefront that once housed a dry cleaners. Darja felt a cold dew of sweat form at her temples.

"Listen, I'm getting reports every day on everything you two are up to, OK?" Soares said quietly. "People are getting a little worked up, OK? A little squirrelly. My Captain figures you did us a favor with this diner thing. But you've also been running around leading people on like you're a couple of Feds, folks like the chief out in Littleton. And that will most definitely not do, you understand?"

"Sir..." Darja started to say before Soares held up a hand to cut her off.

"Listen, no one's shedding any tears over the diner. But by the same token, no one in my office has any doubts at all that one or both of you clipped those two and didn't bother to call it in. The Massachusetts State Police are not stupid, no matter what the good people of the Commonwealth might want to think. We know exactly who and what Bob Travis is, and believe me, no one's particularly happy that he's decided to set up shop around here. Especially since it looks like he's got some other guy going around planting stiffs. Anything you two can tell me about that?"

"Seriously, sir," Darja said, her stomach in knots. "It's the first I've heard of it. I swear."

"No? Nothing about some hitter named Morton?" Soares asked. "Older guy?"

"Oh, yeah. Jeez. I mean, I met him, sir," Porter said. "Once. But I have no idea what he's up to, I swear."

Soares shook his head at the ground in disbelief.

He sighed heavily, then said, "What do I need to know about this guy, Porter?"

"Just that he's really bad news, apparently."

Soares sighed heavily again. "Exactly what *kind* of bad news are we talking about here, Porter?"

"I can't say, but from what I've heard it sounds like he might be some kind of CIA assassin or something. Maybe military. But as far as I know, he's not working with us."

Soares rubbed his face with both hands.

"OK, listen to me," he said in a stern, fatherly tone. "You two are going to go home right now and write everything down for me, OK? *Everything.* Do we understand each other here? Everything you've done, everything you've heard, everything you've seen, everything you know. And I want your reports in my hands before noon tomorrow."

"Sir, I don't know if..." Darja started to say.

Soares held up a stop-hand again.

"Just do it. Travis has a problem with that, you tell him to take it up with me. Believe me, everybody knows full-well the kind of juice he's got in Washington, but you people are tracking mud into *my* house now. We may not be able to take Bob Travis down, but we sure as hell can make his life miserable. And yours."

CHAPTER SEVENTY ONE

Bruehle went up to the kitchen for a midnight snack. After scanning the paltry selection on hand, he grabbed a banana Frozefruit out of the icebox. He'd gained ten pounds already since he started this job, but junk-food was the only way he could handle all the stress. Well, junk-food, wine, cigarettes and compulsive masturbation, that is.

Bruehle had already worked his way through the entire catalog of licit and illicit drugs in the late Eighties, when he was doing the Rave thing in Europe. He never quite figured out how, but he woke up one rainy afternoon in Rotterdam and mysteriously found himself in the possession of a gallon-sized jar of bootleg tabs of Ecstasy, with which he eventually supported himself for quite some time by selling.

But he also broke the cardinal rule of dope-dealing and got high on his own supply. And all this habit ultimately left him with was a very worrisome tremor in his right hand, intense entoptic hallucinations whenever he closed his eyes, and a left leg that went -- and stayed -- numb, sometime around his twenty-sixth birthday.

That wasn't all the X left him with. He'd also racked up a number of outstanding warrants for his arrest in several different sovereign nations.

Which was exactly why he was now toiling alone in a filthy basement workshop in the middle of Redneckistan, instead of fucking GQ models and pulling down big Yankee dollars in Silicon Valley. So he tended to resort to pharmaceuticals only when absolutely necessary.

Suitably depressed, Bruehle was just about to head back down to the Dungeon when he heard Darja and Porter mumbling away in the living room.

Desperate for distraction of any kind, Bruehle wandered over to see what they were up to. He was certain it was something incredibly boring, but kept hoping against hope that one night he'd walk in just as those two perfect specimens decided to give one another a hearty, no-strings-attached fucking, right there on the sofa. Just as an experiment, to see how the parts fit. And in the heat of the moment, they'd invite him to dive in, and turn it into an anything-goes kind of three-way. It could be a like a team-building exercise.

If not, Bruehle was hoping he could maybe lure Darja out to the deck later for a few smokes and maybe a glass or two of red before he turned in for the night. Unfortunately, Bruehle went into the living room and saw the pair hammering away at their laptops, files and note paper littered all over the floor. Place looked like it'd been hit by a typhoon.

"You two are up late. Pulling an all-nighter?" Bruehle asked,

"Probably," Porter replied.

"What's that you're working on?" Bruehle said.

"A report for Soares," Darja answered. "He got a major bug up his ass, and now he wants a full report on everything we've been doing since we started."

"Skipper OK with this, Sails?" Bruehle asked, skeptically.

"I'm sure he wouldn't be. But Soares says he's gonna sic the hellhounds on Travis and the rest of us if we don't give him exactly what he wants," Darja said, ruefully.

"And give it to him by lunchtime, to boot," Porter added. "Which means we gotta type this all up, then print it all out and then get it down to him by noon tomorrow."

"Why don't you just send it by email?" Bruehle offered.

"Email? What the fuck is email?" Darja asked.

"You're a bloody savage. You know that, Lundquist?" Bruehle snapped. "Just come down and fetch me when you're done working that up. I'll take care of it for you."

"What if Soares doesn't have this email thing to get it?"

"He has it, don't worry about that."

"I'm just fucking with ya, Bruehlie. I know what email is," Darja quipped as she hammered away at her keyboard.

"I don't suppose you feel like helping us get all this stuff together, do you?" Porter asked.

"No, I wouldn't want to intrude," Bruehle answered. "You two look like you're having so much fun there on your own already."

Darja scoffed. "Suck my titties, Bruehle."

"You don't have any," he reminded her.

Porter and Darja got their reports pieced together around 4:30 in the morning and Bruehle sent them off to Soares. The Lair was dead quiet, so they decided to catch a few winks on the sofa and loveseat, respectively. It was shortly after 9 AM when Bruehle burst in the living room, banging an old wooden spoon on an even older saucepan.

"Hey, hey, get up, you two! Rise and shine! *Carpe diem! Aufwachen, aufwachen! Schnell, schnell!*" Bruehle shouted as he shook the pair out of their slumbers.

Porter stirred quickly but Darja batted Bruehle's hand away, advised him to go fuck himself and rolled over on the couch. Bruehle shook Darja again. She rolled over on her back and squinted at the sunlight peeking in through the blinds.

"Jesus, Bruehle. Can't a ho' get some shuteye around here? The fuck's so important already?"

Bruehle was on fire with his new scoop, whatever it was.

"You guys're not going to believe this: the guy who owns the studio Cutter's Mill rehearsed at had motion-activated surveillance cameras put in. It seems he got sick of the local crackheads trying to nick all his gear."

"So, what do we got during the time in question?" Porter asked, grabbing a stick of Dentyne from the pack he kept in his jacket.

"Well, we have Conroy and Adam go into the studio at 8 PM. And someone else coming around about three hours later. Care to guess who that was?" Bruehle said.

"Don't keep us in suspense," Porter said as he yawned and rubbed his eyes.

"None other than one Susan Driscoll," Bruehle answered.

Porter looked up. "Adam's girlfriend? I'm feeling another shoe about to drop here."

"Well, the video-feed seemed to mysteriously glitch out shortly after she entered," Bruehle explained. "But the cops searched her apartment and found a knife, caked with what looks like human blood."

"Sounds too good to be true, Bruehlie," Darja said, still laid out on her back on the couch, shielding her tired eyes from the glare with the back of her hand.

"My feelings exactly," Bruehle said. "Initial tests show no prints, but it was found under her bed, wrapped in a black bandanna all done up with skulls and pentagrams."

"Someone's setting the poor bitch up," Darja said.

"Well, they're doing a damn fine job of it, Sails. Driscoll's on tape at the murder scene and that's almost certainly the murder weapon sitting there underneath her bed. The cops are telling the papers she killed her boyfriend because he smacked her up, and they're citing your complaint as evidence. And they're claiming she killed the other one because he was a witness. So unless she's got a bulletproof alibi for exact time of death, I'd say she best start shopping for something sleek and sexy in orange."

"Where is she now?" Porter asked.

"Source has her at Quincy PDHQ."

"Is that it?" Darja said to Bruehle. "Is that what you woke us up for after we were up all night?"

"Oh, you poor baby," Bruehle pouted. "And no, you very nasty bitch, it is not. You two need to sashay on over to Derry right off, because something's waiting there that could crack this entire case wide open. Go on, out with you! *Go! Go! Leave!*"

CHAPTER SEVENTY TWO

Mitchell Kern had stopped cooperating with the police once Adam and Conroy got carved up, and all calls to his office were redirected to his lawyer. So Zaina had asked Travis to make a few calls to some friends in Washington, who in turn got some people to lean on the manager, and lean on him hard.

And so an enormous overnight box arrived at a Mail Boxes Etc. in Derry, which Porter and Darja went out to retrieve after their talk with Bruehle.

The box was filled with all of the materials Kernstock had been collecting for the Cutters' Mill press-package they'd been working on, in anticipation of the band's debut album.

There was even a very polite and deferential little note from Lillian, asking pretty-please that all the materials be returned to Kernstock as soon as possible. Darja got the distinct impression that whoever Travis got to lean on Kern and his people scared the living shit out of them.

Now a riot of photos, flyers and clippings of Cutter's Mill were scattered across the big conference table in the Batcave. There were some homemade t-shirts and some stage banners and the rest, but those were largely ignored. Bruehle set up a large, lighted magnifying lens and the agents and the analysts took turns scouring every photo and flyer the band ever produced.

"Is this Quattro person especially patriotic?" Zaina asked.

"I don't know. We'll have to ask him," Porter answered. "When we find him."

"Well, he's wearing a shirt with the Gadsden flag on it in a number of these photos," Zaina replied. "The design with the coiled snake that says, 'Don't Tread on Me.'"

"The one that's big with truckers and hillbillies? Isn't this guy some kind of part-time academic?" Porter asked.

"What are you thinking?" Bruehle asked Zaina.

"That it kind of looks like the Apophis snake," Zaina said as she stared at one of the band photos. "Coiled."

"Here's another redneck kind of shirt," Darja said. "It says 'NRA.'"

270

"That doesn't stand for the National Rifle Association," Zaina noted. "That's the old logo for the National Recovery Administration. It was part of the New Deal initiative during the Great Depression."

"NRA might also mean 'New Rites of Apophis' here," Bruehle said to Porter.

"Could be. But if this guy was in with them, he hid it pretty well," Porter replied. "His apartment was bare when we went to interview him. There was one weird thing, though,"

"What's that?" Zaina asked.

"There was a spot of black wax on his coffee table," Porter explained. He said it was from his girlfriend's crafts, but now we know there isn't any girlfriend."

"Black candles are often used in occult rituals," Zaina said, a dark hint of suggestion in her voice.

"Yeah, I'm liking this guy for Apophis, more and more," Darja said. "I'm liking him for Gary and I'm liking him for the rest of the band."

"That little guy?" Porter said. "Why? Why kill his meal-ticket? What's his motive?"

"The cult's his motive," Darja answered. "All this could be part of some Satanic ritual thing. I don't think he's acting alone, but he's our common denominator here, Porter."

"So he's in on this with other Apophis freaks?" Porter asked.

"That would seem to follow, yeah," Darja said.

"I dunno. I'm not buying it," Porter grumbled.

"Let's write all this up for the board. We don't have to all agree on the motives, but I think we have enough to pin the murders on Quattro with Apophis acting as his accomplices," Zaina said.

Holy shit, Darja thought; Zaina backed me up. The bitch actually backed me up. And against Porter, no less. Next thing you know we'll be getting our nails done together and going out on double dates.

Right on, Zaina. Mark the calendar.

CHAPTER SEVENTY THREE

Darja's phone rang in the middle of the night. She wasn't exactly sure what the hour was, but it was undoubtedly ungodly.

She had taken to keeping the cellphone next to her pillow on the bed, but somehow it had fallen onto the floor and become tangled up in her nightgown. Which, through some act of extraterrestrial intervention, had slipped from its hook on the wall and wound around her phone like a turban. The phone must have rung several hundred times before Darja finally got the damn thing into her hand.

"What?" Darja mumbled into the transmitter.

"Where is you at, Sails?" Bruehle asked, in what he probably thought was a black American accent.

"I'm on the French Rivera, having my toes sucked by an oil tycoon. Where the fuck do you think I am, Bruehlie?"

"No, seriously. Where are you?"

"I'm in my apartment, Bruehle. In bed. Sleeping. It's three in the fucking morning, for Christ's sake."

"You better get up here straight away. Porter too. Zaina's on her way right now."

"Why, what's going on?"

"Gary Sutton just washed up on some place called Tenean Beach in Dorchester. It's looking like somebody blew a hole in his face and dumped his body in the ocean."

• • •

The mood was bleak at the Lair. Darja, Zaina, Porter and Bruehle sat at the kitchen table and looked through copies of a fax Bruehle received from a contact in the Boston Police. Porter had brought coffee and donuts, but no one felt much like eating.

"So that's it, huh? After all we went through trying to find this guy?" Porter said.

"Exactly what else were you expecting, Porter?" Darja snapped. Where else did you think this guy was going to show up? We talked to everyone who knew him. He wasn't a fugitive. If he were alive, don't you think we would have known about it well before now?"

"Well, I still think we need to work a timeline then and figure out who did this. Who kidnapped him and killed him."

"What the fuck, Porter?" Darja barked. "Are we homicide cops all of a sudden? This entire case was an exercise in futility from the very start."

"I think Porter's right, Darja," Zaina said. "We don't need to solve his murder, but I think speculation would be very useful for the work going forward. I think we can use this as a case study that could help us in the future, with other subjects."

Darja looked set to unload on Zaina but Bruehle ran interference.

"So what's your thinking here, Zaina? You've obviously had time to think this over. What do you think happened?"

"I think it's apparent that, because of his father's work and because of his background, that Gary Sutton got himself involved in something he shouldn't have," Zaina replied. "And because of that, someone, most probably someone involved in intelligence, decided he needed to be silenced."

"So how do you think this all went down?" Porter asked.

"I think it's entirely possible that it involved elements of the military," Zaina said. "I think Kevin Stuart was sent in to create a diversion and that the flash was from some kind of exotic grenade. Gary was pulled off the stage by operatives standing in the crowd, then taken out of the club while everyone else was still reacting to the flash."

"What about this aircraft people said they saw there?" Porter said.

"That was probably some advanced type of helicopter or hovercraft. Possibly even a Harrier-type vehicle. I think the sound of its rotors would have been drowned out by the loud rock music, which is why no one heard an engine. There's a fire escape around the back of the building that the object was seen over. I think that is what was used to load Gary into the vehicle. It was probably something that a very highly-trained team drilled for, before the action."

Everyone sat back and considered Zaina's theory. It all sounded entirely plausible, but it didn't feel right. Not even to Zaina herself.

"OK, so what about all the other stuff, like the other musicians in the band?" Porter asked.

"Well, this is what I mean," Zaina explained. "We may not be able to catch Gary's killers, but I think we still need to continue to work on all that. As I said, I believe it's very important to the overall mission."

"Excuse me for a second," Darja said. "Do you mind if I ask you a rhetorical question, Zaina?"

"Please."

"Alright, then; where in the *motherfuck* is Travis?" Darja barked, non-rhetorically. "Does anyone know where the fuck he is or where he's been? Has anyone actually spoken to him about Gary being dead?"

"I believe Mr. Travis is traveling at the moment," Zaina said, wincing at Darja's rage.

"No offense, Zaina. I know the two of you go back a long way. But for a guy who is so goddamned anal about everything being done his way or the highway, he always seems to leave us twisting in the wind an awful lot. Porter and I are the ones out there getting our asses *literally* kicked, and we still don't know a fucking thing about all these fucking mind-mutants and poltergeists, and all this other insane bullshit that everyone seems read-in on except us."

"Darja, please..." Bruehle said.

"Bruehle, do me a favor and go suck a dick, OK? Don't you fucking 'Darja, please' me. Never in my life have I ever served under someone who gives less of a shit about the people under his command. The people he's supposed to be looking out for. Porter and I have people out there trying to kill us, *literally* trying to fucking kill us. And the fucking CO is off twiddling his fucking thumbs somewhere."

Darja stood and hooked Porter's left arm with an angry right hand.

"Porter, come on. Let's go."

"Darja, what are you...?" Porter said, stunned by this turn of events.

"Porter MacKenzie Dunn, you get your pussy-whipped ass out of that fucking chair and you walk out that door with me right now!" Darja screamed. "If you don't at least have the balls to show some fucking solidarity here and now, I'm going to fuck off for good, and none of you will ever see my face again!"

Porter got up, which seemed to calm Darja down just a notch.

"Listen; Zaina, Bruehle, whichever; You get that crusty old fuck on the phone and you tell him that his little golden boy is dead as a goddamn fucking doornail," Darja shouted. "Then you tell him that he'd better get on the ball or the rest of us are all going to be washing up on a beach pretty-fucking-soon as well. I'm not going up against those psycho cult freaks again unless I know someone -- *anyone* -- has my back on this. Let's get the fuck out of here, Porter."

CHAPTER SEVENTY FOUR

Darja woke in the early afternoon to a loud, insistent rapping at her door. For a moment, she thought Travis already bounced her check and the landlord was here to evict her. She grabbed her Glock, went over to the front door and peered through the view-finder. It was Sam.

What the fuck was he doing here?

Darja opened the door with the safety chain on.

"What can I do for you, Dr. Sanderson?"

"Well, you could let me in, for one. I need to speak with you, Darja. It's urgent," Sam said.

For a moment, Darja wondered if Sam was here because Travis ordered him to kill her. Why the hell not, right? It would make as much sense as everything else that's happened since she started this fubar of a job.

"Please, Darja. We need to talk."

Darja slipped her Glock into her bathrobe pocket and let Sam in.

"Thank you, my dear. I appreciate it," Sam said as he took off his driving gloves.

"What do you need to speak to me about, sir?"

"I talked to Bob this morning. He knows about Gary Sutton, but more importantly, he's asked me to convey his very deepest apologies to you personally. He's been out of the country on some very important business pertaining to Bifrost, and he's very disappointed that he hasn't been there for the team."

"It would've been nice if he called and told me that himself," Darja replied.

Sam held up a sympathetic hand. "I know, I know. Sometimes Bob has trouble expressing his true feelings, especially if he feels like he's at fault. But that doesn't mean he doesn't care. He's just in a very delicate position at the moment. But he wants you to know he has nothing but the absolute highest praise for how you and Porter have performed out in the field."

Darja fell silent. She couldn't imagine Travis having the absolute highest praise for anything.

"I understand the stress you're working under, Darja. You've had a very rough go at it. If you need to speak with anyone, I can put you in touch with some excellent counselors."

"Well, to be honest, sir, I think I'll be just fine once total strangers stop trying to murder me," Darja said. "Oh, and murder my partner, too. I think once a bunch of cult weirdos stop shooting laser-cannons at us, or quit sending psychotic hitmen after us, that things will really start to perk up some. Call me crazy, but that's just kind of the way I feel about it this morning."

"Perfectly understandable, my dear," Sam said calmly. "If you like, I'd be more than happy to write you a prescription for something to help take the edge off."

Darja had to admit that particular offer was tempting. "I'm going to make some coffee, sir," she said. "Would you like some?"

"That sounds terrific. I'd also appreciate it if you could put that weapon away while you're at it."

Darja and Sam sat and stirred their coffees on the living room chairs that came with the furnished apartment. They exchanged chit-chat before Sam's demeanor changed. He looked like there was something he'd been waiting to tell Darja.

"You know, Bob and I first met back in the Sixties. I had hoped to become a famous surgeon like Christiaan Barnard one day, but somehow I ended up a headshrinker," Sam chuckled. "Apollonia says I'm being punished for sins I committed in a past life. But it really all came about as a fluke. The Army needed more psychological people than they were able to find, so Bob Travis dropped in out of the blue and made me an offer. I had a psych minor in my pre-Med days and that was the sum total of my qualifications. But you know how it works with the military. Sometimes they just need warm bodies."

Darja wondered if Sam was going to tell her his Vietnam sob-story now. One of the reasons she didn't do her full twenty was because she couldn't stand to hear any more fucking Vietnam sob-stories from people she had to answer to.

"The truth is I was damned happy to go to Vietnam," Sam continued. "You see, my wife — well, my first wife — had been pregnant with a baby girl. I was over the moon. Couldn't *wait* to be a daddy. But you know how it is, always working crazy hours, sometimes round the clock. And then I found out she'd been drinking while she was pregnant. And I also found out she had been stepping out with another man while I was at work. And one night, the two of them -- my wife and this other fellow — get drunk, get into an argument and the next thing you know this man has beat my pregnant wife nearly to death. In my own house. He kicked her in the head so many times that they actually had to induce coma and remove a huge chunk of her skull, just so all that pressure wouldn't crush her brain."

"Ohmigod," Darja gasped. This certainly wasn't how she was expecting to start her day.

"She lost the baby. She was six months pregnant at the time and miscarried. All over the emergency room floor. I was on shift at the time, right upstairs. Framingham, you know. Everyone I worked with knew exactly what had happened. I'd never felt so humiliated in my entire life. Which is exactly why Vietnam seemed like an all-expenses-paid vacation. Of course, things hadn't gotten as bad then as they later would," Sam said grimly.

"Oh God, I'm so sorry, sir. I'm so, so sorry," Darja said.

Jesus. This almost made Porter's horror story sound like a sitcom.

"But I thought about that baby girl, Darja. I thought about her every day," Sam said, a tone of urgency in his voice. "Hell, I still think about her every day. But I used to imagine what she'd be like on her first day of school, when she was a teenager, when she was in college. Just played the whole life story out in my mind. And I hope you'll forgive me for saying this, Darja, but in my fantasies my baby girl grew up to be so much like you. Oh, I imagined her being a tomboy, because she wanted to be just like her daddy! And then she grew up to be such a strong, independent woman, just like you. I always thought that maybe it was because my wife was so weak."

Darja was wrecked. She was really hoping she wouldn't start blubbering in front of the good doctor here.

"And when you first walked into my office that day, I was dumbstruck," he explained.

"It's as if you'd walked straight out of my day-dreams. And when I went back and looked at your file, why, I nearly had a stroke! When I made allowance for the time-zone difference, I couldn't believe my eyes; You were born the very same day my baby girl died in that emergency room, just minutes later!"

Oh Jesus; there go the waterworks, Darja thought.

"And all I could think was that when my baby girl's spirit left her unborn body, it descended into yours, Darja. Please don't ask me to explain it. It's a mystical force that we're not meant to understand. I realize this sounds terribly presumptuous, but how could that possibly be a coincidence? We're all beholden to forces far beyond us, and sometimes those forces seek to test us. They seek to test us, and mold us and shape us through those tests. But I need you to know we all believe in you, Darja, and we all know that great, great things are in store for you. You're one of the bravest human beings I have ever had the pleasure to know."

Oh God, Darja thought, that is the most beautiful, most touching thing she's ever heard anyone say to her in her entire life. Even if this whole entire scenario was just creepy as all fuck.

"Now, I remarried when I got back home and we had two fine boys that have grown up to be very fine young men, Darja. I hope you can meet them one day, I honestly do," Sam said emphatically. "And I hope that they'll make me as proud as you do. I don't know why I felt I had to tell you all this, but maybe I'm telling you the kinds of things that Bob feels in his heart, but just can't bring himself to say out loud."

"I understand, sir," she said, sniffling now like a flu ward.

"Good. I believe in you, Darja," Sam said as he firmly clutched Darja's shoulders. "Nobody thinks you're broken or inferior. Exactly the opposite. But let's keep this a running conversation, OK?"

"Yes, sir. Thank you, sir."

"Good girl," Sam said and smiled warmly. "We'll talk again soon."

Darja showed Sam to the door and they said their goodbyes.

She went into the kitchen and poured herself a fresh cup of coffee. Then she sat down at the breakfast counter and bawled her fucking eyes out.

CHAPTER SEVENTY FIVE

"Bruehle, why don't you play us that clip?" Zaina said.

The four were sitting at the conference table in the Batcave, called in by Zaina to discuss the latest break in this insane clown-car of a case they were struggling to get a hold of.

Bruehle got up and walked over the video station and popped a cassette into the VCR. He scrolled through the playback trying to find what he was looking for, stopping and starting at annoying intervals.

"Jesus, Bruehle. Couldn't you have set this up before the meeting?" Darja whined.

Bruehle flashed Darja the finger with his left hand as he worked the remote with his right.

"OK, here we go, kids." Bruehle stood triumphant by the monitor, his arms folded. Whatever it was, he sure was proud of himself for finding it.

The last five seconds of a yogurt commercial played, then a black anchorwoman appeared on screen.

"An arrest has now been made in the shooting deaths of two men at the Road Stop Diner in Burlington last week. Witnesses said they saw a man arguing with the two victims before shooting them and speeding off on a motorcycle."

"What the fuck is this?" Darja exclaimed.

The mugshot of a greasy-haired biker appeared onscreen. His right eye was badly swollen and his face was bruised.

"The accused gunman, Steven Joseph Parnell, Jr. of Dracut, is a member of the Chrome Commandos MC, a biker gang authorities have linked to drug running, extortion and prostitution," the anchorwoman continued.

"Police are now speculating that the two victims were members of a rival organized crime syndicate operating in eastern New England. Their identities have still not been released to the public."

Shots of the parking lot outside the diner came onscreen.

"The shootings have residents of Burlington in fear that big-city crime is now moving into their small, suburban town."

Bruehle paused the tape.

"It looks like Loroles probably bribed someone, probably someone working in the kitchen at the diner, to tell the police they saw this man commit the murders," Zaina said. "Obviously by doing so it shifts attention away from their own culpability."

"What about the fact that they were driving around in a fucking Loroles company car?" Darja countered.

"They address that in the clip," Zaina replied curtly. "Play the rest of it please, Bruehle."

The frozen anchorwoman came back to life.

"But one of the questions that arose from the investigation was why the two victims were in possession of a company car owned by the computer manufacturer Loroles, whose headquarters is out in Waltham. Police sources report that Loroles claims the men were subcontractors with one of the firms that provide security for the Boston branch office. The security firm claims that the two victims had lied about their criminal histories and had taken the car off the grounds without permission."

Bruehle hit the pause again.

"And they were just holding that weed for a friend, honest," Darja quipped.

"Someone's going around and cleaning up," Porter said. "Tidying up loose ends."

"That would be our analysis of the situation as well," Zaina said. "We'll proceed with the appropriate recommendations to the interested parties."

Darja wondered why Zaina always had to talk like a damn robot. She liked it better when she thought the bitch was mute.

CHAPTER SEVENTY SIX

Porter pulled up at Grace's house and noticed that all the lights were out inside. He thought she might have gone somewhere, but her Subaru was still in the driveway.

Concerned, he unsnapped his holster and cautiously approached the house. He could see a light was on in the kitchen, one of the low-wattage decorative lights Grace used as accents.

She usually left the front door unlocked when she knew Porter was coming over, but it was locked tonight. So Porter rang the doorbell and waited. He finally heard the shuffle of her bedroom slippers on the tiled hallway floor and was taken aback when she opened the door on the security chain.

"Grace," Porter said. "Is there something wrong? Is everything OK here?"

"He's dead, isn't he?" Grace said through the crack in the doorway.

"Can I come in? Please?" Porter asked, feeling he shouldn't need to.

Grace undid the security lock and walked into the main hallway, leaving the front door open behind her. She went into the kitchen and started a fresh pot of coffee.

"No one called you?" Porter asked.

"I turned the phone off. I was out most of today," Grace replied.

"Out where? Work?" Porter asked.

"How did he die?" Grace said, avoiding his question.

"Gunshot, execution style. His body was found in Dorchester Bay."

Grace froze for an instant at Porter's bluntness, then studied the coffee as it dripped. When the carafe was full, she poured two mugs and sat down at the table with Porter.

"I don't feel anything right now," Grace said. "When Gary left here, he left it all behind. I can count the number of times Gary called since he moved out, probably on my fingers. He never took my calls. We had a terrible fight the night he left. I wanted him to go back to school but he was so intent on pursuing the music instead. I tried to convince him that he should at least have something else to fall back on, and he accused me of being unsupportive. Do you know what Gary said to me on the day he walked out that door?"

Porter mouthed, "No," silently and shook his head.

"He said, 'You are dead to me.' And I was. He'd only call when he needed money. Of course, we had to speak whenever he ended up in the hospital..." Grace trailed off, then muttered, "Men and their secrets," and got up from her chair.

She poured the rest of her coffee into the sink and rinsed out the mug. "Do you keep me a secret from your team, or whatever it is you call them?" she asked, staring out the kitchen window.

"No, I can't keep secrets from them," Porter said. Grace nodded as if she'd confirmed some long-held suspicion.

"I think I'm all cried out for Gary," she said. "I spent a lot of nights alone, crying for him. He really knew how to hurt people, me most of all. But he was my son. When you first came to the house, I thought you were coming to tell me he was dead. I mourned for him then. I knew it was just a matter of time."

Porter stared into his mug. He had nothing to say.

"When will they release his body?" Grace asked.

"I don't know. I hate to have to tell you this but you're probably going to have to ID him at the morgue It's a murder investigation now, so you'll probably have a lot of hassles to deal with."

"I know. I've been there before, Porter," Grace said, with an edge. She immediately softened and asked, "Do you have somewhere you need to be tonight?"

"I'll be here as long as you want me," Porter answered softly.

"I can't be alone tonight," Grace said. She got up and walked to the bedroom.

• • •

The next morning Grace and Porter lay in bed, lost again in their own inner monologues. Porter lay on his back and put his hands behind his head while Grace lay on her side, idly tracing her index finger across his neck and chest.

Suddenly Grace stopped, sat up and pulled the comforter towards her chest. She looked at Porter as if waiting for his permission to speak.

"What?" he asked. "What's wrong?"

Grace frowned, closed her eyes tightly and summoned her courage.

"He wasn't really my son, Porter," Grace said. "I mean, I adopted him, but I wasn't actually his birth mother. Glenn was married when I went to work for him. He was already going to leave his wife, but she got pregnant. She wanted an abortion when she found out about us, but it was illegal back then. So she gave birth and then walked out of the hospital. No one had any idea where she went. So I spent most of my life raising another woman's child."

"Did Gary know who his real mother was?" Porter asked, somewhat stunned.

"He found out just before he moved out for good. He tried to contact her, but she wouldn't reply. Probably because she had so much to lose."

"Why? Who is she?" Porter asked softly.

"Alice Keyser. The writer."

Jesus. Even Porter knew who Alice Keyser was.

CHAPTER SEVENTY SEVEN

Porter left Grace's and drove back to the Lair. He arrived around noon and walked into the kitchen, where was greeted with the frostiness he'd come to expect from Zaina and a lip-curling expression of disgust from Darja.

"For fuck's sake, Porter," his partner barked. "You smell like a goddamn whorehouse. Don't you have the common decency to shower before you come over here?"

Zaina shot the two of them some withering eye-daggers, shouted, "What is *wrong* with you people!" and stormed out of the kitchen.

Porter threw his head down in shame.

"Man, I'm so sorry, Darja. It's been crazy," he muttered.

"I bet it has, manwhore," Darja said, arms crossed in judgment.

Porter's attention immediately shifted to an open box of donuts on the counter. He tore into a honey-dipped and downed it in three bites. He did roughly the same with a Boston creme, and then wiped the sugar and crumbs from his mouth.

"Hey Darj, feel like taking a ride?" he said, as he popped the cap off a lukewarm coffee.

"Not 'til you wash Mama-san's stink off your balls, Richard Gere."

Freshly showered and shaved, Porter changed into one of the spare outfits he kept at the Lair, and he and Darja hit the road to go see what Alice Keyser had to say for herself.

"How's she holding up?" Darja asked as they made their way to I-93.

"She's in shock, but she knew it was coming," Porter replied.

"You realize what you're doing is totally fucked up, right?" Darja asked, pointedly.

"Listen, I never signed anything saying I couldn't do whatever I want in my own free time. And I'm in love with her, OK? Drop it."

Porter gave Darja the latest news while they drove south, about Gary not being Grace's real son and the rest. Darja was unusually silent while he spoke.

She waited a minute or two before she spoke up.

"Mind if I ask you something, Porter?" Darja said, in an unusually somber tone. "Something you may not necessarily want to hear?"

"What?"

"Don't you think there's something seriously *off* about this woman?" Darja asked. "I mean, she finds out her son is dead...."

"Adopted son," Porter interjected.

"OK, so she finds out her *adopted* son is dead, and her first impulse is to spread her legs for the guy who gave her the bad news? That seem like normal behavior to you?"

"Darja, like it or not, she's giving us information we need," Porter said.

"She's doling it out, Porter," Darja insisted. "You bone that bitch and she rewards you with another scrap, like an obedient puppy."

"Whatever gets the job done," Porter said, feeling unfairly wounded by his friend and partner.

"What job?" Darja asked, incredulously. "The guy we were supposed to find is in the fucking morgue."

"Well, then it's our job to figure out who put him there," Porter replied defiantly.

"You're fucking crazy," Darja said, shaking her head in disbelief. "You know that, don't you?"

"Then I'm in the right line of work," Porter snapped.

CHAPTER SEVENTY EIGHT

Alice Keyser was the author of the blockbuster bestseller, *He Will Live Up in the Sky*, the supposed true-life account of an alien abductee. According to Keyser, she was impregnated with a human/alien hybrid who was then stolen from her womb to go live with the space aliens. The tearful climax of the book comes as Keyser meets her young child aboard a spaceship, just as the UFOs are about to return to their home planet.

The book was made into a TV movie, despite squeals of outrage from the scientific community. It made Alice Keyser a very rich woman, and was followed by a sequel in which she claimed her husband was kidnapped and murdered by the CIA for threatening to reveal the truth about the government's involvement with the aliens.

That book made the best-seller list too, despite the fact that Keyser couldn't produce a single scrap of evidence to back any of her claims. It all felt very real to her readers, regardless. And now Porter knew why.

Porter and Darja drove up to Keyser's castle-sized home in the tony burg of Marblehead, a mansion paid for with what the pair now knew to be lies.

The bitch of it was that Keyser now had enough material for another sequel, this one ripped straight from the headlines. The abduction fad was fading from the daytime talk shows, but there was enough real mystery around Gary Sutton's death to get any producer's attention.

The fact that his very existence contradicted the premise of her first book was certainly a problem, but not one that a clever publicist couldn't paper over if it meant another bestseller.

The pair walked the long path to the front door and rang the doorbell, which sounded like it was echoing in a cathedral. Darja was expecting some kind of butler to answer but Alice Keyser herself opened the door and said, "Well, you're all here sooner than I expected."

In fact, Keyser looked more like the help than the home-owner. She was dressed in faded clamdiggers and a well-worn white cotton blouse. Her mess of grey hair was wrapped in a red bandana. She looked much older than her years and while not exactly fat, had the kind of shapeless excess poundage Darja often associated with bag ladies.

"Ms. Keyser, we're with the Special Investigations Group. I'm sure you know by now that your biological son has been declared dead," Darja said.

"Yes, I heard about it on the news," Keyser said.

"Our condolences, ma'am. We understand that you'd been in contact with him," Porter said.

"Of course. He was blackmailing me," Keyser replied bluntly. "Please, come in."

Porter and Darja followed Keyser to her living room, whose footprint was almost as big as Grace Sutton's entire house. Darja was surprised their voices didn't echo. In fact, the acoustics in here were quite good, which was lucky because Alice Keyser had a very interesting story to tell.

"The first time Gary ever called me he left a message on my machine and said it was time I faced the truth. That I'd made a fortune on the back of his misery. Gary had a real flair for melodrama, as I'm sure you've probably figured out by now."

"How did you respond?" Darja asked.

"My agent strongly advised me to give in to his demands. He said the negative publicity would destroy me. So I've been sending Gary money every month, supporting his degenerate lifestyle. How else do you think he got by? That pathetic little rock group of his?"

"So in doing this, you were essentially admitting that your books were all lies then," Darja said forcefully.

"No," Keyser replied, in a sharper tone. "I *am* a multiple abductee, I have been since I was a very young girl. You see, it's only because of the aliens that I was able to have any children at all. I was born without a uterus. That's why the aliens chose me. Gary was part of a hybrid experiment using human and alien DNA. The government was trying to stop it. The Jesuits and the Illuminati were all in on this, too. The British Royal Family, you see, needs the blood of hybrid babies. They drink it as their communion wine during their solstice rituals at Stonehenge. It gives them the demonic power they need to contact the Reptilian and Dracoid races."

Porter and Darja both suddenly realized they were talking to a full-blown psychotic. This woman had suddenly lapsed from being relatively cogent to seeming totally lost in her own nightmare world.

"My husband found out about their plans," Keyser continued. "So the Illuminists forced him to leave me and marry one of their mind-controlled sex-kitten spy-whores. A filthy little spy-whore from a bloodline of generational Satanists, cannibals and pedophiles, stretching all the way back to Atlantis; that's the kind of scummy little slut they chose to raise my beautiful hybrid baby. See, the Atlanteans were once shape-shifting Dracoids themselves, but they had lost their ability to disguise their true appearance because of the ultraviolet radiation from our sun. That's why they need hybrid blood. They always need fresh alien DNA to maintain the illusion that they're human. But I had no idea the good aliens had given Gary back because I'd been kidnapped and locked away in a mental asylum by a gang of Men-in-Black."

"Your husband, he, um, knew about this?" Porter said, utterly ineffectually. He hadn't the slightest clue how to engage with this level of madness. Darja just stared helplessly.

"Glenn was my rock, my savior," Keyser said. "He was the only one who knew the whole truth, about the aliens and the breeding program. He understood because it was his *job* to understand these things, OK? But he would still come to see me, even when he was under that dirty little tramp's thumb. Glenn told me who she really was, that she had whored for the Zionists in order to entrap men they wanted to compromise with her sexual witchcraft. He wanted to get away from her, but the little bitch said she would slit his throat if he even tried. And then she would sacrifice my baby to the evil alien races. You see, baby blood is the most powerful, because it's the purest and least polluted. So Glenn would sneak me photos of Gary, he'd bribe people to smuggle them into my cell. But the British branch of the Illuminati have eavesdropping technology you can't even imagine. The evil aliens have been seeding their technology to the Vatican and the Illuminists for years and years. You see, that's why the good aliens are breeding hybrids. They need people like Gary to fight against the evil aliens when they come to take us over at the millennium."

It seemed for a brief moment that the lucid version of Alice Keyser was struggling to poke her head through these dense storm-clouds of madness.

"I don't know why Gary thought he had to threaten me," she said, utterly despondent. "He was my only child, my baby. I would've done anything for him. I would have given him everything I have."

"Do you have any documentation of your dealings with Gary?" Darja asked, desperate to bring this pathetic woman back down to Planet Earth.

"No, I gave him blank money orders that I bought at the Post Office. But I told him all about his father, what he did for the government. The kind of man he was. How he worked on secret projects based on alien technology. Glenn was a genius with an IQ over 200 and they killed him for it. To keep the technology secret. If any of it ever got out, there would be a worldwide civil war."

"And, um, how did you end up committed to a mental hospital in the first place?" Darja asked, as if the answer weren't already screamingly obvious.

"I was found naked in a field after one of my abductions. Overseas. You see, the good aliens are from the Pleiades and they don't understand our earth-ways. They don't understand our customs, our morals. They don't understand them because they see nakedness as holy, because they aren't contaminated by original sin. They didn't realize that I would be arrested. It caused a huge scandal. So some Luciferian sodomites from British Intelligence ransacked our house and stole all my diaries, all my records of my contacts with the Pleiadeans and their prophecies of the Millennium. But that was only because I made the mistake of telling the truth to a man I later found out was a Mossad agent posing as a reporter for a British tabloid. Glenn was told in no uncertain terms that I had to be dealt with or they'd hand the both of us over to the Satanic Reptoids."

Darja softly said, "I understand," even though she hadn't understood a single, solitary word this nutcase had said.

Keyser suddenly stared at Darja as if she was seeing her for the first time and wondering how the hell these leather-clad demons got inside her house.

But the channel soon changed again, and the author returned back to her delusional confessions.

"In any event, the CIA and Mossad were furious when Glenn swore that he would stand by me. But the Illuminati, you don't say no to those people. Glenn was drugged, they had dirty movies of him with his underage whore. They had doctored photographs of him to make it look like he took part in child sacrifices to the Reptoids because his dirty teenaged skank was also a high-ranking priestess in the black magic. So they finally forced him to go along with their plan. He would marry the whore-spy and she would steal my hybrid baby. The so-called doctors were all Men-in-Black. All of them were murderers, hoodlums, criminals. They told me that I would be raped and beaten by the other patients there, just to terrify me into silence."

Porter had gone numb with this woman's ranting. How the hell was she able to keep a roof over her head, never mind a palace like this?

Someone was clearly taking care of Alice Keyser and keeping her out of the limelight. Apparently her books still sold and the TV-movie was a sleeper hit on home video. And that meant one hell of a lot of money that someone had to look after.

So there was obviously a motive and a vested interest in keeping the Alice Keyser cash-machine running smoothly, and that seemed to depend on making sure no one found out that Alice Keyser was totally insane.

The question then became, did these same people kill Gary? Did he pose some kind of danger to keeping the scam going? Porter tuned back into Keyser's oddly-literary rambling.

"The Men-in-Black finally made good on their threats. When I fought back, they'd just pump me full of drugs until I was worse than a zombie. Then they put me in a basement where I was beaten, raped and tortured thousands of times. All day long. Police, judges, lawyers, famous people. government people, movie stars; they all took turns raping and violating me."

Keyser looked as if just recounting these unbelievable horror stories was making her relive these traumas. Her eyes pleaded for these two strangers to believe her and validate the suffering that was more likely inflicted by the demons inside her own head.

"It's their religion, don't you understand? Rape and murder are sacred to them because the Reptoid aliens feed off of our fear secretions. They can't manifest on this earth plane without them."

Keyser turned and clutched her fist to her mouth, as if trying to summon the strength to continue.

Porter was afraid that she might actually have a full-scale nervous breakdown right here in front of them. Keyser may be able to use these insane fantasies as a shield for a while, but sooner or later the pressure will build to such a point that she'll simply melt down.

"Anyway, it took me a long time to remember who I even really was when they finally let me out," she finally said, utterly spent.

Porter and Darja sat in silence while Alice Keyser stared out the window, seemingly unable to acknowledge the true source of her grief; losing her son at birth, and again now in death.

"Ms. Keyser, may I ask who handles your business affairs? For your books and so on?" Porter asked softly.

"Certainly. Mitchell Kern. In Boston," Keyser replied.

Mitchell Kern. Of course.

CHAPTER SEVENTY NINE

Darja and Porter got into it the minute they backed out of Alice Keyser's driveway. They'd had to bite their tongues while the madwoman ranted about lizard-people from Uranus, but Porter felt as if he'd finally cracked this case, and gotten to the bottom of it all.

"So Gary basically wins the lottery when he finds out who his real mother is. Even better, she's completely out of her mind and can be easily manipulated," Porter said.

"Probably," Darja muttered.

"What I'm thinking is that Kern arranged all of this, the payoffs and the music career. I'm thinking Gary's career wasn't going anywhere until Kern hooked him up with Cutter's Mill and made him a local legend. All to keep his real goose laying the golden eggs," Porter surmised.

"Sounds reasonable to me," Darja replied.

Darja noted how Porter was avoiding the real scoop to emerge from Keyser's soliloquy. She could tell that maybe the accusations about Grace had gotten under his skin. It couldn't hurt to find out.

"So what do you make of all that, Porter?" Darja asked.

"What do I *make* of it? I think the woman belongs in a straitjacket. What do you make of it?"

"What about all those things she said about your new girlfriend?"

"What about them?" Porter snapped. "You think she sounded even remotely rational?"

"Probably not, but it can't hurt to look into it," Darja suggested.

"Look into what?" Porter asked incredulously. "That Grace Sutton is actually a voodoo sex-priestess from Mars?"

"No, the other stuff. The stuff about her working for a honey-trap."

"Well, for your information, I checked that out already, Darja. She actually does work for a software company."

"A legitimate one? You do know that most of them are just intelligence fronts, right?"

Porter actually didn't know that. "Well, I'm going to get an expert opinion."

"Meaning what?" Darja said.

Porter produced a small tape recorder from his inside breast pocket.

"Meaning I taped the entire interview and I'm going to play it back to Travis."

"If he ever shows up again, you mean," Darja replied, sourly.

"Right," Porter acceded. "Well, whatever. If he doesn't, I'll try and get Sam's opinion. Hell, maybe I'll even ask that Morton guy about it."

"Don't you think we should be shaking Kern down instead?" Darja asked. "The fucker held out on us."

"We have plenty of time to do both," Porter said.

• • •

Porter and Darja had returned to the Lair after picking up some Boston Market for supper. Bruehle was as keen to eat a real meal as he was to hear about their interview with Keyser, and the three of them sat down at a table covered almost entirely by takeout containers.

"All right then, you miserable bastards. Out with it, I want to hear every word that came out of that woman's lips," Bruehle said as he slathered a mound of chicken, mashed potatoes, onion rings, corn and green beans in gravy.

"Every word?" Porter said, poker-faced. "Crap. I forgot to take notes. Did you, Darja?"

"You kidding?" Darja snapped as she buttered a roll. "I wasn't going to dignify that crazy cunt's bullshit by taking notes."

"Oh, come on!" Bruehle cried petulantly. "Have you two gone insane? You have any idea how many people would cut off a limb to get a chance to pick that woman's brains?"

"Well, it was all Gary-this, blackmail-that, flying saucers-this, anal probes-that, bla-bla-bla," Darja said, eyes fixed on her plate.

"What else you need to know, Bruehlie? The bitch is cuckoo for Cocoa Puffs. Nothing she said made a damn lick of sense."

"Not to you, maybe. But you don't know the field! Goddamn it, Darja!" Bruehle protested.

"Sorry, buddy," Porter said as he sawed at a chicken breast with a flimsy plastic knife. "It didn't really seem worth the trouble."

"Yeah, sorry," Darja said, and eyed Bruehle deviously as she sucked at her straw.

Bruehle threw his fork down in disgust, sat back in his chair, crossed his arms and stared angrily at Darja and Porter.

"Oh, but there was one thing, I think..." Porter said

"What? What one thing?" Bruehle asked, brightening a bit.

Porter got up and went to the coat rack. He carefully retrieved his micro-recorder and cupped it in his hand before sitting back down at the table.

"OK, Bruehle, listen. Darja and I are very sorry for not taking notes. The truth is we never planned to."

"Huh? What do you mean?" Bruehle said, incredulously.

"We never planned to take notes..." Porter said, and then arced his arm above his head and dramatically placed the micro-recorder in front of Bruehle. "Because I decided to tape the entire interview instead."

"Oh, Jesus Lord, you two total-fucking reprobates!" Bruehle said, his face aglow.

He picked up the recorder and wagged a scolding finger at Darja and Porter. "I'm getting you back for this one, you evil little sluts. You just wait."

CHAPTER EIGHTY

Bruehle pressed play on the tape recorder, and they all ate their supper accompanied by the dulcet tones of Alice Keyser's madcap ranting. Zaina had come in to listen, and Darja noticed she perked up now and then at certain buzzwords. Bruehle, for his part, hung on Keyser's every word. It was as if every unhinged theory he'd read on USENET was now being validated by this disturbed and lonely woman.

Porter heard his cell phone ring and realized it was still in his jacket pocket. He went over to the rack, fetched the phone, and answered it.

"Porter, it's Soares. You people were looking at a music promoter in connection with that dead singer, right?"

"Yeah. What you got?" Porter asked.

"Well, now I got a dead music promoter, still sitting at his desk inside the Boylston Grove. Or at least his remains are. And I also got a nasty arson fire and an evacuated office building to boot."

"What else do you have, Sergeant?"

"You should be asking what your friend Kern has," Soares said. "He's got a tiny little hole in the back of his head, and a great big hole in the front. So it looks like someone did the guy execution-style, then torched his filing cabinets too. The sprinklers did their work, but someone obviously wanted his records gone. And I don't mean his gold records."

"What about the staff?" Porter asked.

"Out to lunch for a birthday party. Lucky for them."

"You giving any of this to the press?"

"Oh, hell no," Soares scoffed. "As far as the good people of Boston are concerned, he died of smoke inhalation. So what I need from you is any information we could use on this."

"In all honesty, I don't know anything about it. We were actually going to go out to see him tomorrow."

"About what?" Soares asked.

"About the fact that Kern was not only Gary Sutton's manager, he was Gary's real mother's agent."

"Whoa, back up, back up. What are you talking about?"

"Gary Sutton's actual birth mother is Alice Keyser, the author," Porter said. "Gary was blackmailing Keyser and Kern told her to give Gary the money."

"Wait, wait. Why was Gary Sutton blackmailing this woman again?" Soares asked.

"She wrote a best-seller about how Gary was some kind of alien experiment, and that after he was born the aliens took him back to their home world," Porter said.

"OK, but this is a science fiction book, right?"

"Well, technically. But she sold it as a true story."

"When did you find all this out, Porter?" Soares asked.

"Well, we found out that Alice Keyser was Gary's real mother this morning, then we went to see her in Marblehead, where she told us the rest."

"OK, so let's establish a timeline here, Porter," Soares said. "Someone tells you this morning that this big-name client of Mitchell Kern's was secretly the mother of another one of Mitchell Kern's clients who got murdered, and then Mitchell Kern gets flash-fried in his office a few hours later? Who told you about all of this?"

"His stepmother."

"And who did you tell?" Soares asked.

"Just Darja," Porter said, in a near whisper.

"Who's the stepmother? That Grace Sutton woman?"

"Yeah."

Silence.

"Porter, do you remember that discussion we had about keeping our lines of communication open?" Soares finally asked.

"I know, Sergeant. It's just that we've been running around trying to get on top of this."

"OK. Here's my problem, Porter; this isn't just one murder now, it's two. And it's looking very much like a conspiracy to commit murders of prominent local citizens. And now you tell me that you've been sitting all day on a very solid motive, not only for Sutton's murder, but now for Kern's. This is totally unacceptable, do you understand that?"

"I know. I'm sorry, Sergeant."

"Never mind 'sorry,' Porter," Soares said, clearly very angry yet still calm as ever. "Consider this your second warning. Next time you pull this shit on me, I'm going to arrest you, your partner and your boss for obstruction of justice."

"I understand," Porter said, miserably contrite.

"From now on, you call me first whenever you hear anything relating to these murders, OK? Not Bob Travis. Not the Joint Chiefs of Staff. Not the Vatican College of Cardinals. Me."

Soares hung up without saying goodbye.

"What the fuck was that all about?" Darja hissed, arms locked tightly across her chest.

"It's about you and I going to prison if we don't start keeping Soares up to date about this case."

"What was the first part, Porter? What did he call about?"

"Yeah. Well, he said someone offed Mitchell Kern at his desk and then torched his office."

Darja glowered at Porter with what looked very much like actual hatred as she got up from the table. She grabbed her jacket and stormed out the door.

Porter knew exactly what she was thinking. He was actually starting to think it himself.

CHAPTER EIGHTY ONE

Porter stood in the clammy and badly-lit waiting room outside the morgue at Carney Hospital, waiting for the medical examiner to arrive.

Carney was a charmless, sprawling mound of concrete and glass that straddled the border of the gritty Boston borough of Dorchester and the upscale hamlet of Milton Village, where George Bush was born.

They had an appointment to view Gary's body at 1:30, and it was now ten to two. Darja was still clearly pissed off at Porter, so he kept a wide berth from her. Grace and Katie both sat and fretted beneath a silent television. Soares had accompanied them but had wandered off to find out where the examiner was.

Porter was checking his watch when his cellphone rang. It was Sam.

"Porter, I need to speak with you. In person," Sam said.

"OK, I'm at the morgue at Carney Hospital now," Porter replied. "Can you meet me here?"

"I'm actually at Carney right now as well," Sam said.

"Well, come on down, then."

"I'd rather not. This is a time for the family. My presence might bring back too many bad memories for Gary's mother."

"Well, what would you like to do?" Porter asked.

"I have an office here, in the psychiatric wing. Go on up to reception and I'll have someone bring you to me," Sam advised.

Peter went and spoke softly in Grace's ear. "I have to go talk to someone. I'll be back in a bit."

"Where are you going, Porter?" Grace asked, her voice slightly panicked at the prospect of viewing Gary's corpse without Porter.

"Not far," Porter said, reassuringly. "You've got some paper-work you have to deal with, anyway. I won't be long, I promise."

Porter went up to Sam's office to update him on what he'd learned since they last spoke. He told Sam about the data Grace Sutton had been giving him as well Alice Keyser, her connection to Mitchell Kern, and how Keyser was in fact Gary's biological mother. And he finally forced himself to confess that he'd been sleeping with Grace.

"What do you think?" Porter asked.

"I really don't know what to think, to tell you the truth," Sam sighed heavily, as he leaned back in his chair.

"You had no idea about Keyser's connection to Gary?"

"I didn't even think to look. Why would I? If all of this went on in England, it would be very hard to look up here. We're talking the days when a mimeograph machine was high-tech in this business. I don't think most hospitals over there would have gotten any kind of computers until at least the mid-70s."

"Well, I was referring to your other line of work, Doc," Porter said, more bluntly than he intended.

"Oh, no. I had no reason to doubt... well, Gary never said anything about Alice Keyser being his real mother at all. He did have those books, though, that I do remember. But he had a lot of those kinds of books. There were quite a few out at the time."

"Is it possible that none of this is true?" Porter asked. "That Gary and this Keyser woman and Gary's adoptive mother are all lost in some collective delusion over the disappearance of Gary's father?"

"I do know of cases where a loved one's disappearance can drive people insane," Sam replied. "Is it possible here? I suppose so. Is it likely? I don't think so. Gary's father was involved in very sensitive work. Based on what you told me, I think the mother — the *birth* mother — began showing symptoms of paranoid-schizophrenia in her mid-twenties and that became a major problem for the people he worked for. And that would have become a major distraction for Glenn Sutton. It looks like they found him a new wife to care for his son and very quietly put the old one out of harm's way. You said she was hospitalized?"

"Alice Keyser told me that they threw her in an English asylum for several years and then paid to keep her quiet about it when she got out."

"Who's her publisher again?" Sam asked.

"Bluestone," Porter said.

"Ahh, yes. That's definitely a CIA shop. I actually prepped with the guy who runs it. Nice guy. Hell of a tennis player."

"So basically you're saying that the CIA is Alice Keyser's publisher, Sam?"

"Publisher? Hell, they probably wrote the books for her. There was a lot of concern at the time about the Soviets somehow making use of all the alien abduction stuff, so they poisoned the well with a bunch of disinformation. By the time they were finished, most people were put off the topic. But you're obviously more worried about Grace Sutton and not Alice Keyser, correct?"

"Do you think what Keyser says about Grace is true?" Porter asked sullenly.

"I really don't think that Central would let someone with those types of skills run off to go play suburban housewife, Porter. It's actually a lot harder than you might imagine finding good people to work those operations. But then again, the CIA were pretty good matchmakers. It's one of the reasons they were so successful with the early computer-dating services. My guess is they simply let Grace distract Sutton while they solved the problem of his wife."

"Well, that would certainly explain a lot about her reaction to Gary's death."

"Don't be too hard on her, Porter. She's had a very difficult life."

"Do you think she ever loved Glenn Sutton?"

"I'm not sure I can answer that, Porter. I really don't know her well enough to judge. The fact that she stuck around so long after his death to raise his son certainly speaks to some kind of devotion on her part. What you really want to know is if she loves you, if she's even capable of it."

Porter looked down at his hands and said nothing.

"Let me just say this, son; it might be wise to put a little daylight between yourself and this woman. Gary's case is closed and you're wading into some very murky waters now. Women like Grace Sutton are experts at luring men into their webs. I've got no reason to doubt her sincerity, but I can see the effect this is having on you and I think it may be best if you make a clean break."

"By the way, how did you know Gary's body was being held here, Doc? Did you get called in on this?" Porter asked.

Sam smiled sagely then said, "Let's just say it's my job to know these things, Porter. After all, Gary Sutton was officially still my patient."

CHAPTER EIGHTY TWO

A tall, thin, graying middle-aged man with tired, dark eyes greeted the group at the door of the viewing room. He introduced himself simply as 'the ME.' Darja wondered if he got those eyes from seeing so much death. She almost expected to hear him sound like Boris Karloff, but he came across as mild, pleasant, and thoughtful.

"You're here for the boy who washed up at Tenean, I take it," the ME said.

"Yeah, we brought his stepmother and his girlfriend along to make positive ID," Darja said. "We just wanted to have a look first, just so we can prepare them for what they're about to see."

The ME's dark eyes looked regretful. "I think that's probably a good idea. The body is in pretty tough shape," he said.

The ME lifted the nylon sheet on the grisly remains of Gary Sutton. His long dreadlocks had been tied back with a piece of red ribbon, given him a weirdly ragdoll-like look. His body looked oddly inflated, as if half-filled with air. There were ugly purple gouges all over his body, leaving the impression that passing sea-life had been snacking on his flesh.

"Doc, why is he all bloated like that?" Porter asked.

"He'd been in the water a while. That's what happens."

Soares grimaced as he noticed a big chunk of the side of Gary's face was missing.

"Looks like a hollow point, execution style," Soares observed.

"Looks like," the ME concurred. "Our prelim has all the damage you see there happening before he went into the water."

"His skin color is very weird," Darja noted, pointing at splotches of greenish-pink and greenish-purple.

"Yeah, that's a real mystery," the ME replied.

"Any theories?" Porter asked.

"Maybe some chemical agent, something leaching from a boat the body came in contact with," the ME mused. "The Harbor is still a mess, even now. All kinds of nasty things floating around out there."

"How did you ID this as Gary?" Darja asked.

"From photos his manager sent us," the ME said. "We were able to make a positive match based on the tattoos," pointing to small tribal designs Gary had on his shoulders and upper arms.

"Why don't we bring Grace and Katie in so we can get a positive ID," Porter said finally.

Katie entered the morgue and looked at the body for a few moments.

She then stepped back and pointed gravely at it, as if the very sight of it deeply offended her.

"That... that's not him," she whispered in horror.

"What do you mean?" Soares said.

"I mean *that's not Gary*," Katie hissed.

"How do you know?" Soares asked.

Katie seemed on the verge of hyperventilation, her face contorted in horror and disgust. After a few minutes, she finally forced herself to calm down and explain.

"About a year ago, there was a fight onstage at a show in Hartford. Gary got buried underneath a bunch of guys. Only there was a broken beer bottle underneath his left arm. He needed forty-two stitches to close the wound. It was the most disgusting thing I'd ever seen in my life. He needed a transfusion to replace all the blood he lost. It's why he always wore long sleeves onstage; he was embarrassed by the scar."

"Did you know about this, Grace?" Porter asked.

"His mother paid for it all," Katie sneered, with palpable disdain.

Grace winced at the dig.

"And there are records of this?" Soares pressed.

"I can show you *photos* of it," Katie sneered.

"Doctor, would being in the water like that somehow obscure the scar?" Soares asked.

"Actually, it would make it more pronounced," the ME replied. "Scar tissue tends to expand when the skin bloats."

"Do you see any evidence of a major scar or surgery on his left arm?"

"No, none," the ME said.

"Doctor, this is part of a classified investigation," Soares said, fixing a serious gaze on the man.

"Please don't discuss this case with anyone else. And please make sure no one is allowed access to this corpse to anyone unless they talk to me first."

The ME simply said, "Understood," and walked away.

Soares then took Katie back to a halfway house in Weymouth, where she was undergoing a court-ordered detox. Darja gave Porter a weary look when he told her he'd meet her back at the Lair.

Porter and Grace left Carney together and departed for her house. Grace was silent for a while, her brow furrowed. Porter snuck glances at her as he navigated the city streets, scanning for the onramp.

"How can this be?" she finally asked.

"I don't know," Porter said.

"It looks like him, but it's not him. I recognize those tattoos. How is it not him?"

"I can't say."

"Can't or won't?" Grace said, sharply.

"I can't. I have no idea what we're dealing with here."

"It's evil, whatever it is," Grace said. "What if the crazy old bat was right?"

"What do you mean? Alice Keyser?"

Grace nodded and said, "What if Gary really is up there? With them?"

CHAPTER EIGHTY THREE

While Porter and Darja were headed south to ID Gary Sutton's body, Bruehle was headed north to talk with Mac Cullen again. Cullen had e-mailed Bruehle under a fake name and dropped a number of cryptic hints before actually identifying himself.

Once open contact was made again, Cullen told Bruehle that there was someone he needed Bruehle to talk to, but only on the condition that the rest of the group not be involved.

Bruehle arrived at Cullen's cabin shortly before noon. The elevation wasn't exactly alpine here, but it still made Bruehle a bit light-headed. He knocked on the door and waited. It swung open as he was about to knock again, and Cullen peered out, his face etched with fear. He looked past Bruehle to the long driveway, scanned the trees behind Bruehle's car and finally looked his guest in the eyes.

"Come in," Cullen said, and locked the door after Bruehle entered.

"What's all this about, Mr. Cullen? Is everything OK here?" Bruehle asked.

No sooner did he speak than a face emerged from the shadows. It was a pretty but pale and drawn face, hazel eyes and full lips framed by long ringlets of brown hair. The face belonged to a petite young woman, dressed in a sleeveless 'Sonic Youth' t-shirt and ripped blue jeans.

"And who are you?" Bruehle asked, slightly taken aback by this surprise appearance.

"This is Gina, Mr. Bruehle," Cullen explained. "She's the one who introduced Gary Sutton to Cutter's Mill."

The young woman nodded at Bruehle.

"OK, pleased to meet you, Gina," Bruehle said. "Could you tell me how exactly you happened to arrange that?"

Gina spoke softly and chose her words slowly and deliberately, "I was dating their drummer at the time. Warren."

"Warren Cortese? Quattro?" Bruehle asked.

"Yeah," Gina whispered.

"And how did you know Gary Sutton?" Bruehle pressed.

"We went to school together. Gary, me and Kevin," Gina replied.

"What school was that?" Bruehle asked.

"It was called Sunshine People School," Gina said.

Bruehle stepped backwards, slightly staggered by this information.

Mac Cullen gestured to an area with a couple of futons and said, "Tell you what; why don't we all just sit down and relax? I'll put some fresh coffee on."

Bruehle, Cullen and Gina sat in the living room area of the cabin and sipped at their coffees. Gina had brightened up a bit but still seemed very, very nervous.

"Gina, could you tell me how long you were at Sunshine?" Bruehle asked gently.

"The whole time," she replied. "From kindergarten to eighth grade. They closed the school before I could advance to the high school classes."

"So how well did you know Gary? From what I understand he was only there for a year."

"No, that's wrong," Gina said. "He was there the whole time too. But Kevin didn't start coming until he was in fifth grade."

Bruehle mulled this over for a moment then asked, "How well did you know Gary, then? Were the boys and girls segregated?"

"No. Actually, I was paired with Gary for the last few years there."

"Paired? Paired how?" Bruehle asked.

"They selected students to pair up. I forget exactly why," Gina said. "They had us do all the activities with our partners, all the tests and the experiments."

"Was it all a boy-girl thing, these pairs?"

"No, not really," Gina said. "It was based on all these compatibility tests we had to take. I have no idea why they paired me with Gary or why they paired anyone else, really. There's a lot that was never explained."

"So you were very close then," Bruehle suggested.

"You could say that, yeah. I lost my virginity to Gary when I was twelve. That was one of the so-called 'experiments' they ran. Quite a lot by that point, actually. It was all videotaped."

Bruehle shuddered. He knew where that particular road was going and decided to get off it.

"Can you describe what your day was usually like there?" he asked.

"It was very, very hectic. We did, like, two hours of exercises every morning. Jumping jacks, push-ups, stuff like that. All the classes together, even the really small kids. We played a lot of soccer. We probably could have beaten any school in the state. Then we'd do another two or three hours of musical practice."

"Musical practice? What kind of practice?" Bruehle said.

"Classical music. We were trained on different instruments. I played viola, Gary played cello and Kevin played bassoon. It was really intense. I hated it. I get nauseous when-ever I hear that kind of music now."

"Were you ever told why you had to do this, Gina?" Bruehle asked.

Gina shot a glance at Cullen, silently imploring him to bail her out.

"From what I've been told, the working hypothesis there was that psychic powers are linked somehow to sound waves, Mr. Bruehle," Cullen said. "The faculty seemed to believe that the most effective psychics had keenly-developed hearing and senses of pitch. A lot of the work they were doing used sonics, radar, ULF, ELF, Faraday cages, things like that."

Bruehle nodded and said, "OK, so two hours of exercise and three hours of musical training. What about academics?"

"They did some classes, I guess regular school stuff," Gina answered. "But that kind of dipped off after a while. The experiments kind of took over. And they got really bad with all of it towards the end. I kind of got the feeling that we weren't giving them the results they were looking for. So the instructors started doing really bad stuff to us."

"What kind of bad stuff, exactly?" Bruehle asked, only to be answered by a silent glare.

Cullen cut in again. "Gina is an experiencer, Mr. Bruehle. Just like Gary."

"Is that true, Gina?" Bruehle asked.

"Yes," she said meekly, staring into her coffee. "We all were."

"Gina, Gary claimed he was first abducted at his house coming home from school in third grade. Did he mean from Sunshine?"

"No, he wouldn't go home after school from there," Gina said. "We didn't really ever leave Sunshine. There were parents' days where they could come and visit. But we never went home on break or anything. It was like prison. Worse."

"So that story wasn't true then?" Bruehle asked.

"Gary was a world-class liar. He lied about everything. All the time. You never knew what was up or down with that kid," Gina explained.

"Gina, do you mind if I ask what your parents do? Do for work, I mean," Bruehle inquired.

"My mom and my dad were in the Army. All of the kids at Sunshine had parents that worked for the government in one way or another," Gina explained.

"Gina, I don't know how much you know about Kevin's situation at present, but we have reason to believe Kevin is being manipulated by some kind of remote control technology," Bruehle stated. "Do you know anything about that?"

"No, but I knew they were doing a lot of tests with remote influencing at the school. Do you know about Becky Hadley?" Gina asked.

"No, who's that?" Bruehle asked.

"That's kind of a big local story in Massachusetts, Mr. Bruehle," Cullen interjected. "A girl came home on break and killed her mother and father then went and killed another man in another town. The girl's father was an executive for a major pharmaceutical outfit. So was the other man she killed. From what I've heard both men were going to turn state's evidence against a new antidepressant the company was developing."

"Why were they going to do that?" Bruehle asked.

"Nobody knows, the whole thing disappeared from the news once those facts came out," Cullen said.

"Becky was a couple years behind Gary and me," Gina revealed. "I know for a fact she was part of those experiments."

Bruehle changed course again. "So what about Quattro, Gina? How did you meet him?"

"I met him at a Lemonheads show in Albany."

"Really? That doesn't seem like his kind of music," Bruehle said.

"He was working with the opening band," Gina explained. "He was their drum roadie."

"What band was this, Gina?"

"I don't remember. I think they were also from Boston, though," she answered.

"When was this? What year, I mean?" Bruehle asked.

"It was 1988. He just came up and started talking to me out of nowhere. Plus, he was with the band. Took me backstage and then to a party at the motel they were all staying at."

"So you were what, 18?"

"Still 17 then, actually," Gina said. "I had a fake ID."

"So you met Quattro in 1988, then," Bruehle said as he tried running the numbers. "Our information has it that he moved down south at some point between then and joining Cutter's Mill."

"Yeah, Tampa. I spent some time with him there, but I was trying to get my degree. So I moved back. He got back in touch when he came to Boston and we went on and off for a while. But he had changed a lot. He was into all this weird shit."

"Occult kind of stuff, you mean?"

"Yeah, occult stuff." Gina replied. "Drug stuff. Weird sex stuff. He was getting into group-sex, bondage, shit like that. Hung around with a bunch of freaks who thought they were vampires. I didn't go for that kind of thing. He also wasn't around a lot. Never told me where he was."

"I'm told you broke up with him late last year," Bruehle noted.

"Yeah, but we weren't really a thing by that point. He was too busy fucking all those disgusting skanks who follow that stupid band around. They're all sick in the head."

"Who is?" Bruehle asked. "The band or the groupies?"

"All of them," Gina explained. "They're all totally messed up. Gary had really turned into a major asshole. His girlfriend started doing a lot of heroin and whoring herself out. Those two thought they were the new Sid and Nancy or something, just a total cliche. I'm just surprised they didn't end up killing each other. Well, maybe she ended up killing him, I don't know."

"So what about Sunshine, Gina? Did you and Gary ever discuss that at all?" Bruehle asked.

"Gary acted like he never knew me once he joined that band. I think he was embarrassed by me."

"Why would he be embarrassed, Gina?"

"I don't know. He was trying to pretend he never went to Sunshine. It's not something to be proud of, really. The rest of the band weren't down with his UFO trip at all. Then Kevin got arrested and Gary cut all ties with him. That's just the way the guy was. Ruthless."

"Do you know a Doctor Sanderson, Gina? A doctor who might have worked there?"

"No, I don't recognize that name. I never knew who anybody there was. The teachers never gave us their last names. Most of them made us refer to them by their rank, like Sergeant Joe or Lieutenant Jane. Stuff like that. But they didn't wear uniforms or anything."

Bruehle reached into his travel bag and took his IBM laptop out. Cullen and Gina sat and watched as he fiddled around for a bit. Bruehle finally presented the computer to Gina. Onscreen was a gallery Bruehle made of the Polaroids Porter had gotten from Grace Sutton.

"Gina, do you recognize any of these kids? Any of them look familiar to you at all?"

Gina pointed to a very young girl and said, "That one does."

Bruehle clicked on the thumbnail, and a familiar face filled the screen.

A small girl held a card that read, *'Regina- Lot 7301.'*

Gina pointed to the screen and said, "That's me."

CHAPTER EIGHTY FOUR

Porter had a lot of work to do but Grace beckoned him back into bed again. Had he not been so frazzled, Porter may have thought twice about what Darja would say about the grotesquely inappropriate timing of having sex with a woman who just ID'd her stepson's body.

But he figured this day had been some time in coming for her and that she might not see much of a future for the two of them once all this was over. She was a middle-aged woman who had lost her entire family now, and didn't have a lot of opportunities left to start a new one.

Grace was needy to the point of actual violence. She clutched Porter so tight to her chest he had to lift himself away just to breathe. She was physically strong and made Porter feel as if he were wrestling with a python. But it wasn't love anymore. It barely counted as sex.

When it was over the two lay on their backs as always, panting and drenched in sweat. Grace's brow was deeply furrowed, and she seemed to be silently rehearsing a speech in her mind.

She stared hard at the ceiling and seemed to be mentally counting down to a new revelation. Then it came.

"I worked for them, Porter," Grace said, clutching a handful of comforter to her breasts.

"What do you mean?" he said, genuinely puzzled.

"I didn't meet Glenn Sutton by chance. I was an operative. I worked for an outfit in Boston before I met him."

"Outfit? What do you mean, 'outfit?'"

"What you might call a honey-trap outfit. Blackmail. Stuff like that," Grace said blankly.

Porter was struck dumb. His throat began to close up.

"I grew up in Maine, out in the woods, Porter. Real *Deliverance* kind of country," she confessed. "My mother died of breast cancer when I was a freshman in high school. I was an only child. My father was a heavy drinker and he started taking his grief out on me. I ran away when I turned fifteen and came down here. I lied about my age and got a job at the makeup counter at Remick's in Quincy Center. I lived with this college girl over a bakery in East Milton Square. Her boyfriend was an older guy who used to come over all the time, and after a while he started talking to me. He'd tell me how pretty I was, how mature I was for my age. Then it turns out this college girl didn't actually go to college and her boyfriend was on the hook with some Federal agency or another. He ran a prostitution ring that specialized in servicing the local politicians. It was an intelligence gathering operation, I'm not exactly sure who it was for, but they were thrilled when I told them I was underage. The hotel rooms were all bugged, there were cameras, everything. Boston politicians were easy marks, most of them were hopeless drunks who couldn't keep it in their pants. Now and then someone would bust in, tell some poor bastard the girl he was screwing was a minor and get him under their thumbs forever."

Porter's heart sunk. Alice Keyser had been telling the truth about Grace after all. At least in part.

"So, what about Glenn Sutton?" Porter asked, dreading the answer.

"They were very worried about his wife."

"Who's 'they?'" Porter asked.

"The men he worked for. Alice was a mess, Porter. Just a total, ranting, raving mess. She'd been abusing prescription diet pills, painkillers, booze, everything, for years. When they moved to England she started fucking everyone she could get her hands on; men, women, school children, street people. Talk was she even started bothering the neighbor's dog."

Porter snorted with involuntary laughter.

"Seriously! Glenn was humiliated, mortified. Finally, she ended up getting arrested for indecent exposure and child endangerment when she was found sleeping naked in a school playground. I mean, she was just an absolute train-wreck."

Grace paused, then added, "I suppose you'd call it bipolar these days. But Glenn's work was extremely sensitive. The people he worked for couldn't afford a scandal. I was looking to get out of the game, so they sent me over there to work in his division and I was told to... do what I do. They rewrote my entire history, made me a college graduate. Changed my name, my birthdate, my family, my Social Security number, everything."

"So you weren't 26 when you met him."

"No," Grace scoffed. "I'd only just turned 18, Porter."

"And what year was this?" Porter asked.

"1970. Just after Gary was born."

Jesus. Well, there's one mystery explained at least, Porter thought. She doesn't look like she's in her early 50s because she's only 42.

"But I fell in love with him, Porter," Grace said. "So, so much in love. Glenn was brilliant, an actual genius. I mean, he was an expert in... everything. He could hold down a conversation with anyone on any topic you could think of; science, politics, sports, movies, cooking. Everything."

She frowned, as if she'd had a new and painful realization.

"Gary inherited his charisma from Glenn, but not his intellect. I think his mother's drug abuse badly affected Gary in the womb. Gary always struggled in school and Glenn just couldn't understand it. It was his one blind spot. He just didn't have the patience to understand his son. I think Gary was dyslexic, but he was never diagnosed. But his genius was creative, from a very early age. Especially the music; he could play any instrument you could think of. That's something else Glenn didn't want to acknowledge."

"So how did it work out with the CIA and your marriage?" Porter asked.

"When we came back here, they would send someone over to talk about Glenn, usually once a month. The questions could get very... intimate. They were worried that his ex-wife's problems would, I don't know, rub off on him or something. They wanted to know if Glenn was drinking too much, if he looked at pornography, if he ever dressed in women's clothing, if he liked kinky stuff in bed, things like that. Anything that might possibly open him up to blackmail. That went on until he disappeared."

"Did they send different people, or did you have a handler?" Porter asked.

"I wouldn't necessarily call him a handler, but I did usually report to the same person. He was a doctor, a psychiatrist from Boston. He was very nice."

Porter's stomach did a cartwheel.

"This doctor's name wouldn't happen to have been Sanderson, would it?"

"Yes. How did you...?" Grace said, seemingly taken aback.

Porter got up and stepped into his shorts. He dressed briskly.

"I have to go," he said.

"Porter? What is it? What's the matter?"

"There's someone I need to speak with," Porter added curtly, then stormed out of the bedroom.

"Porter! Come back!" Grace called out as the front door slammed behind him.

CHAPTER EIGHTY FIVE

Porter dialed Sam's direct line as he pulled out of Grace's driveway and craned his neck to hold the cellphone while he drove.

"Porter," Sam asked cheerfully. "What can I do for you, son?"

"Well, you can start by explaining why I had to find out from Grace Sutton that in fact you were her handler when she was set up to spy on Gary's father. Then you can explain why you never told me you were a consultant for Sunshine People School."

The line went quiet.

"What do you want me to tell you, Porter?" Sam finally asked.

"I want you to tell me what's really going on with this case," Porter said. "It's all starting to feel like it's all a big joke a bunch of old spies are playing on each other."

"It's no joke, Porter," Sam said, more than a bit disappointed in this turn of events.

"You know what I think? I think there's a lot of whacked-out, hoodoo-mumbo-jumbo garbage going on out there," Porter added. "I think all you people are mental cases and have way too much money and technology at your disposal. I think Grace Sutton is some kind of crazy sex machine that you people placed in my path, for what possible reason, I haven't a clue. But I think she still works for you, and I think you and Travis are running some kind of evil CIA mind-control experiment out there."

Silence.

"You hear me?" Porter snapped.

"Porter, I'm going to be frank with you," Sam said, still trying to sound fatherly but sounding a bit less so now. "You've been poking around a lot of areas that a lot of very powerful people would rather you all leave be. And yes, I have kept information from you. Quite a lot of information, in fact. I've had to, Porter, because you simply don't have the proper clearance to know about certain things."

"Yeah? And what about that school?" Porter snapped.

"Yes, I did consult at Sunshine People School when they first opened," Sam said wearily.

"But a lot of doctors did, Porter. They were talking to quite a lot of people at the time. To be perfectly honest, I didn't even remember doing so when you brought it up. And that was well before the MK programs were put into place. But I had nothing to do with any of that. I didn't even hear about it until after the school was shut down. As to Grace Sutton's claims, I honestly have no earthly idea what that woman is talking about, Porter. The only time I've ever spoken to Grace Sutton was during Gary's hospitalizations. And that's all, I swear to you. On my children's lives, I swear to you."

Porter was silent.

"You hearing me, Porter?" Sam said.

Silence.

"Porter, I'll come to New Hampshire tomorrow and we can clear this all up, OK?"

Porter pressed the 'end' button and tossed the cellphone over his shoulder into the back seat.

CHAPTER EIGHTY SIX

The four sat at the kitchen table, nursing tall cups of coffee and ignoring a platter of buttered croissants. A pale sun peeked through the dirty windows, heralding the start of another bleak New Hampshire morning.

Then came the faint sound of tires on gravel, then confident footfalls on the concrete back stairs. Sam came in, wearing a wool overcoat with a fur collar, leather driving gloves and a trilby hat. He stopped, put his hat on the counter, peeled off his gloves and took a seat.

"Listen, before we get started here, I just need to clear the air. As I told Porter yesterday, there are things you haven't been told. And there's a very good reason for that, OK? Despite what you may think, officially speaking you all are working for a private contractor, not the Federal government. That's important to remember. There are things I and Bob are simply not allowed to tell you about. We could be held in violation of our secrecy oaths if certain facts ever leaked out. That means *prison*, people. I'm truly sorry it has to be that way, but I don't make the rules. Do we understand each other here?"

The four either nodded or muttered their assent, but without much enthusiasm.

"Good. Thank you. I appreciate it," Sam said. "Has Bob called in today?"

"Who knows?" Porter said tartly.

"We haven't heard from him at for a few days now, sir," Zaina said, in a worried tone.

"OK, then what do you have?" Sam asked.

"I'll tell you what we don't have; Gary Sutton," Porter said as he crushed his coffee cup and tossed it into the wastebasket.

Darja finally piped up: "But we do have a body in a morgue that looks like Gary Sutton but is not Gary Sutton. We have Gary Sutton popping up all around the state of Massachusetts like a bad penny. We have half of Gary Sutton's band getting themselves sliced to ribbons in their practice room. We have a girl who was either sleepwalking in a swamp or partying in the Twilight Zone with Keebler elves from Mars.

And we have a dangerous psychotic who looks like Frankenstein's monster running around doing God-knows-what to God-knows-who. And oh, yeah; we have a death cult that's also a Fortune 500 company. Other than that? We got nothing."

"Well, I can say Bob has been working to get some capable viewers," Sam said, trying to sound reassuring. "I'm sure that's why he's been hard to reach. He may still be out of the country."

"In the meantime?" Zaina asked.

"In the meantime, I don't think Apophis is going to make any more moves against the team."

"Well, that's comforting," Darja said sardonically.

"Well, what about Loroles?" Zaina asked.

Darja thought Zaina must really be worried about Travis, because she was being so uncharacteristically forceful with Sam.

"Believe me, you've earned your wings on that account," Sam said. "We'd had some extremely vague intel on Loroles' possible activities but this case has forced them to show their hand. We had no idea prior to this just how deep in the black they were."

"So what do we do about this swamp girl?" Porter asked.

"Let Bob worry about it," Sam answered. "He may want to monitor her. In fact, my guess is that he probably will. It's not your problem anymore. Apophis won't make another move on her. She's damaged goods to them now. My advice is that you stay focused on the Sutton case."

"What Sutton case?" Darja spat. "There is no Sutton case. I think Gary Sutton is off sipping margaritas on the beach in Jamaica, laughing his ass off at us."

"Darja, you need to adjust the way you look at this assignment," Sam replied in a mildly reproachful voice. "You're not a cop. You're thinking like a cop, tracking down a fugitive. That's not your job. You are here to gather intelligence for Bob. And you're all doing a marvelous job at it. Absolutely marvelous. The board thinks so. Bob thinks so. It's why he's not here, micro-managing your every move. He trusts all of you."

"So... Gary," Darja said, completely disinterested in everything Sam just told her.

"You have to accept that you're not in control of the situation," Sam said, his impatience slowly rising. "You can't pro-act, only react. It's the nature of the beast. Either way it's clear that this case is most definitely worth the team's attention."

"So what if we never find him? Or if he turns up dead for real?" Zaina asked.

Darja realized she was asking about Gary, but may also have meant Travis.

"Then you hand off all the data you've collected and move onto the next assignment," Sam said. "Bob doesn't want to arrest Gary Sutton; he wants to have him tested to determine if he might possess certain abilities that might be useful to certain parties. But if Gary Sutton is out there somewhere and doesn't want to be found, there's really nothing more we can do about it."

CHAPTER EIGHTY SEVEN

Darja and Porter had stopped at a rest area on the Mass Pike. Darja's anger at Porter had eased considerably, but not yet evaporated. Porter called to check in with Bruehle, then he and Darja hit the Dunkin's kiosk to satisfy their caffeine replenishment needs.

They were sitting at a table in the outside courtyard enjoying the seasonably-warm, beautiful afternoon when Porter's cellphone rang.

"Yeah," Porter said.

"It's Quattro, man. Warren Cortese. From Cutter's Mill? I want to turn myself in."

"Why? Did you kill Gary, Quattro?" Porter asked, his bullshit detector suddenly firing up.

"No, man!" Quattro pleaded. "Listen, I'll tell you everything, I just need to get off the streets."

"Are you near a police station? You can wait for us there."

"No, man, I'm down the Cape," Quattro explained. "I don't have a car. Somebody's trying to kill me."

"Who?" Porter replied.

"Listen, it wasn't me, man. OK? It was these cult guys, they call themselves 'Apophis.' They killed everybody else and now they're coming for me! I think one of our songs set them off or something. You got no idea how crazy those motherfuckers are, man. They got no problem killing cops. Actually, a lot of these dudes *are* cops, man."

"We'll come get you. Where are you now?"

"I'm at the State Beach, near Wellfleet," Quattro said. "I'm hiding out in the fucking marsh, man."

"We'll be there in a couple hours."

"Hurry, will ya, man? I don't have a gun. I don't have a tent. I don't even have a sleeping bag, dude."

"We'll be there. Just hold on," Porter said and hung up.

Quattro hung up the payphone at the snack bar, which was still closed for the season along with the beach itself. He placed his head down on the hood of the payphone and took a deep breath.

His biggest concern now was what he would do for the next two hours until the two investigators showed up.

Quattro turned around to see two very-imposing, stern-faced men in black Adidas track suits standing behind him. One was black, the other white, but otherwise they could have been twins. Heads shaved clean, soul patches, weird piercings and rings. They both looked like the kinds of guys Quattro tried to stay the hell away from.

But the men just smiled, jostled Quattro affectionately and patted him on the shoulders, like he'd just drove in the winning run.

"That was outstanding, my brother. Absolutely outstanding," the Black Twin said.

"Yeah, great work," the White Twin agreed. "You've really earned your wings on this one, brother. We're almost home now."

"Why don't you go down to the beach and relax, brother?" the Black Twin suggested. "Take a little walk and see the sights. We need some time to set everything up."

"OK, if it's cool with you guys and everything," Quattro said.

"Go ahead, man, this place is beautiful," the White Twin gushed. "Just do us a favor and stand guard until we get set up. Keep an eye out just in case a car comes by or something. I'll whistle when we're ready."

"No problem, my brothers," Quattro said cheerily. "You guys are really going to grind those two fucking snoops up, huh?"

"Oh, *hell* yeah," the Black Twin said. "They'll be scraping their asses off the asphalt with a putty knife. I guarantee it."

"Praise Apophis, brother! Praise him!" Quattro said excitedly, making the cult recognition signal of interlocking rings with his thumbs and forefingers.

"Praise Apophis," the other men said in unison, and gestured accordingly.

• • •

Darja and Porter took their coffees to go and hit the road. Both were feeling a tremendous sense of unease, realizing there was a good chance they might be dealing with more Apophis men before sunset.

"So, Quattro really wants to drop the dime on these Apophis dudes, huh?" Darja said, voice ripe with skepticism.

"It looks that way," Porter said. "What's wrong with that?"

"Nothing, except that he's a lying little shit. If he's blaming Apophis for offing his band, then I'm thinking he definitely did them all himself," Darja sneered in response.

"Yeah, but how would he even know about Apophis in the first place? How would he know they're working the area? It's not like they advertise in the papers or something. He certainly has no way of knowing we're investigating them. It's not the kind of name you just pick out of a hat."

"That's what I mean," Darja said. "If he's dropping the dime like that it's almost a guarantee he's involved with them, and probably with the murders too."

"You think it's a set up?" Porter asked, weighing the possibilities now himself.

"I'm just glad we got the Mossberg, all I'm saying. Why don't we fetch it from the trunk before we get there?"

"I've got an even better idea," Porter said and took out his cellphone.

The phone rang six times before it was picked up.

"Soares."

"It's Porter Dunn, sir."

"Where are we at, Porter? What do you got for me today?" Soares asked.

"I think we got a line on who's behind all this, sir. And on who might have kidnapped Gary Sutton. We have a material witness that wants to come in and talk. It's the drummer from Cutter's Mill, Warren Cortese. He says the killers are in that Apophis cult."

"What do you want from me?" Soares inquired.

"We need a little muscle, actually. Just in case this is a setup."

"What do you mean, 'muscle?'" Soares asked, clearly not liking where this was going.

"Backup. Heavily armed, if possible."

"Yeah, listen, I can't assign any state personnel on this, Porter," Soares explained wearily.

"What about non-state personnel, then?" Porter asked.

"Where's this all supposed to go down?"

"Cape Cod. A state beach, near some place called Wellfleet? Parking lot."

"What the hell is he doing down there?" Soares asked.

"He didn't say, sir. I'd guess because he's on the run from these people."

"Why don't you just call the cops down in Wellfleet, have them pick up this guy?"

"He's hiding somewhere. He said he won't come out unless he's sure it's us. Says the local cops might be in on it."

"Porter..." Soares said and sighed.

"I know, I know. Listen, this all stinks to high heaven. But if this guy's really got the goods, we could hand a very major case over to you and your people. This Sutton thing could be just the tip of a much bigger iceberg."

"OK, I'll tell you what. I know some guys down the Cape. State TAC, retired. They do a little freelancing now and then, off the books. If you can get your boss to break open the piggy bank, they might be willing to tag along and watch your backs."

"What do you think they'd ask for a job like this? Say about an hour's work or so."

"Probably about a grand, grand and a half, each. Cash money," Soares said.

"Listen, you tell them I'll pay them myself. Can these guys get suited up and meet us somewhere in an about two hours?" Porter asked.

"Probably. I'll give them your number," Soares said. "But listen, you make sure you call me, hear? Soon as this is wrapped up you call me and tell me exactly what this guy knows. I'm telling you this now, Porter: the chief has definitely reached the end of his patience with Travis and his nonsense."

"I understand. Thank you, sir," Porter said and hung up.

"What was that all about?" Darja asked.

"Soares knows some retired tactical guys he says can probably meet us down there."

"What else did he say?"

"He said time's running out on us, Darj. Sounds like his boss is ready to bring the curtain down on Travis."

"Terrific. That's just fucking terrific," Darja groaned.

"I know. Hey, I need to stop at an ATM once we get off the highway, OK? Maybe a couple."

CHAPTER EIGHTY EIGHT

Quattro smiled as he watched his two brothers lug their gear up the sandy hill. His relationship to the Rites went back quite a few years, but now it seemed as if it was finally paying off. Now they'd see him as a player, as a man willing to do what had to be done for the cause.

He had offered up the required sacrifices to Apophis, and now he was helping his brothers offer up those annoying fake-cops who kept sticking their big, stupid noses in other people's business.

Quattro looked up at the vast, endless skies and sucked in a deep breath of fresh sea air. Savoring the moment, he fetched a big fat joint from a small metal box in his back pocket and lit it with his Metallica *Kill 'Em All* lighter. The weed and the late afternoon sun were making the skies look magical, otherworldly. He took it all as a sign from Lord Apep himself.

Quattro took a long, satisfying hit and closed his eyes, savoring this moment of triumph. Hard work and true faith did pay off, after all. He suddenly felt a bit like his grandfather, an old-school Sicilian who worked his ass off in some shit factory and still dragged himself to mass every day.

Only problem was the dumb fuck was praying to the wrong god, Quattro mused. A dead god. A lying god.

Quattro thought he heard a faint sound; a scuffling noise coming out of nowhere in particular, almost like the sound of a child's running feet. He glanced around and saw nothing. He figured it was the wind blowing through the rushes and went back to soaking up the sky.

He heard it again, turned again, saw nothing again. Maybe it was just his mind playing tricks on him before the big show began.

But then Quattro definitely heard the slapping and shuffling of sneakers on asphalt.

He spun around just in time to see a bald, shirtless scarecrow of a man charging towards him, swinging a rusty old machete in the air. He looked exactly like something out of a horror movie.

Quattro raised his right hand in defense as the scarecrow shrieked incoherently and buried the surprisingly-sharp machete in Quattro's jawbone, chopping most of the drummer's fingers off in the bargain.

The attacker then awkwardly yanked the blade out of Quattro's jaw and screamed gibberish at the sky while his victim staggered.

Then, with all the unnatural strength of the truly possessed, the scarecrow brought the machete crashing down atop the drummer's skull.

The blow cleaved his victim's head cleanly in half.

The two Apophis men broke into fits of hysterical laughter as they watched through binoculars from a nearby dune.

"Holy fucking shit!" the Black Twin said. "Did you see that?"

"Oh shit, that's gotta hurt!" the White Twin cackled.

"Hey, hey; it looks like Quattro's got a splitting headache!" the Black Twin said, and the men bent over double in fits of laughter.

"Oh shit, shit! I'm gonna piss my fucking pants here!" the White Twin said, as he furiously slapped his thigh.

"Praise Apophis! Fucking praise Apophis," the Black Twin said, through gales of laughter.

"Oh *fuck* yeah, brother! Praise him in word and deed!" the White Twin shouted, then raised his meaty arms to the sky.

Several minutes later, their laughter slowly subsided and the two men looked down at the parking lot. Kevin was shrieking like a banshee and hacking wildly away at what once was Quattro's body, which looked like a giant crushed tomato from their position.

The Black Twin cleared his throat, wiped the tears away from his cheek and said, "You got that dart loaded, brother?"

"No," the White Twin said, curtly.

"What? Our orders are to..."

"That freak's a liability. And he smells like an open sewer," the White Twin said. "He's done. You seriously got a problem with that, brother? I mean, for real?"

The Black Twin thought about it for a moment. "Actually, I don't."

The White Twin lay belly down on the dune and took careful aim through the sight of his tripod-mounted sniper's rifle. His companion watched through his binoculars as Kevin danced around the parking lot like a marionette, shrieking wordlessly and swinging the bloody machete at the empty air.

The madman seemed lost in some kind of pirate or Viking fantasy; it was hard to tell which. Maybe he imagined he was Leatherface or Jason. Or maybe he didn't imagine anything at all. Maybe his brain had been so electronically butchered that he was simply driven only by some primal impulse to kill.

A short volley of gunfire echoed across the dune and Kevin's entire head exploded in a cloud of red mist.

The rest of his body froze in place for a moment, then his arms swung stupidly around his waist, like some sick parody of life. Then he fell to the ground like a bag of Tinkertoys.

CHAPTER EIGHTY NINE

Darja and Porter arrived at the rendezvous point off the main drag. They were met by the retired TAC guys, who'd arrived in a mammoth black SUV.

Only none of them looked retired at all; they were all fit, tanned and cop-groomed. Introductions were made and a basic plan of action was laid out and agreed upon.

Soares said these guys were in it for the money, but Darja got the feeling they didn't get many opportunities to throw down with a heavily-armed doomsday cult and were looking forward to some real excitement. They didn't even ask for the money yet, which took no less than eight ATM stops for Porter to collect.

Darja noticed that the tall, muscular, Italian-looking one was kinda giving her the eye. She caught him staring, but he just grinned at her with big white teeth. Yeah, she and Porter would definitely have to take these studs out for a few beers once they'd tossed Quattro's useless ass in the pokey.

They all drove to the beach, which was closed for the season. The tactical unit was familiar with the park and suggested the team split up. Darja and Porter would approach from the commons area where the payphones were, and the other team would circle around and approach from the service road in the rear, just in case they were any shooters looking to take out the pair from the dunes or from behind the bathrooms.

Darja drove into the empty parking lot, looking for the payphones. The sun was getting ready to set and there wasn't any sign of Quattro anywhere.

Then there was.

"Wait, wait. Stop here," Porter said, holding Darja's right shoulder.

He got out of the car, and stepped gingerly towards the gore. Darja drew her Glock and followed a few steps behind.

"It's Quattro," Porter said, wincing at the scene. "At least I think it is. And from the looks of it, Kevin."

"Oh my fuck, what a mess," Darja gasped, as she saw the bloody piles of bone and meat. Her stomach began to cartwheel.

Porter squinted. "It looks like Apophis had Kevin grind Quattro up and then they blew his head off."

Darja stepped closer with the digital camera and took a few shots. She was hoping she wouldn't puke all over the mess and contaminate a crime scene. Then a sudden chill took hold of her.

She lowered the camera and scanned all the high, grassy dunes framing the parking area. They were sitting ducks here. Darja realized that Apophis left this little gift out here as bait to distract she and Porter, and now they were the proverbial fish inside the barrel.

"I think it's time we got the fuck out of here. Like immediately."

Darja and Porter stepped backwards to their car, eyes darting across the dunes looking for threats. Suddenly, heavy machine-gun fire ripped up the asphalt inches away from their feet.

"Jesus Christ! Run!" Darja screamed.

Darja and Porter sprinted towards a wooden guardrail, bullets dogging their feet as they went. They both leaped over it, only to tumble ass over tea-kettle down a sandy embankment. Splinters began flying as the machine gun fire tore up the rail atop the knoll.

A dark olive web of scrub pine branches hovered above their heads, only to suddenly withstand a thick barrage of gunfire as their assailants blazed randomly and wantonly in Darja and Porter's general direction.

"Holy shit! These guys are definitely not fucking around!" Darja shouted.

"Get down! Hit the dirt!"

The gunfire ceased for a moment. Porter assumed they were trying to scope out their target until he heard a loud "whoosh," followed a huge explosion. Those psychos had a goddamn rocket launcher. *They really are insane.*

Darja figured they saw the TAC guys approach from them the rear and blew their damn car up. There was going to be all holy hell to pay for that, for sure.

She didn't have long to worry about that eventuality, because another wall of machine fire again burst through the trees, sending splinters and pine needles down like rain.

"They're shooting high, the dumb fucks," Darja shouted.

"It's their position; they're at the wrong angle," Porter said, shielding his eyes from the flying debris.

"Yeah? Well, they're going to figure that out!" Darja shouted.

Another whoosh, this one a lot louder, which meant it was a lot closer.

"Down! Down!" Porter shouted.

Not a hundred feet away the Explorer exploded. Porter scrambled to cover Darja, out of pure instinct. They felt the heat and the blast wave, but their position shielded them from flying shrapnel.

Oh well, Darja thought, there goes Batmobile Number Two.

Then suddenly, silence.

"Wait: they stopped," Porter said.

"Yeah, they're fucking with our heads down here," Darja replied.

The machine-gun fire then resumed, this time aimed at the top of the embankment. Dirt, sand and needles sprayed everywhere. Porter pulled his jacket over his head and hugged Darja's head to his chest. Sooner or later, one of those bullets was going to get lucky and ricochet right at them.

Darja raised her head from Porter's chest and screamed, *"Jesus-fucking-Christ! Why don't you assholes just come and shoot us in the head with a regular gun like normal-fucking-people! What the fuck is your fucking problem!"*

Suddenly, a fresh fusillade of bullets severed the top-third of a light pole, sending a heap of wood, pine needles, metal and glass crashing down through the branches. Glass and sparks flew everywhere as the blunt end of the entire mass — light fixture and all — landed straight atop Porter's right thigh.

"Argghhhhhhhhhh!!!!" Porter screamed out in pain.

Porter rolled onto his side, writhing in agony. Darja stood dumbly, just for a brief moment. Then her training kicked in.

She rolled Porter onto his back so there wouldn't be any undue pressure on the wound. Porter was moaning loudly and his sweat-drenched face was contorted in physical agony.

As she surveyed the damage, Darja wondered if the shooters were planning to charge their position or were just reloading, because the gunfire fell silent again.

Porter's leg was a total fucking mess, and it looked like a massive compound fracture. The branches broke its momentum, but the weight of that stupid thing may well have shattered his femur completely. Porter's tan chinos were painted scarlet in a terrifyingly-short time.

"Porter, if we don't do something about that leg, you're going to bleed to death," Darja said, the heat of panic rising in her voice.

She couldn't help thinking about how she'd been a part of the biggest war machine in human history for nearly a decade and never even came close to experiencing this level of violence. But despite her terror, she was well-trained and knew what had to be done.

"This never happened," Darja said as she quickly whipped off her jacket.

Then, to Porter's agonized amazement, she lifted off her white cotton blouse. She wasn't wearing a bra and clearly didn't need one.

"No jokes about being a carpenter's dream, now," Darja said as she quickly slipped back into her jacket and zipped it up to her neck.

She glanced up at the embankment for signs of the gunmen and turned back to Porter.

"Listen, this is gonna hurt like hell, but it might just save your life, OK?"

Porter nodded weakly, and Darja then wrapped her blouse tightly around the top of his blood-soaked leg.

"*FUUUUUUUCCCCCKKKK!!!*" Porter howled. The veins in his neck and head looked close to bursting.

"Holy shit, Ports! I think that's the first time I heard you curse," Darja said as she struggled to adjust the tourniquet.

"Oh fuck, fuck, it hurts!" Porter cried.

Darja mentally ran the numbers and knew the odds of Porter going anywhere were less than nil. She spun around, searching for options or escape routes.

Then Porter's cellphone suddenly rang.

"What the fuck?" Darja said, nearly bursting out laughing at the absurdity of a cellphone ringing in a war zone.

"G-g-get it," Porter moaned.

Darja fumbled with the phone then snapped, "What!"

"Hello there. Don Morton again."

Darja cupped her hand over the transmitter.

"It's that fucking Morton guy."

"T-t-take a message," Porter croaked. Darja burst out laughing.

What a trouper, cracking wise while bleeding to death in a ditch.

Darja then put her ear back to the receiver.

"Are you there, Mr. Dunn? Hello? Hello?" Morton said. "Mr. Dunn, I'm standing about eight-hundred feet from your position. I'm going to dash over and fetch you two from the bush there. So when you see a handsome fellow in a tan windbreaker and plaid slacks coming your way, please don't shoot him, OK? Then we can all have a chat."

CHAPTER NINETY

Morton's head appeared at the edge of the embankment shortly after, eerily backlit against the dusky sky by the sodium-lights in the parking lot. He scanned the area with a flashlight to make sure there were no signs of immediate danger, then gingerly shuffled his way down the sandy incline. He stopped to scope out his surroundings like an old pro before greeting Darja and Porter.

"Hello again. Why, you must be the world famous Darja Lundquist," Morton said, smiling genially.

His smile quickly morphed into a concerned frown once he had a look at Porter's shattered leg.

"How are we doing there, old boy?" Morton said, attempting a tone of encouragement. "Not banged up too badly, I hope."

"You with Apophis, Morton?" Darja demanded. "Is that what the fuck this is? You come to negotiate our surrender?"

"Oh, hell no," Morton said and smiled warmly. "There were two gents back there who *did* work for Apophis, but they've been, let's just say, released from their contract."

"What the hell's going on here, then?" Darja said sharply.

"Well, I'm afraid I mucked things up a bit," Morton said, sounding genuinely apologetic. "I didn't count on those two boys up there hauling out the heavy artillery. You two must've really cheesed them off."

"You could say that," Darja said grimly as a passing ocean breeze brought with it the unnatural stench from the burning vehicles.

"Well, I had to wait for those chaps to get into position before I could approach," Morton explained. "Once they got that big .50-cal out, they were so focused on killing you two, they weren't expecting an approach from the rear."

"I'll bet," Darja said, so not in the mood for this guy right now.

"Luckily, I had just enough daylight left to pop them both a few quick ones. Even if they'd seen me, I'd still have had the drop on them. Those big rigs aren't exactly maneuverable, you know. And it's not like they'd hear me coming, what with the earmuffs and the racket and all. Piece of pie, really."

Morton may as well have been describing a badminton match.

"Why are you even here it all?" Darja asked, incredulously.

"Well, call it kismet, I guess," Morton said. "I'd had those two tagged as muscle for a murder ring, and your longhair up there was a bit of a player in those circles."

Morton paused and winced again at Porter's leg. "We'd best get our friend here to the hospital. On the double."

"You'd better call a medic," Darja said. "I don't think he can walk on this leg."

"I keep a first-aid kit in my car," Morton offered. "We can get a proper tourniquet on that leg and hopefully stop the bleeding. I've also got a few emergency ice packs. Instant jobbers. Amazing things, really, don't need to be refrigerated. Be back in a flash."

Morton climbed up the embankment and came back a few minutes later with a surprisingly-large white case emblazoned with a red cross. He set up two battery-powered lanterns and got out the needed supplies.

Then Morton and Darja worked together like a surgical team to get Porter's leg wrapped up well enough so that he wouldn't bleed to death before the paramedics even got there.

Darja was a bit taken aback to see that Morton actually kept glass vials of morphine in his kit, which he injected with a disposable syringe. Porter's agonized expression relaxed and his breathing slowed to a more-normal pace. Morton then took the injured man's pulse, using his wrist watch.

"So should we try to get him up that hill, sir?" Darja asked.

"I wouldn't recommend that, my dear," Morton said. "Let's have the pros handle that."

Morton reached out and wiped a thick glob of blood from Darja's forehead with his thumb. "You got a bit of... blood there."

Thank you, sir," Darja said, touched by his concern.

"Sorry about your friends, by the way."

"We didn't know them," Darja said. "They were just freelancers who came along for back-up."

"What a shame. Poor bastards. Ugly business," Morton said, in a genuinely-regretful tone.

"Crazy-fucking-business. I definitely did not sign up for this kind of shit," Darja said emphatically.

"You never do," Morton sighed.

An ambulance came along after ten minutes or so, flanked by a massive convoy of police cruisers from a number of municipalities.

Morton had to wave his credentials at every scowling face that crossed his path. Darja stayed alongside Porter, who'd lost consciousness as the paramedics worked on him.

They weren't especially overjoyed when Darja informed them Morton had shot up Porter with a syringe of morphine sulfate. And she didn't much care for their portentous expressions as they loaded her partner into an ambulance. This movie sucked the first time she saw it, but now she was terrified that Porter was going to lose that leg. Or worse.

Morton appeared out of nowhere and placed a comforting hand on Darja's shoulder.

"You can ride with me. No room in there," Morton said, jutting his chin in the direction of the ambulance. He'd dropped the whole jolly-prep act now, thankfully.

They walked in silence to Morton's car. Darja couldn't stop shaking. She wasn't quite in a state of shock, but she was getting close to completely losing her shit after everything that just happened.

She'd never dealt with anything remotely like this. She'd never, ever even been shot at before, certainly not with a goddamned .50-cal.

This was insanity. This was utter and total mass insanity.

CHAPTER NINETY ONE

Morton drove slowly but intently through the maze of emergency vehicles. The flashing lights weren't helping Darja's state of mind any, especially since Morton had to stop every sixty feet to flash his DIA shield at some jerkoff asshole or another.

They finally broke free of the circus and cruised out into the cool night air. Morton was talking quietly to Darja. She had not one single clue what the fuck he was actually talking about, but she found his smooth baritone to be very calming, especially without the hale-fellow-and-well-met bullshit act.

But Darja couldn't stop thinking about Porter and that little girl of his bleeding out on her bathroom floor. She knew full well what a little altar-boy bitch Porter was, so he'd probably think this was all some kind of divine retribution for his sins. If he was even still conscious, which she very much doubted.

All the insanity they were chasing was finally catching up with them. Darja began gnawing furiously at her thumb, and beads of sweat on her forehead temples felt cold and clammy.

She was finally able to focus on the meaning of Morton's words.

"You OK? You going to make it?" finally broke through the static.

Darja was finally able to form actual words of her own.

"Porter... he's going to be in surgery for a while?"

"I'd imagine so," Morton said softly.

"Listen, sir, I know you don't know me from a hole in the wall, and I don't want you to think I'm crazy or..."

"I've only ever heard good things about you, my dear," Morton said.

"OK, thank you... thanks..."

"And I don't think you're crazy at all, Darja," he added. "You've been through one hell of a brannigan there. Real D-Day stuff."

"Thank... thank you. But that's not... what I mean," Darja said. "I think..."

"Maybe we should get you to the emergency room, have someone take a look at you..."

"No... what I mean is... I'm really... I mean, this has all been so monumentally fucked..."

"I understand," Morton said reassuringly.

"No, sir, you don't. I mean, I realize we've just met, but I'm... I mean, I'm..."

Morton pulled to the side of the road and stared gravely at Darja, worried now she was going to pop her cork.

"Please; please don't look at me like that, sir. You see... I mean, Porter is..."

Morton frowned, thinking now he should just drop this poor woman off at the hospital and let them sort her out.

"I don't need a doctor, sir. I don't... it's just, I can't sit around in a hospital waiting room right now."

Morton said, "Well, there's a good 24-hour diner a few miles down the road."

"OK, that sounds great. Really. But would you terribly mind, sir, I mean, I know this is going to sound really, really strange but... do you think we could possibly... maybe... go somewhere and *fuck?*"

Darja expected Morton to recoil in disgust, but he just looked more concerned.

Somewhat encouraged by this, Darja proceeded to plead her case.

"I mean, I understand how completely insane that probably sounds to you, sir, but I'm *seriously* about to lose my shit here and I really need... I mean, it's been *such* a long time and I realize we just met, and you probably think I'm just in shock or whatever but I'm not. It's just... I just really feel like I need to do something... *normal* right now."

Jesus. What the hell did she just say to this guy? What the fuck was wrong with her? Her big fat mouth seemed to have a mind of its own at this point.

"I mean... I just really, really need to feel something besides complete fucking *terror* right now. I am just so, so, so fucking *scared* right now, sir. I mean, I was in the military police for eight years, sir, and no one ever shot at me, not even once. No one ever tried to murder me, not even once. But now I've had really, really scary people trying to murder me and my partner several times in the past month alone."

"Less than a month. I mean, I am so, so sorry to drop this on you out of the blue like this, sir, but it's just… you seem like the type who understands what I'm talking about."

Morton was silent, taking it all in as the humiliation and panic hit Darja in waves. She was just about to bolt out the side door to escape but Morton just smiled, patted her knee and put the car back in drive.

"Indeed I do, my young friend. A nice roll-around to clear out the cobwebs sounds like a terrific idea just about now. I'm game," he said with genuine cheer as he pulled back onto the highway.

"I know just the spot. Buckle up."

CHAPTER NINETY TWO

Morton and Darja checked into some scuzzy tourist trap called Sea-whatever and got straight down to business, without any small talk or mind games. This wasn't sex per se, it was crisis therapy. It was a secret truth of the life she now found herself in.

Put simply, sometimes death and extreme danger made people really, really horny. Shrinks had some fancy term for it. Darja read about it in some boring psych class she was required to take for a promotion. There were even studies of certain couples who'd actually go out and commit outrageous criminal acts because it made the sex afterwards all the more mind-blowing.

If she'd had the presence of mind she'd remember the exact terminology, but her objective at the moment was to get completely *out* of her mind, because inside of it wasn't exactly the best place to be at that particular moment.

After a long and exhausting session, Darja fell asleep and Morton quietly slipped out to the deserted pool area to make some phone calls.

After running out to do a bit of shopping, Morton woke her at 10 am with a metal cart carrying styrofoam plates of food from the continental breakfast and, much to her amazement, fresh clothes he picked up for her at a nearby Target.

Darja went in to use the bathroom, and left the door wide open. Morton was tickled by how comfortable she seemed being completely naked around a man she'd only just met a few hours before.

He grabbed a coffee and plain donut, sat down in a patent leather armchair while he enjoyed the comforting sound of a beautiful woman urinating in a motel toilet.

Darja came out of the bathroom, smiled sweetly at Morton, then sat back down on the bed in a kind of lotus position. Morton then watched her studiously pick out congealed bits of semen tangled in her strawberry-blonde pubic hair and flick them against the wall.

Quite a character, this one.

"I just heard from the hospital," Morton finally said, sipping gingerly at his scalding hot coffee. "Porter's finally out of surgery, but we won't be able to see him until around five o'clock or so, maybe later."

Darja silently nodded, then walked over to peer out the blinds at the ugly stretch of highway. She seemed lost in her own thoughts, so Morton took the opportunity to get a good look at the body of the woman he'd just spent half the night engaging in some remarkably athletic sex with.

Not bad, he thought, not bad at all.

Shame about the tits, but the lower half was really top-drawer, especially that nice round ass and that lovely blonde pubic hair.

And she certainly kept herself in nice shape. Not really his type, but she might make for an interesting anecdote in the *roman à clef* he was dabbling with at home.

Darja sat down at the edge of the bed, popped open an 8 oz. carton of Tropicana orange juice and took a swig. She leaned back on the bed and stretched. She sat back up, folded her wrists between her knees and stared meaninglessly out the window for a spell. Morton figured she was considering maybe inviting him over for another round, but couldn't really find the mood.

After a moment she said, "So what's the prognosis?"

"He's stable but guarded. Still in intensive care. He may need a lot more work done to get that leg back in some kind of shape."

Darja nodded then inspected the offerings from the breakfast tray.

"Well, in that case would you mind if we went out for a *real* brunch?" she said, waving a dismissive backhand at the selections of stale Danish and unripe melon.

"This shit... this shit just makes me sad."

Morton took Darja to a steakhouse in Hyannis that served a brunch buffet until noon. Darja seemed hellbent on eating her anxiety away, and Morton watched, silently amused, as she took trip after trip to the groaning board. She ate steak, ham and bacon with her broccoli omelet, a gallon or so of coffee, two bowls of fruit salad and an English muffin.

After brunch, Morton suggested they both walk it off in downtown Hyannis.

It was off-season and the streets were largely quiet, but it was clear the locals were already gearing up for Memorial Day. Darja was quiet and subdued, nothing like the sassy, foul-mouthed hellion he'd heard so much about. Morton knew full well the horror she was processing and gave the woman her space. He'd seen far less trauma than what she was dealing with break hardened men forever, and couldn't imagine how she might deal with it.

There was something about Darja that almost reminded Morton of his second wife, Elsa. He couldn't put his finger on it. Their personalities or appearances were nothing alike, but they both seemed to possess a kind of free-spiritedness, a kind of indomitable individualism. Morton had been with thousands of women, but he never knew anyone quite like Elsa. Or this Darja, for that matter.

Normally, he usually didn't like being reminded of Elsa, because that in turn reminded him of his daughter Karen. And that in turn reminded him of his first wife. Which in turn reminded him that he forgot to call his surviving daughter on her birthday. Yet again.

Morton bought milkshakes at Friendly's and a pint of Bacardi at a convenience store and took Darja to the harbor. They sat for a good long while and sipped their drinks in silence, staring out at the boats rocking gently on the waves.

Morton put in a call to the hospital and was told Porter was finally out of surgery. They took their time getting back to the car and made their way over to visit him in the ICU Recovery unit at CCH.

They got the runaround at the hospital over visiting hours, which forced Morton to flash his credentials at the head of security. When that didn't work, Morton took the man aside and whispered in his ear. Darja had no idea what was said, but the all the color drained from the man's face and he meekly waved she and Morton through without saying a word.

Morton took Darja up to Porter's room then excused himself, telling her he had a phone call to make and that he'd see her later.

Which was fine, since everything else was flushed from Darja's mind as soon as she saw the state Porter was in.

CHAPTER NINETY THREE

Darja stood by Porter's bed in the ICU, her face tight with worry. She stood alongside her unconscious partner, whose un-bandaged leg looked like Dr. Frankenstein's worst nightmare. The skin on his thigh alternated between a dark red and a sickly greenish-black. They'd put the leg at a slight incline of traction, and she was told it was being kept unwrapped for some reason that flew straight over her head. The entire mess was kept in place with all kinds of weird stainless steel clamps and covered in some kind of thick, antiseptic gel that smelled like lilacs. A clear plastic curtain was pulled around the entire bed.

"Knock, knock," Sam said as he appeared at the door.

He came in, held Darja's head in his hands and kissed her gently on the forehead.

"How are we all doing in here?" Sam asked.

"We're alive, I guess," Darja replied, sullenly.

"You two really went through the grinder, I take it."

"Yes, sir."

"What's the prognosis for our man?"

"Not so great at the moment, sir. Apparently, they're very concerned about that main artery in his thigh."

"Don't worry yourself too much, dear," Sam said. "If they were overly concerned, he'd still be in surgery."

Sam took a look at Porter's charts and said, "I'd say you two have an angel watching over you. You've really earned your combat pay this time."

"Thank you, sir."

"I mean that literally, Darja," Sam said. "I've put in for very generous bonuses for the both of you. You should have them in hand within a week or two."

Darja looked at the floor and said, "I really appreciate that, sir."

"Don't be too hard on yourself, Darja. People who've been through far less than you have spent the rest of their lives in mental hospitals."

"It's not just that, sir. It's just that, well, everything has just been so completely screwed up... I don't even know how to describe it. It's like there's some kind of, I don't know, like evil force, or some kind of dark power behind all of this."

"I know, I know. It's an evil world we live in, Darja," Sam said, and placed his hands on her shoulders. "It's a very sick and evil world. But I just want you to know that there are good people out there trying to change that. There are people who are fighting every day to cure a world that seems to be terminally ill."

"Like who, the Salvation Army?"

"In a funny kind of way, I suppose," Sam chuckled. "But I just don't want you to lose hope. People have been watching you, important people, and they are very, very impressed with what they've seen. I know it all seems very dark right now, but there's a light at the end of the tunnel. If you can get there, you'll find people there waiting for you, people who have been through the same ordeals as you, and who want to lead us all to something better, something that can really change the world. More importantly, to heal it. To *cure* it."

"No offense, sir, but this all sounds like Scientology or something."

Sam laughed. "It's no such thing, young lady. Not at all. It's just plain and simple common sense. Don't worry, you'll realize this soon enough. In the meantime, I'm here for whatever you need, OK? Anything at all. And hopefully, Bob will be back at the helm soon and the ship will right itself. I honestly believe that at the end of it all, you and Porter will come out of this as truly formidable warriors for the greater good."

Darja stood in silence, sneaking worried glances at Porter. She had no idea how to respond to any of what she was being told.

"Thank you, sir." Darja finally said.

Sam hugged her, kissed her forehead again, smiled meaningfully at her, and left without saying anything else.

Darja watched as Sam left, then turned to Porter again.

"'Truly formidable warriors for the greater good?' What the fuck is that supposed to mean?" she asked.

Porter didn't answer.

CHAPTER NINETY FOUR

Morton walked back to the lobby, then wandered the halls until he found an empty administrators' office. He locked the door behind him and called his daughter Maggie, whose twin sister drowned in the Saw Mill River three years back, along with her stepmother.

"Hey sugar-plum," Morton said. "Happy belated birthday."

"Thank you, Daddy! I'm so glad you called," Maggie said, with what sounded like genuine cheer.

"Did you get your present?" Morton asked.

"I did, yes," Maggie replied. "Wow, a pink handgun! It's, uh, not something you get every day," she said and chuckled softly.

"Well, I know Steven likes to shoot, so I thought it might be something the two of you could do together. It really is a lot of fun. I think you'll really enjoy it."

"Yeah, he's actually very excited about it. He can't wait to take me out to the range," Maggie said.

"That's great, then," Morton replied. He then froze as he heard his daughter inhale deeply, seeming now to gird herself.

"But I can't help but wonder if there's an... ulterior motive, Daddy," Maggie said, choosing her words very carefully.

"No, sugar. It's just a gift."

Excruciating silence. Another deep breath.

"Are you... are you in trouble, Daddy?"

Morton paused, unexpectedly taken aback by the question.

He said, "I might be."

Maggie got right to the point: "Is it something that might affect my family?"

"Definitely not," Morton said firmly.

"Do you promise?" Maggie asked, pressing him for assurance.

"I promise."

"It's just us now, Dad. You know?" Maggie said, her voice starting to crack.

"I know," Morton whispered.

"I miss them, Daddy. I miss them so much I don't know what to do sometimes. It's like... it's like, I don't know where the other half of my body is. It's driving me crazy, I miss them so bad."

There was another excruciatingly long pause. Morton heard his daughter breathing in deep staccato bursts.

"Daddy... is it... is it your fault?" she finally asked, sobbing. "Did... did they die because of something you did?"

Morton knew she meant Karen and Elsa, but she might as well have meant her mother, too. It must've taken a tremendous amount of courage for Maggie to finally confront him about this, and he admired her for doing so. Even if it felt like a dagger to his heart.

"No. It was an accident," he finally whispered.

"Daddy, please tell me the truth," she pleaded. "Please don't lie to me about this. Please swear to me, Daddy. Please."

"I swear to you, cupcake. It was just a terrible accident."

Another soul-destroying pause.

Morton could sense his daughter nodding, processing.

He could practically feel her gripping the telephone receiver with white knuckles, twisting the cord around her index finger, staring hard at the floor.

Finally, she said, "I love you, Daddy."

"I love you, too. Happy birthday, angel. I promise I'll visit soon. Give my love to Steven and the kids."

Morton hung up the phone, knowing full well now that his daughter knew that he was lying through his teeth to her.

His baby girl now knew that all of it — every heartache, every tragedy, every funeral, everything she loved that had been ripped away from her — was in fact entirely her father's fault.

She knew it all for certain now, but had decided to forgive him anyway.

CHAPTER NINETY FIVE

Darja sat by Porter's hospital bed and stared at nothing as her partner slept, surrounded by a bank of strange electronics, all beeping and flashing stupidly behind the plastic curtain in the half-darkened room.

It was getting near shift-change, and the halls had filled with the sound of cheery banter as staff readied to head on home. But all the chatter did was remind Darja that she wasn't feeling all that cheery at this particular moment herself, thank you.

Darja heard a familiar scuffle out in the corridor and turned to see Travis, looking gloomier than ever. The man nodded ever so slightly at Darja, who rose from her seat as he went to check up on Porter.

"Your little beach party down the Cape is stirring up a Category Five shitstorm, Lundquist," Travis said to Darja as he looked at all the arcane equipment behind Porter's bed. "I've got agencies I've never even heard of ringing my phone off the hook."

"I'm sorry," Darja said weakly.

"Soares has been suspended, pending investigation. The order came down from the governor himself. And the AG is looking into an indictment for the whole lot of you," Travis said sourly.

"What? Why?" Darja asked, shocked.

"Because you just got three very popular retired cops incinerated. Because a state park was turned into a literal war-zone. Because the paramedics had to scrape a human being's mortal remains off the blacktop with actual putty knives. They're not even going to try to identify the TAC team's remains. They're being flown to a special forensics unit because too much of the tooth enamel got melted away. No one down there has ever seen that kind of carnage. Not even in head-on collisions."

Darja just stood there, marinating in shame. Travis returned the clipboard to its slot.

"And you know what I told everyone I spoke to today, Lundquist?" Travis said while inspecting Porter's sutures.

"No, sir."

"I said, 'Get used to it, you goddamned fucking pansies. If those Apophis maniacs really are back in business, this is about as good as it's gonna get.' And that's a direct quote."

Travis turned, put his hands on his hips and looked directly at Darja.

"So which one of you clipped the shooters?"

"Neither, sir. Porter and I got pinned down by that .50-cal of theirs. Don Morton saved our bacon. If he hadn't have show up and take out those gunners, they'd have been scraping us off the ground, too."

"Morton?" Travis scowled. "Who the hell called him in?"

"Nobody, sir. He had a tail on those Apophis mutts, made them for another job. He said it was just kismet," Darja said.

"Kismet, kiss my ass. Morton's been deactivated for years. Now he's sticking his goddamned nose in my business. And he's probably bugging your phones as well."

"He saved our lives, Skipper. We'd be dead meat if he hadn't have shown up."

Travis grunted, then said, "Well, I guess that answers my question about the shooters then."

"What about the shooters?"

"Their deaths weren't especially pleasant, Lundquist. Morton snuck up and popped the two of them right between the legs while they were on their bellies working those weapons. Did it with soft-point rounds."

Darja stifled a snort.

"What the hell are you laughing at, Lundquist? That's a horrible way to die."

"Those two fucking bastards were responsible for five other human beings dying much more horrible deaths than that, sir. And they were doing their level-best to try to make it seven. They got exactly what was coming to them. If it were up to me, I'd give Don Morton a medal."

Travis fell silent and scowled at his charge for quite some time.

Finally, he said, "We'll have a talk about that later. Now, what's all this about the drummer?"

"He's our man for the Sutton hit, Skipper. Seems he was into some real bad shit. Seems he was mixed up with some wacko devil cult down in

Florida as well as Apophis. Bruehle and Zaina are still sifting through all the data."

"So basically, we're left with nothing."

"I wouldn't say that, sir," Darja protested. "We got a lot of fresh evidence to sift through and I think we have some interesting new ideas on how to go after Apophis from Gary's case files. And his killer is off the boards."

"You've got *nothing*, Lundquist."

Travis' cellphone rang. "Hold on... Travis."

Darja saw her boss' stone-face seem to wilt as he listened to whatever bad news was coming over the wire now.

After a sickeningly long pause, he croaked, "I'm on my way."

Darja shuddered as Travis seemed to shrink right before her eyes. He suddenly looked like a very old man.

"Skipper?" Darja said, alarmed.

"I can't talk right now," Travis whispered hoarsely, and shuffled out into the hallway.

Don Morton had come up from the cafe and spotted Travis down the hall. He placed his coffees down at the nurse's station and sprinted over to meet the man.

"Bobby, wait up!" Morton said, slightly out of breath as he caught with the man at the elevator bank.

"Jesus Christ, I'm not in the mood, Morton. I've got somewhere I have to be."

Morton nodded briskly, then gave Travis the once-over. "I'll tag along," he said.

"Morton, for fuck's sake..."

"Come on, Bobby-boy, I've known you long enough to sense when there's real trouble. Let me be your wing-man."

Travis said nothing as Morton followed him into the elevator, down to the parking garage, and finally into the back seat of Khoury's waiting Suburban. They drove away in silence.

CHAPTER NINETY SIX

The apartment looked like a cyclone had torn through it.

Bits of wood and upholstery stuffing, shards of broken glass and ceramic, and scraps of shredded paper were scattered every-where you looked. Several shattered windows were taped up with thick plastic. The walls and doors were riddled with bullet holes from semi-automatic rifle fire.

Travis braced himself and looked into the room in which Sister Esperanza spent her waking hours. The walls were mottled with the congealed spray of human blood.

The attackers had shot Sister Esperanza's father and brother execution-style, before taking turns beating, raping and sodomizing the young blind woman. They didn't come just to murder her, they were here to desacralize her. Travis had no doubt they did so under very specific orders.

They were also organized and armed well enough to take out the coterie of armed guards Travis had protecting this building. All of which meant this wasn't just a random home invasion, it was meant to send a message to him, and him alone.

Two of the invaders were killed by his men and were currently lying half-zipped into body bags inside a meatwagon parked in the alley. Travis had sent Khoury to talk to the local blues, and the man returned to the flat to report to Travis.

"Who were they, Khoury?" Travis asked.

"Cops say they're street soldiers for the Laughing Lobos, out of East Harlem."

"Who uses them? Central?"

"No one I know, boss. Looks like they pretty much took over an apartment building out there, the Cherry Park Estate. Cops said they run their various rackets out of it: prostitution, numbers, drugs, guns, murder-for-hire. All-purpose scumbags."

"Find out who hired them," Travis said.

"On it," Khoury said, and turned to the stairway.

Morton appeared out of nowhere and stepped between the two men.

"Bobby, why don't you let me handle that particular problem, OK?" Morton said. "This is more along my area of expertise."

Travis stared hard at Morton. The two stared hard at each other until some silent agreement seemed to be reached between them.

Morton turned and walked into an empty bedroom. He shut and latched the door behind him, pulled out a cellular phone from his jacket, and dialed.

A wheezy, East European accented voice answered brusquely. "Eight-five-two-nine."

"Yes, I think there might be a gas leak in the basement over at the Cherry Park Estate in East Harlem," Morton said, his voice colored by a touch of feigned concern.

He was answered by a long silence.

"Where?" the voice finally asked.

"That's the Cherry Park Estate. It's located in East Harlem," Morton said slowly and deliberately.

There was nothing to hear on the other line but the sound of raspy breathing. After a minute, Morton spoke again.

"Someone might want to go and check it out. It could spark a terrible explosion. The entire building could come down. Everyone inside could be killed. Every living soul."

More breathing. "When?" the voice asked.

"Oh, I think you should send someone over to look into it as soon as possible. After midnight would probably be best."

Morton heard some papers being rustled.

"One-five-one-six, eight-two-zed-zed-nine-four," the voice finally said.

"Two-seven-four-delta-delta-eight-zeta-zeta-one-seven" Morton replied, carefully enunciating each letter and numeral.

He heard a click as the other man hung up.

Morton emerged from the bedroom, only to encounter a small, frightened child in the hallway, clutching a doll almost as large as herself.

Morton leaned over, beamed at the girl like a favorite uncle and said, "And who might *you* be, sweetness?"

Travis stood in the living room and watched the sad parade of emergency personnel come and go. An elderly Hispanic man Travis didn't recognize then entered the room and bowed his head in respect.

"Don Travis?" the man said. "Señora Munoz would like to speak with you."

"Of course," Travis said. "Bring her in."

Sister Esperanza's mother walked in like a chastened servant who'd somehow failed her employer. Her face was purple with bruises and her left eye was swollen shut. Heavy gauze cloth bandages were wrapped around her head and her right arm was tied in a sling. A crocheted shawl was draped over her shoulders and trailed behind her as she walked.

"Señor, it was terrible, terrible..."

"My God, woman. What did they do to you?" Travis gasped.

Señora Munoz ignored the question and focused on the more pressing issue of her daughter.

"The police said she lost a lot of blood, Don Travis. They were not hopeful. Señor, last night Esperanza said the angels have been offended and must be appeased. She had prophesied that such a terrible thing was about to happen."

"Señora, your daughter will get the very best medical care in the world. She will recover from this, you have my word."

"Gracias, gracias, Don Travis. I will leave you be now."

"Thank you, Señora. Please let me or my men know if there's anything you need. Anything at all."

Travis waited for the woman to return to her bedroom before he called out into the outer hallway.

"Evan, tell those goddamned paramedics to get their fat, lazy asses up here with a stretcher and get Mrs. Munoz to the hospital immediately. For Christ's sake, what the hell is wrong with those people?"

Travis took another look around the ruined flat. He walked into Esperanza's small, spartan bedroom. The only furnishings were an ugly, pipe-framed twin bed that looked like it came straight from a Victorian workhouse, with a small wooden table alongside it.

Travis spotted Esperanza's Bible there. He picked it up and saw there was pink Post-it note placed inside. He opened to the marked page and saw neat, tiny handwriting that read, *'Don Travis -- 57: 1-2.'*

The passage was from the Book of the Prophet Isaiah.

> *"The upright person perishes, and no one cares. The faithful are ripped away and no one takes it to heart. Yes, because of the evil times, the upright is taken off; he will enter peace, and those who follow the right way will find rest on their beds."*

Travis felt a black sheet of ice fall from the ceiling and wrap itself around his soul.

CHAPTER NINETY SEVEN

It was after midnight when Sam got back to his hospital. The night nurses were on duty, but otherwise the halls were empty.

Sam really enjoyed being here at this time of night, enjoying the quiet and the subdued lighting. He found he could do some of his best work here when he wasn't distracted by a hundred different things going on at once.

But the warm glow he felt inside wasn't just from the tranquility and peace this place instilled at this time of night. It was the immense feelings of love and pride he felt for those two extraordinary young souls he'd come to know and love as if they were his own children.

Sam had spent the better part of the last quarter-century learning to really see inside the human heart, and he knew these two were special. He knew it from the moment they first walked into his office. He knew these two spirits would come to see the world as he saw it, and would eventually come to stand by his side and make all things right and good once again.

Bob may not have realized it, but now Sam realized his old friend had been guided by higher powers and the purpose of it all was to bring these two warriors into Sam's fold and go forward with him into a better and brighter future. And now his old friend's task was complete.

For his own part, Sam knew he had to work harder than ever before, which is why he came here. He unlocked his office suite, turned on his secretary's desk lamp then went to unlock his office.

He entered the room and switched on a lamp and was startled to see a figure, half in shadow, sitting at his desk.

"Don! What are you doing here? I wasn't expecting you."

"Oh, I just thought I'd drop by, Sam," Morton said, in a pleasantly neutral tone. "See how things were going with you."

"You scared me there, sitting in the dark," Sam said, obviously rattled.

"I'm sorry, Sam. Rude of me," Morton said, genuinely apologetic.

"What's going on, Don?"

"Bob Travis is dead, Sam," Morton said.

"My God, Don. What happened?"

"Someone creeped Bob's safehouse and did him in bed. Or *someones*, rather. It looks like there were probably about four of them. They also iced one of his bodyguards. The ex-SEAL."

"Do they know who it was?" Sam asked.

"Not yet. But I do know who ordered it. In fact, I'm going to handle the situation tonight."

"Jesus, Don. Who was it?"

"Why, it was *you*, Sam. You know that, old boy," Morton said, smiling warmly. He stood up and smoothly slipped a .32 revolver from his coat pocket.

"Don, what on earth gave you that idea? I mean... that's just crazy."

"No, it's all actually very clever, Sam. Damned clever."

Morton motioned Sam to sit down.

"Go on, sit down. Have a seat, Sam," he said, like he had a secret he was dying to share with an old friend. "I have a story I'd like to tell you."

Sam sat. His eyes darted around the room, searching for relief. He didn't find any.

"This all started when a mental patient tried to kill a rock star," Morton said, his smile still warm and friendly. "Both of whom you treated, Sam. You see, young Gary Sutton was out there, digging around, digging into his past, trying to find out the truth about his missing father. But instead, he found out that you wrote his real mother's books for her. He found out you secretly devised those experiments at Sunshine. Gary was not only blackmailing his real mother, he was blackmailing you."

"And the hell of it, the sheer bloody hell of it was that all of that money was going right up his girlfriend's nose," Morton added. "That had to have rankled a man like you, Sam. So you fried Kevin Stuart's brain and programmed him to kill Gary. Only something truly weird happened, something you couldn't possibly plan for. So you had to improvise."

"Go on," Sam said, smiling beatifically now.

"So that weirdness put old Bob Travis on the case, and he eventually sent his Mouseketeers over to talk to the legendary Grace Sutton. And that could screw everything up for you altogether. So you got a bit fancy and had Grace seduce Dunn and feed him scraps, so you could control the information flow. Only the great black widow finally got sick of playing someone else's tune her whole life, and started playing her own. Which ultimately is how Porter got those Polaroids that Gary had found in the crawlspace, the photos his father hid before he was killed. And if they kept following that little breadcrumb trail, it was going to lead right back to your doorstep."

"You're definitely way, way off-base there, Don," Sam said dismissively. "I had nothing to do with that filthy whore and her sick mind-games. That woman is poison."

"Well, maybe, maybe not," Morton said, willing to concede the point. "Either way, you and your friends badly needed a diversion, so you created one. Well, you've been creating diversions all along, but you needed a big one. So you orchestrated that little stunt down in Bridgewater, which kicked off a whole media circus. Except something else happened you didn't plan for; I got involved. I also got involved with your little backcountry rendezvous, and your big human sacrifice racket," Morton said, the barest tinge of disgust creeping into his voice.

"By this point, things were getting very hot for you, Sam," Morton continued. "You knew Bob was getting paranoid, and you knew he'd fold if you hit him in just the right spot. So you sent two of your men out to kill Lundquist and Dunn, only you didn't plan on them having the moxie to punch those boys' tickets first."

"Wrong again, Don," Sam spat. "I would never send anyone to kill Darja and Porter. I love them like my own flesh and blood. Those men were sent out to test them."

"Is that so, Sam? Test them for what? Chicken pox?"

"To test their resolve. To see if they were strong enough to do what needs to be done. And they passed with flying colors," Sam crowed.

"Then you're further gone than I thought, Sam. Well, be that as it may, you got desperate for this case to get closed. So you blew a hole in your Gary-double's head and dumped the poor, unfortunate bastard in the harbor so it will eventually wash up and ruin some poor beachcomber's day. The stiff's so rough by the time it's found that you never thought it would be questioned. But you didn't know about Sutton's recent surgery, and so you couldn't plan for that either," Morton said, with genuine disappointment over Sam's sloppy planning.

"So you and your disciples decide it's time to bring the curtain down, once and for all. You kill off two of Sutton's bandmates and frame some poor groupie for their murder. But all that just turned out to be a complete waste of time and resources, because Sutton never told them anything that could lead back to you. You'd already found out that the girlfriend didn't know all that much, so all that was left to do was kill their manager and torch any files that might connect the dots. For your grand finale, you had your men kill off your Judas Goat inside the band, and throw Kevin Stuart overboard for good measure. You also order them to kill — oh, excuse me — I meant to *test* Dunn and Lundquist, but surprise; I come along again and save the day."

Sam sat back and steepled his fingers.

"But you've got another racket going," Morton said, the smile suddenly gone. "You've been using your access to all the mental hospitals and headshrinkers in town to sniff out remote viewers, influencers, whatever. You've put together quite a team. But you knew Bob Travis had a big leg up on you with his little nun in the Bronx. Your viewers are good, but she's the best. She'd eventually smoke you out. So you order her killed, too. But you fail again, Sam. I mean, your batting average on this little caper of yours is just for crap, old boy."

"All good things must come to an end," Sam said, exhaling heavily. "I suppose I should have killed you too."

"Easier said than done," Morton said, without emotion.

"Perhaps," Sam said, in an insinuating tone.

"I thought long and hard about this, Sam," Morton said, like he'd been brainstorming on a new sales presentation. "How could a good man like you go so bad? Then it hit me. You were making a king's ransom off Alice Keyser's books, but you were extorting her, bleeding her, breaking every single rule you once lived your life by. You were already sick with guilt over your first wife and everything that had gone down at Sunshine, and I think all that guilt eventually drove you insane. It drove you to the dark side. So you started hawking viewers on the black market, viewers you were ginning up with drugs and surgery. You had the proceeds from that, your salary here, your Loroles stock and your government pension. You had all this money and had no idea what to do with it all. So why not revive an old doomsday cult and blow up the world that had always failed to live up to your exacting moral standards?"

Sam decided he'd had let Morton dance in the end zone long enough. The man was impugning his faith now.

"You think I'm evil, Don? That Apophis is evil?" Sam spat, his voice quivering with anger. "Those old Apophis men were the absolute cream of the crop, the most honorable, the most capable, the most decorated men in their fields," Sam said, counting out their virtues on his fingers.

"They were the backbone, the foundation, the men who kept the entire military running. And the same holds true of the new breed. You think these men are thugs, goons, Satanists? Oh, you couldn't possibly be more wrong, Don! They are the kind of men who never think twice about putting their own lives on the line, for sacrificing themselves to the greater good. These are *real* men, Don. Men who know in their hearts that this world has been broken to bits and needs to be fixed. At whatever cost to themselves!"

"Give me a break, Sam. That little G.I. Joe cult of yours made the Manson Family look like the Girl Scouts," Morton said dismissively.

"Oh, you don't *understand*, Don! The sacrifices, the rituals, the transgressions, the things Apophis was so hated for? It was all *necessary*, Don!" Sam said, riled with passion. "It was shock therapy, can't you see? Exactly what any good doctor is compelled to do when a patient becomes unresponsive!"

Sam's face was red and blotchy as his passion rose.

"I dedicated my life to serving my country, Don, but who the hell was I serving? Criminals, traitors, degenerates, cowards! A generation of the most disgusting, most degraded, most despicable men this world has ever produced! Not *even* men! Nothing more than maggots feasting on a rotting corpse!"

Sam paused to catch his breath and collect his thoughts before swooping in for the big finish.

"This era, this age, is *over*, Don. Can't you understand that? Apophis isn't trying to bring about the end of the *world*, we're only trying to bring about the end of this sick, rotten system. It's ending already, Don."

"Apophis didn't cause that. We simply want to help put a terminal patient out of its misery so we can move on to something new, something better! This world must be purged, must be cleansed by fire, or there's no hope left for anyone! It even says so in the Bible! Don't you remember your Sunday school, Don? How Christ on his cross had the letters "INRI" inscribed above his head? Do you know what that *really* means, Don?" Sam asked.

"No, but I'm sure you'll tell me," Morton sighed.

"It's an old Latin term; *Igne Natura Renovator Integre*. It means, 'All Nature Will Renewed By Fire.' That's not ancient history to us; It's our mission, our credo!"

"Do you really think you're telling me anything I haven't heard a thousand times before, Sam?"

"Oh, how could you possibly understand? You've never believed in anything, Don," Sam said, suddenly deflated. "You never cared about anything but your own selfish desires. Fuck and kill, fuck and kill. That's your epitaph, Don."

"That's where you're dead wrong, Sam. I care a lot. I care a lot about protecting this country from men like you."

"From men like *me*? What about from men like *you*? Men like you are exactly why this world is so sick, Don! For Christ's sake, I've spent my entire life trying to heal human suffering, but you? You've spent your entire life causing it! You're like a black hole, Don. You've utterly destroyed everyone who's ever been foolish enough to trust you. And yet these delusions of yours allow you to pretend you're still joshing it up with the plebes at Annapolis, while you're running around out there creating nothing but chaos and misery!"

"Finished yet?"

"You're pathetic, Don. You really are. You prance around thinking you're some kind of superhero when you're just a scared little boy," Sam said, miserably. "Oh, it doesn't matter, does it? I suppose you're just going to kill me now anyway."

"Oh, you're not getting off the hook that easily," Morton said. "You're going down for all of this, old boy. And then you're going to watch from your prison cell while I tear down everything you've built, especially your new and improved Apophis. Hell, I can't wait to get started."

"I hate to have to break the news, old chum, but that will never happen," Sam said. "If you don't kill me now, then an Apophis man will surely do the job once I've been arrested. We have disciples everywhere now, Don. *Everywhere.* You really think Loroles is some kind of one-off? We have disciples in more big firms than you can imagine. Hell, the way things are going now we'll be running Central before the decade's up. Maybe even the Pentagon, who knows?"

"Well, I guess we've got our work cut out for us, then. Oh, before I forget..."

Without warning, Morton leaned over and pressed his gun against Sam's shoe and fired a round into the center of his foot.

There was a howl as the doctor fell from his chair and rolled onto the floor. Tears welled in his eyes from the pain as he screamed at the man who was standing over him, watching impassively.

"Jesus Christ, you lunatic!" Sam screamed. "What the hell did you do that for?"

"I really don't know, Sam. Just to see how you'd react, I suppose."

CHAPTER NINETY EIGHT

Darja slowly maneuvered her brand new Bronco through some very challenging terrain in Boston's tony Back Bay neighborhood. She had no idea where she was going, and the gloom, the drizzle and the low glare of the old-fashioned streetlights weren't making her life any easier.

Worse, the bumps from the cobblestone street were bouncing the car's suspension around, stabbing needles of pain into Porter's injured leg.

"Cobblestones? Really?" Porter winced. "Can't Boston afford actual pavement?"

"I think it's supposed to lend the place Old World charm," Darja quipped.

"How about you, Bruehlie?" Porter asked. "You're from the Old World. Find any of this charming?"

Bruehle chuckled. "I'm keeping out of this one."

"Crap, we're already like a half-hour late, Darj," Porter said.

"I'm sorry, but I can't tell any of these fucking buildings apart," Darja protested. "Where are we supposed to be going, Bruehlie?"

"Over there, with the big awning," Bruehle replied.

Darja pulled into the vacant spot in front of the building and a valet flagged them down. She gave him the keys and the trio collected themselves under the awning.

Bruehle was dressed in a black collarless dress suit, with a dark grey collarless shirt. He looked like the best man for a gay wedding being held on a lunar base.

Porter was wearing the three-piece indigo blue tuxedo that had been mysteriously sent over to the Lair via courier. Bruehle had looked up the brand and said the thing retailed for five thousand dollars. Porter looked like he belonged on a billboard, except for the crutches and elaborate metallic leg brace.

"How do I look?" Darja asked, as she brushed imaginary dust off her slinky black evening gown.

"You look really, really hot, Sails," Bruehle said. "For real. I'd totally do you."

"Aww Bruehlie, that's the sweetest thing a thirty year-old man who's never touched a vagina has ever said to me. Thanks, guy," Darja said, and gave him a friendly push.

The three walked into the private club. There was a handsome, balding, bespectacled young man in some kind of Village People-looking naval uniform sitting at a desk and smiling helpfully as they approached. Darja noticed he and Bruehle seemed to make some kind of telepathic contact for a moment.

She also noticed that Ensign Elton's head seemed to rock ever-so-slightly as he spoke with Porter. Either he had some kind of neurological tremor or he was falling in love. Porter announced the party, and Elton looked up the trio's names in an old-fashioned kind of ledger book.

Suddenly, the let's-all-be-pals smile fell from his face.

"Could you excuse me just one moment?" he said. The three stood back as the man picked up a black telephone and murmured into it. They gestured and murmured at each other, suddenly feeling like gatecrashers.

But then Ensign Elton hung up the phone, beamed at them once again, and said, "Someone will be with you in just a moment."

A moment was right.

Suddenly, Chief Warrant Officer Freddie Mercury came bursting through the swinging doors marked 'Staff Only.'

Freddie was dressed in a white, full-dress uniform, the kind high-ranking officers wore to funerals. Just slightly gayer.

"Good evening, friends. My name is Omar. Would you please follow me?"

Omar walked over to a set of carved oak doors and held them open. The lobby was soon filled with very loud bar chatter and glass tinkling.

"Please, right this way," he said.

The three followed Omar through a noisy cocktail lounge filled with a lot of very wealthy-looking people getting very soused. Darja noticed that Porter was getting pretty nimble on those crutches, which was a good thing. Because as the situation currently stood, his doctors still weren't optimistic that he'd ever be able to walk on that leg again.

The group trekked from a noisy cocktail lounge into a noisy dining room. Darja was wondering exactly how big this fucking building was.

They walked through another set of heavy oak doors and went from cacophony to almost-total silence. The back hall was dimly-lit by lamps shaped like old-timey gas lanterns. There was a polished brass elevator door with an old clipper ship's helm embossed upon it. A helm being known as a 'steering wheel' to land-lubbers.

The group all crammed in the rather snug elevator, which Omar operated the way they did in old movies. They went down three floors and Omar ushered them out.

They stood in a small lobby decorated with carvings that looked to Darja like Medieval-cathedral kind of stuff, only weirder. But Bruehle spun around and stared up at the decor like he'd just discovered a lost Pharaoh's tomb.

Omar knocked four times on the kind of door you'd usually only ever saw in a Dracula movie. The door opened and Omar whispered to a figure on the other side. Darja was definitely starting to lose her patience with all this cloak-and-dagger crap. The figure gave Omar some kind of electronic wand and he turned to the visitors and said, "If you don't mind, it's only a formality," in a profoundly apologetic tone.

Darja noticed Omar wore a wedding band and wondered if he were the token-straight hire here. That enormous cum-catcher on his upper lip there could just be an ethnic thing, she figured.

Omar then stood at the door and waved the guests in. Darja was starting to wonder if they'd all end up in some creepy-ass satanic temple and be forced to drink chicken blood, or kill babies, or something. But they just walked through yet another hall to yet another oak door. Omar knocked three times again. This particular door didn't have a handle or a knob.

But the door swung open all the same, and cocktail party noise filled the dark corridor. Omar stood and kept the door ajar.

"You can go in now," he said, beaming at his company.

The room looked like any upscale bar to Darja, only decorated with weird nautical motifs, sea monsters and mermaids and shit like that. The decor was all very warm golden-orange, an effect accentuated by the cozy lighting.

The guests were all dressed in evening wear, some going so far to wear white dress gloves. Diamonds, pearls and gold jewelry sparkled and clinked everywhere you looked. Neither Porter nor Darja nor Bruehle had any idea what the hell they were supposed to do in here.

A voice then rose above the din.

"There you are!" Don Morton shouted. "We were starting to get worried! Come, come," he said, waving a beckoning hand.

The three followed Morton through a dense wall of wealth and finally to a heavy maroon curtain, which Morton ceremoniously pulled aside. Behind it was a large circular booth with mirrored walls.

"Porter, old boy, you'd best sit on the outside. Scooch over, will you, dearest?" A glamorous, middle-aged Eurasian woman in a blood-red dress scooched.

There was another couple sitting at the booth, an older man with graying hair and gold-rimmed eyeglass sitting with a younger, attractive woman with huge hoop earrings and very close-cropped blonde hair. The pair looked like a prosperous Hollywood accountant and his former actress wife.

The table was set with unopened bottles of Cristal and Perrier. The party all wore semi-formal dress except Morton, who was also wearing a tux.

Morton entered the nook and closed the curtain behind him. The newcomers were stunned as the noise outside went quiet.

Morton smiled knowingly, then said, "Amazing, don't you think? I had it custom made. Maybe you and I can have a chat about that later, Herr Bruehle."

"Now that we're all here, let me make introductions all around. This lovely young lady here is Ensign Darja Marie Lundquist, with whom I had the great privilege of fighting beside at the now-legendary Battle of Wellfleet Beach. And this courageous young grenadier here is Darja's comrade-in-arms, Midshipman Porter MacKenzie Dunn. Our man here took some heavy flak on that fateful day, as you can plainly see. And this here is the intrepid radio-man, Herr Gunter Herbert Bruehle. Now Darja, Porter, Gunter..."

"Bruehle!" Bruehle shouted out.

"...Bruehle, permit me the very great honor and pleasure of introducing you all to the next Director of the Defense Intelligence Agency, Rear Admiral Louis Edward Brauner. You can call him Ed. And his better half here was christened as Camille Adele, but prefers you call her 'Millie.' And tonight, we are also honored with the presence of Lady Miss Mika David, international star of stage and screen."

Bruehle shot Porter a look. He didn't notice.

"Now, I don't know about you lot but I'm wasting away here, I'm so blasted hungry."

Morton opened the curtain and shouted, "Omar, for Heaven's sake, man! We need food in here! Get your godless heathen ass in gear and bring us rations before we all die of starvation! Chop-chop, Effendi!"

They all ate and drank and talked with great gusto. The food was downright orgasmic. Darja never tasted anything like it before, and had no idea what kind of cuisine it actually was. No wonder they hid this place from the public.

Brauner's wife was a Virginian like Porter, so they seemed to have a lot to talk about. The Mika woman and Bruehle really hit it off as well, since she'd spent a lot of time in Germany in the Seventies.

Mika seemed very sweet and was quite the name-dropper, but Darja kind of got the feeling that maybe she might actually be a guy, or was at least born one. Something about the voice. Hard to tell.

However, it soon became abundantly clear to Darja that this little get-together here was for this Brauner guy's benefit, not theirs.

He and Morton asked them all a lot of questions, about Gary Sutton, about Travis, about Celeste, about the UFOs, about Soares, about Sam, about everything. It seems Travis had been keeping a lot of people at the DIA in the dark with his Bifrost project, even though it was all being financed by the DoD.

Brauner was subtle, but extremely thorough with his friendly little interrogation. Darja figured that he and Morton were probably recording everything being said here tonight. These fucking spooks, it's like they can't help themselves.

Darja did notice there was one very conspicuous aspect of the case neither Brauner nor Morton had asked about, and that was Grace Sutton.

Darja figured that Grace was working for one or both of them all along. Maybe they had their suspicions about Sam and were feeding Porter information through Grace to bait the trap.

Worse still, Grace didn't even visit Porter in the hospital, had stopped talking his calls and then apparently split town. But Porter was still hopelessly in love with her. Even if he realized now that Grace Sutton was just a professional doing her job.

'Her job' being Porter.

CHAPTER NINETY NINE

The Brauners had an early flight, so they excused themselves around one. Ed told the group he'd be in touch and Darja thought that felt vaguely like a threat.

Morton told his remaining guests that Mika had a *pied à terre* not two blocks from there and suggested they wander on over for a nightcap. Darja told Morton she had to use the little girls room first, because she drank so much wine she was about to pee all over her new dress, and it was dry-clean only.

Darja stood at the gorgeous marble and brass bathroom sink console, which she reckoned cost more than the people who clean it every night make in a year. As she touched up her makeup, a woman in a maroon crushed-velvet gown, jet-black hair and paper-white skin came over to the other sink and rinsed her hands off.

The woman then stared at Darja in the mirror with very intense, very creepy dark eyes. She reminded Darja of the Bride of Dracula, especially with that bright red mess of lipstick around her mouth.

Darja looked directly at the Bride.

"Have we met?" Darja asked in a firm tone.

The Bride didn't answer. She just placed her cold, wet hand on Darja's shoulder and creepy-eyed her some more.

"Sorry hon, I don't dine at the Y," Darja said, gently pushing the crazy bitch's hand away. "I'm flattered, though. Truly."

The Bride said, "I have a message for you."

Darja put her lipstick down and leaned against the counter-top, arms folded.

"Really," Darja said, skeptically. "Who's it from? God?"

"The message is this: you passed the test."

"Oh, goodie-gumdrops," Darja said, smirking. "And here I'd studied so hard for it. Anything else?"

"They'll be waiting for you, Darja," the Bride said, then turned and marched out the door. As she left, another woman — who was not creepy-looking — passed on her way in.

"Damn," Darja said to the not-creepy woman. "That chick needs to cool it with the diet pills."

"Who doesn't?" the not-creepy woman shrugged, then stepped into a stall.

• • •

Mika's *'pied à terre'* was actually a townhouse bigger than the house Darja grew up in. Apparently, Mika quit show business to become tarot reader to the stars, which Darja figured was just a different kind of show biz.

The joint was filled with photos of her with pretty much everyone you could possibly think of; rock stars, politicians, actors, authors, models, athletes, tycoons.

Darja wondered how many of them this kooky dame had actually fucked, then figured she probably fucked all of them.

Mika also kept a well-appointed bar in the middle of her ginormous living room, and mixed up a pitcher of martinis for her guests. Porter thought martinis tasted like lighter fluid, so Mika served him an exotic Thai beer, which he downed quite a few of.

Mika had already slipped into a very racy satin nightgown. Her tits looked real enough and there was no sign of a dick, so Darja started to think maybe she was wrong about her. Then again, she might have had it chopped off. Darja figured it was none of her business anyway.

They all relaxed on the faux leopardskin furniture and Morton gave his guests the latest news on the case. With Travis gone, Ed Brauner had tapped Morton to take the reins at Bifrost.

Sam was in custody. The Feds were confident they had him dead-to-rights on tax evasion, but didn't have enough to build much of a case on the conspiracy charges. There just wasn't enough physical evidence. They were also looking hard at Loroles before they ran smack-dab into a wall of very expensive corporate lawyers.

The Khourys' faith required them to observe forty days of mourning for Travis, so they still wouldn't be around for a while yet. Morton wasn't really certain if they'd want to return to work at all now that Bob was dead.

Darja could see how badly Porter wanted to ask Morton about Mommie Dearest, but she also saw how much the topic seemed to torture him.

Maybe it was all the trauma they'd been through together -- and a lot of it was surely all the booze -- but Darja soon found herself snuggling up to her partner a bit on the couch, careful to avoid his bad leg. Porter didn't seem to mind. In fact, he idly ran his fingers through Darja's hair, which she had to admit was getting her kind of wet.

But Darja also felt sorry for Porter as well. He seemed like one of those guys who seems like he should have everything in the world going for him, but had some kind of curse on his life, the kind of curse that you read about in old Greek myths.

And he was such a fucking altar boy about everything. He was so desperate to do this insane fucking job right and yet all he ends up with is a crippled leg, a dead boss and a broken heart.

That's what this rotten fucking system always did to guys like Porter.

She also started to wonder if that Alice Keyser loon wasn't right after all about that Grace Sutton. Maybe she really is some kind of alien pussy-witch. She certainly didn't look anywhere near her age and she sure as hell put the major whammy on Porter, a guy who surely has lines of much younger and prettier women waiting to get into his pants.

Who knows, maybe that evil whore is the product of some effed-up CIA experiment. Darja knew for sure now that much stranger things have happened.

Darja also wondered if maybe she should go sit somewhere else, because all of this bullshit was seriously starting to make her fall in love with this dumb fuck now. He wasn't even close to her type, no matter how good-looking he was.

Plus, she was the first to admit she had major daddy issues. And while she'd pretty much fuck any guy who asked nicely enough, she'd only ever been in love with her old CO.

So yeah, it was definitely time to get up and stand out on the balcony or something before this whole thing got out of hand. If she didn't take control of this situation now, she was going to fuck everything up forever.

They made such a great team, and had been through so much crazy shit together in such a short time, that a relationship could only jeopardize it all.

Time to put the big-girl pants on and stop this crazy train before it ran right off the tracks. OK, on the count of three, ready? One, two, th...

Darja buried her face into Porter's chest and wrapped her arms around his waist. He leaned down and kissed her head. They fell asleep in each other's arms.

• • •

Morton signaled to Bruehle to join him out on the balcony while Mika went off to bed. The two men smoked Bruehle's rancid French cigarettes, sipped at their martinis and generally enjoyed the misty night air.

They spoke about Germany and Amsterdam, and all the interesting places around the world they'd been. Morton told Bruehle of a wild weekend he'd spent in Berlin that led to him being barred from entering the country ever again.

Bruehle was chuffed that this real-life James Bond here didn't talk down or condescend to him, even though Bruehle wasn't even a rookie in his game. Bruehle couldn't get a handle on this guy's personality, though. It seemed to change from setting to setting, like some kind of chameleon.

Maybe that was a spy thing.

They got to talking about Travis and Sutton and the whole mess they left in their wake. Morton had some interesting insights on Travis, and told Bruehle a couple war stories about the guy that were actually pretty unsettling.

They talked about Sam and how evil he became and how insane his secret fortune had driven him. Morton said that Sam was once a very honorable and decent man, and that Travis and himself were the dangerous lunatics, but somehow it all got turned around.

But Morton also said that the intelligence racket was full of people just like Sam, if not even worse.

He didn't say much about Apophis, probably because he didn't want to cast a dark cloud over a very enjoyable evening. But he did let Bruehle know in no uncertain terms that the war had only just begun.

"Mr. Morton, there's one question that keeps nagging at me about all this," Bruehle said. "I realize that so much of what we've seen was all orchestrated for our benefit. But there's still something else I need to know."

"Hit me," Morton said, as he blew smoke rings into the night.

"What do you think really happened to Gary Sutton?" Bruehle asked.

"Do you really want to know my honest opinion?" Morton replied, staring off into the distance.

"Of course I do," Bruehle said.

Morton frowned thoughtfully for a moment, then pointed to the clouds.

"I think he's up there. In the sky."

9/11 and its Speech impediment

Made in the USA
Monee, IL
13 June 2020